ZOTIKAS

SPARKS OF REVOLUTION

BY

TOM BRUNO
&
ROB STOREY

A15 Publishing
PO Box 66054
Hampton, VA 23665
www.A15publishing.com

ISBN 978-0-9989005-6-8

Table of Contents

EPISODE 1: CLASH OF HEIRS

Table of Contents (continued)

EPISODE 2: HIGH RAILS OF ARDAN

Table of Contents (continued)

EPISODE 3: ATTRACTION AND REPULSION

Table of Contents (continued)

EPISODE 4: A LIGHT IN THE DEEP

EPISODE 1:
CLASH OF HEIRS

CHAPTER ONE

Bags' broad hand hovered above the throttle of the mag-lev raider. Kieler watched him, both of them tense and ready. Years of waiting would come to an end in minutes, perhaps seconds. Bags never shifted his eyes from the narrow, rain-streaked windscreen. He searched the darkness for the signal.

In the cockpit of the unpainted metal sled, sweat and rain had scented the air with the metallic tang of rust. A lull in the downpour created an unnerving quiet as their low-slung craft hovered silently in the very bottom of the V-shaped track. The iron and magal track was built for much larger vehicles—not that the raider was tiny. It could, when the now-empty cargo bay was loaded, hold enough food pirated from a freighter to feed a borough for a week.

Lightning flashed, illuminating the face of Kieler's companion. Bags, his dark blue eyes unblinking in his blocky face, didn't look anything like a rebel. He looked like a family man, a determined family man intent on fixing a chair or some other mundane task.

But Bags wasn't just waiting for a signal; he was waiting for justice. When he spoke, his voice was low and cool despite the heat and tension. "Storms came late this year."

Kieler grunted. For weeks they had waited restlessly for the winter storms to roll in from the Northeast Sea and the mountainous continent of Ardan beyond. Had the storms not come today, the last possible day, Kieler's chances of succeeding tomorrow night were slight.

1

EPISODE 1 – CLASH OF HEIRS

Following his friend's gaze out the windscreen, Kieler stared into the darkness, peering through his own dim reflection. His dark brown hair and brown eyes vanished in the dim light, but he could see his face. There was nothing remarkable about it, allowing him to go unnoticed when necessary.

Lightning struck Garrist Ring miles off and far above, momentarily dispelling the ghost of his visage. The upward sloping sides of the huge track to their left and right blocked most of their view, but straight ahead the flash of light silhouetted the dominant tower of Garrist Ring, the spires of the Executive Chair's palace.

"Don't act upset," Bags challenged Kieler's supposedly sour mood. "You're excited to be doing something, same as me." His big face was pale in the dim light. A clenched jaw muscle twitched. "Tomorrow you'll be in the EC's palace, way better than hiding in that hole we call home."

His accomplice was right. Despite the twist in his stomach, Kieler felt like a coiled spring, and he liked it. "The nethercity has been my 'home' since I was eight. You're a newbie."

Now Bags grunted and leaned forward, as if he could see more than darkness and raindrops. He didn't take his hand away from the throttle. He replied slowly, "Doesn't seem much use in bragging about how long you've lived in our starless hell under the Plate."

"I'm not bragging. I'm just saying we've waited a long time for the chance to strike back at these highborns. Stealing the sigil tonight starts the machinery of revolution Movus has been putting together for years. It's the first step toward you and I living in the light of Rei again." After a pause Kieler added in a mutter, "And the first step in getting your wife back from that prog Telander."

Bags made no audible reply, but Kieler could feel the heat rise from his friend.

A long, silent time passed. Other than the distant lights of Garrist Ring, which they glimpsed when the clouds scudded out from in front of the high-rise district, only the occasional lightning

CHAPTER ONE

illuminated their view as it flashed closer. It didn't matter. The high sides and curve of the track blocked any view of their actual target. The storm swirled in and the metallic tinging on the top of the sled resumed.

Their target was the Cortatti compound, and Kieler knew from studying the extensive maps provided by his mentor Movus, it was both a fortress and an oasis in the industrial northeast section of the Isle of Threes. Unlike many Houses of the Omeron, which possessed rich villas on the continents, or penthouses in downtown Avertori far from their economic centers, the Cortattis lived where they worked. Surrounded by their weapons factories, foundries and the rail yards, which supported their industry, their residence and administrative headquarters rose monolithic from the rough neighborhood.

Kieler had seen the colossal six-sided structure from the promenade on Garrist Ring. If he compartmentalized his thoughts, Kieler could almost admire the efficiency of House Cortatti—as much as any feeling human could admire a family who had killed every person in House Ortessi just to elevate themselves.

But the Cortattis worked. Other houses, like Telander, which continued to drain profits from their vehicle manufacturing monopoly, now spent their days in idle pleasures—or perversions. Kieler had nudged Bags' anger by bringing up that House Primes were often untouchable by the cumbersome legal system in Avertori. While to most people Borgus Telander's penchant for women-not-his-wife was just a rumor, Bags could confirm it firsthand. That Bags was still alive was a testimony to his simple wisdom over his passion for revenge. Borgus Telander would casually eliminate problems like Bags should they threaten his perverse fetish.

Despite the long silence, when Bags spoke Kieler realized he had been dwelling on his last comment. "Will she want me back when we do bring Telander down?" Bags didn't look away from the windscreen, but Kieler felt the intensity radiating from his friend. It was a perceptive thought: that things happen emotionally to violated women. And just as profound was Bags' simple certainty that they would succeed.

"Yes, Bags. Regardless of what Telander does. Everything you told me about her says she is a solid, dedicated woman. She is building up an emotional citadel that only you can enter."

Bags flicked him a glance, gauging Kieler, a hint of moist eyes and a hard smile. "You don't know nothin' about women, Sparks!" Bags snorted, using Kieler's Coin name. "You never even had a girlfriend." Bags' smile faded into a tight line. "But I believe you about my Eznea. She'll be right. We just gotta get her back."

Kieler detected the catch in Bags' voice that gave away how hard he was trying to convince himself.

Two lights blinked on in the middle distance. Before he could point them out, Kieler was slammed back in his seat by the rapid acceleration as Bags slammed forward the throttle.

They had thirty seconds.

When a full-size powercoach accelerated, the motion was barely perceptible. Both heavy freighters and powercoaches rode high in the V-shaped track. But their own raider sat along the bottom—low, sleek, and a mere fraction of the mass. When Bags hit the throttle, they hit the back of their seats.

An empty cargo hold, a high-velocity magnetic impeller, and a frictionless suspension—they were built for speed.

Kieler had no doubt this was the fastest conveyance on Zotikas.

Hurtling down the long, gently curving slot, velocity increasing, all Kieler could do was hope that the two guards at the gate ahead were distracted by his apparently inebriated co-conspirators. Across from the gate they'd be crashing were two pubs frequented by a literal army of guards as they got off duty from the Cortatti complex. Two of Kieler's squad mates were to stagger over from one of the bars and call the men out of the guard shack. His third squad member was to provide the fireworks—a fake lightning flash just as they passed. The guards just needed to have their backs to the tracks.

At just over 400 miles per hour, the low metal ship in which Kieler and Bags sat would sound like thunder and a sudden, violent wind as it passed. In this rain, it would be past the guards and out of sight before they could possibly turn around—as long as they weren't looking in the first place.

As they approached the massive gates that regulated powercoaches and freighters entering the Cortatti domain, Kieler got to see the barrier for less than a second. Then they shot beneath it. The gates did not extend into the groove of the track. Presumably, an impeller couldn't be built small enough for a ship their size. Kieler had his late father to thank for that bit of engineering.

A brilliant flash exploded above the rim of the track to his right. It was the magal-luzhril blast to add noise to their sled's high-speed passing. His men at the gate would swear to the guards that they were almost struck by lightning.

The instant they passed under the gates, Bags threw the throttle from full ahead to full reverse. They were thrown forward into their shoulder restraints, now decelerating at the same breakneck rate at which they had accelerated. They now had thirty more seconds to slow down or smash through a weapons factory dock. Though uncomfortable, Kieler decided that this rate of deceleration was far preferred to that of impact.

Most troubling, Kieler would have to go after the Ortessi sigil without knowing whether they would have an unwelcoming party at the end of the line. If the guards at the gate hadn't fallen for their thunder and lightning ploy, they would telegraph the keep and this would be a short mission. The curve of the track took them through a maze of rail yard switches and industrial stockpiles. Kieler looked up at freighters looming a full three stories on parallel tracks as they flew by. He was strangely detached, watching with absolutely no control as they slowed through three-fifty, three twenty-five—

"Bags!" Kieler hissed. "Is that freighter parked on *our* track?"

Bags pounded the throttle back against the stops. All they had time to do was brace for impact. The metal wall of the looming freighter rushed toward them... and flashed darkly over them. Their raider was designed for that very purpose, to pirate these freighters from below.

With no time for congratulating themselves, a whole train laden with cargo seemed to fly at them. Again they skidded under it, but the weight of the cargo lowered it just enough that as they passed through, there was a *crack* and then a fierce, short shriek of metal on metal.

Bags glanced over at him, his raised eyebrows making his long face look longer. "I think we lost the hatch handle."

Relief, and the comic look, made Kieler spit out a laugh. If that was the worst they suffered tonight, it would be a good night.

Their speed dropped through 250 then 200 as they whipped between the parked freighters. Eventually they slowed to where their passage was a mere whisper.

But now the end of the line sped toward them.

"*Bags!* End of the line!"

Bags pressed back on the throttle so hard that Kieler thought it would bend, but it was already full against the stop. Through clenched teeth he growled, "I see it. Not much I can do."

But even though they looked to be rapidly closing on the dock wall, they were decelerating at the same rate at which they had launched. With one last lurch, they stopped just feet from the metal dock. Next to them loomed the enormous hulk of an ore hopper.

They turned and grinned at each other.

"Beats hiding in that hole!" Kieler quipped. He unstrapped. "I'm outta here. See you in forty-five or I won't see you at all."

CHAPTER ONE

"I'll get this sled turned around on a nice, quiet siding while you go for your walk. Good stars, Kieler!" Bags called.

Kieler chuckled at the superstitious blessing. He darted out a hatch in the bulkhead behind them and scrambled up a ladder. In moments he was atop the craft. With a running start across the roof of the sled, he jumped and grabbed the top of the V-track. On the next track hovered the huge freighter. As he pulled himself out, he saw that the front of their craft was just feet from a shock absorbing bumper. Perhaps their doom was not as imminent as it had appeared.

Then he saw that just on the other side of the bumper was the wall of a factory.

Kieler jogged down the dock under a loading crane suspended over the freighter in rusty, frozen sleep. The rain slid off the oiled cloak he had pulled up over his head. He also pulled on a dark mask, a trademark of the Coin, the underground organization of which both Kieler and Bags were a part. He probably didn't need the mask; if he was caught, Kieler was dead with or without it. Undoubtedly he'd be sent straight into the Arena without trial.

Nevertheless, his mask, so much a part of his identity, gave him a certain amount of comfort. Despite the dark and the rain, he felt strangely exposed without it.

This entire industrial complex was built directly on the solidity of the city-spanning Plate, the divider between the sunlit city above and the never-lit city below. Kieler sidled along the back of the aged factory to an ugly, open metal staircase that switched back and forth up several levels until he gained the topmost landing. There he found a door, locked.

He glanced back down to the dock and cluttered rail yard as he extracted a pick set from under his cloak. Rain and rust. Darkness and corruption. The complex looked skeletal and lifeless. But through the falling rain, Kieler saw Bags easing the raider slowly backward toward a switch where he could turn around. Stealth, not speed, was his objective now.

EPISODE 1 – CLASH OF HEIRS

The lock offered no challenge and opened within seconds. He shoved a small rock in the door so that it would not re-latch.

Passing through that door was like stepping from hell directly into heaven. He stood in the rain at the edge of the immense garden on the Cortatti estate; everything was perfectly manicured, as if the greenery were built to precise specifications rather than allowed to grow.

Luzhril lanterns in ornate fixtures lined cobbled paths that wound through lush grass, sculpted topiary, and perfectly symmetrical trees of equal height. From his current position all he could see of the main residence was a hazy glow through the drizzly rain. The garden was enormous.

The budget needed to maintain such opulence—the garden alone—would feed many of the hundreds of thousands of outcasts living under the Plate. Kieler admittedly would prefer wealth to poverty, but he knew that the Cortattis had gained and maintained their riches through the blood of others. Much of their income came from the production and sale of weapons, and they promoted those weapons through the Arena, their "entertainment" facility. Bloodsport.

Kieler couldn't understand how such a thing was tolerated. Human life sacrificed for the sick pleasure of others.

He kept off the path and ran through the trees toward where he knew the Cortatti stronghold would be. After a quarter mile jog, the keep seemed to coalesce in the haze, first as a vague shadow, and then—despite his preparation—as a ziggurat that both awed and daunted him in its sheer immensity. The main keep stood thirty stories high and glistened in luzhril-lit splendor—fountains, terraces, and unfortunately guards. They patrolled the terraces that surrounded the smooth stone edifice. Despite the carefully scripted beauty of the grounds, the monstrous residence had no large windows to view them, as if windows were a weakness to be kept to a minimum.

CHAPTER ONE

At the points of the hexagonal keep, six bastions rose to three-quarters of the keep's height. And atop each bastion, more guards.

The object of his mission lay in the library at the base of one of those towers. Movus had provided the intel on this secret approach. Without it, Kieler believed entrance to the keep would have been impossible. What connections Movus had before he was exiled, and what he had done to necessitate that exile, he had never shared with Kieler.

He spied what he was looking for: a line of shrubbery, again perfectly trimmed, leading from near the tree line to a statue nearer the citadel. He worked his way through the trees to where the shrubs came closest. The rain blurred every image, and despite the bright lights, he felt sure he was not seen as he scuttled out of the trees and dove behind the bushes.

It was then a long, hard low-crawl to stay beneath the short bushes and out of the line of sight of the tower guards. A hundred yards found him at the edge of a paved circle around the statue near the headquarters of Cortatti power.

Indeed, the keep itself was not his immediate destination; it was the statue. From the cover of the bushes, Kieler dodged over to the pedestal. He glanced up at the marble sculpture. Of all the gaudy, vainglorious monuments, this one was of a Cortatti in military uniform with a maggun, the magnetic rifle for which they were famous, held up like an object of worship.

Diminished in comparison to the keep, the statue was still thrice life size. The large pedestal bore a dull metal engraving:

FOR THOSE DEFENDING
LOVED ONES BY THE
USE OF THESE WEAPONS

EPISODE 1 – CLASH OF HEIRS

As Kieler pulled out a simple iron magnet—not its more active form magal—again he wondered, *How did Movus learn of this?*

He touched the magnet to the inscription in sequence to the only singly occurring letters: W – A – R. And with a soft click, the base unlatched and swung open to reveal a descending ladder.

He climbed down into a passage just under the garden level. The deep darkness forced him to pull out a short rod with a small shard of luzhril fastened to its end, though he was aware of how it highlighted him. He walked toward the citadel through the narrow corridor. *Who knows of this passage besides Movus? Feleanna Cortatti?* Feleanna was now the very ambitious defacto leader of House Cortatti, since her father was said to be quite mad.

As he walked the tunnel, Kieler shed his mask and outer garments, uncovering a Cortatti guard uniform. From a distance he wouldn't be out of place. Up close, he'd have to take his chances.

The narrow corridor led two hundred yards straight under the garden and into a lower level of the weighty edifice above. It ended at another ladder going up. The passage's purpose seemed to be an escape route, though obviously it might be used to reenter the main building in secret as well. Its only defense was its secrecy, and that had been compromised.

Kieler left his mask and cloak and climbed, pulling back the latch to a trap door in the ceiling. He cautiously put his shoulder to the hatch. It took more effort than he expected to lift and peek out. He saw immediately that the floor around it was expensive tile, probably from the quarries of Eastern Coprackus. No wonder the hatch was so heavy.

A strong pungency struck him as he climbed into a wine cellar. He saw that the edge of the secret hatch abutted a wine rack against the wall. Inside the rack was a well-hidden latch used to open the trap door from above. It was cleverly and precisely made, and Kieler appreciated such devices. He noted its location for his return trip, but on a hunch left the hatch open. Instinct told him this room would not be on a patrol route.

Again he wondered who used this entrance and how often.

His musings did not cause him to slow down, however. There was no evidence that the guards from the powercoach gate had alerted the main residence, but if a patrol spotted their ship in the rail yard below, it was best that what he must do be done quickly. At least the rain and the shadow of the freighter would make the sled very difficult to see.

The door to the wine room opened out to a tasting area. It was cool, and the redolence of fine wines saturated his nose. This scent, though exquisitely pleasant, somehow reminded him of the stale rank of a pub he frequented in his information trade, The Bottom of the Barrel. The alcoholic stench of that pub was an acquired tolerance.

No one was about. He exited the wine chamber and followed the map Movus had provided and Kieler had memorized. He moved with certainty through the exquisitely tiled lower level of the Cortatti keep. This southwestern side was mostly residential. In fact, the map showed Feleanna's suites to be two and three floors directly above the wine rooms.

The administrative and intelligence headquarters occupied the north side of the keep. Kieler would stay well clear of that as it was sure to be even more heavily guarded.

This lower corridor was cool with several heavy wooden doors on either side. He passed one door on his right hung with a sign that was strikingly out of place, considering the residential feel of this part of the building. It read: **STAY OUT OR DIE.**

Not on Kieler's route anyway. He continued toward the stairway that led up to the great hall on the main floor. He spun silently onto the stair and had gone but five steps when he simultaneously heard and saw the feet of two guards coming down. Instantly he about-faced and was off the stair, backtracking down the tiled hall. There were two doors close, both locked, and then the STAY OUT door. Figuring it locked, he nevertheless tried the lever as he passed. He was shocked to have it swing open.

The guards were chatting, about to round the corner from the stairs.

Be caught, stay out, or die.

He chose to risk dying.

Within, Kieler swung the door closed quickly, slowing it an inch from the latch and then pushing it gently shut. His quick glance around had revealed little, but no instant death came upon him. Instead, the room was quiet, lit by a single source far across the room and shaded by a curtain.

The voices in the hall were faint but did not fade. The two guards had stopped somewhere outside the door. He leaned close to the heavy door to try and hear words but could not.

Move on! he mentally commanded, focusing on their presence beyond.

What if they come in here?

What is in here, anyway?

Accompanying that thought came the uncanny feeling that he was not alone. He turned his head slowly, eyes adjusting to the dimmer light, and saw a faint silhouette against the backlit curtain.

CHAPTER TWO

The part of the room in which Kieler stood was like a waiting room but with only one chair and one low cocktail table, stacked with books. But separating the waiting area from the much larger portion of the room were dark metal bars, spanning floor-to-ceiling, that he hadn't seen in the low light. The entire chamber was covered with a rich carpet. Within the barred area was an ornate bedroom set, a full wall of bookshelves, and a curtained private area from which the light shone.

These details he noted incidentally as he tried to pierce the gloom and see more of the man standing not three feet behind the bars. At first he thought the shadow might be a statue, still as it was. But then he noticed a halo of thinning red hair and the slightest motion of his shoulders. Hands behind his back and eyes shadowed, he silently watched Kieler.

What kind of criminal gets this kind of quarters?

Chilled and at a loss, Kieler didn't know whether to speak first or wait. He could not tackle the man, regardless of the bars. The man could easily cry out an alert before Kieler reached him. And besides, a prisoner of sorts, he could have called out already had he wished. Waiting for the eerie man drove Kieler crazy. He broke the silence with a whispered question, "What are you being held for?"

Despite the shadowed face, Kieler knew the man smiled slightly. He didn't whisper but spoke quietly enough that the guards could not hear. "I hear a voice." His pitch was oddly high.

An answer or an observation?

EPISODE 1 – CLASH OF HEIRS

Torn between wanting to get moving and not wanting this man to sound the alarm, Kieler searched for the right thing to say.

"Hearing voices is not a crime," Kieler remarked cautiously.

The man cocked his head, regarding him—or listening. "Especially when the voice is the truth." Another uncomfortable pause. "But no one else seems to hear this voice."

Having no idea what to make of that, Kieler once again wondered what to do. He could still hear talking in the hall outside. It seemed—had this been a normal conversation—that the man should be asking Kieler a few questions like, "Why are you hiding from the guards in the middle of the night?" or "What are you doing here?"

But something wasn't normal about this person.

Finally, the man did ask a question—a question as unexpected as his behavior.

"Do you want to hear what the voice says about you?"

There was silence. Complete silence. The guards had moved on. Kieler was ready to run. Yet now his curiosity was piqued. And the question remained; would this man give him away?

Kieler didn't have time for distractions. He peeked out the door, found it clear, and left. He hadn't answered the man and he hadn't time for strange discussions. He ran down the empty hall.

Listening carefully this time, he hit the stairs and bounded up them three at a time. At the top, a different kind of disorientation hit him. There seemed to be nothing in front of him. A single dim light shone behind him from the wall above the stairs, creating a small semi-circle of light that faded into darkness before him. Above him was a cavernous space so high it seemed to be open to the outside. For a moment he was reminded of the main cavern beneath the Plate. That cavern, several miles across, hosted Karst, city of exile.

Then he saw lights far away and knew this, though enormous for a building, was not miles across. The lights marked the far side of the Cortatti great hall, dimmed for night. The lights also pinpointed his target: the bastion at the far east corner.

Before crossing the open space, Kieler faded to his left and into the shadows. He looked up and back at the second floor to watch the promenade that overlooked the great hall. Double doors and windows, darkened, were probably Feleanna's quarters. As he watched, a patrolling guard passed indolently by those doors and continued farther south along the high promenade. The guard was bored. Kieler could almost imagine the man's thoughts: *Why am I here? No one would ever dare to intrude on the Cortatti estate.*

Kieler grinned, and the thrill of what he was doing rose in him.

Kieler dared.

And he would dare much more at tomorrow night's New Year's gala—provided he succeeded here tonight.

Once the guard was gone, Kieler forced himself to stride confidently across the open area. Movus' map had led Kieler to expect big, but the magnitude of the great hall could not be gauged from a mere blueprint. As he crossed, he looked up and actually staggered with vertigo from the emptiness above and before him. The ceiling, and he knew there had to be one, was not visible. The great hall must have been open the full height to the top of the ziggurat.

The lights of the far wall, like pinpoints of stars, eventually resolved to show four rows of columns. The bases of the immense columns were the size of buildings themselves, and they disappeared upward toward the obscured ceiling.

He was awed.

Disgusted at his own reaction, Kieler almost spat. This was typical of the gross opulence and pride of the ruling houses. They must appear imposing beyond limits, untouchable, unapproachable. As an archaic saying went, "Thus they lived, mere mortals; thus they ruled, immortal."

EPISODE 1 – CLASH OF HEIRS

But he knew them to be men, with fears and insecurities, hoarding wealth and holding it close so that no one could wrench it from their clutching grasp. And the Cortattis, through violence and deception, were one of the few houses that could actually maintain such grandeur. Most of the rest of Avertori was in steep decline.

He smiled grimly. Here he was, about to steal a symbol of house power from the most heavily armed, well-guarded, ruthless house in history. And this was only the preamble. This was just preparation for nothing short of a revolution.

Glancing up again, he kept his focus on the lights on the nearing side of the empty gallery; acting out a courage he did not feel. He felt exposed despite the keep's vast dimness. At least he was moving. Poor Bags, sitting back there minding their ride, was probably pacing the cargo hold.

Kieler reached the far wall and found the columned entryway to their main library. He checked it clear and dashed up to the library doors at the base of the tower. He slipped the bolt with a tool from inside his fake uniform jacket and passed inside.

Again the only proper descriptor was "awe." The library went both up and down, every wall of the hexagonal room filled with shelves and books. Kieler had always heard people talk of House Cortatti as mindless brutes—a stereotype Movus had warned Kieler not to believe. Most people would be surprised that they could read. But that they maintained such a well-appointed library—that surprised even Kieler.

In the center, hanging down from the ceiling, was a globe lantern, mostly shuttered. But enough could be seen through the shutters for Kieler to realize it held a cut stone of high-quality luzhril the size of his head—a fortune in itself. The shutters were undoubtedly magal, regulating the energy of the globe for safe use. An unbridled globe that size would be so intense it would cause a sunburn in a very short time.

The light escaping from the suspended lantern allowed Kieler to make out the various artworks displayed around the center of the athenaeum. While he was not a student of art, he was certain each piece was phenomenally expensive. As he passed through the center to the stairs on the far left wall, he could tell another thing too: the art was coordinated. Each piece was carefully placed and set to match in style, size, form and genre. They were on display not only as a show of power, but appreciation. He wondered who had arranged the place.

None of these pieces were what he sought. The cases of jewelry and ornate weapons, paintings and carvings—none were as valuable to the Cortattis as the single item he was after.

He climbed a wrought-iron stair to the top level and a recessed alcove. Another locked door barred his way, and this one Movus had assured him he could not pick, its lock being both shaped and magnetically coded within. But the door was simple dark glass.

Listening for a patrol and hearing nothing, Kieler smashed a hole through the expensive glass and reached his hand in to open the fancy and useless lock mechanism from the inside. The security design was manifest arrogance.

Inside a small sitting room were three fine chairs and a table on which to place their coveted treasures for admiring. Kieler exposed the chip of luzhril on his sheathed rod. He quickly found a small but heavy case on a shelf. The metalized glass was designed to sustain and display four house sigils. Each piece was crafted of the finest luzhril jewels, each unique in the colors of an ancient house. He opened the heavy, magal-lined lid and the gems of each piece flashed to life—a dramatic and inspiring effect. The symbols were designed to be worn on the formal attire of a House Prime as a statement of authority and authenticity. But none of these was the Cortatti's own signet. That they possessed these heirlooms was evidence of treachery.

With a burst of anger, Kieler wanted to scoop out every one of the signets, each representing an extinct house, exterminated by Cortatti in the past. But Movus gave the orders. And he claimed the signets were much more useful in the possession of the Cortattis as a means to damn them, to convict them when the time was right.

But Kieler needed one of these symbols of house legitimacy.

He picked up a jeweled signet in the shape of a six-pointed star, alternating between three long and three short points. The long points of the star were decorated with glittering green luzhril and the short with a lovely golden amber, the stone of time. This iconic shape symbolized history and was the preeminent mark on books and art that preserved the rich achievements and foundational principles upon which a more visionary Omeron had been established. This was the sigil handed down to the successors of House Ortessi.

That the Cortattis held this jeweled emblem was only rumored. The fire that destroyed every member of family Ortessi was officially deemed an accidental tragedy. But every house knew who had arranged it. And every house had looked away from pursuing justice because of the personal cost. To do what was right would have attracted the retribution of House Cortatti. No one wanted to add their own sigil to this growing collection—it wasn't worth the risk.

Kieler's thoughts translated to his fierce grip on the sharp-pointed clasp. He almost drew blood from his own hand before the pain cut through his anger to his rational thought. Time to get out of here. He had what he needed.

He took a long last look around. There were so many artifacts of unimaginable value in the room around him. He licked his lips. To take even one more piece—not to have but to sell—would change his fortune forever. But Kieler had a higher calling; he wanted to bring down this corrupt regime, not become like it. Besides, the other pieces were known to belong to House Cortatti. Possessing one would incriminate Kieler.

This piece, this signet, was not supposed to be here. They could accuse him of nothing without incriminating themselves.

He tucked it into the pocket of his coat and turned to leave.

CHAPTER TWO

He spun out of the private collection room and pulled up short—almost crashing into a guard. The man stood in numb confusion, staring at the broken pane of glass. They stood frozen, mutually shocked, trying to process implications.

While the lackadaisical guard could not fathom that his cushy job had just turned into a nightmare, Kieler reached an actionable decision: He smashed the guard's face with the palm of his hand.

He had intended to knock him senseless, forestalling any reaction by the guard. But instead, the man fell backward, losing his maggun down the metal stairs. Whether he was conscious or not, the metal gun on two stories of metal stairs clanged and echoed as loudly and effectively as any alarm bell.

Kieler flew down after him, barely touching every fifth step.

He dashed from the library and hit the grand hall—and hesitated. He didn't want to cross that open area. But it was the shortest and surest route back to the secret exit. He ran.

Before he was halfway across he saw guards coming from the sides to investigate the odd alarm. One was coming straight toward him.

Kieler didn't slow but called out to the approaching man. "It's Corwain! He fell down the stairs and hit his head. I'm going for help!"

The guard, not recognizing Kieler but also not able to believe he could be an infiltrator in the dead center of the keep, stopped and motioned for Kieler to stop. "Who's Corwain?"

Kieler passed him running and called back, "The new guy. Get a doctor!"

The man started chasing Kieler, slowly at first. "Who are you?"

But Kieler had run out of names and diversions. He poured on the speed. He heard the whine of a maggun being powered up. He started veering randomly to make a harder target, opening up the distance.

EPISODE 1 – CLASH OF HEIRS

"Stop that man!"

The first maggun bolt was fired from the man he had passed. It went wide in the dim light, but not so wide that it didn't add adrenaline speed to Kieler's feet.

Other alarms were ringing now. Real alarms. Before he reached the stairs, he saw lights come on in the long suite of rooms on the second level. Feleanna Cortatti's rooms.

He reached the wall and bounded down the stairs. Grabbing the banister he swung around the first landing and glimpsed a guard coming up. Kieler launched himself, using the high ground advantage and his plunging momentum. Catching the unready guard full in the chest with both feet, the guard flew backward all the way to the next landing, never touching a single step on the way down. Kieler kept his momentum and swung completely over the rail to the next flight of stairs. That man didn't follow and Kieler kept up his headlong descent to the bottom.

By the time he reached the corridor, he could hear footfalls from every direction getting close fast.

A guard popped out several yards in front of him as Kieler reached the doorway to the wine tasting room. The man's maggun was already spun up, and as he leveled and shot, Kieler dove out of the corridor, accidentally tackling one of the wine tables. Fumbling for footing, he half crawled, half lurched to the storage room door, knocking over two more tables on the way. He found his footing just in time to crash through the storage room door.

Behind him, a guard fired. The bolt missed Kieler but several wine bottles exploded in front of him. Kieler stepped full speed into the liquid. As he slipped, he twisted.

His heightened awareness caused time to slow, and he had the prescience to wonder as a leveled blade passed inches above his falling face. He gawked at the inconceivable, fierce beauty of the woman he was about to collide with. Her bold, chiseled features were outlined by a wild halo of crimson hair. To further add to the incongruous vision, Kieler saw she wore nothing but a gossamer nightgown reaching only to mid-thigh.

Out of control, Kieler landed hard on his left shoulder and slid into her legs. But somehow, in a feat of dexterity he would always remember, she leapt, flipped her sword over, and stabbed downward as she too fell. Whether she had aimed for his heart and missed, or aimed with intentional, instinctive sadism, she pierced the shoulder he had just slammed to the floor.

The blazing pain was oddly incidental.

Escape.

Escape was his only focus. He spun on the floor and pushed off the far wine rack, propelling himself toward the thankfully still open hatch. Wine bottles cascaded down from the shaken rack, bombarding the deadly angel. The only thought he spared for her was: *She must not follow me down.*

Head first into the hole he clutched for the ladder rungs. He caught the second one down—with his left elbow, wrenching the now bleeding shoulder. Despite his focus, his vision blurred with pain. He lurched back up and grabbed the hatch, slamming it closed. The heavy tile sounded like a thunderbolt itself as it smashed down. But that wouldn't be enough. *The woman had to know about this entrance, didn't she?*

She would unlatch it and he would be followed. From a leg sheath he pulled a four-inch blade and jammed it into the latching mechanism, essentially double latching it so that it could not be opened from above.

He slid down the ladder, the pain now fierce. At the bottom he had enough presence of mind to grab up his mask and cloak. Then he ran.

He sprinted down the under-garden passageway. He prayed that as they organized no one but the woman would know of the secret passage. And she would have to get word to the guards outside. He should not find guards welcoming him at the statue entrance.

EPISODE 1 – CLASH OF HEIRS

It made sense. Probably only the ruling family members knew of the tunnel's existence.

He could hear nothing in the corridor but his own footfalls and heavy breathing. The abrupt silence was strange after such violence. He held his left arm with his right. His shoulder burned.

At the other end he climbed quickly into the pedestal of the statue and slowly released the catch. Peering through the crack he saw guards running toward the residence. So far, they must have figured he was still trapped inside the keep. When clear, he swung open the door and crawled quickly out. He shut the pedestal door and ducked into cover beside the bushes.

More lights were on at the citadel and sirens blared. He clung to the shadows, crawling toward the trees. It was but a few feet later that glaring arc lights began blazing to life all over the garden and his concealing shadows began to vanish.

He felt exposed, but the bushes still blocked line of sight with the guards patrolling the keep. He had nearly made it to the trees when he saw a guard coming toward him. With no shadows he had only one choice: he dove into the center of the hedgerow and froze.

The oncoming watchman hadn't seen him. Within seconds the running man passed by. Had Kieler reached out his hand he could have grabbed the guard's ankle. But the foliage of the bush hid him. It also scratched the skin of his hands and face like the claws of a wild animal.

As the guard ran on toward the main keep, Kieler crawled out and dashed into the trees. He ran from tree to tree now, knowing more guards might be coming this way to get to the main building. Soon enough they would be coming out from the keep, guided by the woman. He avoided two more of the gathering sentinels and had to break cover to sprint for the door to the steps leading down to the Plate level. Kieler hoped Bags was ready for a quick getaway.

CHAPTER TWO

As he flung open the door he had jammed open earlier, a shout rang out behind him. He'd been spotted.

Kieler swore. *Why not just two seconds more?* He'd have been through the door unseen. But he had the lead, and sheer fright gave his legs strength to take the stairs five and six at a time, guided by his good hand on the railing.

He was more than halfway down the ten or so stories when pursuit came through the door above. One shot pinged down through the metal stairs, but it was so obviously ineffective that they didn't shoot again. They bolted down the stairs after him.

He gained the ground level and sprinted across the dock. Now metal bolts followed him as the guardsmen shot from the landings of the metal staircase. He ran so as to put the crane between him and his pursuers. Magbolts sent sparks showering down as they rang off the metal of the loading crane.

Passing the freighter, he spotted their sled with no small measure of relief. Bags had turned it around, ready to run, and had the top hatch opened enough to peer out. He saw Kieler immediately.

"*Sparks!* Come on!" Bags flung open the hatch and then dropped out of sight, heading for the cockpit.

Kieler jumped down into the deep cut V of the track, sliding down the magal slope. He hit the top of the sled and rolled. Magbolts clanged off the hull around him. Multiple shooters, but no one seemed to have a clear shot as the rain again worked to Kieler and Bags' advantage. This time Kieler didn't go headfirst down the hatch, but swung down, caught himself with his good arm and pulled the hatch closed over him.

"Get this sled moving!" Kieler shouted down. Before he hit the floor of the cargo hold, the raider lurched forward and acceleration pressed Kieler immobile against the ladder. The hammering of magbolts on the hull dropped off within moments. His mask slid out from under his arm and fell diagonally toward the rear of the hold, stopping only when it hit the engine compartment bulkhead. He grunted and tried to pry his head back through the rungs of the ladder.

Eventually he muscled himself down the ladder, and though still in full acceleration, managed to crawl through the open hatch into the cockpit. Looking up through the narrow windshield, he saw brilliant lights ahead: the gate! From the guardhouse, more magbolts pinged uselessly off the hull. Then Kieler's heart dropped as he glimpsed two giant rail guns atop the gate, one pointing toward them and one aimed down the track in the direction they were going. A shell whizzed over their heads and Kieler barely felt its detonation behind them—the guards hadn't compensated for the sled's great speed. A breath later the gates flashed overhead. They were through—still accelerating. Before relief and exhilaration had time to take hold, another shell detonated ahead of them, tearing open the upper right of the track. Magal fragments rained down onto the raider. Had they been a full-size freighter, they would have unbalanced and tumbled end over end. As it was they shot by the ragged hole and out of range.

"Back her off!" Kieler grunted, still on the floor. "We gotta slow down before we hit the curve!"

But Bags was also revved, and though he pulled back on the throttle, he only did so to neutral. The sled skimmed down the magnetic track barely slowing. They hit the first curve at still over 400 and were thrown sideways. Kieler smashed his already hurt shoulder and Bags, straining to stay in his seat, finally reversed the impeller to decelerate without throwing Kieler through the windscreen.

Kieler groaned and fell into his seat.

"Did you get it?" Bags glanced sideways at him.

Kieler reached into his jacket and pulled out the gold and green-jeweled star. "I got it."

Bags whooped and clapped his friend on the shoulder, eliciting a wince and a scream. "You ok?"

CHAPTER TWO

"I got stabbed. I think it was Feleanna Cortatti," he grimaced.

Bags' eyes went wide. "What! Sorry. But you did it! You didn't need good stars; you just needed *one* good star, and you got it!"

"I got it," Kieler repeated, relaxing as they slowed to a more controllable speed.

CHAPTER THREE

Deftly, Bags navigated through a series of quick track switches toward a little-known passage through the Plate. Kieler watched his friend enjoying the feel of the nimble craft. They shared a few moments of elated silence, but as that elation slowly ebbed, Kieler realized he probably wouldn't be seeing his friend and former subordinate for a long time.

Gently Kieler doffed his uniform jacket and wrapped it around his shoulder. It was still seeping, but the wound was amazingly straight, as if cut with a surgeon's scalpel. A deeper hit would have easily killed or dismembered. He shuddered then winced with the pain of movement.

Letting the pain subside, he spoke as the craft hissed quietly in the bottom of the track. "You know, Bags, I'm leaving tomorrow on this mission. I'll be gone a long time if things go well, permanently if they don't." He let that sink in. "You're captain of Slink Squad now. You're going to have to teach one of the guys to do the driving of this little beast while you do the leading."

Looking sidelong at Kieler, Bags frowned. "Gotta spoil the fun, eh? They slowed further and Kieler went on. "Yeah, well, we gotta remember why we fight, each of us. And you have to remember the motivation of your men, not just yours."

His frown turning to a deep scowl, Bags replied, "Mine I'll never forget. Someone steals your wife—" Kieler could almost hear Bags' teeth grinding. He hated to remind Bags of ugly memories, but those memories kept a man focused. "I suppose everyone has some reason for hating the highborns. "Some reasons aren't as bitter. Take Caprice; he never knew his parents. He's just lost. As far as anyone knows, he was born under the Plate."

"Yeah," Bags agreed. "He's reckless. No family. Doesn't really care about living or dying, just what he can get that day."

"Yes, but Bags he *does* have a family now."

Bags mused on that as they slowed to a crawl and pulled into an abandoned warehouse. "Us."

Kieler smiled at him. "Remember that and your whole squad will remember it."

They both jumped out and opened a grate in the floor. Within seconds the two raiders had disappeared from Avertori and were descending through the Plate.

This entrance was one of about thirty Kieler knew of, most of them well hidden. The two men donned their masks and moved quickly through massive conduits, rubble heaps, and tunnels— always heading down. Kieler led almost without thinking, winding through the maze in which he'd grown up. He unsheathed the luzhril shard he'd used on the raid and lit their way. It didn't pass unremembered that when he had found this passage as a teenager he only had a jar of light lugs. Movus had given the luzhril on the rod to him much later.

They leaned sideways as they scooted under the slope of a fallen slab, then climbed up a rock heap and half-slid down the other side. A broken tower angled down, forming a long part of their path, but before the end they crawled through a shattered window and into a hollowed-out space that narrowed into another tunnel that had obviously been dug out to allow men to squeeze through. His shoulder throbbed but keeping pressure on it minimized blood loss, and Kieler knew he would be all right. To properly treat the wound they would need the medical supplies in Movus' quarters. He always had the best.

Once the two men turned into the main tunnels, they encountered other residents of the underground city. Though some still kept time and schedule with the world above, many did not, going about their business at unusual hours. Their passing was acknowledged with a glance or a nod, but Kieler knew the insignia on their masks and even the masks themselves evoked respect and a touch of fear. Kieler had earned the insignia he wore over the right eyehole of his mask. The purpose with which they moved and the blood on Kieler's clothes further increased the distance of those not in the Coin.

Some couldn't help passing close. A grimy man, sweating copiously, pushed a three-wheeled cart up the slope Kieler and Bags were coming down. His face was set and to stop would be to lose upward momentum. As he passed, the front wheel hit a rut in the rough surface and the cart tipped. Kieler and Bags both reacted to steady it, but the motion sent a blaze of light out the top of the high-sided cart.

Light lugs. The cart was packed with various containers, from glass jars to rough urns squirming with the bioluminescent insects largely used for portable light beneath the Plate.

This man had worked hard to collect such numbers of the pests. To lose them in a tip-over would have been a financial disaster.

But his "smile" of appreciation to the two Coin operatives was nothing more than a scowl and a thankful nod.

In the world above the Plate, especially at the Cortatti Estate, the streets were smooth and rubble would have been cleared. But *here,* both the street, the sides of the street, and the ceiling of every tunnel were *carved* out of rubble. If he hadn't just been at the immaculately tended gardens of the Cortattis, Kieler wouldn't have even noticed. Growing up in these wasted ruins of a city—a city long dead before Avertori was built—rubble was Kieler's normal.

The end of this wider tunnel opened onto the perimeter of a space so large it had its own ambient light, albeit weak. Kieler and Bags skirted the edge of the Karst Borough. Noise from commerce, from hundreds of thousands of people living in these ruins, filled the air.

The Plate separating above from below spanned the entire Isle of Threes on which Avertori stood. Why it had been built, Kieler could only guess. Under the Plate, the majority of the population existed mainly in these various boroughs. People settled in these larger hollows out of social need, and even in Kieler's brief years the population had grown as Avertori above declined. The largest and busiest of these boroughs was Karst.

From the low path on which they trod, they could see little of what was sometimes called the Karst Plain, referring to its relatively wide expanse. But their world was also deep—deep beyond knowledge. Kieler wondered if even Movus (who still seemed like the parent who knew everything) had explored the full depth of this dark netherworld. Most exiles took up residence as close to the surface as possible in any area free of rubble. Karst was so wide and open that the Plate itself roofed it.

Kieler and Bags reached the hollowed-out corridor leading to Movus' home under Karst. It was a quiet corridor, with Movus' place being the only residence. His home had the added privilege of a solid stone door with a magnetic lock similar to the one on the Cortatti library, except this one had no glass to break. The two successful raiders knocked, received no reply, and Kieler used his key to let them in, eager to share their success with Kieler's mentor. But as they entered Movus' library, they realized the head of their intelligence network was, as usual, not home.

With hardly a word, Kieler pushed aside a spread of plans on a polished stone table and lay down, unwrapping the crude dressing from his pierced shoulder as he did.

EPISODE 1 – CLASH OF HEIRS

"Leave that to me," Bags rumbled at him. "Leaders are always the worst patients."

"I thought doctors were the worst patients."

Bags' only response was a short grunt as he opened one of many cabinets and withdrew a cleaning solvent and a ceramic bottle hand-labeled "Bio-salve". This was not entirely an unfamiliar process. Other jobs had found them injured worse.

As Bags cleaned his shoulder, Kieler tried to lie still despite his racing mind. He wondered at the bottle of salve. He had innocently asked for some from an Avertoric doctor after one of his incursions above the Plate. The doc had no clue what he was talking about. Yes, Movus knew stuff.

A knock at the door, ignored three times, finally bugged Bags enough to go see who it was. Though he couldn't see the door from the library, Kieler could tell the man pushed his way past Bags despite insistent protests.

"I'll throw you out!" Bags said as the stooped man shuffled into the library.

Kieler leaned his head back on a stack of papers and sniffed the air. "What's that smell?"

Over the man's prog-like snort, Bags muttered, "Dirt, filth and swamp-water."

In a way, Zroom, the room's new and unwanted visitor, had an advantage against Bags' hugely superior muscle: he looked like a decrepit old man. It was hard to hit him and feel good about it.

"Stay away from my patient!" Bags commanded. "You'll contaminate the wound."

With an indistinct chuff, Zroom did stay back just far enough for Bags to work. Zroom was one of the under-Plate's few farmers, raising an exotic crop that was actually quite profitable: truffles. Most of his crop he smuggled through the Plate and sold to House addicts at exorbitant prices. Some of his unusual fungi were said to have psychotropic properties that clarified one's thinking. Nevertheless, they grew in the wettest, rottenest, smelliest parts of the underground. His infused aroma did not add to his already scarce popularity.

"What do you want, Zroom?" Kieler asked, not giving him the respect of looking at him. "Come to tell us how to run the world again?"

"Yup," said the man without a hint of doubt. "You need it. You go off and get yourself stabbed on some reckless raid, and you don't have an ounce of common sense about how to run a new government should you actually manage to destroy the old one."

His heavy lids and saggy, sallow face contradicted his confident tirade. But this was not a new argument. Since both Kieler and Bags ignored him while Bags doused a piece of gauze with the salve, Zroom continued, this time with questions.

"What did you do? Raid Cortatti headquarters? Are you as daft as I've been asserting for all these years?"

Bags shot him an enraged look, and had he not been applying the balm to Kieler's shoulder at that very moment, he probably would have grabbed Zroom by the neck. "How do you know what we've been doing, spy?"

A smile that looked more like a scowl cracked the dirty man's face. "And you're our intelligence squad? We're in worse trouble than I've been grumbling about."

Bags' free hand swiped around in an annoyed attempt to backhand him. Zroom had moved two steps away to avoid just such a lashing.

"Blood-stained Cortatti uniform on the ground isn't much of a hint, is it?"

"Bags..." Kieler warned. "Anything you say gives him more ammunition."

A rumble like a grevon growl sounded deep in Bags' chest. But Zroom had moved to the medicine cabinet and was examining the contents with an appreciative look on his flabby face.

EPISODE 1 – CLASH OF HEIRS

"Stop snooping," Kieler said mildly. "Movus finds out you touched anything and he'll have fifty of us fighting each other for who gets to kill you."

Zroom turned and nodded. "My point made. If you succeed you get to be puppet EC. Movus jerks your strings. And fifty grevons fight over the scraps. What a country."

Kieler winced despite the salve's amazing ability to soothe even as it healed. He winced because though he knew that what he was doing was necessary, he did wonder how the end result would be better. Zroom had hit a nerve.

Interjecting for his patient, Bags asked through clenched teeth. "What do you want Zroom and how can we get rid of you?"

"I want to shape this world. You need my wisdom and the only way you'll get it is if I cram it into your over-muscled heads."

At this Kieler cracked a smile. "Why not use your irresistible charisma, Zroom?"

Another snort. "That's you're department, Sparks. I know you're smart. Bags less so, but not entirely stupid. You should listen to me."

"Why?" both said simultaneously.

"Because not everyone agrees with the Coin. Because you don't know what you're doing. And, because I know how to organize working systems; profitable, organized, sustainable working systems. You two just know how to break stuff and blow stuff up."

Neither responded to the muck-stained farmer. Bags was now sewing, and that *did* hurt.

Eyes closed, Kieler muttered, "I did break a lot of stuff tonight, Bags."

Even though he was concentrating on sewing Kieler's wound closed, Bags replied, "And Caprice got to blow some stuff up..." Pretending to acquiesce to Zroom's superior intelligence, Bags heaved a melodramatic sigh. "Well, you're right again Zroom. You can go now."

CHAPTER THREE

Through the condescension, Kieler noted with pride that Bags, despite his annoyance with Zroom, was quite gently sewing his shoulder while patiently bearing Zroom's abrasive presence.

"Revolution requires forethought, during-thought, and afterthought. All those involve *thought!*" Zroom's tone was acidic. "You just rush into action, stirring up the most violent house on Zotikas with no thinking about the result. We need to organize a government *now*. We need to practice governing *now*. We have the perfect chance to create a free-market system of equal opportunity *down here now,* and aside from the Coin, we're in total anarchy."

"A market system that allows you to make even more money, Zroom, without risking your neck smuggling," Bags poked.

Color rose in Zroom's face, making him look a little like the purplish truffles he sold. "Who else in this hell-hole knows anything about systems! Sparks doesn't remember anything other than waifing around these tunnels trying to survive. And you, Bags, are a bottom-beaten lackey who toadied for Telander until he woke you up by rap—"

So much for patience. Bags' huge fist swung around like a runaway powercoach. Nevertheless, it was astonishing how fast the bedraggled looking farmer could move when he realized he had overstepped his provocation. There were no goodbyes. Zroom ran for the door and out. With jaws so tightly clenched he could have ground off the tops of his teeth, Bags returned to Kieler, who was nauseous with the pain of having two stitches ripped out by Bags' outburst.

Bags' temper cooled instantly when he saw what he had done to his friend. "I'm sorry, Sparks," he muttered. Instantly his eyes were wet. "I'm sorry. That prog— My Eznea—"

In silence Bags finished the rest of the procedure and bound up Kieler's shoulder.

Kieler looked away from the operation now, his stomach not quite settled. He found distraction in a globe of Zotikas—their world—that Movus had evidently found in the depths of the rubble. The ancient globe spun perpetually but was not physically supported in its gimbals. Bemused by pain, he became simultaneously aware of the sheer mass of wrecked city around him. This private library, filled with ancient texts and artifacts, was itself surrounded by rubble—above, around and beneath.

An arm's length in front of him, the vast lands of Zotikas passed in and out of view. Avertori came round into sight, sitting on the island in the center of the world; its unique position at the convergence of three continents and three seas. To the northeast, Ardan; to the southeast, rugged Coprackus; and to the northwest, the fertile plains of Govian.

But the place names on *this* globe were not the same. They were from a different time, long forgotten. And this library and the rubble around it gave testimony to the greater civilization that had once thrived here.

"Can you imagine how huge the city of the Dead Ones must have been?" Kieler mused.

Bags took a moment to reply. He was nearly finished playing surgeon and his fatigue seemed to be catching up with him as his emotional energy ebbed. "Hmm. Couldn't have been much bigger than Avertori is now. Our city covers the whole island and more."

Frowning, Kieler disagreed. "I think it was bigger—not in width, but height. Just looking at how much rubble there is, it must have reached far into the sky. It must have been a truly great civilization."

Bags snorted. "Still fell. We live in their trash."

Kieler shrugged. "Mmm. True, but those times had to be better than these. We've *got* to make this world better..."

Bags said nothing and Kieler guessed they were both thinking of past pain. They weren't the only ones. Bleakness and pain seemed to be engulfing their world. Every person under the Plate had a story of heartbreak.

CHAPTER THREE

Kieler shifted his attention to the gimbals around the globe. Battered but functional, there was little left of the embossed inscription. In the flickering red light of the room, he read what remained: *While we live, let us live.* Movus had suggested it as the motto of the Coin, and the subtly rebellious message was quickly adopted by the underworld organization.

Slumping into a thickly padded chair, Bags closed his eyes.

Kieler rose slowly and turned from the globe to pace slowly around the library. He strode beneath the vaulted stone ceiling toward the center of the triangular room. All three walls were stacked top to bottom with artifacts of such a wide variety that he had difficulty imagining how Movus could have collected them all in one lifetime.

In a corner was a simple spear that bore no markings save a single inscription: *Ride fast. Fly true.* Spears hadn't been used in nearly a thousand years. *Where did he get that?* On a shelf near the ancient weapon stood a cloudy frame with a three-dimensional image of an island burned into the mist. That technology was a complete mystery, not of this era either.

Kieler stopped next to the most prominent of all the collected artifacts: a large, glowing sphere of red luzhril on a pedestal. The sphere supplied light and some heat to the subterranean library. It was not as bright as normal white luzhril, but its rare burgundy color probably made it even more valuable than the Cortatti's library globe.

Turning back to the table they had commandeered as an operating slab, he shuffled through the two years' worth of work that lay stacked and spread before him. Even now he resisted reviewing the documents one more time. The red glow of the sphere and something about the table and its one empty chair brought back a memory.

It was the memory of himself, sitting in that same chair; he must have been about sixteen or seventeen. He was looking up at Movus, who was doing what Kieler had just been doing, standing and staring into the swirling opalescence of the red sphere. Kieler had asked, "May I ask you, why did you have to leave the city above?"

Not replying immediately, something between a smile and a grimace played on his face. "No, you may not," Movus replied definitively. His jet black, straight hair reflected the deep red light, and his very light brown eyes, usually the color of sun-ripened grain common to those of Govian descent, shone with the sphere's light. He looked down at Kieler. "Suffice to say I was treated horribly. I went from prophet to pariah, shunned."

Though he said no more, Kieler could read deep pain in Movus' light eyes, a pain he felt keenly himself. Never could Kieler forget the deaths of his parents, or the highborns who caused it. The reflected orb-light danced with the intense fire of revenge. The look frightened Kieler, though he was already a savvy young man.

Nodding, Kieler returned to the present and realized he'd memorized every detail of the plan on the papers in front of him. It was the first major step of revolution—a revolution designed to end his world's pain and bring purpose to his own suffering. Obviously it would bring some solace to his mentor's hidden grieving as well. That the smelly, arrogant farmer Zroom wasn't a privileged member of those making things happen—that was just as well.

Kieler turned and once again stared into the warmth and swirling luminescence of the unique red lamp, visualizing in his mind exactly how their plan would manifest.

The civilization of Avertori was ruled by the Prime houses; dynasties that had hoarded power for generations. Kieler and Movus had worked out a plan to gain Kieler a strategic position amongst them, a position to strike from.

When House Ortessi had been destroyed twenty years ago in a "mysterious" fire, one body was never found: that of the child Orlazrus, the youngest son. Movus had used his contacts to drop hints that the now grown Orlazrus was planning his return.

CHAPTER THREE

Kieler picked up the sigil from the table and twisted it in his hand, his fingers between the points of the star. The Ortessi Sigil would give his claim great credibility. Only Feleanna Cortatti would know the truth, and she wouldn't be able to say anything without incriminating her own house.

Once rumors had spread, it had been relatively simple to get the other houses fighting over the "privilege" of introducing Orlazrus at court. But spreading rumors had been much simpler than his next task: showing up to the party alive.

"So where's Movus?" Bags asked groggily, not opening his eyes.

"I never know," Kieler replied. "Running the largest spy network on the planet; it's probably best he stays invisible."

"Even to you? But he practically raised you."

Kieler shrugged and walked back to the spinning globe of Zotikas. "I never even saw much of him growing up. He showed up to guide me and teach me: how to observe, how to fight... to dance."

Without turning, Kieler saw Bags crack open one eye. "To dance? Why?"

Kieler smiled. "If you're a good spy captain, maybe he'll teach you someday too."

Letting out a grunt, Bags closed his eyes again. Within moments his breathing evened out into a light snore.

"We're doing something, Bags," Kieler whispered excitedly, not really wanting to wake him. "I'm actually point man for something that will make a difference in our world." He reached out and put a hand on the globe to stop it, but the slippery sphere just kept spinning.

CHAPTER FOUR

It was a pit.

The nethercity was a big, dark hole in the ground where people had thrown the junk of an entire ruined civilization. Kieler stood alone atop an ancient mountain of debris and looked out over Karst. From this vantage he could see the dim outlines of the scattered dwellings below, thousands of hovels of arranged rubble lit by the faint glow of luminescent lichen. Very few were lucky enough to own even a splinter of luzhril. Jars of light lugs bobbed in lines indicating the movement of people through the ever-dark city.

Rising up from amongst the faint lights of humanity were darker shadows of various shapes and heights. Some of these "mountains" reached all the way to the underside of the Plate and indicated a portal through which those above had dumped refuse until they had literally piled it to the top.

The middle of the Karst Borough was interrupted by a gash of even deeper darkness. The enormous chasm, unimaginatively called the Abyss, separated the east side of the sunless city from the west. The only connection was a half-mile section of fallen tower serving as a bridge, though by going out of the way, one could skirt the ends of the gap.

Above, Kieler felt the oppressive weight of the Plate sealing the city like the lid of an enormous coffin. Spiking through the Plate at regular intervals, except for where the expanse of the Abyss dropped into nothingness, were dozens of immense, black columns. These pillars reached from the bedrock far below to the highest levels of the city above. It was these timeless structures, built by a civilization long gone, that formed the cornerstones upon which the great trade houses of the current era had fashioned their Rei-lit metropolis.

But the people below, subsisting on the shadowy plain beneath the Plate, were Kieler's friends—outcasts, just like him. Rejected by the major houses, they fled here, or if they could make it, to some remote outland location beyond the reach of the Omeron. At least they weren't criminals bound for Feleanna's Arena.

This city is reversed, he thought. *The random specks of light and life below are like stars, and the unseen, shallow, metal Plate above like a reflection-less sea.*

Curiously, as he looked up at the bottom of the Plate, in one area he saw faint but definite points of light, different from the weak aura of lichen. It was like a cluster of a half-dozen stars. Odd, but not Kieler's concern as he mustered himself to leave the dim underworld. Dropping his gaze from the wispy light, Kieler wondered if he would ever see this shadow-city again, his home for most of his life. After the raid on the Cortatti compound, he had napped, packed, and finally donned his disguise to climb to this point. Behind him, away from the slope of rubbish leading down to Karst, stood a heavy stone arch, marking the beginning of the main path out of the nethercity.

Years ago, Kieler had made this trip in reverse with his father. In self-imposed exile, his father had led him through the Dragon's Gate, down the crumbling, pillared path and under the Arch of Darkness to dwell in the city of night. Most, like his father, never saw the light of Rei again.

Kieler remembered the fear of that moment, standing in this same spot, a child of eight, clinging to his father's side. His fear now was just as real, but this time it was a result of his own choice to leave.

Growing up here had been a depressing adventure. Kieler couldn't just sit by and watch his father work obsessively on his processes and engines. So he explored. He knew this place. He knew more of this labyrinth of tunnels, passages, crawlspaces, sewers, nooks, hideouts and boroughs than almost anyone alive. This had been his perpetually gloomy playground.

More than once he had become lost deep down below Avertori, to the point of thinking he would never find his way back.

Yet he always had. And he had made a life for himself here. After his father was killed, Movus gave Kieler opportunity and direction through the Coin, despite the infrequency of his actual presence. Kieler had striven for advancement and risen quickly in the ranks.

Now he was leaving his life underground and taking on a new life above, a life not his own, and the life, he thought wryly, of a supposed dead man.

He was point man for a revolution. Most people, below and above, had little hope or purpose in their lives. He had both, and it made the prize worth the risks.

He took a last look at the faint sparks of light below, lights that represented people he knew and cared about. That he was fighting for them, and the respect of Movus, made him proud.

Given it was a pit—it was still home.

Kieler turned and stepped through the Arch.

Before him lay a low-ceilinged subterranean road that led to the Dragon's Gate, a portal between the cities of light and dark that opened to a public square in a rough part of Avertori. As the most well-known entrance, those who lived in the light often threatened their small children with it. "You keep up like that, young man, and I'll send you down the Dragon's throat!"

Kieler didn't want to use this gate. He would have preferred to sneak through one of the most hidden access portals, but he knew he probably wasn't the only one to know even that entrance. And now, as Zroom had pointed out, they had sparked the wrath of the Cortatti's; every gate would be watched. It would be better if he exited into a public place. At least he'd have a chance of getting on his way and shaking off sure pursuit.

The road upward must have been grand thousands of years ago. The fluted columns, now mere stubs, lined the pebbled path every few steps. What esteemed property it had announced, Kieler had no idea. Everything below whispered of something lost long past.

He passed a splintery wood counter to the right of the path between two columns. Behind the counter, in the gloom, was a shadowy crack where the proprietor of this strange general store lived. Al, who Kieler now knew well, sold necessities to the exiles as they filed down this wrecked promenade to their new home.

On that very counter, Al had thunked the first jar of light lugs Kieler had ever seen, frightening them into light. They were a necessity to be sure, but they were also a rampant pest, easily caught once you knew what you were doing. Kieler's father had paid a premium price for those bugs many years ago.

But now, the fact that Al wasn't tending store at the moment made Kieler's journey up even lonelier. He took a deep breath and continued climbing the desolate road toward Avertori and the light of the fading day.

The broken columns on either side of him echoed with greatness and disaster. Beyond the columns lurked dark niches and a shadowed silence—deep and heavy. As the road climbed toward the surface, Kieler could feel the Plate pressing down on him.

His confidence and resolve hardened as he strode up the path through the rubbish-packed landscape. His first identity was Geren, a street-wise magal loader. His face was hidden in fake, unkempt facial hair and he wore rough work clothes. It was a persona he'd used many times in his dealings for the Coin.

EPISODE 1 – CLASH OF HEIRS

What little light there was continued to dim. He could barely see the bottom layer of the Plate as he ascended through it. A vast truss-work crisscrossed between the top and bottom layer. Unexpectedly, Kieler heard a rapid flutter close to his head. He spun to look but saw nothing. *Just jitters,* he thought, but quickened his pace nonetheless.

The last few steps brought him beneath the huge trapezoidal hatch in the upper Plate—the Dragon's Gate. A rust-roughened lever half the length of his body extended from one of the metal trusses. Using both hands, Kieler slowly heaved back on the lever, the hatch above him groaning like a wounded beast and tilting downward into the dim space between the upper and lower Plate.

When a crack of light appeared along the seam, Kieler stopped.

A small brown trennek, a bird common to most of Zotikas, flew up and landed on a thin piece of metal near the crack. It looked back at Kieler as if commanding, *Open the door.*

Kieler was surprised. Birds were rare in the nethercity. It looked at him steadily, and Kieler got the distinct impression that it was waiting for him to say something. It reminded him of another animal—a similar look. He thought, and the memory came back to him: the brown slink.

One time, when his father was still alive, Kieler had been exploring. Cave-ins were common, but this time he was squeezing through a narrow tunnel and dislodged a chunk of concrete. The whole mass to his right shifted, sliding sideways into him and pinning him against the left wall. He could go neither forward nor back. With a jar of light lugs on a necklace, he could look around but could not get leverage on the wall of debris to dig out. Ahead of him he'd heard a scurrying sound and looked to see a brown slink about nine inches tall, standing on its hind legs on a shelf of broken material.

CHAPTER FOUR

It had cocked its head, inquisitively, much like the trennek now, waiting. Slinks were scavengers and normally stayed away. But young Kieler, trapped like one of his light lugs, was very scared of this confident looking rodent.

For over an hour, it just waited, watching as Kieler bloodied his hands digging out packed rubble from behind him until finally, body bruised and fingers raw, he squeezed forward and toward the creature and freedom.

As the boy-Kieler had moved toward the rodent, the slink had looked him in the eye, looked away, *looked back,* then dropped to all fours and slithered away.

This bird was the same way. Many things on Zotikas, and especially under it, were ancient and mysterious. Kieler, for all his love of learning how things worked, didn't pretend to understand everything.

"Well, trennek," he now spoke to the bird. "We'll both find freedom on the other side of this door. Let's go." He hauled back the lever the rest of the way, and the gate pivoted downward, becoming a ramp. Counterweights rose along a truss-piece next to him, offsetting the weight of the massive gate.

He squinted and his eyes adjusted. Then he walked up the ramp into Avertori.

The bird fluttered around his head and up into the shadows *above* the Plate. As he followed it with his eyes, Kieler noted how dimly Rei penetrated these lower levels. Even so, it was much brighter than the preternatural light of the nethercity. The winter solstice and the lateness of the afternoon cast the lower city into a prolonged twilight.

He stood in the middle of a shabby plaza in The Glums, the lowest section of Avertori built directly on the Plate. Party-goers were in full force, and even this dreary plaza was already busy. That was why Kieler had chosen this place; if the Cortattis or anyone else had hired mercenaries to kill him, they'd have to sort him out of a crowd first. He grinned to himself that agents of the Prime

43

houses rarely ventured under the Plate while "criminals" like himself came up more than occasionally.

One reason was that agents of the Coin dissuaded intrusion into the shadowy realm below, often violently. Besides, there was nothing to gain from Karst's poverty-infested populace. But there was another reason as well. The nethercity wasn't always as "tame" as it was now. Wild animals and other creatures had reign over the darker regions below the Plate until even a hundred years ago. Kieler knew the stories of Devolay and Tesaran, heroes of that era that had killed many strange creatures or driven them deeper into regions not inhabited by humankind. As things above continued to deteriorate, more people were exiled below and sheer need raised up men to conquer the regions closer to the Plate.

But though the creatures had died, the rumors did not. And residents of the light were easily frightened by the dark.

Kieler turned and pulled another rust-begrimed lever, raising the hatch and eliciting another groan. It closed with a heavy thump. Then he surveyed the surrounding buildings, looking for the creatures Feleanna may have loosed—the low-life mercenaries with no cause but a few dras.

The Isle of Threes had little real vegetation; instead it was covered with a forest of colossal buildings. Kieler had only been in a real forest once, on the continent of Govian to the northwest. It was two years before his mother died and he still remembered the immensity of the towering trees, magnified by his six-year-old perception.

These man-made skytowers needed no magnification. The tallest columns thrust upward through the Plate and soared over two hundred stories into the sky. From here, however, the sky was mostly occluded by the myriad skyways and elevated plazas that formed the canopy of the city. A few determined shafts of sunlight slanted across the gloom, illuminating the ubiquitous dust of Avertori's lowest level.

CHAPTER FOUR

Like layers of moss and mold at the bases of trees, dreary shops and tenement houses huddled around the bases of the high rises. These scabby structures were filled with millions of residents preparing for the New Year's celebration and a night of revelry. For those who lived this low, the celebration meant nothing more than drinking into oblivion and whatever other debauchery they could indulge in.

As Kieler progressed higher, there would be many other varieties of entertainment, both finer and coarser.

He moved to one side of the plaza and his eyes were drawn to a tower shooting up some distance away. This tower, its three-spired top blocked from view by a tangle of skyways and suspended terraces, supported the palace of the Executive Chair. Tonight, every family with power would be celebrating the New Year in that palace by special invitation.

Kieler had written his own invitation.

From the darkened alcoves of the surrounding buildings, shadows stirred to life, roused by the opening of the Dragon's Gate. These watchers probably knew Kieler's identity as Geren, and his disguise should abate their desire to kill him. After quick consideration, he decided he could use their pursuit to wrap up a few loose ends. As he headed purposefully for a narrow alley, three of the shadows resolved into the forms of seedy men.

To them, Geren was a black market business lackey, supposedly a lowly magal worker by day, but well connected. And that was Kieler's cover, a man who chummed the water so that bigger fish could make deals and move contraband outside the official channels of Avertori's controlled economy. He was a small fry, tolerated but always tailed because of the people he connected. There was no way of knowing whether they would follow him because he was Geren or because they somehow suspected his real identity.

EPISODE 1 – CLASH OF HEIRS

The constricting space of the alley allowed him to exactly mark the three men following him. Two were short and the third was of medium height and far less nervous.

Kieler cursed. Bottom feeders. He expected company but losing three tails might be a problem.

The curving alley led to the crusty base of the nearest tower. Once an elaborately decorated entryway to a posh hotel, the heavy door was now coated with grime. Inside the formerly grand lobby were many establishments considered disreputable, even in this part of The Glums. As Kieler walked across the age-worn black and white tile floor, he glanced up into the hollow center of the tower. Stretching up into the darkness was a shaft ringed by six broken-down elevators. It was like looking up the barrel of a maggun.

After striding directly through the center of the bank of elevators, Kieler walked boldly into The Bottom of the Barrel, a pub with a high opinion of its lowly status. He had to walk around the smashed shell of a fallen elevator car, showcased as the centerpiece of the pub's twisted décor. He moved directly to Ogard, the barkeep and a regular informant for all sides of the black-market trade.

"G'day, O'!" Kieler greeted Ogard. Being loyal to everybody (and therefore no one), Ogard was neither friend nor enemy. Both knew their roles and played them well. Ogard poured a drink, and Kieler threw him a coin.

"G'day, Geren," Ogard returned. "You look as though you're about a weighty errand on this day of light-hearted drunkenness."

"Perceptive as always, Ogard. I'm headin' out. I gotta take a trip to Govian to see about getting a supply chain set up. We found a group of farmers willing to trade off the grid." It was a total lie, but Kieler just wanted everyone to know he was going to be gone for a while.

Ogard nodded, making his mental notes so he could pass it on.

CHAPTER FOUR

"Anyway, the goons are going to miss me." The three tails had entered and stood by the bar rather conspicuously. "My assignment is remote and my little excursion will take some months."

This was news indeed to Ogard, who showed some surprise. "Look on it as a holiday."

"That's how I figure it," Kieler nodded. "I've never been out of Avertori before." *Though if things go as planned, I'll still be here,* Kieler thought. *Just not in The Glums.*

"I'll pass on the tale, Geren, true or no," Ogard said with a wink.

Kieler regarded him with a smile. Ogard was a good lot. He knew the game, managing to stay in business, stay alive and stay in the good graces of both the familial goons and the goons like Geren. Kieler decided he might actually miss him.

Kieler leaned in confidentially. "If you can hold on to that news till tomorrow, I'd appreciate it. They don't like my sort traveling out of sight." He slipped Ogard a few silver ril, the more valued currency of the black market. It was considered an insult to use the paper dras, the official currency of Avertori, for a bribe.

Ogard nodded, quickly removing the coins from sight. It was generous for such a short delay.

As Kieler looked at Ogard, he realized how many people in his usual haunts he wouldn't be seeing for a while, if ever.

The awkward pause was noticed and prompted a vague though genuine smile by the barkeep, "Fare you well then!"

Nodding, Kieler turned and made his way out of the pub in such a way as to keep the crashed elevator car in between him and his unwanted companions. By doubling back, Kieler didn't give them the chance to talk to Ogard. They had to follow him now or lose him.

The Bottom of the Barrel was actually on the ground floor of one of the taller towers in Avertori, reaching some hundred and fifty stories. Kieler noted the irony of this: it would have been fastest to go straight up, but the elevator car in the middle of the pub was in no condition to make the trip. Typical of lower Avertori.

Residents who could afford to live on the upper levels saw little value in maintaining easy vertical access. As a result Kieler's route would have to be highly circuitous.

Now that the news had been planted that he would be gone a while, he needed to get gone. He needed to cut off his tail.

He walked briskly to the nearest InterTram station. He had to laugh at the agents following him. They wanted to be discreet, to blend in, but all other foot traffic was exiting the station to join the festivities in the plaza. They stood out like new guys, which they were, except for the third one. On another night he might have played a little game of chasey with them, but tonight... he just had to dump them.

He walked onto the tram and stood next to the door.

Two of them followed him aboard and took up separate positions on the tram, looking like perfect strangers. They had even chosen spots as physically far apart as possible. More experienced agents would have realized the conspicuous situation and pretended to be friends. The odd agent didn't board but stood a step outside the doors as nonchalantly as if this wasn't the train he was waiting for. Kieler frowned internally.

Just as the doors closed, Kieler jumped off the tram and let the other two embarrassed agents enjoy their ride to the next station. It wasn't a subtle move, but Geren was not subtle.

The train started off and Kieler allowed himself the pleasure of looking back through the windows at the men scrambling for the door. Discarding the masquerade of pretending not to notice his pursuers, Kieler turned and looked the remaining man up and down, outwardly scowling now. At first the man seemed to be pretending to ignore him, but then Kieler got the distinct impression that the man was bored and genuinely uninterested in what Kieler did.

CHAPTER FOUR

The man struck him as odd, though Kieler couldn't place exactly why. His clothes were old, though of good quality and tailoring. He was shorter than Kieler, and his ears and nose were larger than normal. Though Kieler had never seen him before, the man's jet-black hair obliquely reminded Kieler of Movus.

Kieler stroked his fake beard and considered. This was inconvenient. He had to lose this guy before he changed his identity. Then he could pursue his goal on the higher levels of the city without unwanted company.

Striding over to the tram going the opposite direction, Kieler pretended to be unphased. But the cards were on the table, and right now the black-haired man had the better hand. Again Kieler thought this would have been entertaining if the stakes were not desperately high. He would not get a chance like this until the next New Year. No, he thought again, the opportunity wouldn't even be there next year.

Kieler and Movus had painstakingly prepared the ruling houses for his arrival by implanting false credentials with key people. The rumors were peaked; the stage was set. This was his only shot.

CHAPTER FIVE

Velirith stood at a bay window in the top floor apartment of Vel-Taradan and looked out over Plaza Floreneva. The triangular central plaza reminded her of the Theater Tri back home in Velakun. There were many differences, but both plazas were the center of social activity in their respective cities.

Plaza Floreneva was surrounded by three tiers of arched colonnades, which provided covered walkways to the myriad of shops and cafés surrounding the plaza. Many of these were closed now, victims of the various monopolies enforced by the trade houses.

In each corner of the triangular plaza stood a magnificent structure with layered accents of a style that was both dramatic and suggestive of indulgence beyond mere functionality. The Arena, the cathedral and the Oraflora Theater—all were built to bring people together. She noticed, not for the first time, her inward revulsion and intentional ignoring of the Arena.

She forced her gaze east, up the Stair to the left, and sighed a small sigh as she looked upon the claw-like spires that pierced Garrist Ring and supported the Executive Chair's overdone palace.

That palace was her destination this evening. That her habiliments not only made a subtle statement of confidence but were practical as well placed her in the position of being ready early, allowing her this time for reflection. She felt a strange mix of nervousness, peace and excitement in the unhurried interval before heading up the Stair to the Gala.

CHAPTER FIVE

As majestic as the view was, she closed her eyes and shut it out. She needed some introspection before facing the people she would face tonight and doing the things she would do.

Concentrating, she pictured herself, dressed as she was for the New Year's Eve Gala. Velirith had prepared for this evening's party in a very different way than just the primp, preen, and pomp of most of the "noble" ladies. Certainly she had dressed well, wearing the silver-lined, deep blue of House Vel. In an unusual twist of creativity, she had chosen a very feminine adaptation of Vel's traditionally male dress uniform. The long coat preserved some of the flow of a dress, emphasizing her form nicely, but pants gave her more freedom of movement. She wore her dark hair a bit short, curving around to frame her oval face.

I look good, she decided internally, smiling to herself. It was an unselfconscious, non-arrogant assessment. She had, she thought, a more handsome than delicate beauty. And she was happy with that.

She focused further, imagining looking into her own reflective, silver eyes. She noted the smile that played around the edges. She took measure of what she saw: *humor, judgment... mischief. I don't like the judgment,* she concluded, resolving that was something she could change. *But I like the mischief.* And she grinned a beautiful smile of straight white teeth.

Mischief. Usually Velirith despised these parties, but she had to admit, she was more excited about tonight's New Year's Gala than any she had ever attended. It wasn't the fancy clothes, or the fine food, or the "important" people. Certainly every family with any economic influence would be in attendance. But Velirith detested these shows of narcissism.

Her excitement had begun two days earlier with a visit from Moshalli MgFellis. Moshalli was the same age as Velirith. The two had played together as young girls when Velator, Velirith's father, had spent much more time in Avertori but Moshalli's house was not of the same class as Velirith's. That didn't matter to Velirith or her father, but it did matter to many. MgFellis had served the House of Ek as a proximal house for hundreds of years. When House Ek was elevated to Executive Chair, leader of the Omeron of Zotikas, the MgFellis house was, in its own way, elevated as well. Moshalli was unashamedly proud of the fact that her family lived in the tower quarters below the Executive Chair's palace and was always well informed of the happenings in the palace and throughout Avertori.

So two days before tonight's party, Velirith had been writing a play. She was stuck. It seemed to lack the heart of true *Theatre Velaki*. The script lay spread out on the low table before the bay window overlooking Avertori's Grand Stair. The same window before which she now stood, playing back the scene.

Moshalli had surprised Velirith, visiting her chambers in the Vel apartments at the top of Vel-Taradan. The three tower complex of Vel-Taradan served as the ambassadorial and economic headquarters of the Vel family in Avertori. Though very comfortable, Velirith much preferred their home in Velakun, deep within the mountains of Ardan to the northeast.

"Velirith, it's so wonderful to see you again!" Moshalli had bubbled, embracing her. Her excitement was genuine, Velirith decided, if not a bit exaggerated. Moshalli liked associating with those considered influential. Being able to say that she used to play *Heroes and Kovars* with the only heir of the house of Vel and that they were "best friends" elevated her status—at least in her own eyes. Velirith invited her playmate of youth over to the window.

Velirith smiled at her. "Good to see you too, Moshalli." And it was, even if Velirith was a bit annoyed to have her creativity interrupted. She looked into the round, plain face of her friend. The eye makeup was new, and Velirith saw that Moshalli was going for a more exotic look.

"It's been, what, two years? Last year's party I think you were sick?"

CHAPTER FIVE

Velirith laughed. "No, I was just stubbornly immature and refused to go. The rumor was I was sick, but I'm sure you knew better."

"Well, I had heard you and Velator had a fight about it."

"Amazing," Velirith shook her head. "My father and I did have words about it, but we were the only ones in the room. You certainly keep well informed."

Moshalli beamed. "We MgFellis' are at the center of everything. We are trusted to be discreet, and yet sometimes if our family didn't know what was happening, *nothing* would ever get done!"

Velirith regarded her talkative friend and agreed there was a good deal of truth in what she said. Moshalli, however, played it up.

"Like now," Moshalli continued with a melodramatic sigh, pulling a sheaf of papers out of a small satchel. "You know my mother is the events coordinator for the Executive Chair. She assigned *me* to order the dancers for the Family Harmony Dance. My stars, Velirith! Do you realize how difficult this is? How important?" Moshalli's mother, Fechua, was not one to overlook her daughter's social training.

Eyes wide with amused concern, Velirith shook her head slightly.

"Well, think of it! What if Forcheso Parchiki were accidentally paired with Feleanna Cortatti, who everyone knows is trying to bring down his fabric trade by having that awful Sindia Corch intercept his cloth shipments? Or if I accidentally paired Feleanna with this mysterious Ortessi heir, who was supposed to be dead and now shows up twenty years later? Could you imagine the consequences?"

Imagine. Velirith had actually put her mind to work visualizing the scene. Feleanna was a wicked witch with way too many years and ambitions left in her. If she were paired with a leader of a house she was currently trying to eliminate, the result

53

would be dramatic, if not explosive. *It could make the whole event worthwhile*, Velirith thought.

"Or imagine the Executive Chair himself, dancing majestically around the outer circle and ending up with Balfani Telander, that big woman married to the Prime of the power plant house? After the faked magal shortage was exposed, they hate each other!"

Velirith felt the excitement of a new idea coming on. "How do you arrange the dance so that no one is paired with someone they don't get along with?"

"Well, the dance represents social order, families caring for each other—"

Velirith let out a snort of laughter.

"What?"

Between spasms of laughter, Velirith managed to get out, "Come on, Moshalli! You just told me how much everybody hates each other. You don't see the irony of a dance that symbolizes families 'taking care of each other'?"

By her frown, Moshalli evidently hadn't looked past the tradition to see the reality. "In the old days, the groups were completely random. They would just dance with whomever they ended up with. Now we are more careful."

Calming herself, Velirith said, "Go on. Please."

"Well, it's also called the Mystery Partner Dance. You've seen it, but this is the first year you can actually dance in it, now that your father has declared you heir-apparent of House Vel. You know the men are in the outer circle and the women in the inner circle. The two circles move opposite each other, everyone switching partners until a third of the way through the music. Then the music changes, the circles stop rotating, and they dance with that partner for the rest of the song. That way the new partners can talk and get to know each other better."

CHAPTER FIVE

Controlling her rising excitement, Velirith pictured what a fouled dance plan could produce in this time when families were anything but caring.

Ignorant of Velirith's inner humor, Moshalli went on. "The hard part is sorting out who hates who. Once that is figured out, it's actually easier than you think to keep feuding families apart. There are two groups of dancers that never mix; my mother just puts rivals in separate groups. Like Feleanna will be in group 'A' and both Forcheso Parchiki and the Ortessi mystery man will be in group 'B'. They'll never get paired together."

"How does that work?" asked Velirith, suddenly curious.

"Look." And Moshalli explained, placing a sheet of paper with diagrams on top of Velirith's script. The outer and inner circle consisted of about forty dancers each, but as they counter-rotated, Velirith saw how they skipped a person after each short dance interaction, creating the two groups, odds and evens, or 'A's and 'B's. As long as the groups were equal in number, everyone would always end up partnered with someone from their own group. Though simple, it was an elegant, beautiful dance, Velirith admitted, and very old, dating back to when Velik himself had united the diverse tribes living all over the three continents.

But she also saw, more by intuition, that if either circle lost a single dancer or a couple from the same group, group 'A' dancers would be forced to partner with group 'B' dancers. She also noticed the pattern was mathematical. If a specific dancer was taken out at the right time, a preset arrangement of the dancers that *looked* random could actually be arranged to partner-specific dancers with an exact predetermined match.

One sheet of the diagram held blank circles that were to be filled in with dancers' names.

"Moshalli," Velirith asked suddenly, as the patterns of the dance began to come together, "May I help you fill in the names?"

Moshalli was thrilled. "That would help a *lot*! Sure! It shouldn't be *too* hard since mother already separated the groups so there won't be any conflicts. We just have to make sure that every other spot around the circle is filled with a group 'A' dancer and that they are across from another group 'A' dancer."

Her mind racing, Velirith dictated the names to Moshalli who wrote them into the blanks. Spinning the circles in her head, Velirith figured out just who would be paired with whom. And, more critical to her mischief, she figured just which dancers needed to be taken out to alter the results of the "random" dance.

Giggling for different reasons, the girls had a delightful time. Moshalli was in her element, gossiping and seemingly planning this important event. Every tidbit of gossip, Velirith turned into a dance couple, appearing to rearrange at random the names Moshalli blithely tossed out.

"So Callia and Ferdando *used to be* this hot couple, but when neither Ferdando nor Callia were willing to go over to the opposite family in marriage, you can bet the elements heated up! If *I* were Callia—I mean, she's *so* pretty and has some of the most *elegant* dresses—I would never let a man as handsome as that Ferdando get away."

"That's incredible, Moshalli. The stupid things people do. Let's move Ferdando over to this circle on the opposite side of Callia. It's still in his same group."

"Okay." And Moshalli penned it in.

Of course, with the rotation of the circles, and one couple dropping out at just the right (or wrong) time... Velirith paused and looked over at her friend. This dance was important to Moshalli, too important. She didn't seem to realize how superficial all this was, and that she was looking up to these puffed-up frauds as heroes, people she wanted to impress. If Velirith could show her how ugly these personalities really were, Moshalli might see that her own qualities, her enthusiasm and sweetness, were actually more authentic and noble than the false fronts of the people she looked up to.

CHAPTER FIVE

It might hurt her a little to see the dance she cared about go awry, but in the long run, she further justified, Moshalli's self-esteem could really be elevated. *And this will look completely accidental! Moshalli can't be blamed.*

At the end, Moshalli packed up her papers. "I have to get these to the printers. Then I'm to hand-deliver to each family their copy of which position they will start in. It's going to be so exciting!"

"No doubt," Velirith agreed.

"Did you know some of the dancers practice all year just so this dance works perfectly?"

"Really?"

Moshalli nodded vigorously. "You probably don't have to because of your theater experience, but it's true. Oh, I wish our family was recognized for how important we really are. Then I could dance and be swept around the floor by some handsome mystery man. This New Year's Eve will be glorious!"

After Moshalli had left on the private tram that spanned the familial towers, Velirith had sat at her window feverishly writing out the pairings she had arranged. Then she had forged notes from one partner to the other, marveling at how devious her own mind could be.

Now, with the dance beginning in just a couple hours, Velirith would execute her plans at the Executive Chair's New Year's gala. The voice of Discernment in her head seemed to whisper that what she had planned was wrong. But the louder voice of Mischief danced and laughed that this was just what the Omeron needed, a little dramatic revelation of the hypocrisy played out in a Family Harmony Dance. Velirith intentionally chose Mischief and opened her eyes just as a knock at the door pulled her from the replay of Moshalli's visit.

"Velirith, your father says it's time."

"Thank you, An'essa. Tell him that I am on my way." An'essa was not only her bodyguard, but a close friend as well.

EPISODE 1 – CLASH OF HEIRS

Velirith adjusted the collar on her outfit and gently arranged the stack of fake notes in her satchel of woven silver. She hung the bag over her right shoulder and patted it with excitement. *Adding spike to the punch,* she thought.

She took a last look in the mirror, practiced her best look of pure childish innocence, and headed to the private tram to meet her father and go to the gala.

CHAPTER SIX

Kieler swore in his head, but his face remained impassive, even nonchalant.

The last agent slid onto the tram as the begrimed bronze doors slid closed with a heavy thump. Both the doors and the agent impressed him as being old without showing it properly. The doors were artfully and sturdily built, at least a couple hundred years ago. Three layers of bronze trim arched gracefully over the portal, strong and solid but tarnished with time.

While casually pretending to look at the tram doors, Kieler peripherally studied the remaining agent. Kieler couldn't pinpoint why the man struck him as old. His face was youthfully unlined. Physically, the man was below average height, dark-haired, and had a pale, smooth complexion. Perhaps the larger nose and ears, despite his clear complexion, made him look like an older man. And his eyes, while not rheumy, were dull, as if the light in them had waned.

The tram climbed slowly, rising from The Glums toward the brighter, higher level of Plaza Floraneva. These trams were built with a tasteful elegance in an era when efficiency wasn't defined by cutting back on materials or energy usage. The vehicles were beautifully designed, monstrous and enduring. Once Kieler was done redesigning the government, the engineer in him would love to streamline these trams. It was said of the ancient vehicles, "They were proof that with enough magal, even a mountain can fly." Since House Ek's rise to power some eighty years ago, the

59

aphorism was irreverently edited to "With enough magal, Ek can move mountains."

But this man shadowing him did not work for Ek, Kieler was intuitively sure. *Probably Cortatti. But how did he know which gate Kieler would use? Chance?*

Lumbering up the track, the tram approached the underside of Plaza Floraneva. The Plaza's tram station encircled one of the ancient pillars that supported the plaza itself and the upper levels of the city. In The Glums, these pillars were either covered with grime or, near Plate level, covered with tenements and shabby businesses like The Bottom of the Barrel.

Several packed trams approached and departed, spiraling in and away from the station. The tracks hung suspended from the column like curving branches from a tree trunk. This was one of the busiest hubs in the city.

Consciously relaxing his jaw muscles, Kieler thought about how he was going to lose his uninvited companion.

Something else made the man seem older too. He didn't move enough. He just stood there, not looking around, if he was pretending disinterest in Kieler, he was an expert at it.

The tram slowed as it sidled up to a curved platform ringing the spire. When the doors opened, the man got off first and moved a few feet onto the platform and stopped to wait for his charge. Kieler considered just staying on and letting the tram take him to the next station farther west, then doubling back. But he needed to climb the Grand Stair from Plaza Floraneva northeast to Garrist Ring. So pretending to go on would just waste time. If he hadn't needed to get the sigil last night, he would have camped on top of the Charlaise Building and waited for the proper time to hop over to the party. But now, he had to get there before full dark.

His tail was just standing there, completely at ease it seemed, as if he knew Kieler would be coming along and he needn't be worried. It was a little unnerving. Was this guy that good? Maybe choosing such a well-known gate from the under-city was a bad call. Perhaps the Cortattis put their best man on it. The guy was sure to tip off a swarm of Cortatti thugs once they got higher and closer to the palace. Kieler had to lose him now.

The platform was jammed with partygoers. Two more crowded trams pulled up to adjacent platforms and unloaded as Kieler disembarked, and suddenly he saw a way.

Inelegant, he thought, *but effective.*

As the throng from the other trams moved toward the exits and pressed around him, Kieler waited until the flow of traffic had put several bodies between him and his tail, and then, in a moment where two taller men blocked line of sight, he dropped down to all fours and crawled.

He wound his way through the legs of the crowd over to another tram waiting with its doors open and scuttled onto it, keeping his head below the window level. The empty tram seemed to be waiting for a set departure time, which was fortunate.

After half a minute, Kieler poked an eye up from behind a seat and looked across the platform. Most of the current wave of people had passed and his stoic tail was easy to spot, standing halfway up the stairs, looking down and around the momentarily less busy platform. Kieler imagined the man shrugging, thought he saw the agent smirk, then turned and continued dispassionately up the stairs.

There were other exits from the platforms up through the hub to Plaza Floraneva and Kieler found one. He climbed stairs through the interior of the black tower. The line of station doors emptied onto the center of the west side of the triangular plaza. Kieler hovered around the northernmost door and looked across the other station doors and east over the plaza. There was no sign of his enigmatic shadow.

Just to be sure, he climbed to the second tier of shops, found a quiet alcove and scouted the plaza below. Plaza Floraneva was jammed with people. In the corners of the triangular plaza were monumental buildings constructed when Avertori was in its prime, flourishing both culturally and economically. All three structures were of such architectural magnificence that it was a marvel of complacency how well the throngs of partiers could ignore them.

South, and to his right, was the seldom-used theater, the Oraflora, named by the house he would be assuming leadership of this evening, House Ortessi.

The Oraflora was open tonight. Run by the Cortattis, who had taken it over when the babe Orlazrus Ortessi went missing (presumed burned to death), the once famous playhouse was now infamous. Anyone older than the takeover assumed the Cortattis were purposely discrediting the usurped property. The play tonight was *The War Tribes of Ardan*. Where once House Ortessi had accurately dramatized historical events, the Cortatti plays tended to butcher history—with the emphasis on butchery.

The theater itself still presented a dramatic façade; its three vertical marquees stretched skyward with luzhril spotlights already ablaze. When the sun went fully down, the bold marquees would cast stark shadows into the sky, contrasting the brilliantly lit marquees with the darkness beyond. But the performance itself would be little attended, Kieler knew.

Even less attended—in fact, *deserted*—would be the edifice directly across the tri from him in the southeast corner, the cathedral. Kieler didn't know much of its original purpose—Movus hadn't taught him anything about it—but of the three corner buildings, it was the most magnificent. Ornate double flying buttresses adorned each of the six corners of the structure, each buttress and the corner itself topped with escalating towers, eighteen in all. A latticework dome topped the main nave and glittered with oranges and reds as the setting sun refracted through the crystalline panels.

It had been sealed off for as long as Kieler had known. One day, he would like to see the inside.

CHAPTER SIX

The final structure, burgeoning with people, was the Arena to his left. House Cortatti ran this place too, but in contrast to Oraflora, they ran the Arena extremely well—from a business perspective. Originally, it was a place of sporting contests for feats of might and strategy, built in the same century as its two companion structures in opposite corners of the Plaza.

Contests were still held there, but losers left dead and winners only lived to fight again. Supposedly only violent criminals sentenced to death ended up in the Arena. But Kieler knew better.

In his operations with the Coin, Kieler had occasionally used the services of the Lurani brothers, who ran a smuggling ring of medicine and medical supplies from the Glums. The Merckles, who had the state-sanctioned monopoly on health care, had traced the Lurani's down through their own industrial spy network.

The Lurani brothers had ended their lives in a dramatic but sadistic contest held in the very same edifice that Kieler was now surveying. The contraption designed for their demise consisted of two separate tanks with one brother chained to the bottom of each tank. Each brother had a bucket and each tank had water running into it. The men could bail the water out, but the contraption was designed to carry the water one brother bailed into the tank of the other brother. Eventually one drowned the other trying to survive. Wracked with guilt, the surviving brother was eventually pitted against another criminal and killed.

Their crime was far from violent. But the interpretation by the Omeron appointed courts was that it was violence against the people of Avertori in general by undermining their health care.

Kieler caught himself gritting his teeth and stopped. Slink Squad had bought from the Lurani brothers. They had been good men with good intentions. The Omeron needed to be taken down.

The ageless shadow that Kieler had ditched undoubtedly worked for one of the Omeron families. Thankfully, Kieler saw no sign of him in the plaza below.

EPISODE 1 – CLASH OF HEIRS

He looked due east to where the Grand Stair climbed at least fifty stories from the edge of Plaza Floraneva up to Garrist Ring. It was a long climb. But the block-wide stair, adorned with statuary and cafes and tall buildings up the middle of it, was far more difficult to watch than the trams that ascended under the Stair. House Cortatti would be his primary opponent. They knew why he was coming and what he looked like. If they could stop him before the gala, he—and any claim Orlazrus Ortessi might have made—would soon be forgotten.

The Grand Stair curved gently and majestically up to the northeast and ended at the promenade of Garrist Ring. Up the centerline of the Stair ran a stately line of towering buildings, each grand unto itself, owned by Omeron families with sufficient status. Connecting each of them near their tops was an exclusive private tram (for ruling family members only). The tram ran from the Arena, across Floraneva to the first family office building, and then up the Stair to each successive tower until it finally ran above the only bridge to the Palace of the Executive Chair.

The nearest of these family headquarters, Vel-Taradan, overlooked Plaza Floreneva. It consisted of a complex of three graceful towers and belonged to House Vel. Kieler thought it the most desirable location since it was nearest the fading beauty and bustle of Plaza Floreneva.

Looking to the top of House Vel's three towers, Kieler saw the private, suspended tram car (nicknamed the FamTram) leaving the station at the top of one tower, probably taking a load of self-important dignitaries up the stairs to the gala.

I wonder if Velator himself is aboard that tram, Kieler thought. The head of House Vel had been reclusive in Kieler's lifetime, spending most of his time in the mountainous city of Velakun from which House Vel originated. When Kieler was very young, he had learned from his father the tales and histories of Velik, Velator's ancestor and the founder of Avertori some thousand years ago. It was Velik and Boreas who reclaimed the city

64

from the decay and wild creatures that infested the ruins of the Dead Ones on the Isle of Threes.

Satisfied that he had crudely but effectively shaken off his tail, Kieler worked his way north on the second tier of shops. The arched facades surrounding the Plaza Floreneva had been designed to house retail stores. In the flourishing activity of the growing city, this was to be the heart of culture and commerce. The plan had succeeded marvelously—for a while.

Now, Kieler noted one shop in three boarded up, with crumbling tiles and unrepaired chips falling from the arches. The shops were busy tonight, but that was an aberration.

Specialty clothing shops seemed to have suffered the most; their faded signs hung over empty display windows.

A sign over a busy shop entryway read "Cortatti Arms" and in the window a sign touting, "Buy the weapon of tonight's battle: the new Barcleaver!" These shops seemed prolific, though why someone who belonged to a sub-house would need a three-foot-long battle-blade and what good it would be against the Cortatti's magguns... well, there was a reason for the term "ignorant masses".

Before he reached the Arena, Kieler turned right and descended to the Plaza level, striding east across the open plaza in front of it. Myriad fountains and statues adorned the Plaza, but all the fountains were dry, even on this festive eve, save the massive centerpiece of Floraneva. This fountain consisted of several characters. Three shungvaal—the giant, horned creatures of the sea—circled the scene within and spouted huge streams of water toward the center. Back to back in the middle were larger-than-life depictions of Velik and Boreas: Boreas hefting his famed spear and Velik with his bow drawn back. Between the jetting shungvaal and the two heroes were grotesquely distorted creatures: a gnarled grevon, legions of oversized slinks, and a dozen monsters that seemed to be part building or vehicle and part animal.

EPISODE 1 – CLASH OF HEIRS

Tonight, Kieler barely glanced at it. He scanned constantly and inconspicuously for more Omeron agents. Still dressed as Geren, with full beard and work clothes, he certainly wouldn't match the description Feleanna would have issued from their encounter last night. Of course, this outfit would be out of place when he reached the financial district of Garrist Ring.

Street vendors hawked their treats for the evening's festivities. Buskers juggled, singers crooned, and as he neared the base of the Grand Stair, he couldn't help but be distracted by a troupe of unusually talented acrobats. Dressed all in white with red sashes and black masks, they performed elaborately coordinated tricks. As Kieler passed, one of the performers dove from the top of a human pyramid straight at the hard tile of the plaza. With no one there to catch the headfirst diver, Kieler, like the other spectators, thought they had made a deadly error. But in a mere blink, the launching pyramid dissolved into a flurry of bodies and four of its members appeared at precisely the right spot to catch, swing and re-launch the diving performer. He seemed to float and slowly flip before rolling across the tiles back to a standing position and a flourish.

Wadded paper money flew in the direction of their caps as the assembled audience exploded with appreciation.

Kieler climbed. The Grand Stair was a half-mile-long stretch of the most prestigious real estate in Zotikas. Of the shops, restaurants, banks and cafes that lined the sides of the Stair or terraced its center, few of these were closed. They catered to the elite, and the elite lived in the apartments and office towers that graced the centerline of the Stair. Already Kieler felt underdressed.

But covering his features now was more important than dressing up. He could still be a worker on a last minute job until the top of the Stair. He spotted a couple agents as he climbed, men dressed in sturdy but tidy suits with bulging overcoats. They looked up from their papers too often. Lounged by the rails too casually. All the while they scanned the Stair and lacked the purposeful demeanor of workers going home or partygoers heading for an alcoholic destination.

From Vel-Taradan and past the multitude of House edifices, the route was always up. Most people traveling to the topmost plaza would have taken the tram that ran up the underside of the Stair.

As he finally neared the top, Kieler found the deepening shadow of a terraced café. Here he shed his beard, work clothes and shambling gait to emerge in a finely tailored, grey cut of cloth trimmed in black suitable for a Bintle financial clerk. House Bintle had, from the time of Velik, run the banking system. Now corrupt, family members and functionaries were quite common on the Garrist Ring.

He reached into the breast pocket and placed hexagonal eyeglasses on the bridge of his nose. Now he was Niven Wensith, his hair short, his walk the stiff, cocky and brisk stride of a confident, drab accountant needing to get to the Charlaise Building for some final business before the closing at full dark.

As Rei finally retired, its fading beams settling into the Western Sea, Kieler gained the promenade at Garrist Ring. Garrist was a toroid of the highest rising financial structures. A wide walkway circled the inner gap, allowing pedestrians an inspired view straight down to the Plate and an equally inspiring view of the void-piercing spire that supported the Executive Chair's Palace.

That spire stood directly before Kieler as he topped the stairs and was taller by far than even the sky-scratching structures surrounding it on the Ring.

In contrast to the purposely-expansive Plaza Floreneva below, Garrist was imposingly vertical. Between the spire and the inside promenade of Garrist was a dizzying, empty gap from the greatest heights of the city straight down to the very Plate itself. Kieler admired the engineering but loathed the hubris.

There were two standard approaches to the palace of the EC; first, a narrow bridge in front of the Grand Stair spanned the gap (over which ran the FamTram), and second, access to the palace above could be gained by coming up the center of the ancient spire from the depths below. Both choke points were heavily guarded—not so much to prevent deviants like himself from causing mischief, Kieler realized, but to keep the untrusted competing houses from getting too ambitious.

Kieler, however, had devised a third way.

He turned right and angled toward the Charlaise Building a quarter way around the Ring. This alone would throw the Cortatti grevons off his scent. To them, the only way to Kieler's inevitable destination was across that single span. He noticed to his great satisfaction a man leaning against a newsstand reading who glanced up at him, saw the bored expression of an overworked, hope-drained financial pawn fixed inanely on Kieler's face, and looked back down. Despite his intentionally minimal disguise, the proper countenance conveyed the proper profession.

Out of his peripheral vision, Kieler noted at least a half-dozen men more interested in who approached the bridge than in what they were doing that evening. He had to tightly stifle a grin. Others waited at building corners, in arched alcoves, or at shop windows. Either Kieler was paranoid—or egotistical—or there were a lot of Cortatti goons determined to get him.

The sky was darkening and would soon be lit with the fireworks that marked the beginning of the New Year's Eve celebration.

The incognito sentinels thinned out significantly as he left the bridge behind. Without falling out of character, he relaxed mentally. He would make the Charlaise Building, headquarters of Bank Bintle. It was with that thought that he noticed something disturbing—some*one,* actually, leaning spiritlessly against the right side of the Charlaise Building. His tail from the tram was ahead of him.

With forty paces to go, as used to pretending as he was, as much as he had practiced, he slipped out of character.

CHAPTER SIX

His pace must have quickened and he glanced left. A man near the edge of the ring noticed him and suddenly dropped the pretense of waiting for the fireworks. Worse, Kieler recognized the man! It was the same guard he'd passed in the Grand Hall of the Cortatti keep the night before.

At the same moment, Kieler's old tail spotted him, straightened and waited nonchalantly for him to get closer.

Kieler looked back at the man angling towards him, pulling a maggun out from under his overcoat. The Charlaise Building was still thirty yards away. There was no doubt that before Kieler reached the building, the men would intercept him.

CHAPTER SEVEN

On the top floor of Vel-Taradan, Velator stood waiting for her in front of a suspended tram. Her father's eyes widened as Velirith approached.

Velirith smiled, wondering what he would choose to comment on. She inclined her head, "Father."

He paused, obviously considering his words carefully. Velirith had always liked this about him. He thought about what he was going to say, rarely speaking offhand.

"Your smile is gorgeous, but it doesn't quite hide the threat."

She dropped her smile immediately, surprised. It was rare for someone to surprise her, but she knew she got her intuition from somewhere. Even though her father didn't see through people like she could, he knew *her* well enough.

Feigning innocence, she said, "What do you mean, Father?"

"Mmm," he shook his head slowly, "mischief."

He shrugged, as if dismissing the thought. Instead, he regarded her from top to bottom and nodded approval. "You certainly have creative genius, my daughter. You've managed to make our Vel formal uniform look beautifully feminine."

She almost blushed, but instead twirled, unable to curb a girlish delight in the spotlight of her father's approval. The long-cut coat flared out like a dress when she spun. *She*, at least, would look good in the dance.

Her father smiled. "Not that I fear some young gentleman sweeping you up. They may *try*, but I'm certain no one will measure up." She scowled at the last comment. "Funny, you should say that, Father. I have just noticed how judgmental I can be. I'm never wrong about people, but I don't know if I like 'judgmental' as an epitaph."

Seeing she was sincere, he drew her into a warm hug. "Moral introspection, followed by resolve, will serve you well, Velirith."

Buried in her father's embrace, she frowned. Tonight's escapade probably didn't meet the requirements of the first step. *At least my resolve is in place.*

They stepped onto the suspended FamTram and it immediately started northeast and up. Velirith looked down onto the Grand Stair below and watched the throngs hurrying both up and down in the long shadows of the towers lining the edge of the Stair. Rei was setting and everyone was speeding toward one pleasure or another. She felt much more distant than thirty floors of altitude could account for. Their lives were so meaningless—her judgment coming through again—but for that matter, so was hers. She wanted so much for her life to have significance.

They passed through two familial towers on the Stair and stopped inside the third to pick up some members of the Merckle family. Velator stood as Lhea Margríte Merckle and her two sons boarded. Like the Vels, the Merckles were required to attend the gala without their bodyguards.

"Margríte, good evening," he greeted.

"Good evening, Velator." Lhea Merckle, despite being a manipulative opportunist, genuinely respected Velirith's father. Velirith could tell. All the house matrons respected him, except Feleanna Cortatti. Undoubtedly that was because he treated everyone respectfully—despite their deep differences.

Margríte Merckle's sons were a couple of years older than Velirith. That certainly didn't stop them from looking at her. Velirith gave them a straightforward, disinterested look to discourage them from staring or stealing glances at her. She could feel her father taking note of the adolescent exchange. A FamTram gondola was smaller than Avertori's public trams and was supported from above rather than below. It covered a shorter distance and carried a very limited clientele. But tonight it stopped at several more familial high-rises. When Ferdando Ashperis boarded from his parents' agriculture headquarters, she felt the judgment rise in her again. *The coward. He'll get a little taste of judgment tonight.* She suppressed her excitement and tried to ignore the fact that he too was looking at her.

I must look good.

The tram stopped climbing and flattened out over the Garrist Ring. Shortly thereafter they were cruising above the narrow bridge that spanned the empty space between Garrist and the spire supporting the lofty palace of the Executive Chair. From Garrist, the spire branched up and out into three curving fingers between which, far above, was a garden terrace, and in the middle of that terrace, the palace.

Velirith looked down toward the Plate over a quarter mile below. She liked the excitement of heights, and the gaping distance reminded her of the towering city of Velakun that was her home. Velakun was a much smaller city, but more aesthetically developed.

The tram entered a portal in the cream-colored spire and they were soon disembarking to board an elevator. The clear elevators ascended diagonally up the underside of one of the finger spires to the edge of the flared terrace hosting the Executive Chair's air garden. It forced the occupants to look down into the gaping distance.

She loved it. And she loved it more to watch the young men pull back from the edge with vertigo as they rose without visual references. Of course, they probably hadn't used their city as a playground the way she had used her home of Velakun. But when she flew at home, she didn't have such a view.

Rei touched the horizon far to the west as it fell through a layer of clouds. The city spread out around Velirith like a twinkling, three-dimensional puzzle. And the sea, visible from this height on all sides, wrapped around the Isle of Threes like a protective mother.

High above Garrist Ring, they disembarked at the edge of the air garden. Velirith on her father's arm, the group of guests proceeded through the widely spaced trees and statuary toward the stairs leading up to the great hall. One reason she had chosen pants for her outfit design was that the quirky breezes at this height teased the ladies' dresses and had them clutching their hats. But tonight, she noticed, the winds were calm.

Velirith decided she didn't like the palace design. Too ostentatious. Too grandiose. She did appreciate the myriad balconies, though. Every level, both above and below the great hall along the spire, was speckled with both private and public balconies, sometimes with decorative plants to add greenery to the entirely man-made edifice.

From Velirith's previous visits to the palace, she knew the layout. Bored, she had thoroughly explored both upward and downward in the lofty palace, dodging or charming the sparse guards. Most of Ek's sentries remained at the entrances or within the great hall itself. Still, her explorations here didn't compare to those of the hidden ways and intriguing architecture of her home in ancient Velakun.

Together with their small group from the elevator, Velirith and her father made their way through the air gardens. When she was younger, she'd found the trek frightening; now she just found it to be frighteningly bad taste.

Greenery was sparse, considering it was a garden. As the visitors neared the great hall, they were channeled between two rows of gigantic statues, three or four times life-size. On either side of them—*looking down on us*, Velirith thought—were the dark likenesses of... House Ek!

The statues were odd, not just because of their size, but because they were grey. It was a good color for a tacky effigy—

dark, loamy grey, as if the sculptor was short on funds so the material was pulled out of a magal mine, lumped into a mold, and then fired to harden into some stodgy ancestor of Ek Threzhel. *Which is exactly what they did*, Velirith realized. But the *oddest* thing about the score of superhuman statues lining the path to the great hall was that they were very highly magnetic, completely cast of magal.

Velirith shook her head at one particularly stern Ek looking down at her accusingly. It evoked an emotional response she could not help voicing, "*Ek!*"

Because of the proliferation of magnetic statuary, it was well known that one did not wear steel to the New Year's Gala. Buckles, swords, and particularly ladies' brooches that could tear away all had to be non-ferrous. Otherwise, one was suddenly and unnaturally attracted to the masculine figures lining the approach.

This presented a problem Velirith hoped she could overcome. In her satchel was a tiny cord knife. It was a dull, wooden hook with the only metal being an incredibly sharp blade around its inside curve. It was used in theatre when a strap or small rope needed to be surreptitiously cut to bring down a dramatic effect. It could be hooked around a cord and, with the flick of a wrist, slice through a line of fair strength.

Unfortunately, the cutting edge itself was made of steel.

Holding her father's arm with her left hand, she clutched her satchel in her right, fiercely pushing down on the satchel to keep it from flying out toward the magnetic Eks.

Even though the sharp sliver of metal around the inside hook was lighter than a hatpin, Velirith could feel the piece jerking the purse from side to side as the massive statues fought for possession. She gently nudged her father so that she was precisely in the middle of the opposing statues. Though she tried to be graceful, her steps wavered.

Her father gave her a sidelong, curious look, but this time said nothing, perhaps attributing it to her nerves.

CHAPTER SEVEN

They climbed the stairs up to the stone promenade surrounding the great hall and entered through its towering doors, joining the queue for Ek Threzhel's receiving line. Predictably, and the pinnacle of gaudiness in Velirith's opinion, a magal statue of Ek Threzhel himself stood behind the flesh and blood model at the end of the receiving line. It seemed taller than the others and no less repulsive.

Waiting to greet the Executive Chair, Velirith surveyed the huge interior of the great hall. The domed ceiling of the oval hall was easily sixty feet above them. The room was longer than wide, but not by much. In the center was a mosaic tile pattern typical to all Avertori, a large honeycomb consisting of smaller hexagonal pieces. This was the floor on which the dancers would be paired in the Family Harmony Dance. She involuntarily tightened her grip on her father's arm at the thought of the dance.

"You okay, Velirith?" he asked.

She forced herself to relax. "Yes, fine, Father. Just jittery. You know I have trouble with events like this."

Velator nodded, accepting her excuse. Around the dance floor, to both the right and left, were high tables and chairs, all assigned to specific guests. Velirith assumed these were carefully segregated for minimum conflict just as the partnering in the dance was supposed to be.

The assignments did make it easier for the wait staff to find people, especially for the task of delivering New Year's Greetings during the social hour before the fireworks. The tradition of notes, begun long ago, was initially a warm, loving way for families to uniquely express appreciation or well-wishes to another cherished family. Some families still honored the tradition. But nowadays, many used it as an anonymous way to jab or jibe a rival house. It could get brutal.

The tradition allowed for only one greeting from each person, making the note particularly special. Velirith winced inwardly, realizing that the twenty-two notes in her purse would definitely not add to "family harmony." But they might make a point that reform was necessary—no, she refused to delude herself: This was a practical joke for her own amusement and to antagonize people who definitely deserved it.

The first person to greet them in the receiving line was Fechua MgFellis, Moshalli's mother.

"Velator! Velirith! Wonderful to see you," she smiled broadly. *Genuine affection still exists,* Velirith noted. It struck her how similar Fechua's greeting was to her daughter's just two days earlier. Velirith let go of her father with her left hand and briefly embraced her friend's mother. Immediately her satchel swung out behind her, *repelled* by the magnetic statue behind the EC. Of course, that statue would be designed to *push* steel away from the EC, not draw it in.

Her bag tugged at her shoulder. Without looking, Velirith stretched out her right arm to clutch the willful satchel and hauled it back as gracefully as possible.

Fechua seemed to notice nothing and asked if they had their New Year's Greetings ready. Velator handed her an elegant envelope, which she passed to an assistant behind her.

"I'm sorry, Fechua. I'm not done with mine," Velirith apologized. "May I bring it up in just a couple of minutes?"

"Certainly. You're not the only one. Just hand it to the attendant at the table."

The man behind Fechua took Velator's greeting over to an elegantly decorated table guarded by another attendant.

"Velirith, that uniform, you designed it, didn't you?"

Velirith nodded. "Working with theater costumes has serendipities."

"It is both beautiful and striking," Fechua admired.

Striking, yes. "Thank you," Velirith replied. The Merckle trio was just finishing their hellos to the Executive Chair and his wife.

CHAPTER SEVEN

Turning to the EC, Fechua introduced them formally despite the familiar association Velator had with the Executive Chair. "May I present Velator, Prime of House Vel, and his daughter, Velirith."

Velator gripped arms with the Executive Chair and greeted him congenially, despite full awareness by both that less than a century ago, the Primes of House Vel had occupied the position of Executive Chair. Velirith knew her father simply chose not to harbor ill will. And Velirith herself—she didn't care. *Who would want to rule such a petty society anyway?*

She felt her father's quick sidelong glance, checking that Velirith wouldn't do anything unbecoming. One year, when she was thirteen, she pretended an over-familiarity with His Eminence and hugged him ebulliently. His guards, always standing behind him, didn't appreciate the gesture of "affection," but couldn't exactly chastise a thirteen-year-old girl in front of hundreds of guests.

She greeted him with only a sly, confident smile, but did nothing untoward, keeping her right hand tight upon her purse. The Executive Chair returned her greeting politely but warily, as if handling a beautifully wrapped but dangerous package.

The Executive Chair's wife was overweight, but not grossly so. She looked as bored as Velirith would have been had she not appointed herself Alternative Entertainment Chairwoman. Their salutations were cursory.

Velirith read a vague suspicion in her father, but Velator simply led her to their table behind one of the wait staff where she pretended to finish her greeting.

"I'll be right back," she told her father. She strode over to the decorated note table and stood in front of the box next to the guard. She held but a single note in its stylish envelope. She glanced at the attending guard and smiled. He nodded in return, looking at her a bit too long.

"Oh," she said, feigning surprise. There was no name on the envelope. She set the envelope on the edge of the table and used her stylus to scribe the name. As she lifted her hand, the card fell to the floor. "Oh!" she said again. She moved to bend over and retrieve it, then stopped as if realizing the impropriety of a young lady crawling under the table to pick up the note. "Would you be so kind?" she asked the attendant.

The man was more than willing to please. As he knelt and ducked his head, she deftly removed the remaining twenty-one notes—all differing in content, packaging and handwriting—and dropped them into the box. The attendant rose, smiled and bowed. Then he placed her final note in the box for her.

"Thank you very much." Velirith returned the bow with a charming smile. Then, with great composure, she walked back to her table, passing another young man with a belated note heading for the box.

CHAPTER EIGHT

They won't shoot yet.

He hoped. Kieler had considered the possibility that he'd be discovered on the way to the Charlaise Building and decided they wouldn't shoot in the crowded Garrist Ring unless they thought they would lose him. At this point, it looked like they would run him down in about six seconds.

He broke into a dead run to change the intercept point and kept arrow straight as if he were going to pass right by the Charlaise building. His conspicuous speed and the purposeful movement of his first pursuer attracted more unwanted attention. Within a few steps, another half-dozen Cortatti roughs emerged from hidden posts and were angling toward him. They were all running now.

Kieler made the front of the Bintle-owned bank and cut right. Once through the sturdy doors, he reduced to a brisk stride across the large lobby and headed directly for the inner stairwell door. Behind him every Cortatti seemed to burst through the doors at the same time, weapons drawn.

The head clerk gave a shout, "Lockdown!" and dashed for an emergency lever.

Kieler had about two seconds before the stairwell door in front of him would be sealed. He dove for it as the clerk yanked down on a huge brass lever to lock the doors of the building through a complex series of magnetic relays. Behind the general din, he heard magguns spinning up. He hit the door, slamming it open. Once in the stairwell, he spun and threw his weight back onto the door to shut it. Now that he was through, he *wanted* it locked. Within a second of it closing, he heard the very satisfying, metallic thunk of a huge bolt sliding into place.

He rolled right as metal rang. A huge hole split open just inside the handle. Fortunately, Kieler's hand wasn't on the handle as the maggun bolt tore through. He scrambled away before any more bolts hit and ran up the stairs.

That the Cortattis had fired inside a Bintle bank showed how intent they were on getting him. It also showed a frightening confidence that they felt they could wield their increasing power amongst the other houses. Kieler could hear more of the bolts flying below, but he had no idea whether the Cortattis were blasting the door or if Bintle security was laying down fire of its own. Regardless, in less than thirty seconds, all shots ceased. Kieler smiled.

This was a good break. He was trapped. Supposedly. They thought they had him, and sure enough, as he tried a door three levels above the lobby, it too was bolted. The Cortatti goon squad was probably figuring they had only to secure the exits and wait him out. They were sure to send contingents to the levels below as well. But he knew there was only one way to the roof, and he was on his way to it. On an earlier night, he had ensured that no bolt would bar him from rooftop access. In the lobby, tense and heated negotiations would be underway.

Regardless that his pursuit had been delayed and that he had trained extensively for this night, trotting up fifty flights of stairs was still a physical challenge. He shed his outer clothes, but carried them so they would not know whether he had gone up or down. The Bintle lockdown could be overridden, but only one door at a time—so Movus' intelligence reported. Kieler doubted the bank Officer-in-Charge would cooperate quickly with the Cortatti thugs trapped in his building. On the roof, Kieler dropped the spare clothes and went to work. It had taken him many nights over the past weeks to carefully and methodically prepare for this. And he hadn't done it using the stairs either. Behind a ventilation duct Kieler threw back the dark cover and felt a thrill of pride. There, secure against any wind, was the lightweight metal frame of a small airship.

A sharp crack sounded just off the edge of the roof and Kieler dropped to the deck. His heart sunk wondering how they had caught him before he could enact his plan. But then he realized; the fireworks had begun!

A giant sphere of purple and gold lightning expanded in the space between the roof and the Executive Palace, right in the center gap of Garrist Ring. The magal-luzhril burst produced a crackling thunderclap as it expanded, its aura lingering in fading radiance. Purple and gold, the colors of House Ek.

Kieler climbed to his feet and began to ready his ship. The hard rains had slackened but the clouds were still thick and threatening, waiting for reinforcements from the northeast. The wind was thankfully light.

His father had been obsessed with making energy production available on a smaller scale. This obsession had developed because Ek Threzhel had manipulated the magal supply to increase his own fortune. Kieler's father wanted to break the hold House Ek had on everyone's lives by their monopoly on magal. Out of this awesome and horrible obsession had come the engine that now drove Kieler's magnificent little airship. It had also cost Kieler's father his life.

Now Kieler's own life was on the line. He stripped another tarp off three hydrogen tanks stowed next to the empty metal airframe. The inflatable envelope that would hold the gas was still secure and draped carefully around the frame for quick deployment.

He opened the valves on all three tanks, one after another, and could hear the steady hiss of gas entering the envelope. He easily had twice the hydrogen he needed for liftoff, but since there was no second chance, Kieler had flown in backup cylinders. Now that he was expecting company, there were other uses for the excess hydrogen. His ideal plan had been to slip up here unnoticed. A maggun shootout in the lobby was hardly ideal.

At first, the envelope looked as if it were barely filling. He checked that the valves were full open and then left the filling airship while he ran a thin wire in front of the rooftop door. The likely charge out of the door would yank the tripwire. After the airfoil was inflated, he would hook the hydrogen canisters into the trap.

By the light of multicolored aerial explosions, he changed clothes. He had cooled from his ascent despite the work of setting up the airship. Donning his final disguise, the one he had stashed here on the rooftop just two nights ago, he buttoned the high collared dress uniform of House Ortessi. It was a sharp set, he admitted. Most houses had sunk to the loftiness of extremes, having colors and cuts that were gaudy and garish. But House Ortessi had risen to prominence with the classic houses, and thus fell when greed and self-aggrandizement became the style. At any rate, the deep green uniform trimmed with gold was simple and elegant, even if this particular formalwear was not suited for surreptitious excursions. Far too restrictive. He kept the Ortessian sigil tucked in an inside pocket for now.

Stepping over his wire, Kieler listened at the door. Nothing. No—wait, a banging far below. They were opening the door from the lobby!

The airship was taking shape. It was a large, bulbous wing that tapered toward the rear of the craft. It was not simply a balloon. Simple balloons had been tried but were too susceptible to the whims of the wind. They were dangerous and unwieldy. Kieler had created a semi-buoyant craft, which used his father's small engine to provide forward motion for extra lift and control.

CHAPTER EIGHT

To create this forward velocity, a motorized fan was needed. And that motor had been unavailable until his father had made it possible to create one smaller than a man's chest.

The dimples on the surface of the envelope were fast disappearing as hydrogen poured in from the three tanks. Kieler quickly shut down the first one, disconnected it, and rolled it over to another ventilation duct near the door.

Carefully, he balanced the tank on the edge of the duct so that the slightest pull from the wire would send it crashing down and break off the valve, turning the tank into a very distracting rocket. He listened at the door but a moment. He couldn't be sure, but he thought he heard footfalls far below.

He dashed over and disconnected the second canister. While he rolled it into its place for his crude trap, he allowed the last cylinder to finish filling out the airfoil. By the time he was ready for the final tank, the skin was tight and sleek, having formed into shape. He rolled the last canister over and balanced it next to the other two, then gently threaded the tripwire.

There was nothing left to do. Kieler jumped over the wire toward the door to listen for a brief second. He didn't have to try very hard. The slow clomping of exhausted men was close.

Kieler leapt back over the wire, ran to his ship, and slashed the tie-downs. He then jumped into the pilot's seat as the craft began to drift. As he pushed a lever forward, a core of highly purified magal slid into the engine and the fan whirred into motion. Revving softly, his airship started rolling across the roof.

Fireworks splashed the sky, illuminating his short takeoff. The beautiful explosions were a good distraction, pulling attention away from him. He just didn't want to become part of the evening's fiery entertainment.

The ship picked up speed, handling well. He had to be well clear of the roof when they barged through that door. If necessary, he could accelerate more by diving. Upon clearing the roof, the ship dropped sharply, but then picked up enough speed to be controllable and leapt back above the rooftop. He was airborne! No one in Zotikas had a machine like this one!

The airship pulled steadily away. His plan was to climb high above the bursting fireworks and enter the palace via a high balcony.

The high-pitched whine of charged magguns pinged in his ears above the whisper of the rotating fan, and Kieler glanced at the door. It opened cautiously. *These goons have some savvy about them.* One of them gave a cry to watch the wire as three others followed him out. Kieler ground his teeth as once again his plan went awry.

None of the Cortattis on the roof were his original tail. Not that it mattered, but Kieler was thankful. And for the moment his pursuers were more concerned about the trap than finding Kieler. But he knew he had only seconds before they would look around. He pulled up and climbed hard, putting himself above eye level. He could see them so clearly; he was too close!

But they were thinking narrowly, searching the rooftop, behind the ventilation duct, examining the canisters, his discarded clothes, and poking at the tarp that had covered the ship. He was gaining altitude and distance.

It became apparent to them all too quickly that Kieler was not on the roof, and one clever thug looked up and around, puzzled. It took several seconds for him to spot the slow-moving airship, and a couple more seconds to realize what he was looking at. Every second was precious distance, but Kieler was still well within maggun range.

Realization dawned, and with a cry, the man raised his weapon.

CHAPTER NINE

Social hour had already begun. Normally something to be endured, Velirith now eagerly glanced about as she rejoined her father.

"How are you doing, Velirith?" her father asked her again.

Is he suspicious or just overly concerned about me having a good time? He knows I hate these masquerades. She worded her short response carefully. "Being good," she said with a bored sigh.

Velator nodded, keeping his assessing gaze on her for a few moments longer. "Good. Let's mingle. I'm sure there is someone here that even you want to see."

Velirith returned her father's look then shrugged. "Perhaps one." And Velator, satisfied with that response, offered his arm and led her into the crowd.

Velator walked his daughter across the huge hall to the table of an ancient looking couple. As they approached, Lorad and Dia Firstholm roused from the patience of age and became warmly animated.

"Velirith, you look beautiful!" Lhea Firstholm exclaimed. "Oh, and Verr Velator, handsome as usual."

Velator grasped Lorad's arm, exchanging warm, knowing smiles but no words. Then he kissed the man's wife on the cheek. "And you look in excellent health, Dia. I'm glad I got noticed as an afterthought anyway."

EPISODE 1 – CLASH OF HEIRS

"Oh Vel, you've always been handsome, even as a boy. And now your daughter has decided to show the world of Zotikas a hint of her true loveliness."

Feeling a slight blush, Velirith smiled back at Lhea Firstholm. The Firstholms had been and still were unfailing allies to House Vel since the days of Velik. Their seafaring family had prospered under the good governance and peaceful times of the fledgling Omeron. When House Vel lost the Executive, they too lost influence.

Velirith knew how much her father admired them and their loyalty. She also knew Velator's affection was more personal. To Velirith, they were like grandparents rarely seen because of distance and busy lives. If there was but one couple she *did* want to see, it was the Firstholms.

"I miss your skynut cookies, Lhea Firstholm," Velirith mentioned, reminiscing.

"You remember those, yes? Well, I still make them for Lorad, but you would be a welcome guest anytime—no, *soon*, should you find the time in your social schedule," Lhea Firstholm invited. "We do spend most of our time at home by the sea now." Their home city, also called Firstholm, was far to the north, on the northwestern coast of Ardan. Velirith laughed at the implication she *had* a social schedule. "What now? Are you saying you aren't booked solid with friends or even gentlemanly callers? I find that hard to accept."

"Honestly, Lhea Firstholm, I don't like most of my peers. They seem only interested in their own status and estate."

Lhea Firstholm gave her a frank, nonjudgmental stare. "Well, doesn't that put you in an enviable position, my dear? You have the choice of joining in their pettiness or rousing them to reform, don't you?"

Velirith, rarely caught short, had to think about that. Her project tonight was definitely in the category of pettiness. Finally, speaking slowly, she responded, "I'm afraid I hadn't even

86

considered that I could make a *positive* difference." She paused. "I'll have to do something about it, true?"

Lhea Firstholm smiled, her eyes penetrating, and nodded.

Unafraid, Velirith felt a peace within her, an assurance that she indeed would do something. *I wonder how that will play out...*

The conversation between her father and his old friends continued. Velirith politely bowed out with a word from her father, "Don't throw anything off the balconies... or any*one*." His look conveyed both humor and a serious warning.

She wandered around the large, six-sided dance floor. While just moments before she had been wondering whether making herself beautiful might be attracting too many eyes, she now felt completely invisible. With everyone's attention engaged, she, like a little girl, walked the lines of tile edges, foot over foot, as if sneaking back to her room after one of her midnight explorations.

Velirith watched the guests and staff. No one was looking at her, not even the boys. She saw the house staff organizing the delivery of the New Year's Greetings. The employees broke up and spread out into the chatty crowd like a stirring breeze.

She watched the Executive Chair in his purple-gold pomp as he moved away from the receiving line toward the booth set up for his privacy. He seemed to be forcing his smile and walked like he was tired.

She saw a man from the wait staff angling toward Ferdando with Velirith's note on the top of his stack. Looking across the room, she saw his frustrated lover, excited as she read the note she had just received. Velirith distinctly remembered writing that one. *"I cannot bear separation from you, my dearest Callia. I have decided that renouncing my house and joining yours is no shame at all if I can spend my life in your arms. F"*

Callia's sharp features brightened in surprise and happiness. Yet neither of the lovers had the courage to truly renounce their family for their "true love." Velirith could only imagine Callia's reaction when she found out Ferdando got a similar note from her.

Forcheso Parchiki's voice blustered from her right. Velirith turned and saw him waving his note high above his head in his clenched fist. "The nerve! The gall! That woman—!" He was referring to Feleanna, or perhaps her second in command who had been raiding his cloth shipments. "She writes like we of House Parchiki will do nothing to stop her! *'Nudity will be in style this New Year unless another house takes up the slacks.'* I'll—" The rest of his words were choked off in his rage.

Very passionate. Theatrical, even. Velirith approved. She hadn't considered her notes might be read aloud. Feleanna was not yet in the hall. Odd, but convenient since Velirith wanted all parties involved to come together at the climax of her little drama. *I wonder if Feleanna will get* her *note before the dance...*

The volume in the great hall was increasing, her notes adding an angry and excited buzz to the general din.

She glanced back to her father, who was just now receiving his note. His said simply, *"You know I love you, Father. Vth"*

It was the only completely honest note in the batch.

His shoulders relaxed and a small, happy smile played on his lips. He looked up and around for her. When he saw her, alone on the edge of the empty dance floor, he returned her sentiment with his glance. But then, as if realizing something, or perhaps just noticing how animated the room had become, he tilted his head and gave her a curious look. It was as if to say, *What are you up to, Daughter?*

A long, piercing whistle shrieked through the gathering night, followed by an enormous concussive boom that drew out into a crackling rumble. The fireworks were beginning. Irresistibly, the crowd was drawn to the balcony that completely surrounded the great hall. Velator had looked away from her, and Velirith quickly slipped out the back of the great hall and down a service stair. She descended several floors, past where Moshalli and

88

CHAPTER NINE

Fechua had their quarters, and found an isolated balcony that looked out over Garrist Ring. She leaned on the stone balcony rail with its ornate balusters. Velirith suddenly felt wistful.

The feeling of peace she had found in her conversation with Lhea Firstholm still held her, like a seed in the center of her chest. But around that was an indefinable yearning. Why did she always have this desire to be alone? And why did she thirst for mischief? How could she hold two such contradictory feelings simultaneously?

Garrist Ring had dimmed its lanterns below, and the fireworks were in full blossom. But something was odd around the Charlaise Building across the gap. Handheld luzhril torches played around its base, as if the perimeter were being patrolled. Its roof lay just above the low balcony on which she stood.

A barrage of three blue and silver rockets exploded into spheres in front of her: a Vel Salute. Traditionally, each house was honored with at least one rocket displaying the colors of their house. The Vel Salute was eclipsed almost immediately by an enormous yellow blast on the roof of the Charlaise. That burst looked more like a flame than a mag-luz discharge. It was so bright compared to any of the other detonations that it temporarily blinded her. She had been looking right at the building and saw—or thought she saw—a dark, bulbous silhouette against the flash just before the shape dropped down against the darker background of the building itself. Great gouts of fire bloomed into the air above the roof. She felt a slight push from the concussion of the blast, even from this distance.

By the time she got her vision back, she could see nothing of the mysterious shape. Just moments later, the show continued with a spectacular red and orange sunburst that lit the space between her and the buildings of Garrist Ring. The show went on, just as it always did.

CHAPTER TEN

It was the first shot that got him.

He had been staring down the barrel of that maggun, waiting for the inevitable crack of discharge and desperately trying to turn enough to use his engine as a shield. But the magnetic field of the engine only slightly deflected the bolt up and through the inflated airfoil.

It ripped through the hydrogen envelope from one side straight through and out the other. For one intense blink, Kieler reflexively braced for an explosion above him. But maggun bolts were not particularly hot, and the only critical damage was the leaking hydrogen. He was now venting flammable gas in the midst of a fireworks show. Kieler looked back to the rooftop.

The other men, after a moment of orientation to the phenomenon of a flying ship, raised their weapons as well. More shots followed.

There was more commotion, a shout of warning. The men weren't looking at him, but at the door to the roof. A scrawny outline, doubled-over for air and stumbling out of the door. It had to be a Bintle man. In a mere fraction of a second, there was a sound of metal scraping on metal and then a series of pops. The three canisters immediately launched out in erratic paths of flame. One fateful missile arced in a tight loop and slammed into the rooftop right behind the man who had fired that first shot.

An enormous fireball erupted. The gunman was blown off the rooftop, engulfed in flame. From here he would not just fall the fifty-some stories to Garrist level, but many, many more—if he were lucky enough to miss all the various skyways and bridges on the way down. Not that it would matter much to his longevity.

The others, including the bank man, were now obscured by flame.

Kieler looked away in alarm. Of course he knew this could happen. But he wasn't a hardened killer. It shook him.

It shook his craft as well. Though the fireball did not reach him, the shock wave did, propelling him into the gap and toward the palace. The venting gas was misshaping the airfoil, and he was in a rapid, uncommanded descent. Kieler could not reach the damage, nor could he fix the holes if he were able to. He was descending between the Charlaise Building and the spire of the Executive Chair's palace.

I may as well go for it. He had one tank of hydrogen on board for emergencies and it was already hooked into the airfoil envelope. Kieler opened the valve full and gas hissed into the airship. The best it could do was to slow the descent. He pointed his ship at the spire and picked a balcony to crash on—if he made it that far before transfiguring into a rock. Despite the backup hydrogen, the airship barely maintained altitude. He was losing gas as fast as it was going in.

Kieler's mind was full throttle and he revved the engine to match. He knew that keeping the airspeed as high as possible would also contribute to his lift and he might be able to get across the gap—if he didn't run out of hydrogen first—or burn out his engine—or ignite in a firework blast—or get shot.

Engine burnout was the reason he hadn't just flown in at high speed from farther away. A longer flight would have avoided all the unpleasantness of dealing with Feleanna's ground thugs. But his technology wasn't perfect and the compact motor tended to overheat. No need for fireworks if he could blow himself up just as well.

EPISODE 1 – CLASH OF HEIRS

His plan had been a short flight *above* the fireworks allowing the highly reflective skin of his airship to look like just more lights in the sky. Now he was right in the path of the ascending rockets launched from the edge of Garrist Ring, and he was *under* the exploding spheres of color.

On top of that he was leaking hydrogen.

This was just foolish. But what choice did he have?

In his head, Kieler had already worked out a new design that would allow the engine to remain cool, but he had not had time to build that new engine before tonight.

A rocket trail blasted upward in front of him. He throttled back and banked right to give it wide berth but felt the drop in altitude from his loss of airspeed. The rocket passed and he throttled up, aiming back toward the Executive Chair's palace. The shell exploded in a ball of red-orange lightning above. The globe of released energy fell toward him but must have extinguished just feet above the venting hydrogen. Three more rocket trails spurted up to his right. Safe from their climb, he banked left to avoid the sparks from the explosion.

The next barrage came up on both sides. Again safe from their ascent, he found himself right in the middle of intersecting lightning spheres. That he hadn't exploded already was unimaginable. *Could I possibly make this?*

He looked down and saw his luck had changed for the worse. He saw nothing but an approaching dot in a halo of fiery sparks. It was coming right at him. His mind racing, there was no course of action that would make a difference in the one second he had to react.

He braced for impact and heat.

Twenty feet below him, the missile looked as if it hit something solid, deflected horizontally and blasted sideways. It detonated at a relatively low altitude over the Garrist Promenade. Echoes of the explosion bounced off the buildings, and the small, illuminated figures on the promenade ducked and scuttled away from the falling red and green bolts.

A miracle. The rocket must have lost a fin to deviate that drastically. It shouldn't have happened...

He had no time to consider it. He banked left as a flurry of hot exhaust streams climbed to his right. The resultant blasts rained down near him, and Kieler watched one of the ragged holes where he was losing hydrogen—as if he would even be able to flinch if one of the plasma spheres ignited it. But none did.

Time after time, the missiles missed him by an arm's length ascending and by less descending. Surviving another dozen such barrages, he began to feel as if he were encased in an impenetrable bubble.

After dodging all those shells, he pressed through a smoke trail and saw the Executive Chair's tower right in front of him. He banked hard left to avoid hitting it.

He'd made it across! But his hope died as he realized he was below every balcony. The nearest and lowest was still ten ship-lengths above him.

It was at that moment, in a gap between echoing blasts that the hiss of gas from his emergency tank ceased. He began dropping. He was out of hydrogen.

Without a moment of hesitation, Kieler reached up and yanked a ripcord. The weight of the empty tank fell away and he felt the immediate sensation of upward acceleration. Still full throttle, he pulled up as steeply as he could toward the belly of the nearest balcony. He glanced at his motor and was suddenly aware of a red, glowing ring around the magal core. In a flash, he realized the highest threat to his survival was now his own engine—either it would melt down and quit or ignite the hydrogen left in the envelope.

The airship now climbed straight up. He was approaching the balcony, then passing it just as fast. He had no time to jump and too much upward momentum. He wasn't prepared.

EPISODE 1 – CLASH OF HEIRS

He was even less prepared to see the startled oval face of a beautiful young lady leaning on the rail as he passed almost within arm's reach of her. She pulled back but amazingly did not cry out or run.

Then she was gone—falling behind as he zipped straight up past the best, and perhaps the only, landing spot he could hope for. There was nothing above him but the structure of the overhanging palace. And if he hit that, he had nothing to grab onto and would simply fall back into the abyss below.

But he was not going to hit it. As quickly as he had accelerated when he dumped the weight of the spare tank, the ship now lost momentum and began falling. He had no forward airspeed for lift. He was dropping straight back down the tower.

Kieler looked down, perhaps to gauge how long he would live on the fall to the Plate so far below. To his amazement, he saw he was about to hit a tree.

He did hit a tree. It stuck out from the balcony on which the young lady was standing. She had pushed over a large potted tree so that it leaned over the railing.

Kieler pushed himself from his seat and embraced it with open arms. His momentum nearly carried him through the thin upper branches, and one of them scratched a painful cut across his cheek, but they caught him. His wounded shoulder screamed. The airship snagged for a moment, the envelope slowly ripping under the weight of the engine. Kieler, in a moment of panic, grabbed for it. He wanted his airship.

His fingers almost closed on a fold in the fabric, but he began to slip down toward the smaller branches. He didn't need to be reminded there was no visible ground below him. He let the ship go.

It slid off the upper boughs of the toppled tree and slowly fell. Relieved of Kieler's weight but still having lost too much gas, it moved as if in slow motion, sinking as if in water and spiraling awkwardly as the envelope collapsed. Kieler clung with both hands to thin branches, but his eyes followed his short-lived, beautiful machine as it tumbled. It wasn't that far down when, during one of its limping swings, he saw the engine, still full throttle, dripping molten metal.

An instant later the remaining hydrogen ignited.

His fear of falling evaporated in the heat of the rising fireball directly beneath him.

CHAPTER ELEVEN

Despite the immediacy of the danger, Kieler felt frozen in the heat. Then the instant passed and he was scrambling down the trunk like a slink on a pipe. He hurled himself over the balcony rail as the winter-bare limbs of the tree caught fire behind him. Slamming onto his back on the balcony floor, he watched, fascinated, as the ball of fire flew past and continued upward until it blossomed on the underside of the palace. It burned itself out in grasping tendrils of flame. For a moment, all was dark.

His airship was gone.

He slowly turned his face toward the balcony doors.

There stood the quick-thinking young lady, staring down at him. She looked calm, even amused, her eyes sparkling green and gold in the reflection of a firework exploding behind him. He vaguely registered the colors of her clothing, blue and silver. She said nothing, and after a moment, spun and left the balcony, leaving him lying flat on his back.

He would have to find his own way from here.

Kieler felt blood dripping down his face, but the burning cut was nothing to being roasted. It was a precious reminder that somehow... he was still alive.

The tree that saved him was solidly anchored by its planter against the rail. The limbs that hung over were still burning like tiny candles. Whoever found this tree would have an interesting time explaining the phenomenon. He stood, but the adrenaline must have ebbed and his knees buckled, forcing him to catch himself against the balcony rail.

The empty space before him suddenly pressed into his awareness and he felt a wave of cold fear.

My ship... gone.

My life... Standing before the dark abyss below him and the smoking tree beside, the relative value of his life over his ship infused him with a profound sense of gratitude. He wiped the blood off his face with his hand and wiped his hand on the railing. The flow was beginning to ebb.

Kieler turned toward the spire and entered through the balcony doors. Ahead of him was a bank of elevators that would take him up to the great hall. But first, he found a washroom and cleaned up.

The Executive Chair and the real Ortessi heir had actually met once before, one week after Orlazrus Ortessi's birth. Kieler was pretty sure that Ek Threzhel would not recognize him.

On the short ride up the elevator, Kieler marveled that he actually seemed to have made it. So much had gone wrong: his seemingly precognitive tail, then being spotted on Garrist Ring, having holes shot through his airship followed the flight through the fireworks, and finally nearly being roasted like a slink on a spit.

And yet, here he stood.

He wouldn't have made it without the help of that young lady. Cute too. He had been tutored and quizzed extensively by Movus on all the important houses, their leaders and their progeny, their colors and corporations. Blue and silver was House Vel, Velator being the Prime with only one heir, his daughter, Lhea Velirith. Something had happened to all the other members of his family, though Movus had never told the story if he knew it.

So the young lady in blue and silver was probably Lhea Velirith. That she had helped him, thinking quickly by knocking that planter over, was another fortunate circumstance that bordered on supernatural. Why was she down there, with no protection, when everyone else was up at the party? And her unruffled amusement was not typical for such a young woman. That she left the scene when he seemed likely to survive was understandable considering his dramatic and clandestine arrival. His character and intentions would have been highly suspect and potentially violent. *She might still turn me in.* But he didn't think so. Nevertheless, she was wise to leave.

But Kieler suspected she didn't leave because she felt threatened by him. It was almost as if she didn't want to have to explain *herself.*

The elevator doors slid open with a clanking of the twin, highly polished, bronze doors. Kieler stepped out in the persona of the Ortessi Heir, his fine-woven uniform resplendent in green and gold (if a tad crumpled from his exertions). Over his heart he now wore the emerald luzhril and amber sigil of House Ortessi.

He stopped just outside the elevator and stood patiently, using the time before he was noticed to scan the room. The central dance floor, tiled in the traditional honeycomb pattern, stood empty. Everyone milled about on the terrace that surrounded the great hall, looking outward to watch the fireworks. The reception line had dispersed by this time, but because the fireworks held everyone's attention, his entrance did not cause the stir he had expected. Though he knew the elevator doors were heavily guarded at the Garrist level, these had but one guard on either side who spared him only a curious glance.

Kieler spotted the Executive Chair's booth and strode toward it. The Executive Chair was still in it, as if the fireworks he had provided did not warrant his interest. Four guards bracketed the booth and eyed Kieler warily as he approached. He stopped two paces before the seated Executive Chair, bowed stiffly from the waist, rose, and announced himself. "Orlazrus Ortessi, at your service."

CHAPTER ELEVEN

The Executive Chair, who had roused himself to sit closer to the edge of his seat as he noticed Kieler approaching, smiled a bit cynically.

Fechua MgFellis, recovering from her hesitation to introduce Orlazrus, remembered her duty. "Ek Threzhel, Prime of House Ek and Executive Chair of the Avetoric Omeron."

Threzhel commented, "Now the real fireworks begin, eh?"

Kieler allowed himself a slight smile despite the roiling in his stomach. *This man is responsible for my parents' deaths.* Kieler tightened control of his thoughts and noticed the Executive Chair looking off behind him.

Turning, he saw Feleanna Cortatti briskly entering the hall. Resplendent in a gown of red and black, she had tamed her dark red hair into a snappy elegance. Flustered and blatantly fuming, she spotted her quarry safely sheltered in the guarded presence of the Executive Chair.

A giant explosion, both of noise and colored light, surrounded the great hall as the finale erupted around them, thick with the gold and purple that lauded house Ek. Appreciative oohs and aahs followed. As the spheres faded, the crowd turned, murmuring excitedly as they reentered the great hall. Suddenly and together, everyone seemed to notice the man in green and gold standing before the Executive Chair—and Feleanna seething twenty paces away. The excitement of the firework display dwindled into an expectant silence as the crowd froze, staring at the scions of two families who had so much history of conflict, now reunited on such a dramatic stage.

The timing couldn't have been better. Kieler squelched the satisfied smile that wanted to burst out of him and glared murderously at Feleanna. She returned the stare openly, her flinty eyes glancing at the sigil on his chest. He could see the muscles of her jaw tighten as she clenched her teeth, biting down on her fury. She took a deep breath, then shifted brazenly to a more cavalier stance.

EPISODE 1 – CLASH OF HEIRS

When Feleanna turned, head stiffly high in unadmitted defeat, it was a sign for everyone else to breathe again. Immediately two houses came scurrying forward—Margríte Merckle, literally pushing her two boys, one on either side of her, and Gippo and Gamielle Mizgot—although even a "scurry" was not very fast for these two lumbering frames.

It was comical. He knew both houses wanted to take credit for "discovering" the legitimate heir of House Ortessi. His presence destabilized Feleanna's hold on an enormous amount of real estate, antiques, artifacts, and intellectual property previously belonging to House Ortessi. Any reduction of her wealth would diminish her capacity for aggression. Therefore the appearance of the Ortessi Heir would be beneficial to the Executive Chair, who knew Feleanna was after his position. Because the Merckles and Mizgots were dependent on the favor of House Ek, their relationship with the Executive Chair was crucial to their status.

Movus had perfectly played these two houses against each other. Running an agency of spies from beneath the Plate, Movus had earned a reputation as a provider of reliable information across house boundaries. Kieler and Movus had fed one of Mizgot's spies tainted information that Orlazrus Ortessi, the lost heir, was being courted rather cheaply by House Merckle, to be used as political leverage with the Executive Chair. The Mizgots, adept at buying favorable regulatory and financial influence, immediately outbid the Merckles for Orlazrus Ortessi to act as their comrade in gaining the Executive Chair's ear.

Considering Kieler, who gave most of the bribe to Movus, was neither the legitimate nor even the illegitimate son of House Ortessi, the sum was exceedingly generous. But it was the access to the Executive Chair and this evening's gala that he was really after. Access to the inner circle, and the endorsement of two very powerful families.

100

CHAPTER ELEVEN

The Mizgots built the vehicles that rode the rails of the tram and powercoach lines. They had been the largest economic power in all Zotikas at one time—until the economy had declined.

The Merckles were currently rising on a wave of political socialization. They ran health care facilities of all types. Ten years ago the Executive Chair and the Omeron had granted government funds for the Merckles to run *free* clinics. Other medical businesses couldn't compete with free, nor could they navigate the maze of paperwork required of non-government sanctioned facilities. As competitors failed, the Merckles gained patients whose bills were paid by the Omeron.

One family of doctors, the Sendaris, was now living under the Plate. Kieler had met them, and since good medical services were scarce in the underworld, Indis Sendari was making a better living on the black market than he had fighting government subsidies and regulations above the Plate.

Margríte Merckle bustled into range. "Your Chairness, this is the man! My sons and I have been trying to arrange an introduction—"

"We are introduced, Margríte, just now," interrupted the Executive Chair. She looked put off, glancing at her sons.

The Mizgots, finally arriving across the floor, took a slightly different tack. Puffing, Verr Gippo Mizgot rhapsodized to the Executive Chair, "This man is the legitimate owner of our great Theater! Verr Executive Chair, I believe a revival in culture would further solidify your claim to leading the greatest cultural and economic boom since Velik himself!"

The fawning was sickening to Kieler, but that's why he was here—to crunch these insects like so many skynuts. Looking over the two new arrivals, he was surprised that despite Gamielle Mizgot's top-heavy build, her dress was tenuously suspended by thin straps. Perhaps she considered them a touch of elegance.

Rather than let the sycophantic behavior continue interminably, Kieler interjected with intentional softness so that

EPISODE 1 – CLASH OF HEIRS

they had to lean forward to hear. "Hello, friends. Thank you for your kind words. But my claim to my family's past holdings has some obstacles to overcome." He flashed a glance toward Feleanna. "Perhaps the Executive Chair would aid me in the reestablishment of some of my family's property and business. But now is not the time to discuss these things."

The Executive Chair nodded. With half-lidded eyes he looked at the two obsequious families before him as if they were not to be trusted with information as delicate as what was for dinner. He spoke to Kieler. "Good to see you passed the test of getting here. You're not much use if you can't live to see the new year," the Executive Chair said, illuminating the harsh reality. "But you've not re-met any of your family's old friends, have you? Friends, I'm afraid, that didn't help your family much twenty years ago. Perhaps they've changed some. Shall we see?"

Kieler didn't respond immediately. He eyed the Executive Chair with practiced coolness. Below the surface, Kieler realized that while the Ortessis' "friends" had let his family die at the hands of the Cortattis, the Executive Chair himself had let Kieler's mother die in the death trap where Ek processed magal. Tightly controlling his voice, Kieler said, "I think I can tolerate that, sir."

Kieler, of course, wanted nothing more than to be introduced as the Ortessi Heir to every head family. His main purpose in being here was to endorse his legitimacy and improve his sponsorship. These two families just wanted to use him to increase their standing with the Executive Chair. The Mizgots had huge wealth, but were falling in favor so fast that they were more influenza than influential. Other houses were trying to disassociate themselves from them, particularly the Bintles.

The Merckles, on the other hand, were rising stars. Considering they were physicians and obviously politically cunning, Kieler found them alarmingly naïve. Movus and he had leveraged their influence easily because of this quality. The current

CHAPTER ELEVEN

generations of Merckles had never struggled to build a quality business. They had no street wisdom.

Both these families followed sullenly as the Executive Chair moved with his characteristic lack of urgency toward a nearby table.

"These are Borgus and Balfani Telander. They produce the generators and control the power plants of our city," Threzhel offered. Kieler felt his chest tighten at the introduction. Every house in attendance had an indictment against them, but *Telander*—his crime was personal. His secret penchant for kidnapped women, particularly Bags' wife, struck to the heart of why Kieler was here.

The Telanders stood for the Executive Chair, and Borgus extended his arm to grasp Kieler's. The man looked very much like the EC himself. Rounded, shrinking in stature with a puffy face, wearing the same bored expression. Kieler knew that there was little love between these two men. As soon as House Ek had taken office, they had boosted the price of magal. And just this year someone had revealed that the recent magal shortage claimed by House Ek, was actually a fraud enacted to raise the price yet again.

Movus had told Kieler that Balfani, Borgus' wife, resented the Executive Chair bitterly because his price hikes cut into the profits generated by their power plants. Evidently, they also cut into her rather extravagant lifestyle.

Kieler noticed that despite the "hard times," neither of them had starved. He also noticed that Balfani, her face lined with angry wrinkles, was glaring fiercely at the EC.

"I knew your father, Salman," Borgus nodded, referring to the former Ortessi patriarch. "Shame he died so young."

"I'm told his name was Salasan," Kieler replied, recognizing the feeble test to his claim. "But I did not know him. He was killed when I was only two."

EPISODE 1 – CLASH OF HEIRS

Borgus nodded, looking at him with the same half-closed eyes that the Executive Chair used. "So you don't believe the prattle about an accident, eh?"

"No. Only a year ago I pursued what investigation I could, being twenty years passed, and it did not even look like they tried to fake it. It seems it simply couldn't be proven that it was the Cortattis."

"You speak plainly enough," replied Borgus. "You'll never make a good politician."

Kieler took a chance. "Neither will you, sir," he countered with a smile.

The Executive Chair laughed, thankfully, and as he started to lead Kieler away, Balfani Telander made a rather bizarre comment. She blurted, "Don't think you can get in my good graces with empty flattery in a silly New Year's Greeting, Ek Threzhel!"

The Executive Chair gave her a curious look but did not retort. As they walked away, Kieler asked him what she meant.

The Executive Chair shrugged. "Speak plainly or speak and make no sense. I find it better not to speak much at all these days." Then he lowered his voice so that only Kieler could hear. "But don't you get too cheeky, Ortessi. We politicians still need fighters for the arena."

Kieler turned his head to the Executive Chair, but the man wasn't looking back at him. The threat was direct, but the warning at least made it very clear what Kieler's limits were in this new relationship. It all served as a reminder that the Executive Chair was no one's friend. The Chair had no knowledge that he had, indirectly, killed Kieler's mother. Nor would he care if he did. The man's only concern was that Feleanna was getting too powerful. Kieler should be able to use that fear to get into his good graces and exploit him.

The frightening aspect of Kieler's game was that the Executive Chair had played it successfully for fifty-some years. Kieler was a brash, no-name challenger.

CHAPTER ELEVEN

Allies. That's what Kieler needed.

"Should we go see Feleanna then?" offered the Executive Chair rather cruelly.

"No, sir. I want to be clear which side I am *not* on," Kieler answered.

"Good." The Executive Chair seemed to treat the subsequent introductions as a play put on for his own personal amusement. But Kieler was not amused and neither was his alter ego Orlazrus. Nevertheless, the fact that the Executive Chair was actually taking him around personally fitted Kieler's purpose nicely. He was introduced to several more houses.

His final introduction to the Bintles was eventful. The eldest were in poor health and not in attendance. Their son, Carrenten Bintle, a young man only a handful of years older than Kieler, was now in charge of the Omeron's financial system. His wife, Serru, was stunning in an elegant but revealing gown.

"Pleasure, Ortessi," Carrenten Bintle said grasping his arm firmly. "You'll shake things up around here!"

"What do you mean?" Kieler asked.

"I mean we'll see some action. Undoubtedly, Feleanna won't let you dance in here like a stodgy old house incumbent. You're going to have to be on your toes to avoid them being stepped on."

Kieler smiled. The man was arrogant and direct, but he liked him. Only Borgus was as direct, but Borgus was jaded and cynical. Carrenten was looking for adventure, if a bit recklessly. Kieler responded with a prodding directness of his own. "Could my conflict with House Cortatti affect House Bintle in any way?"

Laughing, Carrenten replied, "Well, it might blow the tops off a few more of my buildings. But I don't think so. You didn't miss that unplanned firework, did you?"

Kieler had no idea if Carrenten Bintle knew of his connection to the explosion. Actually, Carrenten couldn't know. But the banking king was certainly amused by the detonation even though it would cost him some dras. *But if you're the guy that prints the money...*

Kieler doubted he hid his own reaction very well to Bintle's words. He replied casually, "I may have caught part of it..."

Suddenly Kieler was aware of Serru Bintle, standing just behind her husband, boring into him with her eyes. Not unfriendly, but certainly aggressive.

"She likes mystery men," Carrenten said, looking sidelong at his wife, who was still staring at Kieler. "I should know. I used to be one."

She spoke curtly, "How did you get that cut?"

There was something not right about this woman. Interesting that it was she who was first to ask about the cut he got in the tree. "Knife fight in the elevator." Kieler tried to look serious.

Carrenten laughed, but Serru Bintle just nodded and licked her lips. "Looks like you fell out of a tree."

There was another laugh behind him, a laugh that he enjoyed hearing. He and the Executive Chair turned, and there, next to a handsome middle age man also in blue and silver, was the girl with the tree.

Still amazingly bored, the Executive Chair muttered, "Velator and his daughter, Velirith. This is Orlazrus Ortessi."

Kieler gave a slight bow, keeping eye contact with Velator and then grasping his arm in formal greeting. He knew instinctively that Velirith had not told her father about the incident on the balcony below. He also noted that unlike the other House Primes, Velator was not wearing a house sigil.

"Pleasure to meet you, Verr Ortessi."

"Sure," Velirith cut in with a blatant scoff. "Conveniently dropped in, didn't he?" She didn't believe he was Orlazrus.

The Executive Chair scowled at Velator's daughter, perhaps at her impertinence, but his next words were those of revelation. "Ortessi, how *did* you get here? My men were at the palace tram station to escort you up and bring you to me. Yet you arrived without them."

"Sir, may I get by with the excuse that my course was unconventional? With several unwelcoming parties, I may have to slip out the same way."

The Executive Chair consented with a grunt, but was obviously unhappy that someone could actually sneak into his palace past his personal guards and Feleanna's thugs.

But Velirith muttered, "I'd like to see *that* departure."

Kieler clenched his jaw to hide his embarrassment. Velator gave his daughter a curious look but let it go, probably fearing the answer in front of the EC.

"Ortessi," said the Executive Chair in a dismissive way, "you've been introduced. You're in the dance, by the way, position twenty-one. See me before you leave." And he walked back to his booth.

Kieler bowed, and when the Executive Chair was out of earshot, Carrenten said, "Sounds like you're in trouble."

Grinning, Kieler replied, "Could be worse. I could have fallen out of that tree your wife had me climbing."

Carrenten Bintle laughed but pointed out, "Look Ortessi, you've avoided a straight answer to every question." Kieler smiled to himself that Borgus had made the opposite comment. "What are you up to?"

"I'll give you a straight answer to that one, Verr Bintle. Coming out at this party has made me completely vulnerable. Feleanna's thugs will follow me wherever I go tonight and they will unceremoniously kill me. So I'm looking for a refuge, a benefactor. Can you handle taking me in for a while?"

Completely taken aback, Carrenten thought soberly. Although he did not look at her, Kieler could tell he was thinking about his wife. Perhaps he feared her attraction to "mystery men." But Kieler thought it something else, as if it was Carrenten's nature to do something just this risky, but at a cost to Serru's stability.

EPISODE 1 – CLASH OF HEIRS

"We'll take you in, Verr Ortessi," Velator spoke up unexpectedly, taking the heat off Carrenten.

"No, Father! He's a fraud!" Velirith blurted with complete conviction.

"Shush, Velirith," Velator said in a steady voice, obviously accustomed to her bluntness. "I have intuition too and I think we should give him a place to stay."

Velirith looked back and forth between Kieler and her father, evaluating. Then she sullenly agreed, but not without a steady, accusing look at Kieler.

Kieler made a mental note to be on guard with her. She seemed to see right through him.

"True to the house of Vel!" exclaimed Carrenten. "Gathering together the wanderers of the world."

Fechua, the social coordinator, interrupted from the front of the dance floor, "The Family Harmony Dance begins in just a few moments! Ladies and gentlemen, take your assigned spots. My daughter and I will assist in placing you in your starting positions. Get ready!"

CHAPTER TWELVE

Velirith spoke to Kieler as they walked out to the center, "You *have* been coached on how to do the New Year's Family Harmony Dance, true? I'd hate for you to mess this up like your arrival. You might end up dancing with someone ugly."

Kieler assured her that he had been well coached, and they split up, Velirith taking a position across the circle from him next to Gamielle Mizgot. The Executive Chair and his wife marked the top of the circle nearest the EC's booth.

Eighty dancers were marshaled into two concentric circles around the center of the hexagonal dance floor; men in the outer circle, ladies in the inner one. The numbers matched precisely, each man with one lady.

When everyone had assembled, Fechua called out, "Please face and address your partners..." The men and ladies bowed to each other.

Kieler was paired with Balfani Telander, but knew that the pairing would be short-lived. It was the final partner with whom one spent most of the dance. Kieler bowed, "My pleasure, Lhea Telander." She bowed back, still looking miffed about something. Kieler considered the strong possibility that her scowl was a permanent feature. He also wondered whether Velirith had cursed him with her "ugly" comment.

Fechua continued, "And prepare to dance with someone new!" Some near Kieler smirked at the "someone new" part, knowing the dance was rigged and that everyone would end up with someone inoffensive. Occasionally a single young lady would end up paired with a hopeful young man, and they would get to enjoy an anticipatory thrill. But mostly the old couples knew they would be paired with some old ally and not a hated rival.

With that, Fechua gave a quick triple clap and the orchestra began playing the traditional, upbeat waltz that had been played for centuries. After the intro, the men immediately skipped counterclockwise one position, and the ladies did likewise in the other direction. Since both circles moved opposite each other, the dancers always passed one person to end up with the next. Thus the two groups, odds and evens, would never mix. If Kieler was an odd, he noted mentally, then Feleanna was an even. They would pass but never dance. The social coordinator had done her research well.

After each one-position rotation, the new partners did a four measure pas-de-deux, bowed, and then rotated again.

Kieler knew he would be watched carefully. After all, every one of the dancers except him had seen the dance if not participated in it. They had likely attended this ever since they were twelve years of age. He had never seen it. They'd be watching to see if he messed up.

But he wouldn't. Movus had been his coach. Knowing that all eyes would be on him, he had practiced in the dim chambers of the under-Plate until he was bored silly with the simple dance. By his third partner, Kieler was sure enough of himself that he glanced around during the rotation.

The Executive Chair, he saw, was not "skipping" one bit. He was sauntering, doing just enough to stay in position so as not to disturb the status quo of the dance. Everyone played their part, practiced and rather dull. And this was supposed to be the highlight of the evening?

About a quarter of the way around the circle, Kieler converged with Velirith. Wary and intrigued with the young woman, he desperately tried to think of something to say in the four measures they would spend together. So much about her was unusual: She wore an attractive variant of the Vel uniform and not an evening gown like the other young debutantes. Her every behavior indicated she wasn't going to play like the other Omeron. And, looking into her face, her eyes were unlike anyone's he had ever seen. Where her father had the silver-grey common to House Vel, hers were so silver they reflected colored light like crystal.

And right now, as they touched hands in the dance, those eyes seemed to convey a very readable, barely-contained excitement. What it meant, Kieler had no idea.

"So you don't trust me," he stated, wishing he could have thought of something more positive.

But her casual answer was an odd denial. "No, truly, I do trust you. I just don't believe you. Whereas you should *always* believe me—just don't trust me." The smile on her enchanting face conveyed her meaning almost better than her words.

Having nothing to say to such a cryptic comment, Kieler watched Velirith spin away from him, still wearing that charming, roguish smile matching the one in her eyes.

Though there were many more rotations before the anticipated change in music from regal waltz to light and playful lilt, Kieler knew he wouldn't be dancing with Velirith again, and he felt an unexpected twinge of disappointment.

It was shortly after dancing with Velirith that something happened.

Kieler heard a short, startled scream and looked over to see Gamielle Mizgot suddenly grab her current partner and press the shorter man to her bosom. Her partner was easily half-a-head shorter than her and instantly turned redder than Feleanna's hair. While the rest of the dancers kept on out of sheer momentum, Kieler wondered at Gamielle's break from the age-old propriety of the dance. Then he saw that one of her slender shoulder straps hung limply down to her waist.

EPISODE 1 – CLASH OF HEIRS

Gamielle wasn't the only one who couldn't contain herself. Kieler bit his lower lip to keep from laughing.

Gamielle half danced, half dragged her runtish partner off the floor and toward the nearest corridor leading to the powder room. Kieler glanced across the circle at Gippo. Gamielle's husband was obviously concerned but not enough to risk looking bad by abandoning his position to help his wife. *The dance goes on*, Kieler thought with disgust.

The next rotation occurred almost smoothly as the couples closed the gap and tightened the circle. Kieler couldn't decide if that was talented dancing or callousness toward the missing couple.

During the rotation, he happened a glance at Fechua just off the dance floor. Her face was a frozen mask of utter horror, her hands stopped in mid-air between claps. In a moment he understood, more instinctively than logically.

This altered the pairings. *Would they now be truly random?* That could be interesting. More alert, he wondered, *What could be so bad?*

With each rotation, spreading both ways from the missing couple, odds were now dancing with evens, and evens were dancing with odds.

Still, things were not horrible. After four rotations, eight couples were mis-paired and none seemed to be particularly bitter rivals.

But it was like a wheel of fate. *Where would it stop?*

Kieler saw Ferdando Ashperis looking down the circle. The handsome young man caught the eye of Callia and they were unabashedly thrilled that they were converging with a distinct chance they could end up together. Callia actually raised her hands to her face to cover a surprised but excited flush.

The onlookers from the sidelines were rising to their feet in a growing buzz of excited murmuring. Other dancers were trying to figure it out, looking ahead to see who they might get paired with.

CHAPTER TWELVE

Kieler spied Forcheso Parchiki, the look of concern on his face twisting into outrage.

As Kieler moved with each rotation, the crowd noise around them grew. Everyone was on their feet.

He suddenly realized, as the music began to transition, that this couldn't be random; it was somehow cleverly deliberate. And that begged the monumental question, *Had the secret planner destined someone for him?*

The intensity of the music grew as if the musicians sensed impending disaster. He tried to peer between the women but now didn't have the angle. There was a long fermata to allow the dancers to adjust their steps to their final partner; the circle made its final rotation, and from behind another large matron came his ultimate partner.

Feleanna.

Kieler lost composure, stumbling into position. This whole thing must have been rigged just to embarrass *him*. But Feleanna was just as outraged, if not more! And the other couples... Kieler didn't know all their histories.

The crowd around them was in uproar. Shouts. "What nerve!" "How indecent!"

Face to face with Feleanna Cortatti, he and she were supposed to bow in the extended notes before the next movement. Neither did.

Her features sharp and her deep red dress exquisite and sensual, the heated flush would have been beautiful—had not every degree of hatred been blazing to consume him. Her flint-green eyes shot daggers, and her perfect smile was more of a smirk that said, "*This night's not over till* you *are dead!*"

Kieler was not prepared. He felt weak but rallied his bravado to counter her deadly glare with a look of arrogant amusement, trying to pretend as if it were he who arranged this whole fantastic debacle.

EPISODE 1 – CLASH OF HEIRS

As the music re-started, they, like puppets to its lilt, came together for the first sequence, the men escorting the ladies around the small domain in which they would spend the rest of their term. Thinking as fast as his confusion would allow, he held her arm and looked at her like a secret lover.

Fuming, Feleanna seemed to be gathering for an explosion. But she held off, like a balloon filling beyond its limits. Her first words, however, were not the vitriol he expected. "How did you get that sigil through the magnetic Eks?"

Caught completely off guard, Kieler fought to hide his surprise.

She bared her teeth again in disdainful mirth. "You didn't know, did you? Which means..." She trailed off, piecing something together. "You ill-witted usurper. That sigil, and Vel's, are the only ones *not* crafted out of precious metals. Velik and the first Ortessi hated the sigils, so they mounted the jewels in a base metal, iron, to evoke humility. You're the first *blatantly* arrogant Ortessi to ever wear a sigil to this gala." She spat a short laugh, letting it sink in that his mission of the night before was, in a way, pointless.

Kieler knew he went red, but a retort came easy to his tongue. "And of course, your contempt of sigils is evident by your coveted collection."

The reference to his intrusion of her home stoked her rage. "No one violates *our* keep and lives. No one mocks *Cortatti!*"

As Kieler processed the information and the threat, Feleanna took advantage of his distraction, and while ostensibly raising her arms to twirl, she speared her fingers into his wounded shoulder.

Since landing in the tree, it hadn't hurt much.

He clenched his teeth and writhed to stop from screaming.

Thankfully, the next few measures had them twirling away from each other followed by a hesitation. He used the respite to push away the pain in his shoulder and regain his situational awareness.

114

CHAPTER TWELVE

Not far down the circle of paired dancers was the ashen-faced Executive Chair and, raging red, Balfani Telander. Evidently, Kieler and Feleanna were not the only victims. Balfani stood stock still, refusing to dance and yet refusing to walk away. Ek Threzhel was lamely moving through the steps, clearly baffled at how to respond to such a calamity. If this had been a rebellion in his magal mines, he'd know what to do. But this was a social crisis.

With a quick double take to the other side, Kieler saw Forcheso Parchiki and Sindia Corch dancing, if it could be called that, on the floor—horizontally. There was no pretense as they all-out wrestled and punched, the nasty Cortatti giving the older Parchiki an even match. Amazingly, no one tried to break them up. The guards looked at each other completely stymied.

Feleanna reclaimed his attention as the next moves brought them close again. She added gloating and cursing as her repartee degraded to base abuse. "You ignorant imposter! You coming here is like checking yourself into a butcher shop on a hook. I'll grind you up like kovar meat!" she hissed. "Maggot infested, fetid, trampled, kovar meat!"

That barrage helped take his mind off the pain. He had, after all, worked with underworld roughs since adolescence. He knew how to insult. "What fetching words. Fetching Feleanna! And what's that fragrance you're wearing? Eau d'grevon? Or have you been bathing in wine? It's quite becoming—"

She, evidently, had not acquired a tolerance for being insulted, and her anger flared into a barely controlled assault. In between what were supposed to be close and conversational waltz steps, she slapped him at the finish of each turn. After the first two, Kieler knew when to duck. He managed to catch and stubbornly hold her high hand, keeping his other hand boldly on her well-muscled hip.

The verbal banter disappeared as they both concentrated on dancing and bashing each other. Even as he did so, he wondered why everyone continued the façade of the dance. *Propriety?!*

She aimed an in-time, close-in kick to his groin, and he had to let go of her hip and yank her to one side to avoid it. The crowd was screaming. While continuing his defensive dancing, he could hear several couples flat out yelling at each other.

What amazed him most was that the dance went on. Fechua must have decided that to stop it would be the worst social faux pas. A glance at the Executive Chair told Kieler the man was befuddled into inaction. No one else dared the authority to step in.

Feleanna was swinging again, and all gentlemanly manners aside, Kieler crushed her high hand in his grip and bent it backward, trying not to make it look obvious to the crowd. He knew if he walked away she would club him and if he backed away he'd look weak. She was probably thinking the same thing about herself.

How long will this dance go on!

Avoiding another kick, he failed to see her free hand until it cuffed his ear. It rang. Trying to gain control, he spun her in close and tightened his hold on her stomach, pinning her arm between them. He heard the breath go out of her. This position meant he was pressed into her back, but at least she couldn't bite him.

Instead, she stomped her heel into his instep. The orchestra crescendoed toward a climax. In fierce pain he spun her away with both hands. Her posterior hit the floor just as the musicians hit the final, accented chord.

The crowd fell dead silent. The dancers quieted too, all except for the Callia girl who was now crying uncontrollably and hysterically shouting, "User! Manipulator!"

Feleanna lay splayed on the floor, her red dress torn, sweat dripping from her face as she propped herself on one arm.

Kieler was in shock. He realized his mouth was open but just then glanced left and forgot to close it. He saw Velirith in her father's arms, smiling sweetly up at Velator.

CHAPTER TWELVE

But Velator was in speechless shock as well. A frozen look of terror was pasted on his face, as if he was holding a demon instead of his lovely daughter.

In the silence, Kieler thought he heard Velator croak, "*How?*

EPISODE 2:
HIGH RAILS OF ARDAN

CHAPTER ONE

A glimmer of consciousness and a streak of sunlight across crisp, white sheets. Warmth and a luxuriant exhaustion tugging him back into his dream. A dream—a dream that was so much closer than consciousness.

He was a child, barefoot, with thick spring grass between wriggling toes. People who loved him, who *adored* him, stood behind him, laughing fondly. *Parents?* He looked up through a canopy of leaves to sky and clouds, green and blue and white, all vibrant and pure.

He stretched, and the sheets almost crackled with freshness.

Crisp sheets?

A confusion entered the vision. He had never known crisp, clean sheets.

Cracking an eye open, his vision continued through a plain, neat, half-hex of a window. A blue dawn, white cumulus, and Rei just chipping through the edge of the sparkling clean window.

He had no idea who or where he was. But it was a feeling of pure innocence and nestling security.

Crisp, white sheets.

It was this bewildering incongruity that nagged his mind into puzzling out where he was.

And the realization fell on him like a boulder falling from the Executive Chair's towering palace.

EPISODE 2: HIGH RAILS OF ARDAN

He sat up quickly on the side of a plush bed, a rush of remembrance flooding into his mind. The debacle of the previous night washed away the warm, clinging glow of a dream so rare and so contrary to his actual life that he knew he'd never experience it again.

Despite the memories, he smiled. A bed. *A window!*

It had been years since Kieler had awoken to the light of Rei. And here he was, on the top residential floor of Vel-Taradan, just below the FamTram station, in a room. He hadn't paid much attention to his sleeping chamber upon their arrival only a few hours before dawn. They had all been in shock from the events of the gala, and his curiosity was at a particularly low ebb.

Deliberately avoiding analysis of the fallout from last night, he looked around his room. Unlike the ostentatious, highborn manor of the Cortattis, this bedroom was graced with the clean lines of sparse furniture that complemented the geometry of the exposed metallic supports of the building. Burnished duralium beams ran in aesthetic contrast to the light blue walls. It was clear that here in House Vel the structure itself was the decor.

Now that he was sitting up, he could see through the window across Plaza Floraneva, his favorite place in all Avertori. It was deserted. In the defunct fountains and across the terrazzo paving, the detritus of last night's revelry was strewn. One early-rising porter dragged a beat up trash can across the plaza, picking up a mere fraction of the bottles, food scraps and wrappings. *What could one man do in the face of such wreckage?*

On the three corners of Floraneva sat the theater, the cathedral, and the Arena.

As his eyes settled on the Arena, the smile slid off his face. He remembered the blunt threat of the Executive Chair: Step out of line and you'll end up in the Arena. The Arena was supposedly for criminals. But anymore, the word criminal simply referred to anyone who was inconvenient to the Prime houses. By any *true*

120

CHAPTER ONE

standard of justice, Ek Threzhel himself should have been featured in the Arena long ago.

Charged as the city had been last night, this morning Avertori's heartbeat with only the merest thrum of power. The generators were nearly silent.

With barely a conscious thought, Kieler's eyes drifted to the left of the Arena, beyond Floreneva toward the isle's north coast. The hulking mass of the magal processing plant could just be seen over the edge of the plaza. The plant, dilapidated but still functioning, was the hub of House Ek's empire—and where both Kieler's father and mother had worked. One day she had gone to work. And that was it. He never saw her again.

A savage nostalgia fanned the latent coals of hatred toward Ek's imperious indifference. It seemed that Kieler could actually see the fire-darkened walls of the distant plant. And he involuntarily imagined the horror of his mother, only a few years older than he was now, trapped in that ill-maintained building while the flames rose around her. He felt the heat that destroyed her and, indirectly, destroyed Kieler's father as well.

Ek Threzhel had certainly spent the minimum possible getting the facility up and running after the inferno. To him, it was just an inconvenient cost of doing business. Though no one had championed justice then, Kieler would change that now.

Joining Ek in the Arena, in Kieler's vision of a just world, would be the she-grevon Feleanna. Besides attacking other houses, her crimes included forcing arms into the hands of thousands of "undesirables," setting the innocent against each other, and selling tickets to the macabre spectacle.

Feleanna. He had planned to stay as far away from her as possible. The very "existence" of Orlazrus was an affront to her. Adding his own personal insults made retaliation a certainty. *Maybe rage will cloud her judgment,* he pretended. But he knew better.

121

EPISODE 2: HIGH RAILS OF ARDAN

Last night she had tried to have him killed *before* she met him. But now that they'd been so cordially introduced, perhaps they could be friends.

A groaning sigh escaped him. Again, he knew better.

After the dance, he had followed Velirith and Velator out of the hall like a wounded slink pup. In a daze—and Velator no less stunned—Kieler had ridden the FamTram back to House Vel's Grand Stair residence. There had been no conversation, nothing clever to say. It was the pathos of a well-performed play that had left them, the actors, completely drained of emotion and sense. Velirith had leaned her head on Velator's shoulder, smiling serenely, perfectly pleased. Considering her obvious disdain of her social position, she had certainly enjoyed the show. But could she be responsible for producing it? Kieler shook his head. The magnitude of what had happened made it inconceivable someone so young could have orchestrated such chaos.

Kieler especially regretted not being able to have a final word with the Executive Chair about Feleanna. The Chair, too, had fled. Connecting with him had been an important part of the scheme that he and Movus had devised. Movus had discerned that the Executive Chair's main concern was the growing power of House Cortatti. Kieler had intended to proffer information and assistance that would help rein in her runaway ambition.

He hadn't even had a chance.

Nevertheless, being invited to stay with House Vel compensated much of that loss. In the context of history, even Kieler admired them. True, they were currently "out of favor" and held only a shadow of their former power, but they were still influential and respected.

He heard a quiet knock at the door.

"Who is it?" he asked.

One of the servants responded, "Verr Ortessi, at your convenience, Verr Velator requests your presence in the main hall. A guest has arrived who he believes you need to meet."

122

CHAPTER ONE

"I'll be there soon," he replied.

He stood up and looked to the chair where he had thrown his uniform the night before. It wasn't there! The Ortessi sigil wasn't there!

A moment of frantic searching found him in an anteroom of the guest suite staring at a freshly pressed and hung Ortessian uniform, with the sigil still neatly pinned to the breast. He had to laugh at himself. Had one night of luxury already made him as sloppy as that? Leaving something as valuable as that sigil just lying around. He had been lucky though. House Vel seemed more interested in acquiring him in total rather than just his sigil.

The uniform hung in one side of an open travel wardrobe taller than he was. Next to it, a half dozen sets of less formal clothes were arrayed, all of which appeared new and tailored for him. He wasn't sure what to make of the fact that someone in House Vel had seen to it that he had clean underwear.

The other side of the travel wardrobe contained several drawers stocked with more hygiene products then he imagined to exist. He selected some of the more recognizable ones and went into the suite's lavatorium to make himself presentable.

A few minutes later he left his rooms and rode an elevator, trimmed in alternating bronze and silver, down to level "P," unsure which floor that would actually take him to. He stepped out onto an elevated walkway surrounding the second story of the expansive main hall. The hall itself was thirty-five stories above the Stair and marked the beginning of the residential portion of the tower. Everything above this reception hall was private family living space with the FamTram passing through its top floors.

From the floor of the hall, ceilings vaulted a full three stories. One immense, reaching arch of duralium and glass framed an almost panoramic view of Plaza Floraneva. The view was so expansive it made Kieler feel as if he were floating above the plaza.

The main hall below bustled with activity. A dozen Vel staff scurried urgently across the tile floor, many of them toting luggage.

123

EPISODE 2: HIGH RAILS OF ARDAN

Attempting to direct traffic was a very striking yet severe-looking young woman, the only blonde-haired person in the place.

Kieler spotted Velator standing in front of the arched window, away from most of the hubbub, having an animated discussion with a straight-backed man Kieler didn't recognize. Putting on the Ortessi air, Kieler strode down the sweeping steps to join them.

"Sir, I don't think this is—" the man with the supercilious face was imploring when Velator noticed Kieler coming up to them.

"Verr Ortessi, I'm glad you're up and alive!" Velator interrupted the other man. Kieler immediately noticed the red in Velator's eyes. Evidently he hadn't slept as well as Kieler, if at all.

"I share your sentiments, Verr Velator." Kieler smiled wanly.

"Have you rested well? A night like that isn't easy to recover from," Velator said drolly as Kieler approached.

"I did indeed. Your hospitality is remarkable," Kieler replied.

"We do what we can," Velator answered with only a hint of his fatigue. "I would like you to meet Arvel, the head of our legal department and my chief political strategist. I believe a man in your situation will soon be in need of his particular expertise."

"It is a pleasure to meet you, Verr Ortessi," said Arvel with a lack of enthusiasm that belied his words.

"Likewise," said Kieler as he grasped the man's forearm. "Though I doubt you could extend the same pleasure to my case."

Arvel's smile thinned, and he glanced at Velator before replying. "You are correct. Your position is extraordinarily precarious, and I've been advising Velator that we should not entangle ourselves in this matter."

"I see," said Kieler, wondering where this conversation was going.

"Nevertheless, despite the extreme risk involved, Velator is adamant that we support you. He believes that you represent a unique opportunity to strike a decisive blow against House Cortatti. Now if this were strictly a legal matter, then I would be in complete agreement with his assessment. But the fact is that House Cortatti is known for breaking the rules, and I simply question your ability to survive long enough for any of my efforts to be of any value."

"Arvel is known for his sensitivity," quipped Velator dryly.

"I see that," Kieler replied, and then asked, "So, other than not dying, what can I do to help?"

"For the time being, the process is rather straightforward. I'll need your signature on some documents that will allow me to act on your behalf. I'll get the process started on your claim to house Ortessi, but even with a high profile case like this, it could be months before things get interesting."

"Isn't there any way to speed things up?"

"We will do what we can, but as you know, the current Ortessi Prime, Orticot, was a Cortatti who married one of the, ah, *violently disinherited* Ortessis. The marriage was an underhanded but working scheme to gain control over House Ortessi. Cortatti will have their legal team trying to block every move we make." He added in a mutter, "And quite likely their hit squad as well."

"Fortunately," Arvel went on, "there is little doubt that this case will go to trial. Almost every house in the Omeron wants a trial like this, if only for the entertainment and gossip fodder. And that's why I am recommending that you leave Avertori."

Kieler tensed. He looked to Velator to see if the Prime of House Vel agreed. Velator stood highlighted by the window behind him, stern and stoic.

Everything Kieler and Movus had planned called for Kieler working his way into the Omeron, first by a grand arrival (which was certainly over-accomplished), then by constant needling and maneuvering. And all of this called for him entrenching himself in the heart of the Omeron, Avertori.

The accumulation of luggage around him now seemed threatening.

Kieler thought furiously. "What's wrong with staying here and fueling a generator with gossip and juicy entertainment? I admit, last night was a disaster, but I didn't leave without a significant measure of 'recognition'."

Arvel rolled his eyes and looked to Velator.

"Orlazrus, Feleanna's not one to take something like this without a response. Her counterstroke will be swift and direct. Harboring you puts us in danger as well. Here in Avertori we are far too exposed. I need to get my daughter out of the way, and you need a place where Cortatti can't reach you. I not only agree with Arvel, I am the one who suggested you come back with us to Velakun."

"Velakun!" Kieler exclaimed. "That's thousands of miles from here!"

"To be punctilious about the matter," put in Arvel, "I actually *don't* agree with Velator taking you back with him. I believe he should abandon you here and protect our house."

Kieler's mouth opened at the blunt rudeness. Both suggestions dead-ended his ambitions to climb the Omeron ladder and then topple it.

Arvel continued as if he were already an authority—or perhaps, *always* an authority. "He should be hidden, not running around Velakun putting our house in Cortatti's crosshairs. We'd be foolish to think Feleanna hasn't already an agent or two in Velakun. This move will bring more."

"We are already a target of Cortatti, Arvel," Velator countered severely. "And if we keep avoiding the conflict, we will ultimately lose. I know it's a risk, but it's one that we have to take for our sake as well as his. I *will* protect the last Ortessi, if he will allow it." He turned stiffly to Kieler. "What do you say, Orlazrus?"

Kieler remembered to put on a considering face; he was processing so many factors. For one thing, though they had met only last night, Kieler couldn't ignore that Velator was indeed jeopardizing the safety of his own family by genuinely offering to protect him. *But Velakun? Stars!* What could he do from there?

CHAPTER ONE

And to make it harder to refuse, Velator was by no means lording his proposition over Kieler as a dictate. He was asking for Orlazrus Ortessi's opinion as an equal.

Kieler answered carefully, but with obvious strain. "I certainly don't want to go back into hiding. It would be a lot harder now that everyone knows I'm alive. And to die abruptly would limit the entertainment value I could provide to so many houses, both rival and potential allies..."

"And it would do my house no good either." He stared out the expansive window. Plaza Floreneva was coming to life now. Some people were stumbling home from wherever they had spent the night. Others had obvious business, even on this first day of the New Year. The railing on which Kieler leaned vibrated more perceptibly now, magal-fueled generators pumping life through the city.

This was the hub of Zotikas. But as he looked out, his trained eye picked out skulking ruffians, even at this hour, watching Vel-Taradan. So his choice: be left here without overt support, or go to Velakun and do what he could to build credibility and a power base remotely.

He glanced at the Arena, and his response, though calculated, was a significant change from his original plan. "I accept your offer of refuge in Velakun."

"As you wish," Arvel sighed. He gestured to a coffee table with several documents in neat rows. "Verr Ortessi, would you care to sign?"

When Kieler finished putting the carefully prepared "Orlazrus Ortessi" signature on the last document, Arvel picked them up and fastidiously aligned them into a neat stack before placing them in his briefcase.

"Well," Arvel began as he grasped Velator's arm, "safe travels. Since you insist on this course of action, I shall do everything I can to see that we succeed."

EPISODE 2: HIGH RAILS OF ARDAN

Grasping Kieler's arm in turn, he continued, "And Verr Ortessi, you should probably write to the Mizgots and the Merckles. I understand they assisted you, after a fashion. It would not do for them to feel slighted. Explain to them that you fear for your safety, which is why you have accepted sanctuary in Velakun. Make sure they know you won't forget what they did for you, and that you still consider yourself their ally. Finally, do keep yourself out of trouble. I would hate to go through all of this inconvenience only to have you die on me."

With that Arvel gave them both a quick bow and strode away. Kieler and Velator watched him leave past a line of porters who were now organizing the pile of luggage.

"You know, Orlazrus, he's not just a persnickety lawyer. He's also a cousin." Velator's expression was a mix of emotions.

Kieler wondered why the man shared this bit of information. It was... human of him. And it made Kieler realize that Velator's life was quite complex. He wasn't just the leader of an iconic house. He was a cousin. He was a businessman. He was a father.

With that thought, as on cue, Kieler saw Velirith padding barefoot down the stairs, still in a nightgown, black hair untamed and reaching for the sky. *Truth, she was cute!* Servants rushed up and down the stair around her oblivious form.

Kieler glanced sidelong at Velator. The patron of House Vel now wore the bemused expression of a loving father that couldn't control his daughter and didn't really seem to want to. Instead of commenting on her incongruous appearance and approach, he remarked quietly to Kieler, "We'll be leaving for Zotika Central within the hour. The Pride of Velik should be ready to depart soon, and I don't see any reason for us to stay any longer. Since you probably weren't planning on a journey, I had An'essa make sure a basic travel wardrobe was put together for you." Velator gestured to the blonde-haired woman overseeing the luggage.

CHAPTER ONE

"I noticed, thank you. That was very considerate and generous. I'll be sure to thank An'essa as well."

At that moment, An'essa cast a fierce gaze, not at them, but at Velirith, who now stopped in front of the two men.

Velirith looked up blearily. "I thought Ani was supposed to wake me."

Her father smiled and raised his eyebrows. "An'essa tried four times. You know she is in charge of coordinating the loading process, not just watching out for you."

Velirith looked around, her eyes falling on the piles of luggage accumulating in the elegant hall. "We going somewhere?"

CHAPTER TWO

Kieler tried not to show it, but he thrilled inwardly. An hour later, riding on the private tram toward Zotika Central, he found it hard to stay in character when he was now privileged to the finest amenities—a radical change from scavenging for the bare necessities all his life. If Movus hadn't coached him, trained his mind to confidence and emotional control, he would not have been able to pull this off. He was an under-city slink, living like a family Prime.

And the *Pride of Velik!* The most elegant, most artistic, most finely engineered powercoach ever created! Again Kieler's enthusiasm for machinery threatened to make him forget his role as Orlazrus Ortessi. *My childish wonder will just have to be part of my backstory,* he decided.

Accompanied by Velator's guardsmen and An'essa, the three house nobles stood within the small tram car as it hung from the overhead track. Most of the trip to Zotika Central was a gentle descent. Kieler watched out the front of the tram as they approached the enormous dome, built by House Vel half a millennia ago as the primary hub of the Omeron transportation system. The powercoach station sat immediately atop the Plate in the middle of the Isle of Threes.

The tram car slid through an open portal just under the dome, and after blinking away the dimness, Kieler saw dozens of heavy maglev tracks spiraling up and out from the station below. It

130

was like descending into a metal whirlpool. The major lines headed out to the three corners of the island where bridges or causeways connected the island with the continents.

The suspended tram, a mere fraction of the size and weight of the giant powercoaches, slid directly down toward the center, cutting perpendicular to the much larger powercoach tracks. As they descended across the great, hollow interior space, Kieler looked up to a public park supported by suspension cables. The park appeared to float in the center of the cavernous station, and from three sides, bridges provided a thrilling, high walk to the elevated esplanade.

The core of the park hosted shops catering to travelers, while the perimeter provided walkways and benches with scenic views of the labyrinthine station. Waiting passengers entertained themselves by observing the complex comings and goings of powercoaches and freighters.

The FamTram slowed to a stop at a platform low under the dome. As they stepped off, a man dressed in a blue and silver messenger uniform approached. He stopped a respectful distance from their entourage and bowed crisply to Velator. "Letter for Verr Ortessi, sir."

A guardsman took it, sniffed it, and handed it to Kieler.

Velirith couldn't seem to stop from muttering a sleepy comment. "Even the messengers have recognized your new 'status'."

Velator ignored her, but the tension lines on his face had returned. He was obviously apprehensive about the missive.

Kieler opened the sealed note and read silently:

Verr Ortessi,
The Merckles told us of the Cortatti mishap. You will find necessities for your trip in your baggage at Platform Ten. M

EPISODE 2: HIGH RAILS OF ARDAN

Kieler showed only calm as he read the short note, but Movus' meaning was clear and alarming. Written in a simple code designed for his spy network, it easily conveyed double meaning.

Each sentence held three bits of information, embedded in three parts of each sentence: the beginning, middle and end. The beginning indicated tense—whether the information pertained to an event that had happened, was happening, or would happen. So since this note started with third person, "The Merckles," it meant he was talking about the future ("You" would have meant now. "I" conveyed past tense.) The middle of the sentence usually conveyed direct information, the true subject, and could be vague or use a code word. But in this case, "Cortatti" was quite clear. They would be the initiators of whatever future event was indicated next. In the final position of the first sentence, the word "mishap" was a direct code word for "attack." Translation: Cortattis will attack.

The second sentence began with "you"; second person indicated it was happening now. Middle, "baggage necessities," not coded. End, "Platform Ten," anything ending with a number indicated reliability of information on a scale from one to ten, ten being a certainty. Translation: Get ready. Use the stuff in your bags. It's going to happen.

This code was not the only one they used, particularly since it was very cumbersome in giving precise instructions. But in a situation like this, where a few words of warning were needed without alerting those around you, it was ideal.

Kieler casually read the last line aloud, holding the note so that it was not hidden from Velator, then tucked it in his coat. He looked up at Velator and asked, "Sir, I arranged for some of my scant belongings to be brought here to Zotika Central. Would you mind having them picked up and brought to your powercoach?"

"No, certainly," Velator replied, satisfied. But Velirith suddenly seemed much more awake, as if trying to figure out what the note really said.

CHAPTER TWO

With a nod and several thousand-dras bills from one of the bodyguards, the messenger hurried off to inform a station porter. The contingent from House Vel proceeded from the small, suspended tram up to the much larger powercoach lines.

The nonchalance Kieler portrayed was completely opposite to how he now felt. Feleanna was striking, perhaps immediately. *But how?* His eyes scanned the powercoach station frantically while he forced his legs into a relaxed and confident stride.

And how did Movus know so much so quickly? Kieler hadn't really arranged for things to be delivered to him. *Movus* had. It was as if he'd known about their departure before Kieler! Beyond that information, Movus had also discovered that Feleanna knew about their leaving too and had already mobilized an attack. He was glad Movus was on *his* side. *But how am I to fight Feleanna? Should I tell Velator?*

That the message was coded was a clear indication from Movus that he should not warn Velator, Kieler reasoned. He would just have to protect his new benefactor as best he could. Suddenly, every passenger and worker in the station seemed to be an undercover thug. How could Feleanna attack a recognized House Prime in the midst of Avertori? Even her rage would not blind her to that mistake. Would it? Every house in the Omeron would band together against her in pure panic. Wouldn't they?

He was so focused on scoping out every porter and patron that Kieler was surprised by the obvious. Rounding a corner, he physically staggered at what he saw: A locomotive the size of a ship, hundreds of tons of metal and glass, hovering a few centimeters above the magal track. Defining the front of the railship was a graceful, swooping "V" of duralium that swept from the bottom tip of the prow, up and back through an expanse of latticed glass, to the full height of the powercoach.

He gasped and his mouth opened in awe.

Velirith laughed and Velator smiled, the tension in his face easing. Kieler kicked himself but instantly realized no harm had been done. Orlazrus, orphaned and in hiding since two years old, would have been just as astonished.

The machine was immaculate. A burnished bronze framework supported the glass of the front viewing area. The same finish swept back into the more heavily clad center section with an open promenade deck on the second level. The rear third of the vessel was built around the engine itself, massive in its solidity. The mammoth drive wheel protruded from the top, an arched cowling covering the outer edge. Kieler knew the powercoach was hundreds of years old. Yet someone still took pride in maintaining this masterpiece of art and engineering, and Kieler appreciated it.

Velator stood and openly admired the machine. "She suits her name, *The Pride of Velik,* even though this giant was built five hundred years after his death."

"Magnificent." *How could we have fallen so far from the grandeur of that era?* Kieler wondered sadly. "And yet we should be so far beyond this ancient engine," he added softly, absently.

"I agree. Innovation withers under our government enforced monopolies," Velator responded.

Kieler cast a shocked look at the man. Never did he expect a Prime of the Omeron to admit the fault of the system that protected his fortune. But Velator was not advocating revolution, or even reform, necessarily. Just the facts.

The Prime turned and led them to a heavy, hatch-like door in the mid-section under the promenade deck. The moment he stepped aboard, Kieler noticed a difference. From his work on his father's compact generators, he knew the *feel* of a well-balanced, well-tuned generator. Though the drive wheel was essentially a mobile, full-size generator, it caused the *Pride of Velik* to vibrate noticeably less than the land-based generators that powered Avertori.

The entry corridor was a tight, confined arch compared to the grand exterior. It also seemed to be constructed with many more metallic bulkheads than were structurally necessary. As he passed through this narrow corridor behind Velirith, he staggered; first he pushed left, then right, noticeably enough that Velator commented.

"You must have something magnetic on your person, Orlazrus."

Kieler stepped through the narrow hall into a wider area and turned to face Velator. "I do, sir." He fished inside his coat. "During the dance, Feleanna politely pointed out my faux pas in bringing the magnetic sigil of House Ortessi to the gala." Kieler held the exquisite jewel tightly and brought it back toward a metal bulkhead. Immediately it dove sideways from a strong push.

Velator raised an eyebrow and smiled.

"She said the only other 'base' sigil was yours, Verr Velator. She seemed to think that casting aspersions on our jewelry translated to our character."

Velator's smile went wry. "She is a smart lady, Orlazrus. Twisted by deep insecurities, but too intelligent to underestimate."

Frowning, Kieler returned his attention to the powerful magnetic arch. "And the purpose of this device?"

"The entryway here is encircled by a magnetic field that mimics the drive wheel. That way, when traveling, none of us are surprised by jewelry or weapons or hairpins flying off our body."

For a moment, Kieler considered and then decided. "Sir, it seems this would also reveal magnetic weapons, but I have to admit, it didn't discover my knife."

Velator waited, curious.

Kieler slowly drew and handed over his blade, hilt first. He was fully aware that unsheathing a blade in the presence of another House Prime required a delicate bit of trust.

Velator's eyebrows rose in surprise. "Very unusual weapon. Looks like black glass, but then, how would it survive a fight?"

"Metallic glass," Kieler replied. "It was a gift from one of my guardians."

Velator nodded. "An artifact then. In the quest for non-magnetic weapons, we often see various ceramic blades. Velirith has one made out of shungvaal horn. Mine is titanium."

He handed back the knife.

A porter entered carrying the bags Movus had sent, and Kieler held his breath. If the bulkier bag held what he hoped it held, it had more metal in it than a dozen blades. But Kieler had sealed it, and the container should be magnetically balanced.

As the porter passed through the magnetic safety field, he stumbled. After a moment of panic, Kieler realized the porter had not been magnetically pushed but had simply floundered under the bulky weight of the bag.

Kieler relaxed as they moved fore of the generator into several sumptuous, two-level staterooms and a kitchen. Here Kieler's luggage was dropped off.

When they moved to the front section of the powercoach, the full grandeur of the coach hit him. The entire bow of the massive powercoach was a glass-enclosed viewing gallery, three open decks high and supported by metal lattice. He tried to act as if he were not overwhelmed.

"I seem to recall traveling in our powercoach..." Kieler feigned remembering. Then he shook his head. "But I was too young. Someone must have told me about it."

Velirith snorted disbelief. As they walked forward into the open viewing area, Kieler continued, "*The Ortessian Glider*, I think it was called."

Kieler watched Velirith break away and stride to the very front of the powercoach. Then, like a little girl, she lithely climbed up into the metal lattice. She perched in a spot where three of the larger trusses came together about twice his height above him. Looking out the front, it was a commanding spot, like sitting in the crow's nest of an ocean ship, but oddly restrictive as the trusses contained her like a lonely birdcage.

CHAPTER TWO

"I recall the *Glider*," Velator nodded, ignoring his daughter's antics. "House Cortatti 'purchased' it from that puppet Orticot they have running your house. They refitted it because it ran much smoother on the track than most of their engines. But they did a poorer job of it. Ostentatious, without class. They still use it. Rudely but aptly named *Spoils of Conquest*. Sorry if it brings back memories."

Kieler dismissed the sentiment. "Remorse and regret serve no purpose, particularly mine. My feelings for my parents and their murderers have always been dealt with from a distance. Reacting rashly will just get me killed faster."

Velator stopped near a divan amid the vaulting glass. "You seem to fully expect House Cortatti to kill you."

"Don't you?"

Velator shrugged, acknowledging him. "But you also speak of your purpose. What might that be if it isn't agitating the grevons to rip to pieces the last of House Ortessi?"

"Is my purpose more obvious to Feleanna than to you, Velator? I come to claim what I can of my heritage, both historical and physical property. To take it back from *her*. As I have come of age and have a boldness in me, I would rather make the attempt than rot unknown in obscurity." Kieler had practiced that little speech. He smiled broadly. "At the very least, it will make another awkward chapter in Avertoric history as the rightful Ortessi heir is disenfranchised by the gross machinations of House Corruptatti."

Velator laughed. "Not afraid of staring the ugly truth in the face, are you, Orlazrus?"

"But foolish enough to get in a fight with that devil on my very introduction to society. I certainly didn't intend to engage Feleanna last night. I want to be bold, not brash."

"Last night was—" Velator searched for a word and avoided looking up into the latticework, "—a mess."

"Considering I've led a life isolated from politics, last night was dumbfounding. And your generous invitation to Velakun puts you in the path of her wrath too, Velator. You know that. Why are you taking me in?"

Velator walked the last few steps to the broad bow-window that looked out upon the long curve of track ahead of them. It spiraled up and out of the tangled city, the end unseen. In moments they would slowly accelerate up that path. Without looking from the window, he said, "I know strength when I see it, Orlazrus. And determination. You will not be easy prey for Feleanna. And I will never run in *her* pack." He paused. "When my great-grandfather was Executive Chair, he attracted two major criticisms. That he took too many risks, and that he did not take enough risks. The second is correct. Without risk there is no progress, no growth. And if we're not growing, we're dying. We men are not born to seek security, but challenge.

"I too should have taken more risks. Instead, I discovered that avoiding danger can be the greatest risk of all."

There was a heavy pause. Kieler knew Velator had been married, but didn't know what happened to his wife. And he thought there may have been a son...

Velator went on. "Zotikas needs unselfish, visionary leadership. The current EC has neither. He's just trying to hold his crumbling empire together until he dies.

"The house of Velik is at one of its weakest points in history. I can hang on defensively, or I can seek strength. I see us as possible allies, Orlazrus. I do not yet know what you bring to the fray. But I know the grevons will attack. And being friends in a fight will benefit us both."

Kieler nodded. "True." And he thought, *Truer than you know.*

"Hmph!" came a disgusted snort from overhead. Velirith dangled a leg from between the bars of the odd metal nest.

Velator turned and looked right at Kieler without looking up at his daughter. "Velirith is obviously of a different opinion about you. I love her dearly, but she disdains the political waters in which we swim. I do too, truly, but we are steeped in them. To stop paddling is to drown."

Kieler looked up at the girl tangled in the beams. "Your daughter does trust me in her own way." *Otherwise she would be more forward in exposing me*, Kieler thought. "I just need to prove myself."

In the silence that followed, a man came in from the back of the viewing room and spoke. "Verr Velator, we are ready to depart."

Velator nodded. "Thank you, Tanik. Let's get underway."

The *Pride* accelerated so slowly and smoothly that Kieler never felt it. It was almost as if the station was slowly slipping backwards, like the hour hand on a chronodial. After accelerating for a moment, the movement was fast enough to perceive easily. Like a hovering hotel, the powercoach circled up the departure tracks to the city above.

Kieler didn't want to speak. He felt five years old and just barely able to contain his excitement. He found himself at the very peak of the prow, leaning into the lattice with his face almost against the window, though the view was only layered patterns of circling tracks. If he could have stood on the prow like a bowsprit, no doubt he would have.

He caught himself and pulled back. Fortunately, neither Velator nor Velirith laughed this time.

As the train reached the top of the complex of spirals, it emerged from the station into the light of Rei in a cloudless sky. Velator sat Kieler in a plush viewing chair on a dais overlooking the world. Then Velator excused himself to go aft and brief Captain Tanik on the events of the previous night.

Kieler had never seen Avertori from this perspective. For many minutes he forgot the threat of imminent attack and lost himself in the grand views. How could Cortatti attack them here anyway?

EPISODE 2: HIGH RAILS OF ARDAN

Powercoach lines were different from the intra-city trams. Passenger powertrains had only one public stop in Avertori: Zotika Central. Freight trains used the many industrial sidings that existed around the city, like in the Cortatti complex. For this reason, the lines passed through the lonely places of Avertori, behind towers and plazas, arching over empty space on elevated causeways.

Now behind the scenes, Kieler felt removed from the usual bustle of the city. The various and disparate towers etched the luminous sky. Except in Floraneva and Garrist, the city was mostly built without an integrated plan. As expansive as the island city was, the hodge-podge development left Kieler feeling purposeless. This incredible city lived only to survive.

What if all the energy put into the building of this city had been unified? What if people could communicate and coordinate to build a city like a work of art?

Still traveling at only a moderate pace, the *Pride of Velik* floated silently above and through the city. A second, inbound track paralleled the one on which they rode, allowing two-way traffic and passing, though they saw no other trains. Every track was bi-directional, providing levitation and a magnetic field for the drive wheel to push against.

Proceeding generally northeast, Kieler looked through the gaps in the cityscape, searching for the northern ocean and the causeway that bridged the Isle of Threes and the continent of Ardan. A day's journey far into the northeast mountains would bring them to House Vel's home city, Velakun.

Before the water came into view, however, near the edge of the city, he saw a siding leading into a service area surrounded by high walls and security towers. A gate like the one he and Bags had passed under blocked the track: It was the Cortatti weapons works. *Hard to believe I was sneaking around in there just a day and a half ago.*

This time they glided past in complete safety, the complex silent.

140

CHAPTER TWO

Once again he looked forward. The towers had thinned, and he spied the ocean. Kieler had seen the ocean many times, but never from the luxurious perspective of a gliding powercoach. They broke through the towers at the edge of the city, and he half-rose, struck by the vista before him.

To the left was the expanse of the North Sea, stretching to the horizon. Northeast and before him was the massive, rising continent of Ardan, building from plains to mountains into the distance. To the right was Ardan's southern coastline, alternating between sheer white cliffs and broken sand beaches. Arrow-straight ahead of them was the deep V of the track, the small channel at the bottom just big enough for a sled, he thought, remembering the wild ride with Bags just two nights ago. There was something compelling about the straight, purposeful span of the fore-running track.

With a swooping, descending glide, they were suddenly on the causeway, ocean close on both sides except for a narrow pedestrian road beside the two tracks. Kieler had left Avertori.

Once onto Ardan, *The Pride of Velik* accelerated to breathtaking speeds, and the miles passed quickly. The Pride was known to be the fastest coach, and despite Kieler's constant vigil for some kind of attack, he was swept up in the fantasy of this trip. Out here on the elevated rails, he couldn't imagine how Cortatti could even get to them. Yet Movus had given the likelihood a rating of ten. Certain.

Growing up in the nethercity, Kieler had experienced few comforts, much less the opulence available to the Prime families. Now, here he was, traveling in the most well-appointed, grandest powercoach on the face of Zotikas.

He could get used to being a House Prime.

But Movus had warned him not to let his guard down. Velirith still perched above, and he could feel her steady gaze upon him.

EPISODE 2: HIGH RAILS OF ARDAN

He could show no uneasiness being in the presence of the Prime family of House Vel. These were the direct descendants of Velik himself, the man primarily responsible for establishing the society that had endured these thousand years. Of course, Kieler's masquerade would be unnecessary if Velik's foundational values were still followed.

Velator's powercoach... Kieler allowed himself a long look around him. This was the finest of all the familial powercoaches. Best in every detail. Built in the heyday of the transportation revolution when the magnetic lines were laid to span the three continents around Avertori.

The segmented windows through which Kieler looked stretched three full decks, embracing the entire front third of the powercoach. Supported by metal lattices, elegant and strong, the glass provided an enormous panoramic view. It was in one of these ingeniously engineered lattices that Velirith had taken up residence. While not built for human nesting, it served as an ideal vantage point.

Kieler realized he was no longer pretending to sit casually, but stood boldly on a wide, raised dais in the middle of the lounge area. He felt as if he was floating through the vista before him, and he had no doubt the dais was designed for precisely that effect.

Besides the handful of comfortable chairs on the dais, there was also a carved wooden table and three free-standing sculptures. Kieler freed his attention from the grip of the vast view, only to have it captured by the sculptures arranged on the rear of the dais. He moved aft to study each sculpture closely. Instantly his consciousness was drawn into them, though he had no idea what they represented.

The first was a life-size bronze of an older man on a throne. His right hand was raised with fingers extended and palm vertical, as if dividing something. His very visage radiated power and authority. Even though it was inanimate, Kieler could not help feeling profound respect for the man to the point where he felt

142

CHAPTER TWO

compelled to kneel in humility before the perfection of the statue. He did *not* kneel, of course. Such an action would be below the Ortessi's station. Even so, he may have dipped slightly before catching himself.

To the right of the bronze was a wooden figure of a farmer or animal herder. The piece was done in the exact style as the first, but because the medium differed it gave the figure a more common aspect, like a friend one would meet while out walking. While simple, the detail of the carved face gave Kieler the feeling he liked the man... and that the man liked or even loved him. That feeling was an intuitive stretch for Kieler, but he felt quite sure of it.

The last statue was in white ceramic, which seemed utterly impractical for two reasons. First, it was on a train, subject to jolts and accelerations. And second, the piece itself was wispy, cloudlike, with thin strands of the material reaching up and around. In the center, the ceramic threads coalesced into a figure—not quite a figure but the *suggestion* of a strong, sinewy spirit. Its right arm seemed to be reaching out as if offering a hand of help, or perhaps beckoning. And the left arm, a mere suggestion itself, swirled out from its body and around as if embracing the world.

All three faces bore a strong family resemblance. In fact they almost could be the same person in somehow different aspects.

Intensely pensive and introspective, Kieler was aware that he was evaluating himself not logically, but more intuitively. These statues brought it out of him. He was so drawn in that he didn't realize he was staring intently into the face of the wooden figure.

Why did this man love him?
Who was he?

CHAPTER THREE

Velirith tuned out everything below her, leaning into the window. Before her and around her, the fertile basin of southwestern Ardan embraced her in a blur of dormant fields. Fed by streams coming down from the mountains, these plains produced apples, amaranth, triticale maize, lentils and rye in quantities and varieties that rivaled broad Govian's abundance. Midwinter's melancholy didn't lessen her enjoyment of these wide lands stretching to the horizon.

Soon the Abiding Mountains would rise up before them— mountains that covered even more of Ardan than the plains, the mountains that sheltered her home, Velakun.

She thought about the future. Though young enough and rebellious enough to have avoided politics so far, she felt as if she were hurtling into political entrapment as fast as the *Pride of Velik* was screaming toward the mountains far ahead.

It would happen.

She sighed. The last heir of House Vel. How had she gotten stuck being the one? And how had it come to this? Her older brother—

She still didn't know how he really died, only that her best guess felt dead wrong.

Now the politics had passed from him to her.

I'd much rather write plays and act in them. There's more truth in my fiction than in the Primes of the houses of Zotikas. If only I could engage the world on my terms. If only people weren't such posers! Like this Ortessi.

CHAPTER THREE

Velirith looked down at him. She was very surprised to see him intently gazing into the face of the wooden man. He was lost in it, much as she had been lost in the sweeping landscape of Ardan moments ago.

She startled.

By truth, he's seeing it! Or at least recognizing that there is a deeper level to the statues. Even her father didn't completely get that. This was a true feeling she perceived in this false Ortessi.

Who is he? She knew he wasn't who he claimed, but that left the much bigger questions of who he was and why he was trying to pull off this poor performance. It took guts—or stupidity—to come out on the stage half-prepared.

Besides his enrapture with the statute, she had seen other truths in him as well—his boyish wonder when presented with something new, like his first view of the *Pride*. And she loved that. It was like he'd lived in a hole all his life and had never seen the sun. When he fell out of his ridiculous role and became a real person, he was a person she could like. She looked at him again and found him still absorbed by the power of the wooden man.

"I'm not going to expose you." Her own words surprised her so much that she clapped a hand over her mouth. The Ortessi actually jumped back as if the statue had spoken.

"What?" He looked up at her. Recovering, he added, "Of course not. There's not much to expose."

"Mmm," she said softly, lowering her hand and musing. "That's not true, but you have to stick to your cover story. Nevertheless, you'll be interested to know *why* I'm not going to dig into your true personage. It's the way you look at the Triad. There's something genuine in you even though you're covering it with this façade. I'll give you time."

"Well thank you very much," the Ortessi replied, feigning amusement. He stood with fists on his hips, looking up at her as if she were some mystic bird speaking riddles.

"That cocky pose is so unattractive."

145

But he was still lingering in the spell of the statues; he obviously wasn't feeling threatened.

She was looking past him and through the sternward windows of the viewing section when she saw it—another powercoach overtaking the *Pride* on the parallel track.

It took her some moments to even comprehend. The *Pride* was *the* fastest powercoach on rail. And the engine that was pulling alongside was obviously not built for comfort. It was built for—*war!*

With a lower profile than the *Pride,* the deck of the battlecoach was fitted with three turrets housing oversized magguns. The sides had only tiny portals in an otherwise armor plated chassis. Like the *Pride*, its drive wheel protruded from the top at the rear of the attacking machine. It was squat, ugly and dangerous—and everything was pointed at the *Pride.*

"*Look!*" she yelled.

The Ortessi spun in alarm. "Get down!"

But Velirith was already launching herself from her perch. As she dove, the first salvo from the magnetic turrets blasted through the windows of the viewing platform. Glass exploded everywhere.

Velirith screamed as the fragments of the windows laced through her light clothes and lacerated her body. She hit the floor. Her arms and midriff screamed with pain. Orlazrus was beside her immediately sheltering her as best he could with his body. Smothered in his uniform, she smelled the thick, musky material on her face. It protected them from the cyclone of flying glass much better than her light clothes.

He pushed her behind the dais as the guns continued to violently relieve the metal frames of their glass. There was a pause in the rending guns' death song. Though the wind blasted through the missing panes and falling glass crashed around them, Orlazrus' shout could still be heard. "To the aft section!"

He swept her up as he too ran for protection.

CHAPTER THREE

She glanced toward the attacking battlecoach, wondering why they had stopped firing. It had matched their speed, and through the broken windows she saw a wind-shielding tunnel being pushed across the short distance between the massive engines. The tube came from the top of the low-profile cutter and smashed against a mid-section bulkhead on the promenade deck. Instantly there was a flash of heat and light where the circle of the tunnel impacted the *Pride*. Velirith flicked her gaze at the Ortessi; he'd seen it too.

Her father and An'essa were running forward, Velirith their only concern. "Back—!" the Ortessi's warning to her father was cut off by a renewed blast of bolts and glass. But the projectiles were behind them, and in two seconds they reached the more heavily clad mid-section. Sweeping Velator and An'essa back with them, they dove into Velirith's cabin.

The second level of her quarters still had glass for about three breaths. Then that glass too evaporated into sharp shards of shrapnel, this time above their heads.

"We're being boarded!" Orlazrus shouted.

Comprehending immediately, her father commanded, "An'essa, seal off the promenade deck! You two, stay here and stay down!" As An'essa turned and sprinted for the stairs to the second level, the metal walls pocked inward from the deafening impact of magbolts. The metal held—for the moment.

"I'm going for the pilothouse. We won't make this easy for them."

Velirith nodded, as did Orlazrus, and Velator bolted down the corridor to climb the narrow stairs to the control room.

The bolts were hitting farther back now, the attackers not knowing exactly where their targets had gone.

"Even though our generator's mag field will deflect them some, those bolts could punch through if they hit the same spot," Orlazrus determined. "Let's get to the opposite side of the train."

147

EPISODE 2 - HIGH RAILS OF ARDAN

Velirith obeyed and started to duck across to Velator's cabin. She slipped immediately and fell flat. She looked at the floor to see that she had slid in a small pool of blood—hers. Strong arms scooped her up and the Ortessi's face was pale with concern as his eyes assayed her midsection.

Orlazrus helped her across and they gained Velator's cabin. He laid her on the bed.

"How bad?" he asked, full of distress. He too was cut, but minorly. She assessed her own condition, afraid of what she might find. The inside of her left arm had a nasty gash as well as many small cuts. Several other pieces of glass had ripped her shirt along her abdomen. She tore away the bottom of her blood-soaked shirt to reveal two bleeding slashes and a third with a finger of jagged glass still imbedded in her side. Instinctively she yanked it out, and immediately another gush of blood sprouted from the wound accompanied by a wave of intense pain.

She heard Orlazrus swear as she fought off fainting. He grabbed the towels off Velator's rack and pressed them to the larger cuts. "Hold those there! I've got to stop those boarders or we'll all die anyway."

She nodded, stunned, but not so much that she didn't wonder how he was going to do that. He bolted down the center corridor. Looking through the open door, Velirith saw him dive into the cabin assigned him.

Now knowing the damage to her body and dealing with it, her mind kicked into thinking what she could do to help stop them from being killed. A second later, Orlazrus emerged from his room carrying the heavy, lumpy bag she had seen the porters load. He moved with certainty down the corridor to the very rear where a heavy door led into the drive section. He thrust it open and disappeared inside.

What is he up to? How does he know what to do? She found herself admiring his definitive action in the face of danger—not to mention his unfeigned protective instinct.

148

CHAPTER THREE

As the pounding of bolts on metal continued, Velirith decided she was not going to bleed to death. She wrapped the towel around her midriff, tied it tight, and got to her feet. Not bad. Her head steadied, and she moved carefully but quickly back through the screaming powercoach. She heard running feet on the deck above her. *Who could that be?*

The *Pride* lurched violently, throwing her toward the bow as it decelerated rapidly. It shuddered and a thunderous groan of metal on metal vibrated through the ship. Velirith guessed that her father had slowed the powercoach to dislodge the gangway the attackers had laid across. Did she also hear a human scream? There was too much noise to be sure.

Entering the dimly lit drive section, she saw the three-story magnetic wheel still spinning smoothly in its casing. Next to the center of the wheel, she saw a ladder leading up to the observation deck. The hatch at the top was open.

Rather than climb that ladder and follow him directly, Velirith chose to climb the ladder near the front of the drive section right next to her.

As she climbed, she passed the promenade deck, and Velirith could see through a partially open side hatch. An'essa faced two of the boarders in a narrow hallway. The first man charged. An'essa feinted with one knife, parried with the second, and spun around him as he staggered past. Before the second man had a chance to react, she had driven one of her knives into his throat. Leaving that knife, she rounded on the first man.

Velirith nearly swooned. She clutched the ladder rung, not fully grasping the violence and blood she had just witnessed. And An'essa seemed so unfazed.

Just then the *Pride* lurched again, this time accelerating sharply. She winced as the sudden movement jarred the wound in her side.

When she opened her eyes again, An'essa was gone and the first boarder was leaning against the wall clutching his stomach.

EPISODE 2 - HIGH RAILS OF ARDAN

The clang of bolts from the attacking coach had moved forward, but now returned to the stern. They must have spotted Orlazrus up top. *Is he drawing fire away from* me? A twinge of guilt and responsibility seared her mind as she realized last night's prank may have been the catalyst for this attack.

Pushing against the hatch at the top of the ladder caused her to wince again. Fortunately the hatch opened toward the attacker's battlecoach, giving her solid cover to poke her head out.

Looking back over the roof of the *Pride*, Velirith saw Orlazrus crouched behind the hatch next to the drive wheel, facing aft. A third portal, closed, lay at the very back of the powercoach. Glancing forward, Velirith saw her father's back through the clear door of the pilothouse. A sweeping cowling enfolded the control room, creating a sleek, slanted windbreak that diverted airflow over the top. The windbreak created a protected channel down the middle of the roof and around the massive drive wheel protruding from the back of the coach. This observation deck was another place Velirith liked to frequent on these trips. But she knew the danger of it too. Just outside the protected corridor, above and to the sides, the wind ripped violently.

Crouched low and intent, Orlazrus pulled a metal device from his bag. About the length of his forearm, the apparatus was encircled with symmetrical coils and linkages for which Velirith had no reference. It didn't look like a weapon, but between her mental state and the short time she had to ponder, she couldn't fathom its purpose.

Orlazrus didn't see her peeking up through the front hatch. He worked extremely fast on the contraption, removing one end. She briefly glimpsed the interior; a shiny, bronze-colored cylinder was suspended within the device.

Magbolts ricocheted around them, poorly aimed. Her father must have been accelerating the *Pride* to outrun them. The squat cutter had fallen behind. The men on top manning their guns seemed clumsy, unused to the sudden changes in acceleration. It

150

CHAPTER THREE

was a small but critical advantage to the *Pride*. Too soon, unfortunately, the cutter was gaining on them once again.

Orlazrus had lined up the flat end of his device toward the center of the *Pride's* drive wheel. He glanced sternward and seemed dissatisfied that the attack cutter was so far back. The soft case that had held his device had snagged on the rail at the edge of the wind-protected area, its carrying straps whipping in the wind.

At that moment, the rear hatch flew open and three figures, all bearing white knives, swarmed onto the roof. One of them was a woman, the flat-faced Sindia Corch.

Orlazrus saw them immediately and rose with his back to Velirith, defending the mechanism he had positioned next to the drive wheel.

Velirith hesitated, feeling her own weakness and doubting her ability to help him. As Orlazrus drew his own blade to engage, a sound behind her caused her to swing her head around to the foredeck. Suddenly the door to the pilothouse flew open and her father staggered out backward and fell to the deck. A single man with a long ceramic dagger dove after him.

While the man was in mid-air, her father twisted right. The knife stroke missed, and Velator caught the man's knife arm. Immediately they fell to grappling on the deck. Velator was hampered by having to control the man's knife hand, and she noticed her father no longer had his own weapon.

Velirith started to climb up out of the hatch to help him, but swooned. Lack of blood in her brain caused her strength to fail, and she nearly fell the three decks down through the hatch to the floor of the engine room. She caught herself on the edge of the hole with her good arm and fought to maintain consciousness, her head lolling with dizziness.

She saw her father managing to get behind and on top of his attacker, twisting the knife arm behind the man's back. Her head spun around and she saw Orlazrus, swiping his blade at a bald boarder. So far they were at a standoff. Behind the bald one came

151

a man in a white shirt, already stained with blood. She couldn't tell if it was his own. He attempted to move closer and attack Orlazrus with his partner, but was unable to pass in the narrow space between the wind and the fast-spinning wheel. Sindia Corch came last and, realizing she was of no use so far from her prey, she fell back and started around the other side of the wheel, circling.

Like a patron of Theater Velaki, Velirith had a stage-side view of the action—a drama in which the players were real, and the danger was real, and yet she felt removed. Her swimming head wavered just above the portal. She realized vaguely that if Sindia Corch came around the front of the wheel and saw her, Velirith would not be able to defend herself.

Just as the top of Sindia's head came into view above the drive wheel, Velirith ducked down holding on to the ladder rung as if it were her only link to consciousness. When she pulled her head back up, one eye just above the opening, Sindia had rounded the wheel and was creeping back toward Orlazrus.

Thank the Truth she's not after my father.

She wanted to warn the fake Ortessi, but her mouth wouldn't respond to her thought. It was all she could do to hang on. Her head lolled back to her father who was sweating, struggling with the man half his age. Velator had the man's face pinned to the metal deck, the knife lying a few inches from his squashed cheek. The younger man was writhing to get away and Velator couldn't get a hand free to finish him off. In moments the man would be free or have the knife.

Velirith closed her eyes and shook her head, trying to regain control of her body. When she opened them, she was looking at the man attacking the Ortessi. The bald man looked behind Orlazrus at Sindia, who was about to strike. Fortunately, Orlazrus noticed the look and must have realized one of the boarders was missing. Orlazrus feinted, the man swung and Orlazrus moved in, pinning the man to the drive wheel cowling and breaking his knife arm. They were within inches of the heavy spokes of the drive wheel, the ends of which were moving as fast as the *Pride*, nearly 300 miles-per-hour.

The Ortessi's bold attack tied him up with the bald man and opened him to attack from both the man in the bloody shirt and Sindia.

Before they could strike, Orlazrus slammed the broken arm of the bald man against the cowling again, dislodging his knife. The ceramic knife fell into the drive wheel and shattered in the spokes. The Ortessi had buried his face in the chest of the bald man as the group was sprayed with shards.

The man with the bloody shirt caught the worst of it and reeled back. He fell, hitting his head on the open rear hatch. Evidently unconscious, he just kept rolling right off the back of the powercoach. Gone.

Sindia had recovered all too quickly. Having shielded her eyes from the shattering blade, she had taken shrapnel to her face and arms. Though facing away from Velirith, it looked as if a piece had gone through one cheek and out the other, blood flowing down her face. The hard woman ignored the pain, grimacing and advancing on the Ortessi.

The Cortatti thug slashed at Orlazrus who pulled the bald man in between them as a shield. Sindia buried her knife into the man's back. The Ortessi then shoved the body at Sindia.

As he fell to the deck, Sindia's knife went with him.

She was now empty-handed, and Orlazrus advanced, intent and confident since he still held his dark knife. Taking a step back, she just smiled a bloody smile and pulled another blade from under her open jacket.

Velirith wanted to get up, to make a difference in this fight. But it was all she could do just to hang on.

Father! This drama was poorly planned. It was impossible to watch both Orlazrus to the stern and her father toward the bow. She spun her head forward causing another wave of dizziness. She turned just as her father's attacker freed a hand and grabbed the

153

sharp blade. Stabbing blindly back and up at Velator, her father had to change tactics.

He didn't react quickly enough. When Velator shifted his weight to avoid the slashing knife, the man on the bottom bucked him off and whirled. Velator fell back as the man leapt at him. Her father concentrated on the descending knife, managing to catch the man's wrist with both hands, but he landed with his head on the edge of the deck—outside the protected area with the man on top of him!

Putting their own man at risk, the gunners on the cutter fired off a quick clip of mag-bolts. Had Velator not fallen, they would have both been hit. As it was, the heavy caliber bolts raked the railing, completely removing a ten foot section above their heads.

The rushing wind blasted the left side of Velator's face. Velirith once again tried to rise and once again could not manage more than a weak attempt. She knew she needed to get down and tend her own wounds. But she could not leave these men. Still, there was nothing she could do! The knife wavered back and forth over her father's chest as he struggled to see out of his downwind eye.

A shout behind her caused her to turn her head back to Orlazrus and Sindia. They were still trading swipes, neither gaining an advantage, both dangerously close to the rotating wheel.

Even though Sindia was yelling, her voice was barely audible over the rush of wind noise. "Fool! You think you can steal a sigil from Feleanna and then flaunt it in her face?"

"Why not? She was stupid enough to keep the sigils as trophies," he shouted back at her.

"By taking it you wrote your own death sentence. Say good-bye."

"Good-bye!" he yelled back. "But *you're* the one leaving."

Orlazrus tried a feint and then a thrust, and *missed*, throwing him off balance. He stumbled heavily toward the drive

CHAPTER THREE

wheel. Velirith gasped. Sindia's foot was closer than her knife and she kicked him in the knee. Collapsing to the deck, he rolled desperately away from the spinning wheel. He nearly hit his head on the heavy brass device he had set up. As he flailed to recover, he entangled himself in the straps of its cloth case.

Sindia pressed down on him, slashing at his legs. Orlazrus frantically fought the bag away from him and threw it at her. She automatically swung at it and her knife hand went right through one of the carrying loops. Raising her hand to dislodge it, the large, empty bag caught in the raging wind above her head.

The ferocious winds filled the bag and yanked the woman by the arm right off the deck. She flew back and over Orlazrus. Aloft in the powerful wind, she was instantly carried away and out of sight in the slipstream of the powercoach. Her landing promised to be less fortunate than Orlazrus' the night before.

Velirith's head wobbled back to see her father with his attacker's knee in his chest trying to push the air out of his lungs. Velator still clutched the man's knife hand. Her father made a desperate move, kipping both his legs up and into his forward-leaning attacker's back. The man was pushed forward, all his weight on the knife hovering above Velator's head—but only for an instant.

Velator wrenched his head to the side. The knife descended into the metal deck, and with a mighty heave, Velator pushed the man up and over him into the ripping wind. He quickly disappeared, the wind literally sweeping the last of their attackers off the deck. Velator caught a remaining stump of the missing railing and used it to pull himself into the wind-shielded area, gasping for breath.

Halfway through a sigh of relief, Velirith heard the *clang, clang* of magbolts on metal. Looking back at Orlazrus, his head between the drive wheel and his device, she realized the attack cutter had pulled abreast of them once again. Their rounds hit

155

everything except the Ortessi. Railings bent, the wheel housing dented, and the rear hatch cover was ripped away.

In the midst of the iron storm, while not calm, Orlazrus was focused. He aimed, and without hesitation, flipped a switch on the rear of the cylindrical apparatus. Immediately he jumped back and the smaller cylinder seemed to vanish. *What was that thing?* She caught only a brief flash toward the cutter. The cylinder must have accelerated extremely rapidly. The rest of the device bucked violently, bounced off the drive wheel casing and flipped over the side.

She poked her head quickly around the hatch to peek at the cutter. A metal-rending screech came from an impact right in the center of the cutter's drive wheel. The wheel wobbled violently. The spokes, easily twice a man's height, caught on the track and launched the back end of the cutter into the air, forcing the front end down. The prow of the cutter dug into the track, and the momentum of the speeding battle engine sent it tumbling back over front, buckling the frame and shredding it into ragged strips of metal. Something in the foredeck exploded in a white hot flash. One thick spoke off their drive wheel, catapulted by the flipping of the cutter, shot like a man-sized magbolt over the top of the *Pride*. It clipped the roof between her and Orlazrus, gouging the heavy metal, and then spun wildly over the opposite side.

Velirith froze, shocked at the sudden and complete destruction and the obvious loss of life of the attack engine's crew. The wreckage disappeared behind them in mere instants as the *Pride* barreled on at high velocity. But though the debris from the attack ship was now completely out of sight, the image of its demise was burned into Velirith's mind.

Velator had run back into the pilothouse to control their rail-ship. It seemed he hadn't seen her during his struggle. She saw for the first time the body of Captain Tanik lying prone on the floor of the pilothouse.

156

CHAPTER THREE

She glanced back at Orlazrus, who was lying flat next to their drive wheel, his head toward the rear of the powercoach looking back at the destruction of the cutter. Her own motives hazy, Velirith realized she did not want Orlazrus to know that she had witnessed his surprising acts of bravery and quick thinking. She ducked back down the portal and pulled the hatch shut over her.

She was incredibly woozy. Forcing herself to focus, she dropped down as quickly as possible and stumbled back toward her cabin. She knew she was trailing blood, but her focus was to stay moving. She could see her bed through the open door, but before she gained it, she saw the floor rise up before her and consciousness drop away as if falling from a great tower into a dark pool.

CHAPTER FOUR

Picking his way through the glass, Kieler felt the haze of destruction in his head. Shattered piles of what had been metal-framed glasswork littered the viewing deck. The cold, constant wind of their progress had organized the fragments into hills of glass and rivers of cleared decking that wound around the floor of the viewing area. The wind whistled around him, but at less than a quarter of the speed the *Pride* was capable of.

It was morning again, the day after the attack, and he knew they must be getting close to Velakun, though he was unsure how close. The deep V track was elevated by angled supports anchored in the sides of the mountains as the powercoach tracks paralleled a great valley. They had been following the river below since daybreak.

Velator had cursed himself after the attack when he found Velirith lying in the doorway to her cabin, soaked in blood. He couldn't be blamed—except by himself. In the heat of the fight, he hadn't realized she had been cut so badly. And Velator's action in the pilothouse had disrupted the boarding party, giving Kieler the chance to set up and launch the magnetic core of his motor into the heart of the enemy's drive wheel. Despite Velator's self-reproach, Velirith was not dead; she was weakened by blood loss but should recover.

Nevertheless, Velator hadn't left her side as he and An'essa cared for her through the night. He had commanded the crew from

CHAPTER FOUR

Velirith's cabin. Sitting across from Velator and his pale, sleeping daughter, Kieler and Velator quietly recounted their perspective of the battle, Kieler intentionally omitting any reference to his magnetic motor core. He did mention that the Cortattis had tried to kill him on his way to the gala the night before. And he told the Vel Prime that during the battle he had fought Sindia Corch, Feleanna's strong arm. If there had been any doubt of Cortatti responsibility, Sindia's participation in the raid dispelled it.

The only fatality had been Captain Tanik, who Velator had known since he was a youth. Losing a longtime friend was hard on him, but Kieler could see that Velator was truly terrified of losing his only child. He was guilt-struck for leaving her and now he was trying to make up for it. She had awoken several times during the night and each time she was given water and fell right back asleep.

They had stopped once in a small village to assess the damage done to the engine and to telegraph ahead to Velakun. After a quick inspection, they determined it was safer to proceed forward slowly to Velakun rather than risk returning to Avertori. Backtracking would mean passing the Cortatti's weapons works and dangers they could not guard against. How many attack cutters the Cortattis had built was unknown. That they had possessed even one was disturbing news to everyone.

Kieler worked his way forward. He found a place near the prow where he could hold onto the metal frame and not cut his fingers on bits of remaining glass. It was, he realized, the same place he had stood the day before, then completely insulated from the force of the bitter wind that now threatened to push him back into the cabin area. The wind stung his cheeks and watered his eyes as he squinted, looking down to the river far below. The valley was deepening into a sheer canyon as they pushed further into the rugged, towering mountains of Ardan. The tracks hugged the mountain to his left.

He thought about his role in yesterday's attack. He worried about how to explain his actions during the raid in such a way as to further his ambitions. And he considered the danger he had brought to House Vel. The path he had chosen would by design bring harm to many others. Revolution was violent. But the current bureaucracy was violent too. Theirs was just a slow, indifferent violence that kept on killing innocent people, his mother among them.

Still, doubt nagged him. *What if there were other house leaders as genuine and generous as Velator and his daughter?* They would suffer loss if Kieler succeeded. If this scheme required him to become completely cold-hearted, he wasn't sure he could do it, despite the determined knot in his gut.

With the airstream racing past, he felt like he was on the open deck of a sailing ship. Only a few panels of glass remained intact above, the wind gusting and washing over him, cleansing him of the guilt he felt despite his noble purpose. He looked down and back, away from the wind.

Behind his station on the bow, the patterns of windswept glass had collected against a large obstacle on the floor. At first, Kieler couldn't determine what piece of furniture it may be. Then he spied the end of a staff protruding from the glass and his mind grasped the fallen shape of the animal herder, the wooden statue. It had evidently toppled and slid forward during one of their rapid decelerations.

The glass had scored the hands and feet and face of the image, though the eyes were thankfully untouched. A long shard was still imbedded deep in the side of the figure, and Kieler felt the urge to pull it out. But it was just a statue, and to try to remove the shard would surely cut his bare hands. Still, he leaned close and saw a dark, sticky liquid oozing from the puncture. Sap? In a statue this old? Surely the life of the tree that gave this wood would have dried out after all these years. Perhaps the nature of this wood kept its lifeblood sealed within the statue, kept it vibrant.

Kieler glanced up and saw the track shifting away from the cliff-side as it rounded a mountain. The powercoach moved to the center of the canyon directly over the river. The curve of track was now supported by a series of graceful double-arches, one above the other, that spanned from one cliff face to the other. Connecting the upper and lower arches were tall, symmetrical columns sculpted into stately trees. Their spiral trunks reached above the top arch with foliage only in the topmost branches.

These were undoubtedly representations of the famed haventhalls of Velakun. With the powercoach gliding through the center of the double-arches, the stone trees formed a regal path welcoming visitors to Velakun.

Though Kieler stood on the solid foredeck of the *Pride*, the sheer height and the wind against his face made him feel as if he were falling away. Having abandoned the solidity of the mountainside, they glided far above the river with literally nothing beneath the arch-supported track. Weak-kneed, he crouched and steadied himself with one hand on the statue.

The canyon curved left around a rocky promontory and—magnifying the feeling of plummeting—the gorge opened wide before him. Directly in front of their fast approaching engine, a wall of water plunged over the top of a half-crescent dam into an icy lake a thousand feet below.

Kieler caught his breath in the frigid air. Seven stone water dragons, frozen in lifelike sculpture, seemed as if they were emerging from the roaring waterfall. Each creature was as big as the *Pride* with long, hoary beards of ice from the frosty mists. The immense dragons appeared to be flying out from the face of the cliff, their ranks of raised wingtips nearly touching each other as the water crashed down upon them.

Water dragons were regarded as mythical, but Kieler's father had told him the tale of Velik's encounter with the leviathans on one of the patriarch's later travels. They had never been spotted since. This monument obviously memorialized that expedition in a gigantic feat of aesthetic engineering.

EPISODE 2 - HIGH RAILS OF ARDAN

So overwhelmed was Kieler with the magnitude of the vision that it took several moments to realize that the track on which they rode led straight into the torrential downwash of water. There were no sidings. And even though they had slowed some, Kieler doubted they could stop in time to avoid getting deluged. An undamaged powercoach may have withstood the force of the water, but the viewing deck was now open above him. Kieler would be washed away!

Panicked, he stood and was about to turn and dash back to the more protected cabins when he noticed movement—impossible movement. Unable to look away, Kieler realized the massive dragons were *diving*.

Bowing their heads and descending slowly, they seemed to fix their frosty glare directly upon him. He shuddered and realized the creatures were not leaving the face of the fall; that was an illusion created by the powercoach's approach. They were descending because rechanneled water was pushing them down, the overflow now shooting out the dragons' mouths in fiercely impressive streams.

Kieler stood marveling as the wonders of Vel craftsmanship and engineering continued to hold him transfixed. And the arrival salute was not over. Something massive was rising up through the falls in counterpoint to the descending dragons.

As if lifting themselves from a deep bow, seven stony heads rose from the face of the waters. Slowly. Regally. Kieler's clockwork mind automatically assumed that the descending dragons must counterweight the rocky visages, raising them up through the water. In under a minute, seven men were standing erect, diverting the water around their carven shoulders to form flowing white cloaks that adorned and covered their lower bodies.

Kieler closed his mouth and shook his head. When it came to "imposing," the Cortattis now paled in comparison to the Velaki. Kieler recognized the countenances as some of the most prominent leaders of House Vel over the past millennia. As the faces shed their watery crowns, they seemed to stare down the tracks, as if discerning the intentions of those approaching their guard.

And now Kieler saw what they were guarding. As the water was forced to divert around the stone megaliths, it revealed a tunnel opening about a third of the way down the falls, directly under the center statue. The *Pride of Velik* could now pierce the cliff face and enter its home.

The watery gate had opened to allow their favored son entrance.

Faced with such majesty, Kieler felt small and exposed. He knew the lifeless faces could not see him, but their grandeur, the nobleness with which they stood, heightened the illusion that they knew exactly why he was here, and that his motives were ignoble.

In rebellious defense, Kieler wanted to accuse his accusers: *These arrogant men are responsible for the mess this world is in,* Kieler justified. But at the moment, he had to admit, they held the high ground.

His pulse raced as the train plunged straight through the middle of the torrent. Again he crouched, and the powercoach slowed further. Heavy spray from the cascading water washed over him as they approached the tunnel. Even though the heads above had opened a gap in the waterfall, the spray itself was far more water than he had expected. Kieler got drenched in the chill brume.

Then he was in the dim of the tunnel.

Soft lights illuminated the way before him, and to his relief, the air of the tunnel was much warmer than the outside air. Still, he shivered. Unable to see the tunnel end, Kieler wondered why it took longer than expected to penetrate the inner cliff wall. Then he realized—annoyed that he missed the obvious—the lake that fed the waterfall was above him! The idea of all that water over his head only intensified his shivering.

The underwater tunnel stretched out before him as he squatted on the deck of the *Pride*. A couple minutes later, the tunnel opened up to a well-lit, underground station with the simple sign:

Arrival Point Station

Velakun

As the powercoach emerged and slowed to a crawl, Kieler stood, shaking. Travelers on the platforms turned en masse to watch the wrecked *Pride of Velik* cruise smoothly into the station with a wet, shivering man in green and gold standing like a refugee on its bow.

Suddenly self-conscious, Kieler was about to return to the cabins aft of the ruined viewing deck. But just as he turned to do so, the beauty of Arrival Point Station penetrated his awareness.

While not as imposing as the stern faces of the stone heads outside, the station's beauty and engineering were no less impressive. Arrival Point Station was essentially an enormous underground dome, the peak of which was decorated with a stained-glass sun, somehow backlit. Around the sun, a deep blue sky and shining white clouds, and nearly reaching the clouds were the spectacularly tall, spiral-trunk trees that also decorated the arches of Velakun's approach, the haventhalls which grew only in this city.

He stood appreciating the subterranean station as the train drew to a stop. Through the crowd of gawking spectators on the platform, a crew of blue and silver uniformed officials pressed through, rushing to assist the injured *Pride.*

From the cabins, Velator moved purposefully forward. With the main portal mangled by maggun bolts, Velator found it easier to step out of the *Pride of Velik* through a large ragged gap in the metal lattice and onto the platform. Kieler followed, and as he set foot on the solid boarding platform, he once again noticed a difference in the ground he stood on: It didn't vibrate—at all. The *Pride's* generators had been well tuned, and the ones powering Velakun must be just as well cared for. Interesting. So many things

164

could cause one of the massive generators to wobble and induce vibration: inconsistent magal, unbalanced spokes, etc. Most of these imperfections simply introduced inefficiencies, but severe flaws or disruptions were disastrous. He thought of the cutter's drive wheel disintegrating as an extreme example.

He laughed at himself. Every time he stepped on new ground he took stock of the character of its vibration, something most people never even noticed. But generators were his father's obsession. And sitting by his father's side, sleeping in a crack behind his father's whirring experiments, these experiences made Kieler who he was.

As Velator's men arrived, he spoke to the one with the most silver on his shoulders. "Commander Scoravik, send the gurney and medical team to my daughter's cabin." Instantly, Scoravik turned, and with a word, three men with a stretcher dashed aboard the *Pride* and down the corridor to her cabin.

"How badly injured is Velirith, sir? What happened?" Scoravik asked.

"She was cut by flying glass. The bleeding has stopped, finally." Velator waved an arm at the destruction around them and added in a low tone only Scoravik and Kieler could hear, "We were attacked from the parallel track. Some sort of cutter. Perhaps the one rumored to be intercepting Parchiki's cloth shipments."

"Cortatti?" Scoravik asked.

"Yes," Velator nodded, "but we'll need evidence. Convene an emergency meeting immediately." He turned and introduced Kieler. "If not for this man, it's likely we all would have been killed. He destroyed the attack vessel. The track will need to be repaired and debris gathered for evidence."

"We'll send out a crew."

The medical team returned, carefully carrying Velirith through what had been the windowed lattice of the viewing deck. Awake, she allowed herself to be attended. Aside from being pale, she was clear-eyed and calm. She smiled at her father and regarded Kieler with an up-down look he would have given a piece of machinery that was acting oddly.

He looked back at her, wondering how much she knew and how she knew it.

Once Velator knew Velirith would be well taken care of, Kieler saw him relax ever-so-slightly. Then the Prime of House Vel focused fully on command. With a quiet calm that belied his grave concern, he directed security forces, coordinated with powercoach administration, and sent messengers with the details of the emergency council meeting.

Kieler stood back, observing the off-loading of luggage and crew, helping when appropriate. He was determined to hide the limp Sindia Corch had caused him by bearing the pain. It was probably a pride issue, but he wanted to show no weakness.

The situation allowed Kieler to watch Velator's command style and learn about his staff. Velator was level headed, listened to his advisors, and then he was decisive. As Kieler was admiring these qualities, he looked past the immediate frenzy around the *Pride* to where another powercoach train of several cars had just docked at another platform.

As the passenger load moved away from the train, Kieler's stomach dropped as he saw, in the mass of people straining for a view of the *Pride*, a dread familiar face looking over the rail of the exit ramp. It was too far away to be sure, but it looked like the spectral face of the man who had always been one step ahead of him on New Year's Eve! *Could it be?*

Kieler was about to go after him and find out for sure when Velator called to him. "Orlazrus, we are about ready to leave for the council meeting. Your witness and account of the events will be crucial. Will you come with me?"

He had phrased it as a question out of respect, but refusing was not a viable option.

CHAPTER FOUR

"Of course, sir." He glanced up at the ramp. The man was gone. Kieler couldn't know for sure if it was his unshakable tail, and that unnerved him even more.

Velator gave Kieler a grim smile of thanks. "Just one last thing and we're off."

Velator turned to address a heavyset man leading a team that maintained the *Pride of Velik*. "Jarovel, my friend, I'm afraid I didn't protect our elegant lady very well this trip. Take her back to the maintenance bay. For the next few days, you'll have to put up with the forensics team as they gather evidence. Then she'll be yours to nurse back to health."

Jarovel nodded, dazed as his eyes moved from one catastrophe to the next. This was his charge, and she was in sad shape.

Kieler had a sudden impulse. "Velator, can you put me on Jarovel's team to help with repairs? I'm very good with machinery and he's going to need the help."

Velator considered carefully before answering. "Perhaps I'm presuming, Orlazrus, but won't you have your hands full trying to reestablish your house?"

It was bracing to be reminded of his mission from the man he was using to accomplish it. "That is my primary mission, yes. But I have seen how the courts work—or don't. It will be weeks between decisions, and the Cortattis will try to block me at every turn. It will be therapeutic to have some hands-on work to keep my mind off the inefficiencies of the system. It would mean a lot to me to be useful."

Again Velator considered, but finally nodded. "Jarovel, can you take on the help? I have a strong feeling this Ortessi knows his mechanisms."

Jarovel agreed, if absently. He was still in shock.

"May I suggest that you don't get too wrapped up in the project, Orlazrus? Limit your time with Jarovel. Your future is a

167

blank book waiting for a creative pen. I'd like to discuss it with you before you over-commit."

Kieler nodded, and Velator said softly, "Move her to her berth, Jarovel."

Jarovel shouted to an engineer on his crew and the wounded but still magnificent *Pride* slid slowly down the track toward the maintenance bay. The three men solemnly watched it go.

Velator turned his back on that issue and led them across the depot, accompanied by two guardsmen. Kieler tried to simultaneously take in the beauty of the station and get a feel for its layout.

Looking back to the west side of the dome, he traced the track on which *The Pride of Velik* had exited the tunnel. Two parallel tracks through the dimly lit tunnel brought traffic from the dam, under the lake, and in and out of Velakun. Opposite the exit tunnel, *The Pride* was currently gliding down a siding and disappearing into a side chamber to the southeast.

As he walked across the passenger platform, Kieler looked down through a large open section and glimpsed a level below. Freighters were docked in that deeper level, some crawling even deeper into the underpinnings down dim tunnels and sidings. While not as vast as Avertori, this complex piqued his spirit to explore the under-secrets and workings of this new city.

Looking away from the rails, he noticed some of the same signs of decay that plagued the capital: benches worn smooth, wood and masonry work chipped and cracked. Lesser quality construction would be structurally failing by now. Still, it wasn't as bad as Avertori.

The long distance powercoach line terminated at Arrival Point Station. But the station was also the link to the smaller intra-city transit, what Kieler had heard called the "podcar" system.

Feeling put off by the vision of the man who had tailed him, Kieler searched for something to say. Awkwardly, he could think of nothing to fill the silence and envisioned Velirith laughing at his poor role playing.

Thankfully, Velator began to verbalize his thoughts.

"Our response to this attack is crucial," Velator thought aloud. "We must prove Cortatti the perpetrator. We must secure ourselves against further attack. And we must rebuild the *Pride*. I doubt I'll be much of a host in the coming weeks."

Velator led the small entourage to a platform in front of a track only a fraction the size of the hefty powercoach line. This was Velakun's equivalent to Avertori's tram system but with private cars.

As they stood next to a semi-circular loading slip, an empty podcar (a flattened sphere hovering on a half-cylinder track) glided off the main track and came to a stop. Velator reached out quickly and punched the latch with his finger. The bi-fold hatch split neatly at mid-car, the top half flipping up, and a door in the bottom half folding down to span the gap between the platform and the car, creating a very short gangplank. The entire top half of the car was transparent, though what there was to see in a tunnel, Kieler didn't know.

He waited as Velator stepped in first, dismissing the guardsmen. As Kieler stepped down into the podcar, he noticed the simple appointments, faded and worn to be sure, but elegant. The craft could hold about six people on a circular bench seat that ran around the entire inner circumference of the car. The seat was padded with dimpled, burgundy leather. The fittings and trim were brass, including the raised dais in the center that supported a single brass knob and a row of numbered brass dials.

Velator pulled a small book from a leather pouch on the side of the dais and handed it to Kieler. It was simply labeled "Address Reference Guide."

"Look up where you want to go in the guide," Velator explained, "and spin the corresponding code into the dials. Then engage the lever." He dialed in a number from memory. "This will

169

take us to the city conference room most of the way up The Empyrean Tower. If you change your mind, you simply disengage the lever and enter a new address, or it will drop you off at the next available platform." Velator engaged the lever; Kieler heard a series of clicks below them, and the podcar slid from the dock onto the main track, accelerating smoothly.

Again Kieler noted the system was a brilliant legacy of a time when skilled workmanship was prized. The wear on the seats and brass reminded him of old, quality furniture, but it had obviously been some time since it had been expanded or renovated.

"Is that the fast track?" Kieler pointed to the track next to them, opposite the loading platform.

"Yes, for the pods not stopping at this station."

"How does it sequence a slower car onto the fast track without pulling out in front of a faster car?"

Velator laughed at him. "Only an engineer would wonder. It's some kind of electromagnetic lockout. But your question confirms one thing: You'll love working with Jarovel—once you get used to his personality."

Kieler smiled weakly and shrugged. Two pods passed before their car jerked slightly and shifted to the far track. Immediately they accelerated and headed into a cluster of large tubes heading up through the vaulted ceiling of the station.

Kieler watched admiringly as the car transitioned smoothly from horizontal to vertical motion and rose through the various levels of Velakun. They passed softly lit numbers indicating levels. Tapping his forefinger on the worn leather of the seat, Velator was obviously pre-occupied. Kieler, trying to maintain stoic dignity, said nothing. After a few moments, Velator seemed to become aware of Kieler's discomfort and broke from his own reverie with a short laugh.

"It's hard to always look noble and officious, isn't it?" Velator smiled. For a moment, Kieler thought Velator was professing to know of Kieler's fraud, but the leader's next comment belied that assumption. "I took over as head of the House of Vel when I was twenty-four. Much too young. Looking 'authoritative' was the most difficult trick, even when I knew what to do."

Kieler's awkward smile held double meaning: relief that he hadn't been discovered and the admission that he too was in way over his head.

CHAPTER FIVE

Wondering how fast and how far they were climbing, Kieler tried to guess the height of The Empyrean. It was several minutes before they stopped at a small station without ever traveling outside. Velator made one more comment before they disembarked into a frenzy of administrative workers.

"Let me tell you my secret to good governance, Orlazrus: Keep the government out of as much as possible. Roads, rails, and personal safety. Those are the basics. Much more and my 'officials' are just interfering with people's lives."

Kieler wondered if Velator really abided by this high ideal.

He led Kieler to a triangular conference room. Already a couple worried officials stood near the door, pulling Velator aside as soon as he entered.

The walls of the tower chamber were pushed out in a graceful curve, the window blinds drawn. Making clever use of space, the insides of the blinds were hung with maps of Velakun and schematics of key towers and structures. Kieler immediately found Arrival Point Station and was fascinated by the many service corridors under and around the transportation hub and an extensive system of airshafts through every structure. Satisfyingly, he also found the generator station, the feed lines to the buildings and podcars marked clearly.

Thinking to correlate the map to the city, he peeked around the blinds and was rewarded with a non-view of dense, white fog.

CHAPTER FIVE

He studied another map showing a top-down view of the whole caldera of Velakun: Center Island (where they were now) hosted the majority of government and commercial buildings. The irregular shaped island was surrounded by "Lake Skyfall," and from the edges of the island, six bridges radiated outward like spokes to the surrounding "Rim." The inside slope of the Rim was dotted with houses. Thus the oval caldera contained the lake whose only outlet was over the seven-headed dam to the west. Kieler frowned trying to figure out what fed the high lake since the map showed no tributaries coming in through the Rim.

He didn't have a chance to ask because Commander Scoravik, Velator's Chief of Operations, entered and immediately began briefing Velator. A steady stream of Velator's leaders and aides hurried into the room, worry and fear on their faces. They took their places around the triangular table. This was Kieler's first chance to meet the people he eventually wanted to influence. He was keenly alert, somewhat nervous, and determined to be silent and listen until he had a feel for how he could make himself look good. Velator quickly introduced him to the heads of his government as they showed up.

After Scoravik came the mayors of the North and South Rims, Palovik and Annavel, showing up together. They were followed by the mayors of Center Isle and East Rim, Deteran and Senova. All were grim in light of the attack. Several aides and city officials arrived, but Kieler didn't catch their names.

An'ovek, Scoravik's captain of the guard, showed up next, out of breath and very tense. He had dusty blonde hair, not quite so light as An'essa but evidently of the same clan.

And last to arrive was the Technical and Utilities Custodian, a man named Hezek, his work clothes crumpled and thin as if he had just crawled out of some access tunnel. Kieler thought his job would have been mostly administrative, but obviously he wasn't afraid to get his knees dirty. All except Hezek wore some arrangement of the silver and blue uniform that designated a position in Velakun's administration.

Velator took his place at a truncated corner of the table with Scoravik on his right. Kieler was given a chair on Velator's left, and the Prime of House Vel began by recapping the attack. He then asked Kieler to add detail from his perspective. The gathered leaders were particularly interested in how the cutter was destroyed.

Kieler scowled inwardly, thinking that ideally he would like to have been hailed as a hero, saving the *Pride* from destruction with the head of House Vel as witness. But instead, *no one* had seen him do it! In hindsight, perhaps it would have worked better to reveal his intelligence and prevent the attack altogether rather than nearly getting killed by magbolts and Cortatti pirates. But to take credit and brag now would force him to explain his portable generator. That treasured secret belonged to him and his Coin comrades.

"I have no idea why that attack cutter came apart," Kieler pretended to admit. He shook his head and grimaced, recalling ruefully the loss of his generator. But the fact that he'd had it and had the knowledge of the polarities of the two powercoach drive wheels made him far more grateful than regretful. Weaponless, he would have been destroyed with the *Pride*.

Then thinking of his airship he added, "From what I've read, prototypes tend to have flaws. Sometimes fatal. I'm just guessing, but maybe firing so many large caliber mag cannons near their drive wheel caused it to destabilize. Anyway, after helping to repel the boarding party, I turned to see the attack cutter pulling alongside the *Pride* and open fire again.

"Then suddenly it seemed their drive wheel flew apart." Kieler used his hands to illustrate as he said, "Wrapped up in fighting, I didn't see the details of what happened, but the back came up, the nose dug into the track and at that speed it flew apart like an egg thrown across the pavement."

174

Kieler shrugged. "Sorry I can't be more specific. In truth, being scared and wind-blasted didn't help my awareness of what was happening."

At least he had hidden the existence of his motor from them. As he took his seat, one of the lady mayors—what was her name... *Annavel*—stared at him as if she'd caught him sneaking into her house. Other than her, Velakun's leaders reacted with enthusiastic praise and encouragement.

"You kept your head very well, young man," Hezek declared.

But Annavel cut off Kieler's accolades. "Why did they attack? And why now?"

Velator handled that one, briefly retelling the catastrophe at the ball. He ended by saying, "Cortattis were hoping to end two bloodlines with the destruction of one unarmed powercoach. Two bloodlines who are in clear opposition to her ambitions.

"And I cannot go without publicly relaying what my daughter told me this morning. She was weak, but I believe she was clear-headed when she told me she saw Verr Ortessi fight off *three* attackers on the pilot deck. On all other details, unfortunately, she was justifiably hazy."

Reaching up and rubbing the wind-burned side of his face, Velator added, "And although I was just fifty feet from Orlazrus, I was so intent on my own problems that I didn't even see him struggling."

The entire assemblage was looking at the red, leathery patch of skin where Velator's face had been exposed to the high-speed windstream.

"Cortattis must be brought to justice and pay reparations!" the lady mayor of South Rim continued, this time with nods of agreement all around.

Velator held up a hand of restraint. "I'm the only one who's had much time to think on this. Let me make a few observations."

Silence fell as they listened to him.

175

EPISODE 2 - HIGH RAILS OF ARDAN

"Feleanna attacked because she was incited and enraged—but that was only the trigger. Ultimately, she attacked because she thought she could get away with it. And the bottom line is: she can. She has influence in the courts. And she has more military might under her command than House Ek. All we have are patrol coaches and telegraph stations spread out across the entire network.

"Nevertheless, she must be held accountable if for no other reason than others will continue to suffer if she is not stopped. The ugly truth is that she's probably not through with us. When we fight her in the courts, we will be her loudest threat and therefore her biggest target. So not only do we need a legal plan, we need a political plan, and most importantly, a defense plan.

"Should there be any dissent about our need for military strength, visit my daughter. Sit by her bedside, as I did all last night, and wonder what would have happened if one of those millions of shards of glass had hit a major artery. Or if one of those magbolts the diameter of my sword hilt had gone through her body. And imagine, had the dice fallen just a little more to their favor, what you would be discussing right now without a Prime in House Vel, and without his daughter. Do you put it past our enemies to stop at assassination? Or do you think perhaps they might have their eyes on our mountain stronghold?"

Silence reigned as the weight of his statements fell upon them.

For the next several hours, they hashed out a broad outline of what needed to be done.

First, they needed evidence to convict their attackers, and they needed to find out if there were more of those attack vessels out there. Then they laid out how House Vel should respond to the attack. And finally, they began the process of increasing Vel's security, including manpower, weapons, and some sort of escort for their powercoaches, both freight and passenger.

Scoravik's strong personality complimented Velator's rather laidback, reason-oriented leadership style. "We not only have to defend the *Pride* and transports, sir, but also our facilities in Avertori, and Velakun itself."

Velator considered his Operations Officer's statement. "Let's look at Velakun's defense first. We haven't been attacked in our entire history, so assuming someone decided to try, how would they do it?"

Scoravik looked at his security chief. An'ovek answered by listing off how they wouldn't do it. "Well, they couldn't really come in through the mountains around the Rim. There's the cold and hundreds of miles of impassable ice and rock. And marching up the Veshun Valley would be a horribly indefensible position. The only way would be to use our powercoach line to try to bring troops in."

Velator looked at Scoravik, "Do you agree?"

Scoravik scowled and nodded. "I cannot imagine any other way. They could destroy a section of the powercoach track itself, isolating Velakun, but that also cuts off their only attack route. They couldn't finish the job. That certainly wouldn't sit well with Feleanna's ambitions."

Velator, his gaze on Kieler too, asked, "Anyone else?"

No one spoke. Kieler's mind considered an attack by air and dismissed it. As he was thinking, he caught Annavel staring at him again.

"Fine," Velator said, "then how do we insure that we don't get a trainload of troops delivered to Arrival Point Station?"

The mayor of Center Isle spoke up, "What if we search every arriving train?"

"Deteran, a train full of enemies in our station is not going to wait around to be searched," Scoravik pointed out.

"True, but perhaps we could ensure that arriving coaches carry legitimate cargo or passengers before opening the Veshun Gate," Deteran continued.

"A checkpoint? Outside the waterfall?" Scoravik mused. "What do you think An'ovek?"

An'ovek was nodding. "Peace has allowed us the luxury of trust. A small delay to check each train outside the gate would be a good compromise, in my opinion."

After some discussion of details, that precaution was agreed upon. They would set up a checkpoint several miles out from Veshun Falls, which would divert trains onto a dead-end track if they failed to stop for inspection.

They also agreed that for now a security detail should accompany every train in and out of Velakun. Additionally, they composed an investigative team to figure out what had attacked them and find proof of who built it. The team consisted largely of engineers, of which Velakun had many excellent ones.

Far into the meeting, during a lull, Kieler found an opportunity to contribute. "Velator, may I bring up something?"

"Certainly."

"That machine that attacked us, some sort of attack powercoach, did anyone here have any idea that such a thing existed?" Kieler asked.

Looking around the room at the mute and shaking heads, the answer was obvious.

Kieler went on. "That machine was a major project. It would have required engineers to design, personnel to build to it, materials, weapons—and for something this groundbreaking, it would have been hard to silence rumors and gossip. And it couldn't have been built overnight. What I'm saying is that you should have heard about it through your intelligence channels."

He saw Scoravik and Velator exchange glances.

"Being an outsider, I don't want to be critical, but you should have had some warning, at least a hint."

An'ovek responded, "A telegraph operator near Avertori reported that something had passed him going the wrong way on the inbound track. We relayed that down the line, but since we had no traffic outbound from Velakun, there wasn't a collision threat."

CHAPTER FIVE

"You need to do better," Kieler stated flatly. "We're talking about espionage, not traffic reports."

Velator replied, "Orlazrus, we work hard here to have solutions to the problems we bring up. Do you have a suggestion?"

Kieler took a deep breath. "I do. The people who hid me and raised me had contacts with the underground in Avertori. I'm sure you've heard of the Coin. I know that group is considered criminal by the Omeron. But they have a spy network that probably surpasses even that of House Ek. The people who live below the Plate cannot afford to be surprised. It was through this network that I learned that now was the best time for me to come out of hiding. They can also seek out information on new threats and even supply weapons—for a price, a *ril* price." *In case any of these cloud dwelling idealists still think their paper dras is worth anything.*

There was a moment of silence, and then most everyone spoke over each other at the same time. The general gist of the commotion was that they would not condone doing business with the subversives under the Plate.

Velator quieted the group and spoke. "Working with criminals is no better than abetting them. But aside from the few people that have been captured and tried, the people living below Avertori are not convicted. Nothing is proven."

"They are exiles," Deteran replied. "It is against the law to participate in commerce with those unaffiliated with a trade house."

Hezek, evidently lacking the self-righteous idealism many of the others abounded in, spoke tactlessly. "Those 'subversives' could probably rule Avertori better than Ek! They're smart. They're efficient. They hit and run before they can be caught. I'll bet they'd sell us good info for a fair price!"

Annavel, the South Rim mayor, bristled and stood, leaning into the table. "We are not stooping to pay them to do our dirty work! For all we know, they were the ones who attacked us!"

"Not likely," Hezek snorted. "No money in it. They go after cargo, *booty*, when trains are going slow. The *Pride* wasn't carrying cargo and was blazing along at top speed. Anything valuable would have been scattered over the three continents in the crash. Besides, they don't try to kill people. Draws too much attention. They do just enough to get what they want without bringing the law down on themselves."

"You sound like you've worked with them!" Annavel shot back.

Scoravik held up a hand, "No Annavel, Hezek is right. This isn't their method of operation."

Annavel didn't sit. "'Buying information' is just a euphemism for 'spying.' That in itself is suspect activity."

Velator scratched his eyebrow and muttered, "Let's not be too holy, Annavel. We don't like to admit it, but we do that already. Evidently just not very well."

Looking from Velator to Kieler and back, Annavel replied, "Are you sure it is wise to admit that in front of this young man, Velator? After all, he's of a different house, and even the position he claims is not proven, is it?"

Kieler sat up, alarmed that this kind of attention had been directed back at him. Things had been going so well—with Velirith absent.

"Annavel—" Velator started, but was cut off.

"I *knew* Orlazrus Ortessi," she declared boldly, pent-up words spilling out. Kieler froze his expression. This was about the worst thing he could hear. "I held him when he was a baby. And he was an *ugly* baby! This man is handsome! That he could be that child is very unlikely."

Out of high-tension silence, short snorts of laughter broke out. Annavel blushed deeply, realizing she had just complimented the man she was accusing of being an imposter.

CHAPTER FIVE

"Annavel," Velator fixed his grey eyes on her. "I have decided to trust him. He risked his life to save ours. Unless you have baby pictures and proof, let's reserve judgment."

She sat in an embarrassed huff.

Hezek stepped in without reserve. "Ortessi, can those underground boys get us magguns too?"

Annavel popped back to her feet instantly. "Oh come on now!"

"What?" Hezek raised his hands as if innocent. "We'll need more magguns for the security details on the trains and for more forces here at home. What? You want us to buy them from Feleanna? They'd explode as soon as we pulled the trigger! At least the thugs under the Plate aren't trying to kill us."

Controversy erupted around the table. Red as she was, Annavel must have realized she was being incited. Evidently, Hezek had goaded her before. She glowered at him and sat back down slowly, shaking her head.

Velator did his duty and stepped in. "Good points, all. Commerce with those expelled from society is forbidden, to condone it would be to bring further negative upon Velakun from House Ek's already less than cooperative position."

Hezek started to jump in again but Velator cut him off.

"That said—that dealing with the black market is undesirable, does anyone have any better ideas?"

There was a conspicuous lack of eye contact.

"Sir," Kieler spoke up finally, "you and your daughter were almost assassinated by a threat you had *no* warning about. *That* is criminal. Whoever attacked had better information. Procuring intelligence is—if not accepted—let's say is very common. The ethics of how to obtain this information should be weighed against the survival of Velakun."

Scoravik looked at his boss, "I agree with the Ortessi. However, I want assurances concerning the reliability of intelligence obtained through this channel."

Back to Kieler, who smiled nervously, "I feel like a liaison to pirates. I admit many of those I heard about under the Plate were just criminals, hijacking and stealing whatever they could to profit by. But the ones who ran their spy business had only one credential on which to stand: the truth and accuracy of their product. As far as is humanly possible, they delivered correct intelligence."

"That makes sense," An'ovek agreed. "If they delivered inaccurate information, they would be out of business."

In the end, it was grudgingly agreed to pay for intelligence on whoever constructed the cutter and attacked the *Pride*. It was also asked of Kieler to find out if they could buy weapons from the underground, considering the only other source was their known enemy. Kieler claimed he didn't know (but he did) and that he would try to inquire discreetly.

And Annavel retreated, with obvious reluctance.

CHAPTER SIX

It was late when they concluded the meeting and rode to Velator's estate.

"You handled yourself well, Orlazrus," Velator complimented, leaning back exhausted in the podcar. "You were bold to speak up on a controversial subject, even when it pointed out a flaw in our strategy."

Kieler felt the simple pleasure of the affirmation while his mind worked the odd angles: Velator was not his friend nor mentor nor father. He was part of the political system that must be destroyed. "I meant no disrespect, sir," he replied simply.

"And you conveyed none. That's what I'm saying. Even though I have no authority over you, I wish all my subordinates handled themselves as well, neither sycophantic nor cowardly. You'll make a good leader."

A snowy night had descended upon Velakun as their podcar pressed out of a tower to pass above the west end of Center Isle.

"Speaking of leadership," Velator continued after a pause, "the Ortessi Leadership Academy is beneath us on the right. You can't really see it through the snow and mist, but Orcad survived the usurping of your house by moving here to Velakun."

Kieler wanted to know more about the Academy, but was fascinated by the snow itself. He'd never seen it before today. "I didn't know snow and mist occurred at the same time."

"Here they almost always do. Our waters are heated from the earth below and are much warmer than the air. It snows because we are in the mountains. But our geothermal heat keeps

Velakun reasonably warm all year," Velator replied. "We even grow limited crops in the winter." They began to pass over the water on the skybridge leading to Vel Estate on the slope of the Northeast Rim.

Through the wet snow that obscured much of the view, Kieler could barely see soft lights from Rim dwellings dancing on the water of Lake Skyfall. It reminded him of the eternal night of the nethercity. But on this city, Rei would dawn. He was eager to see it in clear daylight.

He thought back on today's long meeting. He had played his part well, but he had never considered that someone may have met Orlazrus Ortessi when he was a baby and claim non-recognition of him now! He was quite sure he would never attempt to garner some physical semblance between a babe and the full grown man twenty years later. He decided to ask Velator in a circuitous manner. "Why did Annavel seem so defensive on every issue?"

Velator answered, "She has some reason to. She represents the inhabitants of South Rim, largely working class. Because of the lower sun angles this far north, they live largely in shadow. Thus, the South Rim has less expensive real estate and attracts the less affluent of Velakun. Although I try to convince myself otherwise, it seems they are envious of those better off. She is a product of her neighborhood.

"But as for her specifically questioning your authenticity, well, you didn't exactly come with papers. I choose to trust you, but you must admit we're going to have difficulty proving it in court. The testimony of Merckle and Mizgot will be weak."

Kieler had discussed this with Movus. They had a couple of things in their favor, but still his legal acceptance was far from certain. Movus had assured Kieler the two judges that Ek had bought off would vote for recognizing the new Ortessi. In addition, Movus owned two more judges. But the only play Kieler could talk about to Velator was the sigil.

CHAPTER SIX

"Velator, I have only one original possession from my youth." Kieler looked levelly at Velator. "My family sigil." He looked at it as if hesitating to share it with his new benefactor. Then he handed it across the car.

Curious, Velator examined it gently. It was obviously worn and old. "Ah, yes. The Ortessi sigil. Green luzhril and golden amber. Your very possession of it at the ball gave some attendees a natural acceptance of your identity. Its authenticity can be proved?"

"Yes," Kieler nodded. "I hoped to find someone who knew it well before the attack on my family who would vouch for it, but the green luzhril is so unique it proves itself. Perhaps it would help with Annavel. She probably remembers it well. My possessing it doesn't prove who I am, I know, but considering all else has been destroyed, what *could* actually verify my identity?"

Handing the jeweled signet back to Kieler, Velator nodded. "That crest will help enormously. Thank you for trusting me to hold it. Now that your enemies know you have it in your possession, they may come after you more aggressively. As it is, Feleanna may decide to disprove your claim in court since another attack on your person would be bad for her politically."

Kieler eyed him with doubt. "Do you really think so? The Cortattis got away with murdering my family with barely an alibi. She nearly killed me to stop me from getting to the palace to be introduced, and Ek knows it. And I think your investigation will prove beyond what little doubt exists that she almost killed me, you and Velirith with her battlecoach. I doubt that even proving she attacked us will harm her politically. I think the only thing keeping me alive is you."

A silence fell between them. They both knew he was right.

"I hope Velirith is all right," Kieler muttered, looking at the floor of the podcar. "I'm certain I brought Feleanna's wrath down upon your heads."

Velator stared into the snow outside the podcar. "I hope she is too. I am eager to see her. The doctors at the estate sent

185

word around dinnertime that she was resting well and drinking water to help her recover."

A few minutes later found them pulling through the intensifying snowfall into a station just below Vel Estate.

Before the hatch fully opened, Velator climbed out and strode through the covered station at a fast pace. Guards on either side of double doors read his urgency, and with a nod from Velator, they pulled a lever that slid the doors aside.

Now another aspect of the falling snow hit Kieler: It was cold. He wasn't quite as excited about the cold. He wanted to stop and touch the fresh, white confection, even to childishly taste it, but now was not the time.

He followed two paces behind Velator, jogging occasionally to keep up.

To the right of the broad, slushy walkway, Kieler heard pounding water. Perhaps this was how Lake Skyfall was fed. He paused a moment to look over the rail of a short bridge and found he was looking into a narrow gorge that disappeared into steam. He couldn't see the waterfall, but the roar of it told him it was big.

His glance gave him a quick view of the bridge itself, a view that revealed its peculiar, cut-stone construction, something he'd seen only in Movus' old books. It struck Kieler as odd since almost all construction for nearly a thousand years was done with structural ceramics, invented right here in Velakun. Then he remembered, somewhat abashedly, that Velakun predated Avertori by a great many years.

Pulling himself away from a flood of curiosities, Kieler lurched to catch up with Velator. His feet slid on a layer of ice beneath the slush, and he barely recovered. *One more reminder that this is not Avertori.*

Velator, though twice his age, was hard to catch. Between the snow, his hurt leg and the hurry, Kieler didn't get much of a picture of Vel Estate. Ahead he could make out hazy lights in a multi-tiered complex of structures. Misty shapes of towers and domes rose on ascending terraces up the slope of the caldera, but it was hard to tell the actual form of things. Nothing looked quite real in this fantasy world.

As they approached the solidity of an arched colonnade, Velator stopped beneath the partial cover. Kieler caught up.

"I'm sorry, Orlazrus," Velator apologized. "My feet are so worried about Velirith they've run off with me."

Kieler replied without concern for himself. "It's fine, Velator. Keep going as fast as you need to. I do understand."

Velator smiled his thanks. It was surprisingly light for nighttime, the snow reflecting brightly. Velator turned and resumed his quick-time march.

On the other side of the portico, they followed a winding path through a lush garden. This disoriented Kieler further. *Snow on green plants? The waterways must be very warm.* More mist rose from the pools, streams, and cascading fountains of the garden. All this Kieler noted in a blur as they sped toward a large edifice.

Unsure if he could trust his eyes, Kieler thought he could see slim spires hovering in the swirling snow behind what must be the main residence, shrouded in an ancient ethereal elegance. Velator led them at an angle from the formal entrance toward the right wing. Behind a jutting tower was a small arched door, and the House Prime ducked in with Kieler at his heels. They bounded up a winding staircase, past a landing to the third floor where they entered a stone corridor. The home was quite warm, with no sense of the chill outside.

Velator paused for a moment at the threshold of a single door, and then entered, leaving Kieler standing in the doorway.

Velator approached his sleeping daughter, pale in a dim circle of light from an elegant mirrored fixture of luzhril on the ceiling. An'essa watched over her, and after a few quick words with Velator, she gave up her seat at Velirith's bedside. Velator touched Velirith's cheek gently. She stirred but didn't wake. Kieler couldn't help realizing he was checking to see if his only daughter was still alive. The thought once again crossed his mind that overthrowing the Omeron would bring more violence to many good people. *Is there another way?*

An'essa motioned for Kieler to follow her from the room. Kieler hadn't talked to An'essa at all on the *Pride*. He wasn't sure exactly what her role was, but her bearing implied that she was much more than a servant. She was tall with a precise but relaxed posture with blonde hair that none in House Vel possessed (though An'ovek at the council meeting was light-haired). She also maintained a veil of seriousness about her for which Kieler had no context. She wore a simple coat of deep Vel blue, and even the way she pulled her hair into a tight twist indicated a certain constant tension.

Kieler expected her to lead him with the brisk purpose she always seemed to possess. But as they left the residence into another garden, he saw how tired she was. Even her straight-backed posture showed a slight slump, and her pace was little more than a stroll.

"I'll walk you to your quarters," she said without enthusiasm (nor title). "Then it's my turn to sleep."

Kieler was feeling it too. At least he had slept a few hours on the *Pride* after the attack. After a few moments walking through the blanketing silence, he decided to try to find out something about the enigmatic An'essa. "You serve House Vel with far more dedication than a mere proximal house relationship requires. Why is that?"

She looked at him, studying his face. In a matter-of-fact voice she told him, "House An is much different than the other houses of the Hegemon. We lived in these mountains long before Velik journeyed out to unite the people of the three continents.

"We worshipped the truth, striving for it in every way. The Vel family has always had even a deeper knowledge of the truth,

188

and when Velik himself stood to defend our clan from destruction, we began the tradition of serving House Vel.

"Part of that tradition is a series of trials by which I was chosen to serve the Prime Family—specifically Velirith."

Kieler thought on this. An'essa didn't seem to want to give more than this cursory explanation. So he gently pried on a personal level. "Protecting Velirith, with her independent streak? I can only imagine how hard that would be," Kieler ventured.

"Oh, I doubt it," An'essa replied.

The snow fell heavy but slowly with little wind. Kieler noticed that in his fatigue he had slackened his vigilance in scoping out his surroundings. Vel Estate consisted of many structures: what might be a reception hall, garden sheds, stone bridges, and a large, domed structure that emerged from the mist to the left. A brief lessening of snow allowed him to see that the stately building spanned the height of several terraces, each level encircled by arches and a wide balcony.

"So what's this building?" Kieler broke the silence again.

She replied with an accusing look. "This library was a gift of House *Ortessi*. I would have thought you'd know at least that much."

"I may have missed a few details since I was forced into hiding as an infant." Her doubt of his identity annoyed him.

But she wasn't done. She stopped and faced him, forcing him to stop as well. "I don't even know how to address you, *'Ortessi'*. Velirith has declared you false. I mentioned that House Vel has a very intimate connection with the truth? Well, Velirith has an even deeper relationship with the truth, which she totally takes for granted. She *always* knows when someone is lying. She's *never wrong*. Why she's playing along with you when she knows you're not Orlazrus Ortessi, I do not understand nor agree with.

"My obedience is my duty. But my trust is earned.

189

Kieler thought of several responses to her 'disrespect' but decided he'd probably learn more by just letting her go on. And she did.

"I trust Velator. He has shown me that to the best of his ability and wisdom, he will choose to do the right thing. And this is where a conflict occurs: Velator has chosen to believe you. Perhaps he doesn't spend as much time with his daughter as I do to realize the extent of her ability." She smiled predatorily at him. "And this puts me in the unique position... of watching for you to slip up."

Whether it was her words or a cold breeze down the slope of the Rim, Kieler felt suddenly cold. An'essa turned and walked off, crossing a small arch over a misty stream. The mist turned icy as it rose to touch his face.

He wished Movus had told him more about the An. Once again he realized, *This trip to Velakun wasn't part of the original plan.*

They crossed a final bridge over a deep cut gorge, again with a roar of unseen water below. This one led to a wide plaza with a fountain in the center surrounded by several ornate buildings in a variety of styles from all over Zotikas.

"These are the ambassadorial residences." An'essa led him to a mansion on the northern side, built up into the cliff face of the Rim. "This was used by House Ortessi until Orticot took control. Velator has decided that you should make it your home for now."

He managed to catch himself before expressing gratitude. Technically such a residence should still belong to his house.

Upon entering, Kieler saw that his luggage and the travel wardrobe had already been delivered. The residence was cozily warm and illuminated, once again, by luzhril. *In my whole life I've never seen as much luzhril as in the past week amongst the Primes.* In addition, the walls were adorned with paintings of historic scenes, and several artifacts of varying purposes made up the décor.

CHAPTER SIX

He dismissed An'essa with a nod of guarded thanks. She left without ceremony.

When she was well gone, Kieler kicked off his boots and stretched out on the plush divan. He smiled and shook his head.

It's going to be very strange living in such luxury. But I'll do my best to get used to it.

CHAPTER SEVEN

He started awake to an urgent pounding on his door. Startled, he jumped into clothes and ran to open it.

Velirith. He should have guessed.

"Is that how you treat dignitaries around here, Velirith?"

"No, I *ignore* them. This is how I treat *you*. And why did you take so long to answer? I could have further hurt my arm on your door."

Kieler had to watch himself around her. "Shouldn't you be in bed?"

"I've been in bed for a day. Unless they restrain me—which Doctor Yuric threatened to do—I'm getting up to have breakfast. You almost slept through it." She paused, glanced behind her and continued, "By the way, I'm here to stun you."

He took a cautious step backward. "And what does that mean, girl?" He caught the sharp glance at his intentionally demeaning address of Her Daughtership.

"Watch it, poser. I lost my blood, not my brain. Now come out here."

He rubbed his eyes and stepped out into the brightness—and was stunned. Rei had crested the cloudless Rim behind him and was spotlighting the basin of Velakun. Reflecting off Lake Skyfall and a ring of white snow around it on slopes of the caldera, the sun hit Center Isle from several angles. Tri-cornered towers pierced the sky. From the towers extended wide terraces, and from the terraces waterfalls fell in a complex maze of interlocking streams from the heights to the depths of the soaring city. The towers, terraces and waterways were so interconnected, so coordinated that only the most skillful of architects could have composed such a masterpiece. It was a city built as a city should be built.

Below him, where the slope of Vel Estate touched the waters of the lake, haventhall trees shot into the air, their perfectly formed, twining trunks barren of branches until their high, leafy canopies spread like umbrellas. These too were capped with white snow atop the sturdy, green foliage.

From just below the residence of Vel Estate, an arched skybridge spanned the lake between the Rim and the island, the very bridge they had traversed in the snow the night before. Snow covered the top but had sheared off its sides. Through the transparent upper half, Kieler spotted several podcars sliding silently across the graceful bow of Vel engineering. Five more skybridges, equally spaced, connected the Rim to the island with an elegant symmetry.

As he continued to absorb the magnitude of artistry and design incorporated into the city, Kieler saw that many of the tower terraces themselves were planted with haventhalls, their straight trunks paralleling the obelisks at great elevations.

And at the far end of the lake, only partially visible beyond the cityscape, were the backs of the stony heads that held back the waters of Lake Skyfall like massive guardians. Beyond that, he knew those waters plunged over a thousand feet, pouring over the powercoach tunnel and into the Veshun River.

Rei shining, waters blazing with light, the city stretching impossibly tall and surrounded by lake and Rim—Kieler realized he had stopped breathing and pulled in a deep breath of clean mountain air.

He became aware that Velirith was looking at him, not the view. He tore his gaze away from the resplendent haven in which the Velaki lived and looked at her, still speechless.

193

EPISODE 2 - HIGH RAILS OF ARDAN

"Well, whatever game you're playing, you're not immune to beauty," Velirith decided out loud.

Looking back at her, Kieler silently agreed.

The slightest flush colored her cheeks.

Breakfast was taken on the terrace between the kitchen and the tower that was part of her bedroom. Velirith loved the mornings when snow had fallen, especially when it fell thick and heavy like it had the night before. The rising warm air off the lake already made it comfortable to sit outside. Rei and the warmth of the lake air conspired, already beginning to melt away the scenery while magnifying the waterfalls cascading down the Rim, roaring at high volume.

Velirith took a seat to the right of her father and watched the Ortessi try to figure out his table manners. His eyes darted across the lack of place settings, a glance at her father, at her (as if she were going to help him!), and then to the serving man. Her father noticed Orlazrus trying to find where and when he should sit and pointed mercifully to the seat on his left. Their guest looked pleased (and relieved) and sat, turning his attention to the food coming out. His eyes dilated at the sight of gfrishta fillets and a side of steamed greens. *He isn't used to eating this well.*

Her father looked tired, but his constant glances at her and her apparently solid recovery made much of his stress melt away with the snow. Still, there was an underlying conflict in his eyes as they met hers. He noticed her assaying him and smiled at her. He knew she was always observing. She smiled back.

The men exchanged small talk, "How did you sleep?" "The snow is beautiful." "The food is delicious." Etc.

Orlazrus was evidently holding back, absorbing information and atmosphere in order to calculate how best to fit in. But soon her father began to express what was really on his mind.

"Orlazrus, as I see my daughter alive and recovering well, it strikes me how much we owe you. An'essa and I saw you carry Velirith to safety from the shattered viewing area of the *Pride*. And

194

that cutter didn't just explode of its own accord. Even though I had my hands full, I know you did *something,* and your modesty can't conceal the fact that your quick thinking saved us all."

There's something more he's not saying, Velirith read in her father. She glanced at Orlazrus. He was soaking the praise like a thirsty man in the desert, but he had sense enough not to say anything.

Velator went on. "We're sitting here enjoying the delicate flavor of gfrishta when, had you not been there, the fields of Ardan would be enjoying the delicate flavor of our blood! I am convinced it was that close."

The Ortessi cleared his throat. "I can't help reminding you that the Cortattis were probably incited to attack by my behavior the night before. Feleanna could not let my insults pass unanswered."

Velirith felt that twinge of guilt for her part in sabotaging the dance, but Velator waved off his conciliatory remarks. "She started it. We both know it. And she wanted to finish it." He leaned toward Orlazrus. "You've asked for no reward, but by the end of breakfast, be ready—I'll have thought of something."

Orlazrus faked undeserving very well, Velirith noted. He replied to her father, "You have given me food (exceedingly good food, by the way), shelter, and refuge—from the Cortattis, I might add. And you've offered to get me started on a legal claim to regain my house. Any 'reward' is already given in full measure."

Velator ignored him. "I'm thinking some sort of recognition... It's on the edge of my brain, a magnetic impulse... I'll think of it."

He has something in mind, Velirith perceived. *He's just waiting for the right timing. Why?*

She watched the man in green and gold talking to her father. He was cute, despite being deceiving. *Cute,* she almost gagged in disgust at herself for being so shallow. He was medium tall, solid and muscular, a simple, strong face with no distinguishing

195

features. *What's cute about that*? But then she shifted her thoughts, choosing to honor her true impressions. After all, most people did not trust their own instinct, and that was what bred so much contempt for them within her.

Handsome was more apt. And more than that, she liked him. *Oh, this is really too much*. Did she have contempt for him or like him? She knew he was playing a false game.

She thought a while, staring at him as he talked. He gave an occasional glance her way, but did not engage her. *I despise his lies, but I definitely don't despise him. I like him*. Ok, that was honest. But why? *He truly is brave, he's shown that. First on the Pride of Velik, and second, just by trying to pull off this incredible sham of stolen identity. So why is he doing this? What are his* real *motives?*

She sighed loudly and that drew his puzzled gaze again. Her father too looked over at her as she studied Kieler. *I must believe that despite his deceitful behavior, he has very noble and true motives...* She chewed her lower lip and nodded.

And I can have contradictory feelings. Look at my father— and she did—*I love him, but I hate all the posing and positioning he does when he's playing politics—like right now. I think it shows weakness and I believe he could be more.*

"Hmm? What?" she said out loud.

"Velirith!" her father evidently repeated. "We're talking to you and it seems you're having a fine conversation with yourself. What are you thinking?"

"That I like this claimed Ortessi anyway," she answered bluntly.

Her father was unfazed. He was used to her talking this way. But she looked over at Orlazrus to see his face flushing with red. He was sufficiently embarrassed.

Velator spoke again. "Good. Because you'll be spending more time with him. He's going to Orcad with you."

CHAPTER SEVEN

"Pardon me? What?" Velirith spluttered. "Were you just talking about me as if I wasn't here?"

Kieler and Velator exchanged glances and smiled. "Were you?" they asked together.

Now Velirith could feel herself coloring. Lost in her own thoughts, she had paid no attention to their conversation assuming it was just more posing. She had no idea they had been talking about her.

"Well, that doesn't happen often," she muttered. "Me getting embarrassed, I mean."

As they laughed at her expense, she repeated what her father had said, "Why does he need to go to Orcad? Isn't he an almighty Prime already?"

"Because he is serious about making a difference in this world and admits to gaps in his education. You're getting the education, but seem to care not at all for your role in this world."

"My role in this world?"

"I've often told you, Velirith, that as my daughter and the only direct heir of Vel, you could and should help straighten the crooked path this world is on. But you've been content to show disdain for the political machinations of the ruling class. I'm hoping *that* part of Orlazrus will be a good influence on you."

"But shouldn't you have a larger role in this world too, Father?" She meant it, but knew it would sting. Despite being the truth, she didn't like saying it.

Velator scowled.

"And this faux-Ortessi—" Velirith continued her admittedly overdramatic rail, "he has no real references, no resources, and no real influence. What can *he* do?"

Velator repeated part of her diatribe, "No resources... that's it!" he exclaimed. "Orlazrus, you will attend the Ortessi Academy, but not just as a student. You will also attend as its *owner*!"

"*What!*" Velirith found herself in chorus with Orlazrus.

EPISODE 2 - HIGH RAILS OF ARDAN

Velator explained, "The Academy has been without an Ortessi at the helm for twenty years. What better way to establish yourself than to run the place?"

Orlazrus, with a weak argument intended to fail, said, "But you said yourself, I'm not qualified. I should be a student there!"

"What better way? The Prime family of House Vel would be *extinct* if not for you! Are you open to mentorship? The Academy Superintendent, Entrovel, will stay on, and I will be available as a board member. We can phase you into a more active leadership role, nothing rushed, and as the other houses become aware that you, as a true Ortessi, have resumed control, it will pave the way toward solidifying your legitimacy! Do not deny me this chance to express my gratitude generously."

Velirith found herself rapidly looking from one man to the other. She could see her father was grateful, but this was totally out of character for him. There was more to it. Something she didn't like and that churned sour in her stomach.

And the Ortessi—well, he was pleased beyond his wildest expectations. His schemes, whatever they were, were in accelerated bloom, like an unnaturally early spring.

She simply didn't understand the motivation. Breakfast wrapped up quickly after that with an excited Ortessi grasping her father's arm and thanking him and promising he wouldn't let him down, blah, blah, blah. Velirith said nothing, trying to figure out why her father had spontaneously (a rare but not unheard of trait in him) given the Ortessi control of perhaps the best school on Zotikas.

After Orlazrus had left, she spoke, leaning in close to her father and looking him in the eye. He did not avoid her inquisition. "Father, what was that? Gratefulness does not trump prudence. Giving an unknown upstart control of Orcad?" She shook her head, baffled. "Why?"

CHAPTER SEVEN

To his credit, Velator did not argue with her or try to defend what she knew was untenable. He held her gaze in return. "Velirith, do you think Orlazrus Ortessi has some good in him?"

She squirmed, but answered, "Yes, some."

"Do you think that by giving him a major boost toward legitimacy, which I perceive as his strongest desire, he can easily think ill of us?"

She thought with her heart on this one. *Others in the Omeron—Telander, Ek— they would take the boon and consume it like so much gfrishta. They would simply see it as poor strategy on Velator's part and feel no gratitude or obligation of fealty. But this Orlazrus...* "No, I think he's beginning to like us. To trust us—*you*, at least. But that doesn't make him loyal to you. You know true well that loyalty isn't bought."

"I do. But by showing him kindness and trust, I have nearly doubled the number of houses that are kindly toward us." And his voice had the slightest catch in it, the slightest hint that his confident exterior was expected as a House Prime, but not completely realized.

Again Velirith thought with both her heart and mind. "We have more allies than that, Father! The Firstholms, the An..." She was going through the families of the Omeron trying to think of others.

"Ah yes, the An. You know they are so much a part of our family that I had actually forgotten them. My apology. They are, however, a proximal family, yes? And the Firstholms, certainly, our maritime ally has always been close.

"But do go on, dear daughter. Who else?"

Shaking her head again, she couldn't grasp that no other families were allies of Vel. "Father, we do not make enemies. We play nice, especially you. You are just. I cannot fathom that the rest of the Omeron is our enemy."

He smiled a sad but fatherly smile, expressing his love for her. "What you say is true as far as it goes. We don't make enemies

199

easily, mainly Cortatti by some horrific encounters. And we have survived by treating others well; that is our strategy. But neither have we kept friends, allies on whom we could rely. Who of the Prime families would come to our aid should we need it?"

His voice was gentle, but his jaw muscles were teeth-grindingly tight. As he paused, she pictured their faces at the New Year's Gala.

No one.

Merckle, Terizan, Ashperis, Bintle, Telander, Ek, Parchiki, Mizgot... not enemies, no. But not a sure help in time of need. They would look the other way were evil to befall the respected House of Vel.

"MgFellis?"

"Proximal."

"Yes," then another thought struck her. "But who among the Primes *does* have allies, even one true friend?"

Her father nodded slowly. "It is a sad state. But their insecurity does not make ours less."

"So you buy an ally?"

With a sigh, "No, Velirith. As you said, you cannot buy allies. But the man is ambitious, and we both think he's of a good heart. Kindness plies a good heart."

She began to see how her father could think this way, though she could not. "You're using him," she mumbled.

His expression was that of surprised offense. He replied, "I just gave him the best school in the world and now I'm using him?"

Velirith stared thoughtfully across the water to Center Isle. She could see the theater, and though enormous, it gave her the feeling of a cozy home, secure. To the north of the theater she could see the tower of Orcad. She felt her feelings for her school changing as she looked at it. She had no complaints about her education there, but now she saw the place in a different light—a tool, a piece being moved in a complex, snarled game that no one seemed to win. She mumbled again, "I hate politics."

CHAPTER SEVEN

She thought about who she trusted: her father, An'essa... to some degree Moshalli. She did not trust them because of what they gave her, but because of who they were, because of their character. More importantly, her father's act showed her more about her father. He was generous, yes. Kind, yes. But mostly he was scared.

CHAPTER EIGHT

"Don't worry; little boys are always scared on the first day of school."

Kieler scowled, recalling Velirith's parting jibe. Leaving her at Vel Estate, he had traveled across Lake Skyfall with her father. It wasn't the first day of school, but it was *his* first day.

As they approached the triangular tower of Orcad, Velator pointed out an oversized terrace high up on the east side of the school, just now being bathed in the light of rising Rei. "That is Daybreak Hall, an outdoor amphitheater where we gather for the New Dawn Ceremony, among other assemblies."

The podcar came to a stop at the Center Isle station labeled "Ortessi Academy."

I'm not scared. I'm just... nervous.

Being supposedly Ortessi, he supposedly knew about this place. At some point Movus had mentioned that House Vel was now running the Ortessi Academy. But at the time Kieler was a half mile underground studying the entire structure of the Omeron, every family, every Prime, the Proximal families, manners, history, dance, who hates who, who runs what and—well, a little school over a thousand miles away on a continent he'd never set foot on didn't seem like a high priority. He had never guessed House Vel would take him in and he never suspected he'd be running the school within a week of his ascension from the nethercity.

Fortunately, on the way across Lake Skyfall, Velator gave him a bit of the history. "Orcad was originally founded in Avertori by Oonyez Ortessi, a clan leader known for gleaning useful knowledge wherever he could. Your ancestor, Oonyez, and my ancestor, Velik, shared a passion for learning from the past."

Velator recounted that as Avertori was slowly tamed, driving out the wild and weird beasts that inhabited the Isle of Threes, Oonyez realized the place was a treasure trove of history previously inaccessible to the disconnected clans of Velik's time. The re-claimers of the Isle of Threes were simply dumping the fascinating ruins of a lost civilization under the massive Plate or into the ocean to make way for their own version of progress.

Oonyez had petitioned Velik and his newly organized coalition of tribes to set aside parcels of land throughout the city-to-be as repositories for this history. These properties became the Ortessi legacy and a thriving business of museums, schools and a theater dedicated to recording and learning from the past. The most notable *property* was the Oraflora, the theatre on Plaza Floraneva: prime real estate.

But as society withered slowly, interest in the past also declined and revenues with it. As Velator told of the more recent history, his tone went flat with remorse so heavy that Kieler knew there was more to it than just the straight facts. "Your father, Salasan, was a friend, though admittedly not a close one.

"Along with the general populace, House Ortessi had lost its passion for preserving the past and fallen heavily into debt. Tragically, they had taken to selling priceless artifacts just to pay their Omeron tribute. Museum collections lay un-curated throughout the city, even though the actual property on which they stood was extremely valuable."

Velator paused and looked toward the city sparkling before them in the rapidly melting snow. The contrast between the darkness of Velator's mood and the brightness of the silver city pulled his emotions in two different directions.

In a voice so low with sadness and regret that Kieler could barely hear him, Velator continued, "Enter the Cortattis. Aggressive, unscrupulous—a grevon picking out the weakest and fattest of the herd. Immediately after they pulled off their usurpation of House Ortessi, they sold off whatever assets they could through that puppet Orticot, supposedly the last surviving Ortessi and related only by marriage. Orticot was a known worm commanded by Feleanna Cortatti—but it gave them another seat in the Omeron. Very few opposed the murderous takeover and those who did... suffered."

Kieler felt ill.

The Prime of House Vel took a deep breath and straightened. "One positive came out of the takeover. After the tremors died out, I swallowed my hate and made an offer on Orcad. It wasn't originally for sale. The Cortattis counted the low-enrollment school as a liability rather than an asset and had summarily closed it down.

"I knew this and made a ridiculously low offer on it. The Cortattis thought it was for the land in Avertori where the original grounds of Orcad still stood. But the offer was so low they said we could have the *contents* only.

"Well, that's what I wanted anyway. As weak of a victory as it was, at least it was something. I bought the teachers, moved the whole operation from Avertori to Velakun, and preserved an institution vital to the survival of our society."

Velator finished with a prophetically poetic comment. "If we don't hear our shouting past, its echoes will surely deafen us."

Now, as they stepped out of the podcar, Velator led the way across an elevated causeway to the entrance of Kieler's new school. The main doors stood about a third of the way up the triangular tower with a plaque beside them that read "The Ortessi Academy for Leadership Development." As the only Ortessi in the known world, Kieler felt rather deficient in the "leadership" arena. But the truth was he had led more men as a squad leader in the Coin than the instructors in this building would ever lead. *I'll be fine,* he convinced himself.

CHAPTER EIGHT

Inside the entrance was a grand foyer laid with bronze tiles of intricate, interlocking patterns. Velator walked across the foyer to a handrail and paused, looking both up and down. Kieler followed and was impressed. The space inside the three-sided tower was open from bottom to top, tapering slightly as it rose. Classrooms, labs, dorms and offices faced this open inner atrium, and Kieler assumed they had exterior views as well. Light cut across from outside at various levels in sharp beams, reflected off mirrors, and then to suspended crystals that diffused it throughout the tall chamber. Various objects of art and science hung from wires across the inner volume, and one in particular caught his eye: an airship, in miniature, not too far removed from the new design he had in mind. This one, however, looked to have no motor.

Below him was an open café with scattered tables, a place for students to gather. It was empty now. Students wouldn't be arriving for the new term for another week or so.

To the right of where he stood, in the near corner, was a metal cage that extended upward and to the left diagonally across an inner wall of the tower. After a moment's consideration, he recognized it as an elevator and realized that it must continue down and to the right below him. It traveled much more in the vertical direction than across, but its gentle arc provided an aesthetic Kieler had never considered an elevator capable of. At the top he could see pulleys that directed the elevator cabling into the center of the vast chamber, and hanging from these cables were the light-diffusing crystals. *They not only serve as the elevator's counterweight, but as lighting fixtures! Ingenious!*

And then the final realization, "You're *giving* me *this*?"

Still sober after discussing the school's history, Velator nodded at Kieler's open admiration. "Please make me glad I did."

The plea was not lost on Kieler. It was a big risk for the Prime, and Kieler suspected Velirith had grilled him about it. His councilors would probably be less than excited as well.

EPISODE 2 - HIGH RAILS OF ARDAN

They took the elevator to the top level. The floor of the elevator was made of the same tight metal grid as the sides and allowed him to look below as they ascended. Around the top floor were the offices of the administration, and Velator took him directly to the office with a plaque labeled "Cota Jad Entrovel, Academy Superintendent." Inside was a receptionist, a young man of efficient confidence who bowed to the Prime as he entered.

"Verr Velator," he greeted. "Cota Entrovel asks you come straight in."

They passed through the ante-office into Entrovel's. Apportioned with a similar mechanical motif, Kieler felt the atmosphere as one to inspire creative endeavors. To have grown up here with resources and his already inventive mindset—it would have been a dream!

Entrovel made a slight bow and grasped his Prime's arm. "Verr Velator, my pleasure. Verr Ortessi."

"Cota Entrovel," they both greeted the head of the school with the honorific signifying a master in his field.

"Seat? I understand you gave away our school, Velator?" Entrovel began directly.

Velator seemed to expect the straightforwardness. "Yes, I did. Any questions?"

Entrovel shrugged and leaned back behind the desk. "A few... hundred. But one main one." He looked to Kieler. "Do you want to run this place?"

"I—ah, not yet, no."

"Do you want me to run it?"

"Yes."

"Are you going to give me a raise?"

Kieler looked at Velator for help, but the Prime remained stony-faced. "I—can I do that?"

A smile cracked at the corners of Velator's mouth and Entrovel laughed out loud.

CHAPTER EIGHT

With a wave toward the Superintendent, Velator laughed and said, "This is Jad Entrovel! He won't judge you, but you better know what you're doing and why."

Entrovel, still smiling with his eyes, gave Velator a look as if asking him why he was doing this. He refrained from vocalizing his question.

Though the honorifics and titles were scarce, the mutual respect between the two men was obvious. Velator moved the conversation forward. "So Orlazrus here is eager to learn. We did discuss some of the ramifications of my rather spontaneous generosity. He wisely decided to let things run as they are for at least a term to give him time to see why we do the things we do. Should be interesting to let him see both the decision-making process and the consequences to the students.

"So, Orlazrus, consider Entrovel on loan from House Vel. If he ever leaves the Superintendent position, it will be your loss, my gain. I have plenty of positions where his skills are needed."

Entrovel asked Velator, "So do you want me to introduce him at the New Dawn Ceremony next week before the first day of classes?"

"Yes, better to be up front with the other students than have uneducated rumors running amok."

From the outer office, Kieler heard an intense, muffled exchange. Entrovel's personal assistant came barging in—politely. "Sir, that behavior challenge with Rejin has turned... ah, 'explosive'. Do you want to address it now?"

Entrovel rose with a curt nod. To Kieler he said, "Walk with me now. You'll see what I get to deal with."

As they took the sliding elevator down, Velator excused himself and left them at the entrance. Once alone, Kieler asked the Superintendent, "I thought the students didn't arrive back for some weeks? How can they be misbehaving?"

"Students?" he grumbled through grinding teeth. "Students are easy to frighten into submission. It's the faculty that is difficult!"

They walked into a lab, and Kieler was surprised to see it identified as "Cota Sah Rejin, General Science."

"Rejin is a *Cota* and he's being difficult?"

"*I* am not the one being difficult, nor am I a *he*," snapped a voice from behind a tall lab bench. Kieler felt his face go hot and mouth dry. "*I* was minding my own business when *this* happened!"

As they rounded the bench they saw a smoking, smoldering mess. Bits of glass, a foul stench of rotten eggs, and unidentified liquids dripped from multiple surfaces. The science Cota had her hair in a neat, tight bun, and her face was clean with sharply angled features. But her face and hair were the only parts of her that were neat and clean. Her clothes were splattered with the foul brownish liquid that was everywhere else as well.

Cota Entrovel surveyed the wreckage, breathing through his sleeve to mitigate the gagging odor. He found a towel outside the blast zone and handed it to her. "And you suspect...?"

"Who else?"

"Was he here? Did you see him?"

"Of course not!" she snapped back. "The man is like a spirit of mischief! A theatrical ghost of trouble."

"Then how do you know it was—"

"Who else!" she repeated. Cota Entrovel backed away and shut up. "You want to know how I know? Deduction. Scientific method. Reason! Something he seems to avoid.

"Why does he torment *me?* Why me? Because I'm his opposite? I am logical. I do not retaliate except through you, who have yet to ban him from this establishment. And what does he teach here? Foolishness! Theater? Intuition?

"Nonsense!

"What use are any of those to the minds of our future leaders? He's an atrocious example to our charges!"

She paused to wipe her already clean face.

Jad Entrovel did not speak yet.

She started wiping one mess into another. An angry hiss erupted with another gout of foul-smelling smoke.

"Aagh!" she wafted the towel at the smoke. "And he's so blessed clever! He mixed paraffin and sulfur, suspended it in a sugar solution which he crystallized and then molded into a beaker. When I heated the beaker, *poof!* Instant stink bomb. So simple even he could have done it! But he probably used his prop department for his own personal vendettas again. But why *me?* I have never—!" She stopped, so flustered she couldn't speak.

Beaker-shaped stink bomb... that was *clever,* Kieler noted. *I'll have to remember that trick.*

Cota Rejin must have noticed his admiring look and turned on him. "And who is this rude young man? A spy here for Battle Damage Assessment and a report back to Cota Aurelios?"

Neither man spoke, knowing that whatever they said would rekindle her wrath. Finally, in a low but clear voice, Cota Entrovel replied, "He's your new boss."

Rejin must have looked back and forth between the two of them six times in two seconds. Kieler clamped down on a rogue smile and she exploded.

"Mock me!" she shouted at Entrovel. "I bother no one! I teach some of the most arrogant creatures of the Omeron how to make this world better, and they *sleep* through science! How can anyone sleep through the only interesting class at this Academy?

"Now you bring a student in here and say he's my—what are you doing? What are you saying? Are you in league with that senile trickster?"

Both men were looking down, hoping not to be called on. Kieler wanted to pick up a towel and start helping her clean up, but he was afraid to move.

She stepped up close to him. "What's your name?"

EPISODE 2 - HIGH RAILS OF ARDAN

He opened his mouth but couldn't get anything out through the force-field of her rage. He cleared his throat. "Orlazrus Ortessi."

Her eyes pierced his skull, then began to widen. A flicker of panic, then horror, then resign. She threw the chemical-soaked towel over her shoulder. She plopped down onto a lab stool that was none too clean, but she no longer cared. She looked up at him. "Figures. That man has uncanny timing. All those years on stage, I suppose. It's like he set me up in a three stage chemical process. One, blow up smelly stuff in my face. Two, rage at my boss. Three, rage at my future ex-boss—the one who's about to fire me. Maybe there is something to this intuition thing. Maybe I should quit science and study theater. It works better."

A very long period of silence followed as the only studying going on was of each other's shoes. Finally she asked, "So you're the rumor in the flesh, true? The resurrected Ortessi?"

She actually expected an answer.

"Yes."

"Are you going to fire me?"

"So far everyone I've met here has asked me that." He shot a glance at Cota Entrovel and found him stifling a snicker. He seemed to say, *"Are you sure you want this place?"*

With Kieler and Entrovel as the release valve for her steam, Rejin remained at sub-explosive pressure. Only when they were leaving did she come close to blowing up again, and that was when Entrovel promised only to talk to the accused and issue a reprimand if it was determined the man was behind the mischief.

When they finally left, Entrovel walked Kieler around the science floor. "While we're here, Verr Orlazrus," Entrovel said, motioning to another office on the right, "let me introduce you to another master instructor, a far quieter one." This door said "Cota Chance, Biology."

Jad Entrovel relaxed visibly as he turned into the biology department. He obviously didn't feel on edge with this instructor.

210

Kieler, too, relaxed slightly in preparation for meeting a less volatile professor.

Following Entrovel through a narrow office door, Kieler stepped around him to meet the man seated at the wooden desk. A different kind of shock froze him with his arm half extended.

Cota Chance was the agent who had followed him up from the Dragon Gate.

For the agent's part, the man's eyes widened, but he almost instantly stood and gave a false smile, putting out his arm to grasp Kieler's. "Hello."

Entrovel introduced them with a puzzled look to Kieler. "Verr Ortessi, this is Cota Chance. Do you... know him?"

Kieler, jolting his mind back into motion, still couldn't answer. This man was *everywhere!* This Chance knew Kieler came up from the Plate and how much more? And here he was a Cota?

Kieler didn't know if he should expose Chance as an agent of Cortatti (if he was after all), or if the man would expose *him*. The expressionless, wrinkleless face did not answer Entrovel either, instead studying Kieler as if to see how he dealt with the surprising situation. Stammering, Kieler finally got out, "I- I- thought I saw him in Avertori just a few days ago. But that seems impossible."

Entrovel looked to Chance, looking for confirmation.

Chance shrugged. "Possible," he said.

Entrovel put in, "Cota Chance did just return from New Year's break. Didn't you go to Avertori?"

"I did." Chance sat back down, resuming what Kieler took to be the same bored expression he had seen on the tram in Avertori. "So it is possible he saw me there."

Was Chance a Cortatti agent spying on Vel? But how had he established a cover identity in Velakun even before Kieler himself had known he was coming here? And how could he pass himself off as a Cota of Biology? Nothing about him made sense.

The silence dragged, Chance not deigning to talk, Kieler unable to, and Entrovel not sure why this was so awkward.

"Well," Entrovel finally said, "Verr Ortessi has been given ownership of the school. He's our new boss."

Again Chance seemed to be gauging Kieler, this time with the slightest hint of amusement in his bored eyes. Neither of the Primes had sat down, nor had they been offered seats.

"Okay!" Entrovel said finally. "Let's move on."

Kieler was more than ready to go.

CHAPTER NINE

"I never had a House Prime to order around and turn wrenches for me," Jarovel began. He was much larger than Kieler, in height and girth. He had the frame of a man who was strong because of work and carrying around his own body.

Jarovel sat with his large feet up on his desk, which was really just a workbench at the far end of the maintenance bay. The workbench-turned-desk was covered with papers, sockets, wire bits, parts, pencils, and a huge chunk of unshaped metal. Behind the desk was a sagging cot that evidently saw a lot of use.

Kieler had thrilled to see the *Pride of Velik's* shop as he came down to see Jarovel for the first time. He walked slowly through row after row of dusty, greasy shelves of spare parts and materials; walls filled with tools of every configuration. It was organized chaos. The kind of chaos an inventor thrived in.

He could hardly contain his excitement as he walked back to talk to the Chief Maintenance Engineer, his new "boss." If Kieler would have had a shop like this in the nethercity under Avertori, he could have turned out airships powered by his father's motors in weeks instead of years.

He couldn't wait to get started. He had determined, however, that he would hold his tongue. Just walking through the aged rows of pieces and parts, he had come up with a hundred questions. But he needed Jarovel to like him and trust him, for a couple reasons.

First he wanted to learn from him. Second he wanted to steal from him.

EPISODE 2 - HIGH RAILS OF ARDAN

Kieler knew he didn't know everything about powercoaches, but he was confident in his ability to pick up on how things worked. He did know that the principles that turned the *Pride's* three-story drive wheel were the same ones that turned his backpack-sized airship motor. But he would listen first—figure out this Jarovel—even if he had to bite a hole in his tongue.

Kieler recognized Jarovel's verbal challenge. This was Jarovel's domain, and the Pride of Velik his queen. Velator knew it, and respected Jarovel's expertise. Jarovel would look at Kieler like an inconvenience, someone he *should* respect but didn't. And someone he *wouldn't* respect unless Kieler earned it.

Kieler remembered a fish-seller in Karst below the Plate who had worked hard to establish a network of suppliers and distributors to get fish to the people in the under-city. He was gruff, knew the right people to make his system work, and had become king of his own kingdom. He didn't let people push him around and he got his job done.

An agent of the COIN, not well respected by Kieler, was charged to collect protection dues from the fishmonger. The agent was offended by the fishmonger's lack of respect for his position. He tried to lord it over him. Every time the agent tried to collect, the man gave him grief. He eventually paid, but it was always at the very edge of violence.

Another agent asked for the assignment, respected the work ethic of the fish vendor, spoke his language—not with threats, but by wordlessly hauling crates of fish for the man. It was a humble position. He didn't even ask for the payment his first visit. In fact, he might have grunted three words to the fisher king.

On his next visit, the agent brought the fish seller the name of a new store in a deep borough that would probably want to buy his fish.

And that was all it took. The fish man knew he had to pay the protection payment. He knew what the new agent was there for. And after a brief, five-minute interaction on that second visit, he pulled out a folded paper, the kind used for wrapping fish, but this time used for wrapping money.

It was done. The agent had spoken the man's language. It cost him very little.

So Kieler understood that his response to Jarovel's "disrespectful" comment would define their relationship. Kieler put on his stoniest face and intentionally overacted. "I am a House Prime, therefore arrogant and humorless and completely without practical knowledge of anything. That's why I volunteered to work with you while not reigning over my domain. Of all the residents of Zotikas, I chose to annoy *you*. You may feel honored. I grant you permission."

Looking back at Kieler through his puffy eyes, Jarovel returned Kieler's stony expression. But he couldn't hide the slight crinkling at the corners of his eyes. "I'll bow when I get up."

Though he had wanted to stay silent until sussing out the master mechanic, Kieler couldn't stop one last jibe. "So you do get off that chair sometimes, eh?"

Jarovel's eyes narrowed to where Kieler couldn't see his irises. He was thinking. Finally he spoke. "I'm gonna work you so hard you won't have enough energy to annoy me. Maybe you leave." The man had the slightest accent and Kieler wondered where he was raised if not here in Velakun.

The chair under Jarovel groaned and spun away as he rose. He rocked as he walked down an aisle toward the open work area. He must have been three times Kieler's age.

Kieler wanted to ask why so much stuff had accumulated. He wanted to know what every linkage did. What every gauge measured. What improvements had been made over the years.

But he simply followed Jarovel, who spoke not at all. They came out of the shelving area and Kieler saw a huge crane hovering over the battered *Pride,* ready to lift up whole sections of the massive engine. The necessary investigation was over. It was time to get to work.

EPISODE 2 - HIGH RAILS OF ARDAN

Kieler watched as the Chief Mechanic started surveying the *Pride of Velik* from bow to stern. The bow looked the worst, the glass gone. Much of the metal lattice-work was bent, broken or twisted from high-caliber maggun bolts. Looking at where the damage was heaviest, Kieler concluded that the crew of the Cortatti cutter must have been trying to kill the occupants and take the *Pride* as a prize; there would have been more damage to the drive section had their goal been total destruction of the vehicle.

Jarovel seemed to be tallying every item of damage. The rear of the *Pride* simply had dents and holes punched through her skin, but Kieler realized that to repair those metal plates and structural pieces would be far harder than replacing the glass and lattice.

When the lumbering hulk stopped in front of the huge drive wheel, Kieler heard the man give a great rattling sigh. Thin, long gouges marred the Rim and each of the three massive spokes of the burnished drive wheel. It was miraculous that the impacting magbolts hadn't unbalanced their own wheel. Kieler knew that the wheel had to be nearly perfect to run smoothly. Would they have to regrind it? The job seemed impossible.

Kieler finally spoke without even intending to. "Maybe we should scrap this one and build a new one."

The reply to that comment was not in words. A deep roar burst forth from Jarovel's thick chest. It was guttural. Kieler realized only afterward that he had jumped back from the man about three paces.

But Jarovel was not directing his anger at Kieler. He was frustrated. From behind, Kieler saw the man's ears burning red. Kieler mentally kicked himself for speaking when he had resolved not to.

After inhaling deeply several times and blowing the air out in measured bursts, Jarovel called out to his crew. Five men and a woman appeared almost instantly from different parts of the expansive bay. They stood in silence like a grim assault team.

CHAPTER NINE

"Now that investigators have gone, I want our lady cleaned up. Everything that's beyond repair—gone. If it's critical, or irreplaceable, make rack and we keep it and fix it. Prime-slave," he looked at Kieler, "I don't trust you to know what's irreplaceable, so I want you to sweep up every piece of glass from fore to aft, inside and out. Once she's cleaned of debris, we'll take off the plating and strip her down to her bones."

Kieler had no objection to this menial task. It would be like when he had proved himself to Movus doing the trivial courier jobs better and faster than anyone else until he was recognized and trusted to move up. He would find his opportunities to shine and learn.

But his noble resolve was challenged immediately when, after the instructions were issued, Jarovel turned on him. "The *Pride* is *original* work of art. This vessel built when they did everything great, everything beautiful, everything worked. It is still one of the fastest coaches on the tracks. It is the best on the three continents for five hundred years. It will *not* be 'scrapped' while *I* am Chief Mechanic!"

Kieler tried to maintain a cool composure, but he knew he was cowering under the raging glare of Jarovel.

Kieler did his work with speed and extreme diligence. He inspected every niche for debris and dug out every piece of embedded glass with a tool and brush that Jarovel gave him. He swept and re-swept until the front deck shone clean. It took him all day just to clean up the view-deck. Two others worked on the fore-section with him, Catrovo and Lervik, who removed the damaged furnishings and broken lattice-work. Even the statues were brought to the holding area for pieces to be restored.

To move the bronze statue of the old man on the throne, Kieler got recruited to help. That piece, because of its weight, had stayed erect. The chair of the statue had three major dents from maggun bolt impacts, but evidently the entire piece was solid because there were no holes. Kieler noted with surprise that the seated figure himself had not been hit.

"Let me sweep the glass from around the base before we move it." Kieler knelt before the statue with his broom and dustpan. As he did, the light caught and reflected sharply off the bottom of each of the legs. Attracted by the glint, he looked and saw, near the base of each leg, a symbol engraved, each like a pointed oval. The symbols meant nothing to him, but his curiosity was piqued as to why he only now noticed them. "Have you ever noticed these symbols, Lervik?"

Lervik looked without leaning over and grunted. "I don't see anything."

Looking closer, Kieler realized the engravings were like an old scar he had on his hand, only seeable at a certain angle. In the case of these symbols, the angle occurred when on one's knees. Kieler noted this keenly, finished his sweeping, and stood up. The symbols were completely invisible once again. With significant effort they managed to get a harness under the bronze statue and lift it clear of the *Pride* with the help of the dock's gantry and pulleys.

The end of the day found Kieler's injured knee and shoulder aching, but he was able to appreciate the preciseness of the construction of every item on the *Pride of Velik.* Jarovel, as he dismissed his crew, spoke straight to Kieler. "You work hard, like used to it."

That was a compliment, Kieler decided. "I really haven't had the usual House Prime upbringing."

Jarovel scrunched his thick brow, wordlessly asking the obvious question.

Kieler just grinned. Jarovel's single-minded concern with the *Pride* had evidently precluded him from learning about House politics or the history of House Ortessi. "I'm not only the highest ranking Ortessi, Jarovel, I'm also the lowest."

CHAPTER NINE

By his expression, Jarovel didn't get it. And that raised Kieler's opinion of him. Laughing, he decided to leave him puzzling it out. He slapped the man on his shoulder. "See you later, Verr Jarovel!

CHAPTER TEN

After annoying Jarovel that afternoon, it was Kieler's turn to be annoyed by Arvel, visiting from Velakun. The man was infuriating but undeniably knowledgeable about every facet of Omeron law and process.

They met in a conference room in the library at the Vel Estate. It was a formal room on the third tier overlooking Lake Skyfall and the city on the island.

On his way to that meeting, Kieler managed to speak to Velator and ask him about Chance. Velator told him that Chance had been teaching biological sciences since Orcad had moved to Velakun. And he had been teaching at the original Avertori Orcad before that. Kieler didn't tell Velator why he was asking, but knowing Chance's exceptionally established background didn't help reconcile his behavior toward Kieler.

Meanwhile, Arvel droned on. "House Cortatti will fight you on the statute of limitations, but their main argument will be that their man, Orticot, has a proven lineage, albeit through marriage. They will claim you lack a provable identity."

"Orticot!" Kieler raged, embracing the "entitled heir" role. "He was married to my dead mother's dead cousin! Hardly a claim! They've stripped my family's holdings to finance their aggression! They have *no legitimate* claim, only legal manipulations."

Arvel sat unmoved.

Kieler raved on. "They are *thieves!* Do you not see this truth?"

Like a bored machine, Arvel replied, "My job is to assist you in processing your claim. The truth is irrelevant. The proof and the proper process are the only things that have any hope of achieving the results that Velator has asked me to help you achieve."

Kieler glared at the pompous, and unfortunately correct, High Clerk of Self-Propagating Complications. He was like a priest of the bureaucracy. The only access to the god of government was through his guild. Kieler made a mental note: *When I'm in charge, this kind of person will be made illegal.*

Grudgingly, though, Kieler had to be grateful to Arvel. If Velator had left him to try to find his own way through the temples of government red tape, he would have been lost in the labyrinth and died. In the end, Arvel suggested they proceed stepwise. First, establish him as the provisional Ortessi heir by the testimony of the Merckles and Mizgots, who could only go on adamantly claiming his authenticity or be exposed as the fools they were. Use the sigil as "hard" evidence. Second, once his claim was confirmed, have Orlazrus claim some of the archeological properties that Cortatti considered more nuisances than assets. The theory was to get a foot in the door and keep wedging it open.

Since the Ortessi family had monopolized the history and museum industry, as well as the theater business outside Velakun, the only assets the Cortattis found valuable were the centrally located buildings and land formerly owned by the Ortessis. The museum pieces, from what Kieler could find out, were summarily warehoused somewhere.

After all, there hadn't been much interest in history or theater for the last hundred years. This disinterest in the significant items and ideas of history had led to the weakened state of Ortessi affairs and opened up the opportunity for the Cortattis to take over.

"Consider yourself briefed, Ortessi." Arvel straightened and packed his inexhaustible stacks of papers. "Your first physical appearance in an Avertori court will be in about three weeks. We will have copious guards. And you'll pardon my over-preparation,

221

but before that appearance we will role play your deposition until you recite it in your sleep."

After Arvel left the small conference room, Velirith literally skipped in and plopped gracefully in the chair across the table from Kieler.

"Charming man, Arvel, true?" She smiled her mischievous smile.

"Almost as fun to talk to as that chair you're sitting in."

"But what do you care? It's not your stuff anyway."

Kieler looked at her accusingly. "You were listening outside the door, weren't you?"

She nodded seriously and went on, "Did you know that I can be intuitive about intuition? I amaze myself sometimes. I mean, I was trying to figure out why I don't believe you. The righteous indignation act about how the Cortattis cheated you almost works. It's the right act, but the truth is in the subtleties: the pauses before reacting, the too-careful choice of words."

Kieler was already getting used to her. He just stared at her, chose not to defend himself, and changed the subject. "So you've got your blood back, I see. Or did you have it replaced with vinegar?"

She smiled sweetly and said, "Father told me I'm well enough that tomorrow I am to show you one of my favorite places and then one of your favorite places! Do you want to go with me, or shall I call Arvel back and tell him you'd rather go with him?"

From her, the threat was real enough that Kieler popped up and grabbed her arm. "Let's go now!"

But the humor of the moment vanished when she winced at his touch. He saw the fresh scar from a glass laceration just inside her upper arm.

"I'm sorry," he said immediately, pulling his hand back quickly and lowering his eyes.

Velirith pushed away the pain and muttered, "It won't be the last time you hurt me, I'm sure."

CHAPTER ELEVEN

The next morning was the first time that Kieler had spent much time with Velirith alone.

"I'm not your friend," she declared firmly.

Smiling, he was ready with a response. "But you like me."

"A paradox, not a contradiction."

"How do you figure that? Don't friends like each other?" They boarded the podcar at the Rim station just below Vel Estate. Across from the station was an old kovar stable mostly covered by vegetation and almost a ruin. Velik himself may have started his journey into the rest of the world from that very stable.

Velirith snappily spun a destination into the brass dais and engaged the lever. The podcar moved out over Lake Skyfall within the covered Skybridge. On the lake, much was happening. Graceful sails pulled their small cargoes of men and women enjoying the protected climate within the caldera. Other boats, mostly with flywheel motors, pushed freight and ferried passengers from the island to the rim. Some of these larger vessels were parked at various plots within the lake marked by tiny buoys and a slight darkening of the water below the surface. Kieler had learned that these were farms growing a type of marine vegetable that not only bore a sweet, crisp fruit called *senye,* but whose nutritious leaves made excellent salad greens.

And directly below, perhaps most breathtaking of all, were the tall haventhalls, their trunks branchless and leafless until near the top where they fanned out into a verdant canopy. On this, the east end of the lake, the trees grew well out into the water.

EPISODE 2 - HIGH RAILS OF ARDAN

Between the gaps of the higher foliage, Kieler could just make out a series of mazelike, suspended paths winding from tree to tree about forty feet above the water. Kieler found it difficult to maintain his demanding repartee while being awed with the beauty of Velakun.

Velirith, however, could do more than one thing at a time. "Friendship," she explained, "is based on trust. I don't trust you because you're hiding something from me. You don't trust *me* or you wouldn't be hiding it."

Looking up and back toward the rim, Kieler followed the cables that laced through the skybridge and upward to the anchoring tower near Vel Estate. Like everything in Velakun, the cables not only provided utility by supporting the skybridge, but also a graceful symmetry that wooed the eye. The bridge was enclosed by a clear cylinder that protected not only the tracks but the foot path that paralleled them.

Kieler was aware of the raw excitement of exploration and appreciation of beauty. He tried to remind himself that the beauty specific to Velirith herself was off limits and dangerous to his mission. He finally replied somewhat absently, "Even married couples don't tell each other everything. Sometimes it's for their own protection."

"I don't need your protection and you're dodging the point. You're hiding your very identity. You're playing a part—and not all that well. How can we be friends if I don't even know who you really are?"

"Doesn't everybody play a role?"

"Yes, but I don't like most everybody because of that."

"But you like me? Why?"

Velirith sighed. She stared out the clear top of the podcar back at her home. Not looking at him she answered, "Because whatever you're doing, you're doing it because you really feel it's right. True or not, I don't know. But I like your heart."

They glided over the last of the giant haventhall canopies directly over the water.

"And that's a start," she finished.

The silence of the podcar gliding on the hemispherical track filled the air. What could he feel about her accurate but unconfirmable assessment of him? He had worked for years with Movus preparing for this scheme. Her transparent personality could not charm him off his course. She wanted his trust?...it was not going to happen.

Kieler allowed himself to feel a little sad about that.

Approaching the northeast end of Center Isle, Kieler took in the city. The eastern tip was just above water level, populated with a myriad of docks, floating markets, shipyards, skiffs and barges. The city rose gently into variations of rounded triangular towers, shorter ones on the east end of the island, much taller ones on the west side. Dominating the shorter east end structures was a large hexagonal building adorned with steeply arched entryways. This edifice, elevated by a natural hill, was connected by a broad elevated walkway to the far higher towers to the west.

The walkway, which defined the midpoint of the isle, bustled with foot traffic. The west end of the promenade led into the towers rising steeply to dizzying heights above them. The tallest of these was crowned with a sculpture or statue that Kieler could not completely make out, high as it was. From this and the other loftiest towers, water cascaded down from terrace to terrace forming a skyscape that was more aerial garden than merely utilitarian city.

Kieler absorbed as much as he could of the overwhelming layout before the podcar slid into the tower that anchored the other side of the skybridge a short way onto the island. They bypassed a few boarding slips in the small station and then exited out the other side. Though the car was relatively low in the city, it was still many stories above ground level. The tri-corner tower construction formed valleys over which they crossed, occasionally

225

switching tracks as the podcar confidently bore them toward Velirith's programmed destination.

Below, the residents of Velakun were arriving at the central business district from their homes on the rim. As they passed the large hexagonal structure on their left, Kieler asked, "Theatre Velaki, right?"

"That is where I spend as much time as possible. We'll not be going there today." She broke into dull, highly articulated speech in an excellent imitation of Arvel, "The price of that tour exceeds your trust capital at this time."

Kieler didn't have enough time to decide whether to scowl or laugh before they descended into a tunnel under the walkway connecting the theater with the sky-piercing towers ahead. After the tunnel, the journey opened into a lower level of a fully enclosed mall rimmed with dozens of podcar slips and animated with throngs of people.

"Government section," Velirith announced, seemingly bored.

Lining the wide promenades above were shops and entrances to offices that Kieler imagined extended upward into some of the towers they had seen coming in. But their podcar stayed on the fast track, again passing the slips and eventually entering another tunnel. Kieler felt the car transition from horizontal to vertical motion and wondered which tower they were ascending.

Velirith and Kieler continued upward. With a yawn and without a word, Velirith settled back against the seat with a smug little smile.

The light in the car began to change and brighten.

Kieler noticed his ears popping and wondered how high and how fast they were ascending. "What's at the top of this tower?"

She shriveled her nose at him like the little girl she was fast unbecoming. Instead of answering, she smiled and told him, "You're not ready..."

226

CHAPTER ELEVEN

With a quizzical look he asked, "For what?"

She smiled, and the light got brighter and brighter. Kieler looked up, glimpsed blue sky and suddenly—they were launched out of the dim vertical tunnel and into the air. Instinctively, Kieler grabbed the seat and cried out.

Velirith laughed raucously. As Kieler began to orient himself he thought, *You're no lady!*

"Nope!" she replied, and Kieler realized he must have spoken aloud. She was watching him, not the view, as usual.

The podcar was still rising straight up, but the tunnel shaft was now crystal clear, transparent except for the magnetic guides on which the sides of the cars were supported and propelled. "You could've warned me! And for that matter, the builders of this thing should warn the passengers!"

"Ha! Don't be a baby. I was on the Executive Chair's balcony when you made your grand entrance, remember?"

"That was different. I planned that—sort of... I—this is *magnificent!*" Kieler went from peeved to awe in a heartbeat. Velakun spread around him, thousands of feet below. The tower next to them, and a few others that aspired to these heights, were the only obstructions to an otherwise unimpeded view.

Center Isle was a few miles east to west and a couple miles north to south. Lake Skyfall blazed with the reflected light of Rei. Around the caldera, the slopes of the rim were lined with bright, white houses that shone in the mid-morning sun. Occasionally, someone had painted their house a brilliant red, blue or yellow, and these structures stood out in tasteful contrast.

Besides the haventhalls below Vel Estate, Kieler saw groves of the tall, white trees growing right out of the water in several places around the lake. Spanning the half mile from isle to Rim, the six enclosed bridges originating at Center Island reached across to the Rim at regular intervals like giant arms. The tops of the towering trees were still far below the little pod in which Kieler and Velirith continued to ascend.

EPISODE 2 - HIGH RAILS OF ARDAN

Again Kieler admired the unity of architecture; the buildings were similar but unique to Velakun, most framed by three, bowed-out sides and topped with a garden or majestic domed cap. Terraces graced the sides of the towers, planted with vegetation and traced with flowing water. Kieler couldn't absorb enough of it.

It was so different from Avertori, where competing houses and industries vied to be more opulent or gaudier or more brash or just... more. That result was often a discordant mishmash of overdone architecture. This place was built as a coherent masterpiece, a planned development completed with a vision that spanned hundreds of years.

His attention was drawn to the tower nearest them, the one that hadn't fallen away below them like most of the others during their ascent. They were slowing, and he assumed they would disembark somewhere on this aerial mast. But he was puzzled. He couldn't quite see the edges of this spire. The edges shimmered, as if undefined.

Velirith was still watching him, admiring his admiration. "Do you want to know why that looks so disorienting?"

Kieler cocked his head. No, he really wanted to solve this mirage on his own. Ego, to be sure, but it was what he liked to do, figure out how things work. Suddenly, Rei glinted off the surface and he saw it for what it was. "Water!" he exclaimed. "But how on Zotikas do you get it so high? How does it cling to the surface of the tower?"

"I don't know why the water clings to the outside of the tower. But I know the water is pushed up here naturally through the tower's interior. Some sort of natural spring and cavern system below Center Isle creates great water pressure. Air pressure too. I may show you that later. Not today." At that bit of information she smiled slyly. Obviously there was more to this air pressure story than she was telling.

"Magnificent," he repeated in true awe. He was thrown off again as the tower seemed to tilt toward him. He instinctively

228

pulled back, a silly reaction, but soon realized it was another architectural illusion. The tower wasn't falling on them; the top was flaring out to meet them.

"Wow," said Kieler, forgetting himself—rather, forgetting Orlazrus Ortessi and being himself—he gushed at the beauty of the place. "This is the most spectacular city I could ever imagine."

Velirith was pleased with his genuine praise. "You're going to appreciate Symphony Garden also."

They continued upward as the outward slope of the tower appeared to gently envelop the podcar, which slowed to a stop at a small loading platform.

Velirith opened the top half of the pod, and they stepped out into a garden of water, trees and stone.

The podcar platform stood at the tip of the triangular tower they had ascended. Kieler looked across a wide terrace that spanned the distance between the three tallest towers of the citadel. They stood upon the very top of the first tower. The second tower, some distance away to his left, was The Empyrean, supporting a corner of the terrace, but rising far, far above it. The third tower, on the right, extended several stories above this garden terrace, and Kieler imagined the view of the garden from that tower would be spectacular.

The air here was calm, but the garden was alive with the ringing and rhythms of water on rock. Kieler was speechless, but Velirith whispered, "This is nice. Often the breeze rustles the haventhalls and the subtleties of the water tones are drowned out."

Just outside the podcar, they stood listening between two ponds, flat as mirrors and reflecting the puffy clouds above.

"It's like a symphony," he whispered back, starting forward very slowly. Kieler had heard water and he had heard a symphony, but never a water symphony. He couldn't get his mind around what he was hearing. Runs and trills, percussive beats, xylophone-like melodies, everything tuned to produce harmonies across many octaves.

It was as if there were instruments hidden behind the trees and rocks, but on close examination, it *was* the trees and rocks producing the sound! A waterfall nearby filled a hollowed rock until it tipped, splashing down ten feet to tap upon a hollow log and produce a certain note. A pond overflowed at just the right rate to splat drops on a flat rock in perfect rhythm. Kieler pinpointed one cascade that produced a run of notes over gradually increasing rock sizes. And behind it all, somewhere deep into the garden, was a deep bass thrum, as the main water supply surged up and out from below in a slow, quarter-time rhythm to the overall beat of the concert.

And that was only the audible music.

The visual beauty was ethereal. Symphony Garden unveiled tempting rock formations, millions of gallons of flowing and standing water, and abundant plant life, especially haventhalls. All around the garden, the tall haventhalls reached for the sky, their height amplified by starting far above Lake Skyfall. Looking suspended in mid-air, they formed a backdrop like an amphitheater, evidently planted many years apart. The oldest and tallest lined the far edge of the terrace, and the closer rows stepped down like a choir on descending risers.

Other smaller groves formed islands in the many shapely ponds arranged in just the right proportion to give the place a depth far beyond its actual dimensions. Nevertheless, those dimensions were not small.

Some haventhall groves grew so thick that Kieler could not see into them. Narrow, stony paths entered between the trees and immediately disappeared, enticing lovers to enter their secret, darkening depths.

The entire park was made up of these seductive paths. They wound gracefully through the ponds, next to and behind waterfalls, over stone-arch bridges, between small but steep cliffs, over rocky outcroppings, even into darkened caves cleverly hidden behind freestanding rock formations. With so many forks and splits in the paths, it was a park asking to be walked through and beckoning to be explored.

And so they did. Kieler and Velirith walked slowly, Kieler in complete rapture, starting left and walking near the edgeless pool that encircled the entire terrace. He asked one more question before lapsing into a peaceful silence. "Is there an underwater rail to keep visitors from washing over the side?"

Velirith shrugged. "Jump in and see."

Kieler let the comment slide. The rail-less Rim made the garden seem to float even higher above the basin of Velakun. It was unnerving and increased the silent thrill in the atmosphere. He did not shy from walking as close to the pool as possible.

Their path brought them near water dropping from the rocky grottos, and those too were designed so that as one walked, different themes of the never-ending and ever-changing concert were emphasized simply by their proximity. Kieler stopped under a particular waterfall in the space between rock and water. The fall bounced and surged in a slow *cooshaaah, cooshaaah* rhythm as the water spilled over a cliff just higher than he was tall.

Velirith followed a few feet behind, gracefully allowing him to absorb as much as he was able at his own pace, stopping when he stopped.

On a narrow strip of path between a cliff and a pond, Kieler paused and asked her, "Those haventhalls, why are they so tall? And why are they always growing out of the water?"

"They need lots of water to live. And they must be in water to sprout. That *is* different from most other trees, true? And these trees are not as tall as the ancient ones in the lake. Do you know how they got their name? There's some dispute whether it's from 'Heaven Tall' or 'Heaven Fall'. I feel like it's the second name, 'Heaven Fall'. That seems right to me. They tell kids in school that the first ones fell out of the sky." She shrugged as if unsure what she believed about the myth. But she was opening up. Her young cynicism was occluded by the true joy she felt walking through her favorite place on Zotikas. Even her mischief succumbed to the overwhelming tranquility of the place.

One of the path choices led away from the Rim, and Kieler headed across a very narrow causeway between two large ponds. Even the causeway curved gently, intentionally slowing one's pace and forcing a person to concentrate on the walk itself, not on the outside world. The causeway split near the center of the ponds, and Kieler chose a way that led landward up along a narrow ledge of rock and eventually atop a narrow ridgeline. The way widened near the crest just enough to allow two or three people to sit on the stones that seemed placed there expressly for sitting. So Kieler sat, and Velirith sat on a rock across from him, still looking at him more than the garden.

This spot looked down opposite the causeway on a deeply shaded pool. Some sort of leafy plant floated on its calm surface. Stepping stones led out a few jumps to near the middle of the pond so that one could stand there surrounded by water. Kieler's vantage was also high enough to look out over the edge of the garden and see the Rim of Velakun in the not-so-far distance. But here he was separated from everything else.

Kieler breathed deeply and slowly let it out. He smiled and knew it was a peaceful, relaxed smile. He didn't mind that Velirith was studying him. This place just poked a hole in his façade and let the tension run out.

Finally, he turned to her and said, "See anything worthwhile?"

She smiled back at him. Her smile was relaxed too, as if she had let go of her scorn and disdain for the petty games to which she was exposed as the house leader's daughter. She nodded, her silver eyes glittering with reflected Rei-light mixed with the greenery of the garden.

CHAPTER ELEVEN

Something Kieler hadn't noticed at first was the smell of the place: misty, to be sure, and full of green freshness, but also a lightness to the atmosphere that could not be attributed to mere altitude.

"Cota Aurelios says that you can tell the mood and mind of a person by the paths they choose through the garden." She shrugged. "Me, I feel like the garden changes my mood every time I come here."

The name Aurelios tugged at Kieler's memory, but for the moment, in this peaceful place, he couldn't place it. He thought lazily about the path he chose, settling on this relative high spot. "Can you tell anything about me by my choices?"

She thought about it, looking around. "Nothing specific. But choosing to stop on higher ground with wider views indicates you are looking for control, for as much input as you can get so that you can make the best decisions on how to act. I think it also shows you're not afraid to expose yourself in hope of gaining positive attention. Then again, I'm not as good at this as Aurelios."

Kieler raised an eyebrow and had to admit that hers was a good guess. He did like being able to see around him, to be unsurprised and have time to choose his reactions. He gave her a slight nod of agreement and asked, "Who's Aurelios? And what's he a master of?"

Velirith looked over the pond. "He's my mentor. The Master of Theater Velaki. He knows every major play ever produced in Velakun's history and more. He knows much of their spiritual meaning too."

This intrigued Kieler. He had never given much thought or credence to "spiritual" matters. Not that he disbelieved in a spiritual world, he just hadn't seen how it could be important in getting him to his goals. "If there is a Spirit of Peace, this place is its dwelling."

She nodded, not looking away from the pond.

233

EPISODE 2 - HIGH RAILS OF ARDAN

There was a long period of silence between them, and then Kieler realized something. "Where is everyone? A place this beautiful should be teeming with people trying to get away from it all." They were out of sight of the podcar platform, but he had seen no one and assumed no one had come up behind them.

Shrugging, she stared down at the water. "People are busy. They are more comfortable in a life full of busyness than in a simple moment of peace. If everyone made time to get away from it all, there wouldn't be an 'all' to get away from. Most don't even consider pursuing the Spirit of Peace. I imagine if I had given you a choice of where to go, say a garden, the central generator, or the government district, you wouldn't have chosen the Symphonic Garden."

He had to agree. But he would have made the wrong choice.

Kieler wandered off into his own thoughts and considered how everything associated with the house of Vel was different than he had expected. The nobles of other houses were so predictable. He could count on them to do anything they could to further their own self-interest. This selfishness made them easy to manipulate.

Velator, however, was different. Here he was helping Kieler even though he had little to gain from it. In two days, Arvel, undoubtedly the Vel's most expensive procurator, would be in Avertori petitioning for the return of Orlazrus' House. Kieler's interaction with other houses had taught him that they were petty, self-absorbed and fearful that what power they had was always threatened. Perhaps House Vel's isolated location afforded them such natural protection that they were less paranoid. Most houses manipulated every detail to their advantage, employing intrigues and deception and generally treating others badly.

It had been Kieler's intention to ally with one of the lesser houses and use them as a stepping stone up into one of the more significant ones where he could wield enough influence to bring down the Omeron—the political system that had killed his parents.

CHAPTER ELEVEN

Yet he found himself in the House of Vel. Though not the strongest house now, they were definitely the most notable: This house had ruled the Avertoric Omeron for much of the last thousand years. Yet Kieler was still unsure about his decision. Would this house have enough influence and power left to leverage? And being the most remote house headquarters, would he be able to communicate enough with Movus? And how could he remain active in the Coin? He'd have to figure out a way to visit Avertori more often.

House Vel had been in decline for most of the last 150 years, most obviously when they lost the Executive Chairmanship to house Ek. So in essence Kieler had just jumped onto a sinking ship. Now, he had to make sure that the ship stayed afloat long enough for him to accomplish his purpose.

"Let's go!" said Velirith, suddenly standing.

Kieler blinked, surprised. "Why? I thought you liked it here."

"Yes, but you're not here anymore. You're back out there again. You're in the scheming world." And she waved her arm indicating the world beyond the garden.

Kieler scowled but realized she was right. He needed to focus on his mission anyway, and this enchanted garden spellbound him from that purpose. He stood and they started down the ridge. Following her slim, curving form, they took a different way back, a way that led by one of the water-bound haventhall groves. He craned his neck to look up into the thick branches very high above his head. A split in the path led into the trees. It was so immediately shaded that it caught Kieler's eye.

He couldn't resist a quick look. Ducking into the dim, narrow path between two trees, he squinted to try and get his eyes to adjust more quickly. He stumbled as the stony path rose steeply—something he didn't expect. He went just a few paces and realized the pathway changed from stones to wooden slats. Seeing better now, he looked up and saw the path wound up and around the trunks of the towering trees, a virtual aerial maze with benches and hidden nooks at various spots high above his head.

The draw to explore was suddenly interrupted. "Oh no you don't!" Velirith grabbed him by the arm. She had realized he had deviated from her lead and had run up behind him.

"But it's so—"

"Come back out in the sunlight, and I'll tell you," she insisted. She quickly dropped his arm as if his touch were contagious.

Bemused, he followed her out, more than a little wistful.

She stood for a moment, shifting, and Kieler thought she looked the most uncomfortable he had yet seen her.

"What?" he demanded.

"Well," she started hesitantly, "there's some... folklore about these trees—not all haventhalls—just this particular grove, that, well..."

Kieler was totally perplexed and amused. She seemed embarrassed.

"Oh, never mind!" And she stormed off toward the podcar.

This time Kieler gently caught her arm, mindful of her injury. "Oh no, Lhea Velirith. There's more to this. I've never seen you flustered, so this must be good. Though I can't imagine..."

She was truly red-faced now. "Oh, it's just a folktale! It's stupid." She started to say more but instead she snapped her mouth shut, as if trapping the words she didn't want to say. He tried to pry it out of her, but she refused to utter another word.

So intrigued was Kieler that he tried a feint. "Fine. I'll just ask your father why you chased me into that haventhall grove." He shrugged and strode off down the path as if dismissing the whole thing.

He was surprised to be hit with a shower of tiny, gravelly pebbles. Ducking, he turned back, ready for another onslaught. But Velirith was storming past him.

236

CHAPTER ELEVEN

"You'll do no such thing!" she huffed, trying to act older and nearly pushing him into a stream on her way by.

Kieler was unable to respond through his laughter.

He followed close on her heels, and as they rounded another rock outcrop, he suddenly bumped into her halted figure. "Hey! Sorry, I—"

He saw why she stopped. As Kieler spoke, a man turned from a low, interior wall and looked up at them. Chance.

Again.

Infuriatingly, he again did not seem surprised. In his left hand he held a pickaxe, sharply honed. Defensively, Kieler stepped in front of Velirith.

It was she who broke the silence. "Cota Chance, why are you chipping at that wall?"

Now Kieler saw what the man had been doing—chipping at a waist-high retaining wall. Water gently overflowed the entire length of the wall from a small pond behind it. On the ground next to the wall was a small, cultivated garden sheltered from the wind and watered by the pond.

Chance had collected a small bowl of wet clay chips from the surface of the wall. Kieler's curiosity almost outweighed the unnerved feeling he got whenever this man showed up.

Chance looked back and forth from Kieler to Velirith, and the look made Kieler aware of how close he had stopped to Velirith, and how genuinely playful their interaction had been just moments ago.

"Why such a sudden shift of spirits? You were having such a good time."

So the man had been listening—if not intentionally watching them. The realization raised Kieler's hackles as much as the man's pale, unwrinkled face. Why didn't the man look aged? Chronologically, he had to be at least fifty based on what Velator had told Kieler of the man's past.

EPISODE 2 - HIGH RAILS OF ARDAN

Kieler repeated Velirith's question, "What are you doing up here?" Kieler knew that as a Cota the man could take offense at his aggressive tone. But he seemed incapable of rousing to any kind of emotion at all.

With his pick, Chance gestured to the leeward side of the wall. The angle of the wall blocked the wind but reflected sunlight off the water. On the ground before the wall grew a long cluster of succulents, green even in winter at this altitude. "I'm fertilizing my garden."

"With wall chunks?" Velirith asked.

Chance shrugged. "I am a botanist. I powder the chunks because the minerals in this wall enhance the growth of this alovea."

Velirith gave Kieler a look—and he wasn't sure how she conveyed it to him—that said, "*He's telling the truth.*"

But Kieler had an insight of his own. "But that's not all you're doing, is it?"

The most the man ever did was hint at a smile. "I am talking to a young man and young woman who seem to be enjoying a walk in the garden together, despite the gravity of the world around them."

Somehow, that seemed threatening to Kieler—no, not threatening, condemning, as if he were not doing his duty.

Kieler wanted desperately to confront this fraud, but the man had better credentials and legitimacy than Kieler himself. He knew he wasn't what he appeared to be, yet Kieler couldn't expose him. *Perhaps that's how Velirith feels about me.*

Velirith spoke very deliberately, watching Chance. "Well Cota Chance, we're going down to the underpinnings to show the Ortessi something he will be very interested in."

The man's lifeless eyes actually betrayed a flicker of emotion: surprised concern. Then it was gone. Another shrug. No verbal response.

CHAPTER ELEVEN

Kieler wanted to go. He felt nervous. The least reason was the pick in Chance's hand. The pressing reason was that the man gave him the creeps.

"Cota Chance," Kieler said, his voice tight, formal, "we'll see you at the New Dawn Ceremony. Goodbye."

"See you," and the man watched them go. Kieler could swear the man seemed nervous himself.

They quickly walked the rest of the way to the podcar. They passed between the two entrance ponds, their surfaces rippling.

As they approached the pod, Kieler stopped and looked back, wistfully hoping for a taste of that peace he had felt before they ran into Chance. It eluded him, and instead a general feeling of uneasiness persisted. A light breeze arose and Kieler heard an ethereal sound, eerie and mournful. It seemed to be coming first from one side of the terrace, then moving around it as if following the wind. "What's that new music?"

"The edges of the garden have hollowed pipes of haventhall branches, tuned to make those harmonies."

Kieler wished they could stay and listen, but he wanted to get away from Verr Chance. And something else was bugging him. He closed his eyes to block out thoughts of the unnerving Cota. And he felt something. Vibration.

He opened his eyes and knew the rippling of the ponds was not caused by the breeze.

"We need to go to the generator station," he said flatly.

Velirith turned on him, gaping. "Aw, you guessed it! That's where I'm taking you for your favorite place."

He gently but urgently pressed her toward the podcar. "No. Something is wrong."

She looked at him very strangely, and he knew, even though his mind was on the generators, that she was wondering if perhaps he was as intuitive as she.

They climbed in the podcar and closed the hatch. Velirith dialed an address into the podcar and engaged the lever.

"You've known Cota Chance for a long while," Kieler began, preparing for his loaded question. "What's your read on him?"

She looked at Kieler, analyzing in her uniquely perceptive way. "Cota Chance wasn't surprised to see us. In fact, he wanted *us* to see *him*. And he wanted you to know he was watching."

Kieler nodded as the car began its descent. He wondered aloud if Chance would follow them intending further trouble.

Velirith shook her head, sure of herself again. "If he wanted trouble, the garden would have been the perfect place." After some thought, she continued, "Cota Chance has always been an odd instructor. I know he is competent in his field, steady as clockwork, and more competent than he even lets on. But I've always felt there was more to him. Something not quite... good."

It suddenly occurred to Kieler that Velirith would be a great partner in some of his more elicit dealings. She read through the haze of deception much more quickly and clearly than even Bags did. And Bags had quite a bit of experience. His look must have betrayed his appraisal for again she smiled at his unstated compliment.

"Thanks," she said, and then added just loud enough for Kieler to hear, "Fraud."

The podcar slid down the invisible rails, magnificence all around them, but Kieler wasn't gawking now. He was calculating. Velirith would study him until she had him all figured out. It made him question himself, *Was this going to work?*

CHAPTER TWELVE

Generators.

Kieler's heart was a generator.

His father had created magnificent generators. Magnificent in their compactness and efficiency. And more importantly his father had also created the concentrator that purified the magal into a much more densely energized material. If Ek Threzhel had wanted to help the world develop, rather than protect his little corner, he would have encouraged the development of compact generators. Smaller generators would have affected the world in great ways.

Small towns and remote places across Zotikas could not get the massive generators like the ones in the cities. It was cost prohibitive or impossible to transport the giant components. But a generator that Kieler could haul in his backpack, or any size in between—such an innovation would revolutionize small town economics. Kieler's father had envisioned an economic revival comparable to the early years of Avertori.

But Threzhel had quashed that with his small-minded thinking and, according to Movus, the killing of Kieler's father.

But Kieler couldn't afford to think about that now. He smashed down the memory of his father's death.

The podcar fell in a controlled plummet from the light above to the tunneled darkness below. Kieler knew his perceptive leaps were limited. But when it came to generators, he had been around them his entire life, and he knew when something was off beam. He had felt the smooth, almost imperceptible pulse of Velakun's heartbeat. Compared to Avertori's pulse, strained and palpitating with age, Velakun's generators ran like a man in his prime, sure and well nourished. At least until now.

The workmanship on the Velakun generators must be outstanding, built back when the guiding principles were precision and improvement. But like the podcar, all of Zotikas was falling, its decline accelerating.

History was odd, he thought. Five hundred years was a long time. It had taken about that long for the Avertoric Hegemon to reach its peak from a ruined isle, and it had taken about that long again for it to deteriorate to the point where it was about to fly apart. But 500 years was nothing relative to the Dead Ones. Kieler knew from growing up in their ruins that they had built a great civilization that had thrived for far longer than a thousand years. But they had been gone for far longer than that. Nothing guaranteed the Avertoric Hegemon would not go the way of the Dead Ones.

Adding to his anxiety, the lights outside the podcar flared, brightening unnaturally. Velirith looked at him, knowing he was right, and concerned about whatever he was concerned about. For her to be concerned about anything beyond her plays and pranks seemed unnatural to him too.

The podcar swooped from vertical to horizontal, traveled another forty seconds, and came to a stop in the large entranceway to the generator station, well below Center Isle's surface. A gate and gatehouse ran from floor to ceiling.

"We'll have to check in," Velirith told him as they ran forward. The vibration beneath their feet rattled the metal gates ahead of them.

Velirith stepped up to the gatehouse window, peered in and frowned. She tried the door and couldn't get in, but Kieler found the gate itself open and they dashed into the power plant complex.

They needed to alert someone, but the fact that no one was around made that impossible. Running through the administrative hallways, they shortly came to the main dome that held three

CHAPTER TWELVE

industrial generators equally spaced in a triangle under the wide dome. Long catwalks and rails for service cranes connected the spinning, horizontal wheels. The nearest generator, labeled with a huge "1", had its magal fuel rods pressed full into its outer circumference. Except for the absence of operating technicians, everything looked normal.

But everything didn't sound or feel normal. And as they stood next to the number one generator, a sickening *creak* of metal groaned out of the wheel and the vibration they had both felt from a distance became a full-fledged shaking, making it hard even to stand.

Kieler knew what was happening and he even suspected why. "They're all over-revving!" he found himself shouting. "We have to disengage the magal pushrods. Now!"

They leapt up the stairs and clanged down the catwalk to the control pedestal of the # 1 generator. Beside the pedestal was a large, red, electrical lever-switch marked "ALARM." Without a thought Kieler yanked it down. Klaxons blared, not helping him think, but he hoped they would sound throughout the city.

Velirith was wide-eyed but cool-headed next to him. "There has to be a disengage switch or even emergency disengage lever!" he shouted. This close and looking down on the flying wheel, the noise hurt. Velirith scanned, but Kieler knew what he was looking for. On the panel was a series of three switches that when thrown consecutively would electromechanically shut down the generator. He punched them without hesitation—and detected absolutely no change. He looked at Velirith with dread.

He looked around the back of the control pedestal and found a metal panel peeled off and a bird's nest of wires yanked out. Panicked, he started to try to figure out the wiring and realized it would take longer than they probably had. He looked around and scanned the catwalk.

There! Against a vertical beam was a lever as tall as he was, clearly marked "EMERGENCY STOP." Linkage led along a catwalk

243

that ran over the spinning wheel and then radially outward to the control rods. It was entirely mechanical.

He leapt for the lever and yanked it down. It had probably not been used in literally hundreds of years. It did not yield to his initial pull, and he braced his feet against the rail and pulled with everything in him. It moved two inches and stopped cold.

Instantly, he knew something blocked it. Looking down he found a metal bar the size of his little finger stuck through the mechanism and bent around in a loop, making it impossible for him to dislodge without great strength or... *tools!*

He searched his surroundings again. "Velirith, I need a pry-bar! Anything." He knew there was desperation in his voice. The wheel in front of them was now screaming, literally pulling itself apart. Nothing burned because a well-built generator had no friction; they were magnetically suspended. But the radial forces at the speeds this thing was turning would stretch steel spokes until they tore apart. And with each spoke weighing several tons and moving way too fast, when the wheels tore apart they would rip through *anything*. If *all* the wheels came apart, it was possible to take out enough of the foundation of the citadel to bring the tower above crashing down.

And there wasn't a tool in sight. He strained desperately to untwist the metal bar but couldn't even budge it. He looked for a way to unhook the lever and pull directly on the physical linkage, but it was all too strong without tools.

Velirith was tugging at his coat sleeve; she had an idea. She shouted, "The alarm lever?"

After a quick moment of incomprehension, Kieler looked at the metal lever the length of his forearm, the switch he had thrown to sound the alarm—which they could now barely hear. If he could break it off, he could use it. He jumped to it. To get an angle on breaking it off the hinge, he had to disengage the switch, and unfortunately that silenced the alarm.

244

CHAPTER TWELVE

It didn't matter. Someone would come. But undoubtedly too late.

Kieler and Velirith got their first break. Prying the switch 90 degrees to the way it was supposed to swing snapped the hinge pin, and the metal bar came free instantly. Together, he and Velirith pried open the bar blocking the emergency stop lever from moving. Within seconds they were able to pull it apart enough to pull it out from the mechanism.

Kieler yanked the man-sized lever again. This time it came down, and the linkage pulled the magnetic rods out from all around the circumference of the spinning wheel housing. With the first motion of the extracting rods, the wheel slowed, no longer being pushed by the rods. It was still spinning fast, having no physical friction to slow it, but the induced magnetic fields of the coils were electrically dragging on it, slowing it. They were out of danger. On this one.

After a moment of relief, Kieler noticed one last horrifying problem: The electric coils were drooping. They were melting! Way too much induced current from the overspun wheel.

That wasn't a problem anymore on this decelerating generator, but the other two couldn't be far behind. If the other generators' coils started arcing and dripping molten copper onto the spinning wheel, it would only accelerate the disintegration.

Exchanging looks of near hopelessness, Kieler told Velirith what she already knew, "Two more to go."

He took a second to think, then, "You take this pry-bar to generator three on the right. I'll get another from the alarm at generator two over to the left. There has to be one there. Do the best you can. Or better yet: Run away!" But Kieler knew she wouldn't run, even if he had no reason to think otherwise.

She grabbed the bar out of his hand and bolted down the catwalk. They could already hear the generator screaming. Their chances of making it in time were almost none.

Kieler bolted for #2.

EPISODE 2 - HIGH RAILS OF ARDAN

He thought about Velirith as he ran. Despite her selfish immaturity, he liked her. But she would probably die. He would too, but he had accepted that risk a long time ago. Did he bring this on her? This had to be the Cortattis doing. They probably killed the guards and infused...

Kieler brought to conscious thought the only explanation he could come up with to explain what was happening here: concentrated magal rods had been inserted into these older generators. They were not designed to run this fast.

Did Cortatti now have some form of his super-generator? Or just the purified magal? Perhaps they were using it on just their bigger generators. Perhaps that was what made their cutter so fast.

His flash of thoughts ceased as he approached the next control pedestal. The claxons suddenly blared again. *Smart girl!* She didn't need another alarm switch for leverage, she had the first one. So she had thrown the alarm at her generator to alert the city. *Or had she thrown it to let me know she made it?*

He looked across the dome in the over-bright, glaring arc-light from the wildly revving generators. At the other generator he saw Velirith's tiny form busy at the emergency lever.

She had beaten him despite recovering from her own injuries. With his limp, he justified, she could hardly jibe him. Despite imminent death, the thought made him smile as he ripped the alarm switch off the side of his panel. This generator was indeed in the same shape as the last—wires ripped out, bar wrapped through the Emergency Stop lever.

There was one terrifying difference: These generator coils were already dripping metal!

Electricity arced across shorting coils. The ones below the wheel didn't matter, but the ones above were melting onto the spinning rotor just below his feet. The molten metal wasn't doing what Kieler had expected, off-balancing the wheel. Instead, the wheel was flinging the liquid metal off at high speed in random

246

directions! The arcing and dripping metal created fireworks and a volcano together.

Then, just to make it more interesting, he realized that the saboteurs had wrapped the bar through the mechanism *twice* on this one, leaving little to pry at. What else could he do?

Frantically, he worked his makeshift pry-bar into the bent metal. He hadn't been working five seconds when a stream of molten copper flung from the wheel and splattered on the column next to him. Liquid metal splashed onto his skin and clothes. Molten heat seared his face and hands. He screamed, falling to his knees and dropping the pry-bar. It clanged down through the catwalk to the floor below.

"Velirith!" he screamed impotently over the noise. The pain was mind obliterating, the hot metal cooking the skin on his hands and the left side of his face.

He stood, trying yet to think through the pain, to think of something he could do to shut down the groaning, screeching wheel beside and beneath him.

A streak of metal shot out below him, ripping out the catwalk supports. As the catwalk fell, Kieler felt the wheel hit the housing and disintegrate in every direction beneath him. A million pieces exploded outward from the hub, and Kieler fell with the ruined catwalk. Blackness, as the lights of the dome went out. Blackness, as his head hit something metallic.

CHAPTER THIRTEEN

If this were the afterlife, it was dominated by pain. Soft noises, a nearby crackling and popping, and the rustling of clothing. He tried to open his eyes and the right one came open a little.

Sparking lights and the soft glow of distant luzhril. He wondered if Velirith had been sent to the same afterlife destination. Her annoying gibes might take his mind off the searing pain.

His head swam in a sea of pain and dizziness.

A silhouette passed in front of his right eye. Not Velirith. A round head, looking at him.

A short eternity later he felt something cold press against the left side of his face, and his eyes shot open again from the pain. He must have passed out again. The crackling had mostly died away, and the face looked to be that of Chance, floating above him. Something pried his mouth open—not that he could put up even a mote of resistance. Then a thick liquid went down his throat. Instead of gagging, he swallowed the bitter pulp.

Then things really got weird. Even with his eyes closed he saw faces: Movus, Velirith, Chance, Bags and Feleanna. He cringed back when Feleanna seemed to slap the left side of his face. Then Velator hovered over him, accusing him of killing his daughter.

Kieler screamed.

And then he was opening his eyes again. The pain had lessened, but the left side of his head felt like fried kovar meat. The light still dim, he heard muttering. Spirits?

Although it sounded like a conversation, it was but one voice. Chance again?

CHAPTER THIRTEEN

"Shoulda let the lousy slink die."

"But he wouldn't have died. Just been an ugly cripple."

"Shoulda killed him myself."

"Ah, ah, ah! Boreas would know!"

"He doesn't know everything."

"He knows how to keep you alive."

"Or kill you."

"Shut up and tie him."

The muttering stopped when Kieler tilted his head to see the speaker. This time he was sure he saw Chance's face hovering over him. Through the haze and dizziness, Kieler saw—no, *perceived*—a hideous shadow superimposed over Chance's face. Searing pain rippled across the left side of his head. Was the man torturing him?

The apparition reached up and pulled something from the side of Kieler's face that he hadn't realized was there, and agony anew shot through his brain. As he wandered into consciousness once again, he became aware that the left side of his face was itching as if from the bites of a million spit-fleas.

Despite his own condition, the first thing he found himself wondering was if Velirith was still alive. Then he wondered if he himself was still alive.

No crackling. No rustling. No muttering. Something close creaked then fell with a *clang.* The dim glow of far-off luzhril was the only light.

As his awareness grew, the itching intensified. He tried to reach up to push away what must be a swarm of insects. He found he could move neither arm, both tightly immobile against his body.

Horror overwhelmed his mind at the thought of what could be crawling on his face, the intense prickling, not being able to swat them away, not being able to see them. It was as if something were eating the muscles and tissues of his face.

He squirmed in panic. Screaming, he raised his head and looked to his right into a jumbled, tangled mess of metal and mechanisms. The catwalks and copper coils were a packed mass of rubble, reminding him of his home under the Plate.

Velirith was in that mess.

Thrashing and nearly mad with the crawling itch, he looked left and saw someone running toward him through the islands of less densely strewn debris. He stopped writhing, a tiny hope and an enormous desperation competing within him. It was An'essa!

She was above him in moments, her usual stoicism replaced by an expression somewhere between confusion and revulsion as she gazed down at him. Before she could speak, and in spite of his own agony, he found himself shouting at An'essa.

"Velirissh! She was at the number three generator!" Though his voice came out slurred and distorted, he pointed with his eyes and a jerk of his head, his meaning clear.

An'essa's horror melted into terror as she began to grasp that her charge was in the middle of that destruction. She bolted for where the third generator should have been, vaulting into the wreckage.

In moments she was out of sight, obscured by debris.

In agony and frustration, Kieler screamed again.

Why is she leaving? Why didn't I tell her about Velirith after *she helped* me *?*

What's more important: my mission or Velirith?

EPISODE 3:
ATTRACTION AND
REPULSION

CHAPTER ONE

Velirith couldn't quite understand what was going on, her mind cloudy and the light very dim.

Her father spoke to a man lying on the floor of the wrecked generator complex. "We're not untying you."

Confused, Velirith stood next to Velator and Dr. Yuric and examined the grotesque figure at their feet. The man on the ground seemed to be missing half his face. The burns on one side were so severe that the blackened skin was shriveled and sunken beneath his eye, highlighting the shape of the skull beneath. The hair above his left ear was burned away, and a greenish, translucent goo covered what remained of the red and black skin of his scalp. That same greenish substance was plastered on every part of the left side of his face. Bits of pinkish-brown skin seemed to be bubbling under the paste. Some part of her realized this man had only a few minutes of agonized life before him.

His hands and arms were bound hastily but tightly to his torso with ragged strips of singed green and gold cloth. The clothing not covered by the bindings was also spotted with burn holes. And finally, his legs were bound together around partly burned pants with strands of copper wire, likely from one of the shredded generator coils.

An'essa stood by Velirith, mute. Velirith looked around at the twisted catwalks and chunks of metal, trying to remember where she was and why she was here. She shook her aching head,

252

trying to force herself back to full consciousness. She heard the man at her feet moan and open his eyes a bit more.

"Why?" the man cried. In obvious pain, the man's speech came out airy and slurred.

Velirith looked at her father. "Did you and Doctor Yuric bind him? Who is he? Is he dangerous?"

Velator glanced at Velirith, a mix of horror and concern on his face. "No, of course not. We found him this way."

Minutes ago, An'essa had brought Velirith, dazed, out of the wreckage. Her father had hugged her tightly, and Velirith had assured him she had only been knocked out but was otherwise whole. Still muddled, she joined her father and the doctor as they had turned to gape at the writhing body, foul smelling and disfigured. Detached, it was as if a part of Velirith's mind was intentionally denying her comprehension.

Velator looked at her again, realizing something. Sympathy—for her, not the man—seeped into his eyes. "Daughter," he said softly, "This is Orlazrus."

Wires connected in her brain, and cognition flooded her with horrified shock. "Nooo!" she screamed. An'essa grabbed her, steadying her. Her father stepped in front of her as she felt herself lurch toward the man on the ground.

Orlazrus spasmed toward her. He seemed to see her for the first time and relaxed. His uncontrolled writhing eased, her safety a balm to him.

Velirith inhaled in a burst of short, sharp gasps. With Velator blocking the sight of the ruined man on the ground, she eventually began to regain some control of her emotions and voice.

"Father! He *felt* the generators shaking apart! He knew what to do! He saved the first generator and I ran to save the second while he went for the third." Her words tumbled out.

"My lever wasn't blocked. I was shutting it down when a part from his generator flew over and knocked the catwalk out from under me. I fell. I hit my head. He told me to run away, but I didn't. He was trying to save us. *Again!*" She was blubbering, now looking past her father to the twisted form. "*And why don't you want to untie him?*"

"Velirith," her father held her face to make her look at him. "It's not that we don't want to. It's that Dr. Yuric thinks he is bound to keep him from further injuring himself. The green paste seems to be some sort of healing salve."

She looked over to Dr. Yuric. "You mean you don't know? Maybe it's still burning him!"

Dr. Yuric shook his head in consternation. "I've never seen this compound before. The tissue beneath the salve is not receding as it would be from a toxin. And strange as it may be, his face looks to be healing already."

The doctor held out his examination rod, its luzhril gem shining on the patient. He leaned toward the disfigured man. Velirith cringed back farther behind her father. Orlazrus groaned and croaked out an unintelligible word that Velirith interpreted as her own name.

"We need to get him to the med-center," Doctor Yuric declared.

"The medics have been alerted, but with no power to the podcars, they'll have to carry him the whole way," Velator added.

The doctor nodded, and for the first time Velirith became aware that there were a great many rescue and response people moving through the debris looking for other injured.

"Father, I believe the Ortessi and I were the only ones in the whole complex. I don't know where the workers went."

Velator nodded comprehension but said, "I hope no one else was caught in here. But Orlazrus didn't tie himself up. Someone else was here."

Velirith puzzled on that as Hezek, Chief of Facilities, approached.

"What have you found, Hezek?" Velator asked.

CHAPTER ONE

Hezek, casting an uneasy glance at the hideous Orlazrus, reported. "No other casualties so far. But the generator next to where we found Verr Ortessi is completely gone. It looks like the one where Velirith was found was also destroyed by this one coming apart.

"The generator by the administration offices is still intact, but overstressed. We might be able to get partial power out of it in a few days. Best I can tell you for now, sir."

Four men came and gently lifted Orlazrus onto a pallet. He moaned again as they carried him off.

"An'essa, go with Velirith to the hospital. Make sure she's treated and examined for any other injuries."

Velirith didn't resist. She wanted to be going where Orlazrus was going. He was the bravest, most self-sacrificing fraud she knew.

CHAPTER TWO

She wept on and off until evening. She kept visualizing the black, cracked skin under the translucent green goo that covered the side of his head.

Admittedly she didn't know this man well, this man who called himself Ortessi. She hadn't had long enough to open him up and find out what was really inside him. And she hadn't had the chance to open up to him either. She suspected, from his selfless actions in addition to her intuition, that a heart of pure luzhril burned inside him.

But the outside of him didn't agree with the inside. He always wore a mask—and that mask was so badly burned that she knew his chances to live were small. Once in the medical ward, the staff wouldn't even let her look at him. They wanted him to rest and keep stress to a minimum.

In a room down the hall from him, the doctors gave her medicine that made her drowsy, but her own pains and worries kept her awake for a long time. Worry that this mysterious man might die before she got to see him, before she got to know him. And before she got to thank him.

Eventually she drifted off and didn't wake until early the next morning. Feeling much better, she woke with a determination to see the man she always hesitated to name, knowing only his false names. She would not be refused. Like a powercoach, she charged down the med-center hallway.

How has this blasted con-artist made himself so important to me? Especially when I value truth so highly and all he represents is lies?

CHAPTER TWO

She had questions... and thanks. Maybe some answers would come out in his last confession. She wiped away tears before she opened the door to his room.

Why do I care for this deceiver?

Her first reaction when she looked at the sleeping man was sheer puzzlement. First, lying alone in the sterile Center Isle Hospital bed, he looked anonymous. He had no family and nothing to identify him in the homogenous surroundings. No uniform. No false bearing.

And it didn't look like they had done anything for him, except perhaps sedate him. No dressings covered his grizzly face. He looked grotesque. They hadn't unbound him; in fact, they had *re-bound* him with sterile bandages.

They *had* cut away his shredded and burned uniform coat, but that only made him look more nameless and unidentifiable.

But why hadn't they cleaned him up?

Her father came up behind her and leaned against the door frame to Orlazrus' room. Velirith examined the Ortessi's face. Now peeling and floating in the green gel, the blackened skin was still untended. The muscles underneath, which she knew had been shriveled by heat and made him look skeletal yesterday, seemed to have filled in some. And was that new, pink skin showing through the cracks in the curling burned skin?

She looked back at her father, her face an unvoiced question.

Her father walked up behind her and put a hand on her back. "No one knows why he isn't dead, Velirith. But everyone agrees the green gel seems to be making him better, even though he thrashes trying to get it off him when he's awake."

Questions flooded her mind. "Who did this to him? The green stuff?"

Her father shrugged.

She turned away from the Ortessi and her father, controlling tears as she looked out the hospital window. Iliss,

257

EPISODE 3 – ATTRACTION AND REPULSION

Zotikas' moon, was a tiny, white crescent over the Rim, clinging desperately to its feeble light as Rei burned away the night.

"Who attacked our generators, Father? Cortatti?" she asked, still gazing out the window.

"Probably," her father agreed uncertainly.

After several long, slow breaths, she turned and looked at the man on the bed again, almost unidentifiable. Unspoken, she asked herself the most troubling question of all, *Who is he?*

When she saw him the next morning, the Ortessi had obviously been tended. Medical staff had picked some of the flaking black skin out of the gel, and the general shape of his face seemed to be back. It wasn't just missing like the day before.

Though the doctors on Center Isle kept him sedated, he thrashed against his bonds and even screamed once, scaring her. His eyelids, lashes gone, fluttered in tortured sleep.

She sat by him.

For the first time in many years, she felt sorrow. She felt many other things, too—violated for one. That someone could strike at them this far from Avertori.

She wondered how.

She wondered what her father would do about it.

And she wondered what *she* would do about it.

She spent much of that day watching Orlazrus, giving him water when possible, though sedation kept him from full consciousness. Grotesque as his face had become, it was fascinating. Sometimes she thought she could *see* a section of skin move, like it was filling in. Bubbles seemed to form down by the skin and work themselves slowly to the surface of the green goo.

And it stank. Burnt hair. Sloughing burned skin. The green substance itself smelled bad, like some nasty boiled vegetable.

After two hours, a mood of anger hit her, and she took it out on the easiest target.

CHAPTER TWO

"You stink," she told the unconscious man. "You bring destruction and fear to *my* city? How dare you. Clothed in your green cloak of lies." She spat the words out between tears.

She looked around and listened. The hospital was empty. If all three generators had shredded at high speed, this facility would probably be full of casualties—if it were even still standing.

"Thank you," she whispered. "You who had no reason to die for us. Sometimes I think you resent us, or hate us. And yet without a second of consideration you put yourself in danger. For us."

She thought about how much she disdained politics and realized it wasn't the concept of politics she hated, the core goal of which was a smoothly running society. What she disdained was the selfish political maneuvering in which the Prime houses engaged. If everyone looked out for everyone else, if they served each other, it would be better for all. Isn't that what Orlazrus had just done? Served her and her city over his own needs, even his own life?

But did Velirith herself think that way? Orlazrus was right about one thing; as long as she was insulated, both by age and distance, from the responsibility of governance, she could be irresponsible and spoiled.

Destruction and fear. Yes, he had brought them to her city. And she resented him for that. But they were realities that other families, like the true Ortessis, had to deal with. Perhaps she would have to do something about these abhorrent realities too.

Velirith couldn't think straight, or feel straight. Emotion was stuffing her nose and pouring out her eyes. She took a kerchief and blew her nose loudly. Orlazrus' body jerked, startled, but he did not wake.

She laughed. She thought it funny when he felt pain or surprise or embarrassed. But there was a line. And his gruesome face, with its sunken cheek and scorched skin and burned away hair—that was way over the line.

EPISODE 3 – ATTRACTION AND REPULSION

"You'd better live, you brave fraud, just so I can torment you." And to improve the mood of her vigil, she started thinking of all the jibes and pranks she would play on him should he live.

On the third day, in the late afternoon, Dr. Yuric stated that he believed Verr Ortessi would live. It was miraculous, yes, and his recovery was far more rapid than normal.

A week after the generator disaster, they moved Orlazrus from Center Isle Hospital to Vel Estate.

On the following morning, overlooking Lake Skyfall, the Ortessi sat looking at her from across the breakfast table. Velirith took a deep breath and asked him directly, "Okay, Miracle Man, how come you're not dead?"

Most of the time, his face remained bandaged. But at times, like now, his raw skin just needed to breathe. The new, healing skin was bright red, as if it had been steamed.

And he was eating. Granted it was pureed grains and strained senye, but it had only been a week, and he was *eating*. "You can always tell if I'm lying right?" Orlazrus asked in reply, trying hard not to move his jaw much so as not to pull the tender skin of his cheek.

"Yes."

"Great," his voice raw through gritted teeth, "Try this answer: I don't know. I don't know how I still have a face."

"Well, don't you have two of them? Is the second as handsome as the first?"

Her victim accepted the verbal slap and compliment with a reddening that managed to momentarily match the colors of the two halves of his recovering face.

Velirith continued, examining the very pink, baby-like skin that had replaced his rugged man-skin. "But you suspect something, don't you? You know something more that you're not saying."

She could see him clench jaw muscles and gauge his reply. "Yes. But what I think makes no sense. I was definitely hallucinating

260

and any suspicion I have I'm not going to share because I don't know the... implications."

"Consequences," Velirith said over his last word. "You more accurately wanted to say 'consequences'. Because your conjectures could expose more of your true motives."

He glared at her and dabbed tenderly at a bit of mash that had flecked the new skin of his left cheek. She took that as confirmation of her insight.

Where his hair had burned away, her father's barber had delicately trimmed both sides to nearly match. He looked like a soldier, clean cut and wounded.

The fact that he was no longer missing part of his face after almost no time at all baffled everyone, especially Doctor Yuric, who had studied under the best physicians on Zotikas.

The gelatinous greenish paste had been consumed by the returning skin, almost like nutrients for an insect colony. He did look odd—the new skin so soft and pinkish, not tanned and weathered by life and Rei, and not whiskered like the right side of his face.

His healing and his bound state were total mysteries. And it was clear to Velirith that they were a mystery to Orlazrus too, but somehow for a different reason than for everyone else.

Meanwhile, the bowl of Velakun was abuzz. The Velaki, in isolation and protected by miles of mountains, had been attacked. It was more than unnerving; it was terrifying.

Velator had given the city workers time off—everyone except those repairing the generators—legitimately stating that he wanted no further strain on the power system. None of the arc lights worked, of course, and they were the main source of light on Center Isle and much of the Rim. Only luzhril still shone. At least luzhril was more plentiful here than Avertori.

Podcars still hovered where they had stopped when the generators had flown apart. Most terrified were those residents of

EPISODE 3 – ATTRACTION AND REPULSION

Velakun who were traveling the towers of Center Isle vertically and had to be hoisted up or down to the nearest service port.

Velator's leaders, once apprised of the events and both Orlazrus Ortessi's and Velirith's role in them, suspended much of their obstructionist bickering and agreed that building defenses was a must. Even Annavel had backed increasing their weapon supplies by "any rapid means possible."

But that, Velirith's father told her, was not easy. Cortatti, the probable perpetrator of this attack, also controlled the weapons monopoly. If the Ortessi's contacts under the Plate could provide magguns, it was now welcome. Unfortunately, the current supply was much less than the sudden demand. It would take time.

So Velirith found herself wondering how this fake Orlazrus knew all this underworld intrigue. She found herself involved with politics despite her natural abhorrence. And she blamed *him*.

She didn't care if it wasn't logical; she resented that *he* had popped her little bubble world. The fact that she liked him and admired his courage made it far worse. Here he was changing her world, destroying her peaceful insignificance, and rousing her to an activism she didn't want to activate.

She would make him pay.

The start of Orcad was delayed a month and the electric lights had been out an entire week. Students who would have started school that week enjoyed the leisure of time, many of them boating on the lake or hiking the Rim. Anything that didn't require electricity.

As a credit to Hezek's competency, he had Generator One up and running on the seventh day—but only at *half* its usual speed. As a show of solidarity, Velator ordered that all non-luzhril lights be turned out at the Estate. Never mind that they had a lot of luzhril, the darkened security lights were just one more intrusion into her world brought by the *Ortessi*.

Two enlightening ideas had surfaced to illuminate Velakun. First, Hezek had scrambled the city's maintenance crew and was

CHAPTER TWO

coordinating with Jarovel to connect the generator from the *Pride of Velik* to the power grid. Power lines and regulators needed to be laid and connected. Once operational, it would enable a majority of Center Isle to operate, including the podcars. And it should be done just before Orcad began.

The second idea was an obvious one: Light the Starstone. During festivals the huge stone bathed both city and Rim in a spectacular sparkling light in which party-goers could comfortably revel.

But there were technical difficulties. It took power to activate the device that controlled the magal and shield that regulated the Starstone. The power-fail "safe" mode kept the stone subdued. Hezek reported that the extreme power surges before the generators came apart had caused major damage to the activation mechanism.

Velirith preferred to blame the Ortessi for this as well—and for her childish attitude toward the entire affair.

So the day before the start of Academy, with winter still thick and white on the slopes outside the caldera, Velirith and her father had a conversation in the estate garden. The moment of quiet fellowship with her father reminded her painfully of their time together after her mother and brother died.

"Why? Why must I share both morning martial arts *and* a full engineering round with the Ortessi? I do not want to associate with him that much."

"Yet during his convalescence you spent even more time with him, yes?" her father answered.

"Yes. But I'm tired of him now. He'll live. He doesn't need me."

Velator took a different angle, "Why is An'essa with you even more now?"

"For my protection. And, yes, I believe you when you say that *they* are out to get us." She paused and added in a mumble, "I visited the *Pride* yesterday." Seeing their magnificent coach

263

stripped down to her decks brought back a clear mental picture of that battlecoach overtaking them on the plains of Ardan. The *Pride* was like a badly wounded patient, the thrumming drive wheel her still beating heart. Sadly, even that life was being pumped out to power the city.

Her father nodded. "Your protection is the first reason. He's put his life on the line for you in the past; I believe he will in the future."

Velirith looked up into the canopy of haventhall branches while looking into herself. She readily admitted, Orlazrus probably would protect her again. *Crazy imposter.*

She changed tactics. "But why expose me to someone I've told you is a fraud?" Velirith, to be honest with herself, knew this wasn't the real reason she didn't want to spend too much time with Orlazrus. The real reason was she already felt too close to him.

But Velator did not question her fraud assessment. Instead, he used it against her. "Isn't that a good reason for you to keep an eye on him? If, as you say, he's not who he claims, then you'll be there to catch him when he slips up. If he's just pretending to be Ortessi for the inheritance, well, it's a dangerous game considering his chance of success. And I think you'll agree with *my* intuition. He's not here just for the property; there is something noble in him."

Again agreed. But that didn't make him less dangerous.

Her arguments weren't working. She realized something niggled her sense of her father's transparency. She tried opening that door. "You're not telling me the whole reason, Father. You're manipulating me with reasons you know I'll accept."

Velator looked unfazed. "Didn't take the intuitive genius in you to figure that out, did it? I am a statesman and a diplomat, Velirith. I know how to negotiate. Start with reasons that sound good."

"And so the real reason is..." Velirith left the blank for her father to fill in.

CHAPTER TWO

He smiled, giving in too easily. "You'll be a good influence on him. A truthful influence."

Looking into her father's eyes, searching, she drew out her next word, "And...?"

Her father had to look away to avoid laughing at her I'm-gonna-get-to-the-real-reason-somehow attitude. He turned back but leaned forward to whisper in her ear. "He'll be a good influence on you, if you're careful."

She pulled back. *"Him?* Only if you want me to become a worldly deceiver!"

Velator shook his head. "No. I want you to pick up his desire to make a difference in the world around him."

Her pious stance changed to the stunned realization that her father had slipped a truth in on her that she hadn't seen coming. He had led her in with sound reasons and snared her with a clincher: The Ortessi *did* want to do something great. It didn't change the fact that he was using them to do it. But it changed her attitude.

"I want reparations."

"What?" Velator finally balked at her capricious tactic. "You sound as if I've wronged you somehow."

"Having to put up with that man, yes, you have. I want to take more theater and less engineering rounds. Those I'll never use."

"You already do."

"No I—well, perhaps I do. But I bet I'll use theatrics even more if I ever really have to play politics."

Velator flushed at the implication that he was "playing" politics. "Young daughter, if you want to add more theater, you do it in addition to what you need to take at the Academy. Deal?"

She tried to hedge. "But I don't need to take engineering *this* round, do I?"

"How many rounds have you put it off already?"

265

EPISODE 3 – ATTRACTION AND REPULSION

She winced. The truth was: *a lot*. Moreover, since the Vel legacy depended greatly on their engineering prowess, her ability to interact with engineers was indispensable. She sighed, deciding that his permission to spend more time at the theater, though a meager concession, was the best consolation she would get without a blow-out argument—which she didn't like having with her father. She grudgingly accepted her sentence.

"You know, Velirith," an amazed look glazing Velator's face, "this will be harder when you negotiate with people who don't love you."

She scowled, thinking those days would probably come.

CHAPTER THREE

The first day of Orcad, Velirith found herself still agitated. Orcad was a very exclusive school, priding itself on student-centered, in-depth education. But whether traditional and exclusive or just one of the mindless trade schools most youths were corralled into, Velirith didn't want to be programmed, period. Knowing herself and her strength of will, she was certain that she was mentally and spiritually armed against being remolded or remodeled. But to have to tolerate accountability to teachers and the interactions with other students—especially the Ortessi—well, it made her edgy.

If her brother hadn't died, he'd be a few years ahead of her and acting in this role of 'protector' that the Ortessi was assuming. The thought, that this fraud was assuming her brother's role, further annoyed her.

The Ortessi had returned from a trip to Avertori tired but excited. *Why?*

She knew from Arvel that their two days of legal filings had been as boring as talking to ceramic walls, and with identical results: none. So she strongly suspected that Orlazrus had received good news from someone else, someone not on his official agenda.

And why do I care!

But she answered her own question. *Because he's using my family. Because he doesn't trust me with his secrets. And because at least he is doing something!*

She was annoyed. And she was agitated.

Agitated and annoyed.

EPISODE 3 – ATTRACTION AND REPULSION

She hoped she didn't run into that poser at the New Dawn Ceremony.

The beginning of the year ceremony took place in the open air terrace of Daybreak Hall. It jutted from the east side of Orcad's tower.

Before dawn, she took a podcar over to Center Isle. Gliding over the northeast side of the city, the car passed the tower in which Orcad was housed. It was a well-kept structure overlooking the theater district, striking because it stood on a prominence apart from the other towers crowding Center Isle. Ceremonial luzhril torches already glowed on Daybreak Hall. It would be a clear, cool morning.

Gazing up to the Rim, she could see the first glimmer of Rei glinting red off the Artist's Towers. She wished she could be up there today, thinking and enjoying some solitude rather than beginning a round of engineering.

She had programmed her podcar to stop a few blocks from Orcad Tower to allow herself a short walk to the Academy. She walked slowly through the cool pre-dawn, breathed deeply, and remembered the day before, after talking with her father, when she had spent time alone outside the Rim in the ruins of the rock theater. It was a quiet, special place and just being there brought her a spirit of peace. She seemed to communicate with that spirit and found herself calming dramatically.

But the composure and peace she had garnered there were dispelled within five minutes of her arrival at the Academy.

"You." Velirith sighed.

"The place *is* named after me," the fake Ortessi said with mock arrogance. He leaned against the main entrance of Daybreak Hall. Half his handsome face sported a very spotty beard (which also annoyed her) per doctor's orders for him not to shave yet. He straightened from the grand, arched, haventhall-wood frame embossed with the words: *Through This Door Pass the Future Leaders of Zotikas.*

CHAPTER THREE

"Why *you?*"

Orlazrus shrugged. "Your father knows I'll look out for you."

"Ha!" Velirith turned away, but she couldn't argue with him. Whatever he was, he was telling the truth about that.

They entered the roofless, sloping terrace of Daybreak Hall from the top, back row. The Ortessi made to go down and sit in the front row of the open-air theater, and as soon as he was committed to that course, Velirith split off and sat in the last row with her back against the tower wall.

From the top of the rows of seats all the way to the east-pointing tip of the terrace behind the lectern below, spear shafts lined the edge of the low terrace wall. Rough chunks of dim luzhril were lashed into the haft-ends of the spears, their points symbolically buried in the "ground," indicating they met in peace. The spears varied in weight and decoration, and Velirith knew that each one was as authentic to the original clan it represented as historic study could make it. Some were original, a fact that the now extinct Ortessis had probably taken great pride in.

In the pre-dawn dimness, students and faculty cast long shadows as they passed in front of the glowing luzhril spear hilts on their way down to their seats. Velirith shivered, not with cold, but with a clear imagining of the original clan representatives gathering from all over the three continents for that pivotal moment.

It had occurred much like this nearly a thousand years ago; she felt the realness of it every year when she began a new school term. No, not on a terrace in her beautiful city, but in a circle of rocks on a chilly winter morning just outside what would become Avertori. In fact, before Orcad had moved to Velakun, the New Dawn Ceremony was conducted on Govian just off the Isle of Threes in what was believed to be the very spot of the original convocation. And it was the leader of her "clan" that had spoken at that historic meeting, the founder of modern civilization: Velik.

The Academy Chairman, Cota Jad Entrovel, played the part of Velik. Even as she imagined the original setting, she seemed to feel the tension between clans, both now and then—some had fought each other, vied for land, and some would vie for power in this future society. The tension gathered between her shoulders and neck, bunching in a tightness she couldn't dismiss as simply huddling against the chill of the morning. And there was another tension too, an anticipation. Rei would rise at a well-planned moment in the ceremony, its rising symbolizing the new hope of a new year both then and now.

Cota Entrovel casually but confidently approached the lectern and looked up into the shadowed faces of students from all three continents.

"Verr and Lhea," he began, "we stand before a new era like travelers on the gangway of an ocean vessel. We journey forward in time with a definite purpose; with hope, with skills and stores and resources that make it quite likely we will achieve great things. But we stand here also with our fears."

Entrovel looked around as if looking into the faces of fellow clans-leaders. "I say to those fears here present, 'You are not invited. Flee! For our hopes and desire for peace and prosperity will crush you!' It is our hopes that will prevail when we send our fears to flight.

"Look around at the faces of people just like you. People, I believe, that come from the same roots, roots that likely drive deep into the rocky soil of the Isle of Threes before us. Roots of the same tree. Roots that make us family."

Velirith did look around. Some of the other students did also, but most listened as if this ancient pomp and ceremony had no bearing on the lives they would live, lives that would be more like the feuding clans of pre-Avertoric society than the flourishing civilization that was born from that stirring historical event.

If those here present would just buy into what Cota Entrovel were saying and believe it as truth without the cynical worldview to which they clung... She surprised herself by believing it was possible.

CHAPTER THREE

"I'm asking you to treat each other as family. As if those gathered here were a clan itself, *our* clan." He looked down at Orlazrus in the front row, studying him before moving his silent gaze to others in the amphitheater. Finally, the man representing Velik looked all the way up to where she sat. And he smiled. It might have been odd to see a smile on such a serious occasion, but Entrovel conveyed a true friendliness appropriate to bringing people together.

"We make our own destinies. And if they are in alignment with the Truth, then they are blessed. Truth dictates peace. It dictates faith in a better future yet unseen. It demonstrates love, for in love there is value, true meaning, in a sometimes hostile world.

"Look around at your family, and think on how we may best serve one another. We go into an uncertain future. But one thing we *can* determine—how we will treat each other, and how we will react when we feel as if we were not treated well. Grace and Truth will guide us. We will rule the Isle of Threes, and we will rule this world with Grace and Truth."

To this point, the address was the same as every year, the same, perhaps, as it was in that cold clearing nearly a thousand years ago. But from this point, Cota Entrovel spoke specifically to how these ideals applied to another year of students struggling with academics at the Academy.

"From all over the three continents, we gather to make life better for those we love. I ask you to extend that love across traditional house lines and look at those within this tower as your own house. It is this unifying spirit of which Velik spoke. And it truly is this spirit that will take us into a new adventure across a new sea.

"Many of you will be leaders of your house someday. Remember these words. Words not of your Academy Head-chair, but of the man who really did bring those of very different clans, cultures and agendas into unity with the words he spoke.

271

EPISODE 3 – ATTRACTION AND REPULSION

"They allied in submission to a common purpose. And they created a thriving civilization that brought out the best of their uniqueness for the benefit of all.

"I point to you, Ek Connigar, and I remind you that your house was once but a rough clan of miners, digging in the ground for elements. Your roots are in the mountains. Still today that tradition and strength runs in your house line. And I remind you that it achieved its greatest worth when it was used with a heart to serve the common goal, to tame the Isle of Threes and build Avertori out of the ruined city of the Dead Ones." Ek Connigar, Velirith knew, was the *sixth* child of Ek Threzhel. Traditionally it was the firstborn who trained at Orcad. The lesser-born sibling slouched and did not look up to meet Cota Entrovel's gaze. Velirith read his resentment in bold letters: Connigar regarded himself as a token presence here, of little worth. And there was much truth to his self-assessment. He carried a casual arrogance before him like a shield to his insecurity.

"Tarawy Firstholm," Entrovel turned his gaze to a tall, young lady in the third row. "You are named for the remote sea-city from which your family originates. When your sea-wandering ancestors joined the cause of Velik, they gave him great credibility and led many others to follow him. Your presence here is an honor in a long line of honorable presences, you being the fifty-fifth in an uninterrupted line of attendees to Orcad."

Tarawy tensed at the attention drawn to her. She was young for her height and this was her first term—her first *day*—here at the Academy. But Velirith sensed that the young woman was pleased with the attention of being recognized and acknowledged so early in the ceremony.

Cota Entrovel continued his litany of attendees, specifically edifying either the person or their family. *He knows his history,* Velirith admitted. And it felt good to hear the exceptionally good things the families were known for. There was much good in Zotikas, and Entrovel chose to focus on it during this ceremony.

272

CHAPTER THREE

Velirith was mentioned along the way as one who "had the same eyes for Truth that her many-times-great grandfather Velik had." A fitting and perceptive observation, she thought.

But as the list went on, she realized that the Ortessi hadn't been acknowledged. Did Entrovel suspect the fraud as well? Or was he saving him for last?

It was, Velirith sadly saw, the last position for which Orlazrus' introduction had been saved.

"For twenty years this Academy has been without an attendee with the name Ortessi, the name of its founders. The Ortessi family had the foresight to preserve our hindsight, to encapsulate the lessons of the past in museums, in theater, and in this Academy. It is this Academy that endures. All eyes will be on you, Orlazrus Ortessi, to prove that the lessons preserved are lessons learned, lessons that will renew our faith in an uncertain future." His voice seemed to fade and Velirith was uncertain if she heard the Chairman repeat, "All eyes are on you."

Orlazrus, for his part, sat solidly determined-looking in his front row seat. Velirith shook her head, *all part of the act.*

But the Chairman straightened suddenly, as if thinking of an idea. "Verr Ortessi, I'd like to ask you to say a few words. Come up here, please."

The solid and determined look changed to a frozen-like-ice look. Velirith giggled and couldn't decide if she was glad she was hidden in the back or wished she was up front to watch him squirm.

For a long sequence of seconds, Orlazrus didn't move. When he did, it was very slowly, as if he was willing his mind to engage and think of something profound to say. Eventually, he stood mutely next to Entrovel, who moved out of the way of the lectern so Orlazrus could stand behind it.

Oddly she both felt bad for him and closer to him and her heart beat faster in empathy. He was a real person. A person who

273

knew fear and had experienced loss and was taking action as best he knew how. But she was also reveling in his stage fright.

When no words were soon forthcoming, Entrovel prompted Orlazrus with a question. "Verr Ortessi, the students before you come to this Academy for many and varied reasons. Some because it is a life-long dream of theirs, many because it is a dream of their parents—or a requirement by their parents. Why are you here?"

Velirith leaned forward, eager to hear the response.

The question got Orlazrus' brain moving. "I—" he cleared his throat. "I have long known of this prestigious institution but I," he paused, "I really just want to learn how things work when they work well and how to make them work better."

Velirith slumped back. He hadn't made himself a fool as she had hoped. His answer was decent and, she noted, truthful as well. *The stinker*, she pouted. At least he wasn't a great statesman and orator besides his other hidden talents.

Entrovel patted him on the back and sent him back to his seat. "A hope-filled answer, Verr Ortessi. Well said." Entrovel moved on. "For us to bring continuity to an ever-growing body of history takes a dedicated cadre of men and women. Our staff deserves the highest commendation, and for our new students, a worthy introduction.

"But before I introduce our regular faculty, we are particularly honored to have in special attendance Cota Aurelios, Director of Theater Velaki, true master of the theatrical arts, particularly as they relate to our unique heritage here in Velakun." He paused for the ensuing applause, and Velirith was again on the edge of her seat in hearty approbation. Her mentor stood slowly, his theatrical robe unfolding around his aging body.

She loved that robe. Standing there in front of students who did not know him as she did, the robe showed colorful scenes of life—of love and death, excitement and perseverance. But she had seen the robe stretched out. When he extended his arms, the

CHAPTER THREE

scenes showed more depth, angelic beings holding up the arms of a toiling farmer. The light of knowledge pouring into Velacon, the designer of Velakun's famous dam. It was like the plays Aurelios produced; if one looked deeper, there was more going on than on the surface.

"Cota Aurelios is an extraordinary friend of mine—" Velirith noticed a deep scowl on Cota Rejin's face, "one who still amazes me with new insights and—err, *activities,* despite his respectable age." Velirith chuckled at the intimation. Her "mischievity" could likely be credited to her association with Aurelios. "He preserves a spiritual history often overlooked in a student's training. I encourage you with the strongest recommendation to spend any free hour learning the knowledge contained—not in the massive theater structure which Orcad overlooks—but in the hearts of those Cota Aurelios has trained."

That's me, Velirith realized. It was so easy to take for granted the special attention Cota Aurelios had given her over the years.

"Triose, my friend, please stand." Cota Entrovel gestured to the only other instructor besides Aurelios clothed in a robe. But the plain grey robe of Triose was different, looser. His blue eyes sparkled with humor and alertness. "I'm very thankful to call him my friend, for as an enemy, I would lead a fearful life. He specializes in training the body to fight. He is the best. A man of few words, in fact, no words! And yet, you will not find a better Cota in the arts martial in all Zotikas. For you new students, his 'playground' is the Martial Terrace."

"The mind, future leaders, is equally important in your training. Please don't try to prove me wrong during your evaluations." A soft chuckle ran through the assembly for those who got the joke. "Lhea Rejin is in charge of the programs dealing with disciplines of reason."

She stood, her snug black clothes and sharply carved nose accenting her stern countenance.

EPISODE 3 – ATTRACTION AND REPULSION

"Her focus is on the sciences because she believes, as do I, that the creator of this world did not create haphazardly. This world, in fact this universe, is designed under a set of laws so precisely aligned that to alter certain constants in the slightest degree would change our entire existence—perhaps even *preclude* our existence. Study her teachings well, for the physical world is determined by the principles science has discovered, and most exciting, by the principles some of *you* will discover. Science is an adventure itself."

The Ortessi made the slightest tilt of his head as he studied Lhea Rejin. The thought crossed Velirith's mind again, *He's fascinated by the sciences. Odd for a man supposedly raised in hiding...*

Entrovel continued his introductions, and Velirith noted the sincerity with which he edified and uplifted both apprentices and Cota. The recipients of such praise usually beamed in the spotlight. It was clear why he was a leadership expert. She noted the contrast to herself—how close she was to being cynical of the depraved state of society. *Why aren't men like Entrovel in charge of the government?*

Velirith noted Cota Chance when Entrovel spoke briefly of his biology expertise. The man sat with the same inscrutable demeanor she and Orlazrus had seen when they encountered him in Symphony Gardens. It bothered her now—his unreadability. Velirith was used to reading people in big, bold print.

Cota Entrovel moved on, his voice beginning a slow crescendo as Rei edged closer to breaching the Rim behind Entrovel. Suddenly, Velirith noticed a peculiar odor, familiar somehow as a memory from the theater though she couldn't quite place it. It grew more pervasive and she looked around to see if others had noticed. She tensed, anticipating, and looked down toward the front.

Cota Aurelios was looking up at her and, despite the distance, she could read his expression. *What is he up to?*

CHAPTER THREE

"...and so, future leaders, fellow clansmen, I now declare this year to come—"

Rei burst over the Rim and shone fully on the terrace. As its light hit the amphitheater, the seats were suddenly and completely engulfed in an instant dense fog. Velirith could barely see the row in front of her.

Yelps, followed by shouts and demands, filled the impenetrable cloud. The attendees cried out, many fearful. Some apprentices moved, floundering for the stairs up to the door. Others stayed put, disoriented.

Velirith leaned back against the wall and laughed. For a long time.

That sly slink.

"Stay calm and stay where you are!" Entrovel bellowed, using an impressive, commanding voice. "We don't need any more *theatrics.* The fog is harmless and part of the ceremony!"

An unexpected part, Velirith was certain. She knew what it was now, though few others here would. It may look like fog, but it didn't smell like fog. It was a gas called *pousha,* and it was used for special effects in plays, though rarely. It turned from transparent to opaque when exposed to bright light. She'd never seen it used outdoors. *But what better mischief at a sunrise climax!*

The cloudy gas was persistent—perhaps the valves were still open on the supply tanks. Some students reacted well; others didn't. Some laughed, others accused or complained or shouted how inappropriate the fog was. Velirith thought it perfectly appropriate: The New Dawn Ceremony symbolized the hope of a new year. The fog symbolized how hazy that hope may be.

The assembly dispersed as slowly as the fog. After the opening ceremony, Velirith trudged slowly up to Cota Rejin's Engineering lab. She was chagrined to find the Ortessi shared the same round for the next eight weeks and their daily martial arts lesson as well. New to "his" Academy, he seemed to follow her around like a grevon pup would its mother.

277

EPISODE 3 – ATTRACTION AND REPULSION

The laboratory smelled of harsh sterilization and an underlying odor of something foul. Orlazrus, noticing her sniffing the air, commented, "At least most of the stink bomb has dissipated." Though curious, Velirith didn't feel inclined to ask details.

Cota Rejin intimidated Velirith. She was very smart and stern. *Disciplined* was a good word for her. Rejin's world was one of unrelenting logic ruled by formulas. Velirith lived in a world of instinct and intuition.

As they walked out of Rejin's lab, Cota Entrovel pulled them up to his top floor office for a private counsel session.

"You two are here specifically because of Velator," Entrovel began, "and you *will* get special treatment."

Velirith felt Orlazrus sit up straighter, pleased with the status of recognition. But she knew that was not where Entrovel was going with this line of thought.

"By this I mean that I will hold you to a *higher* standard, and part of that standard is knowing your motivation. You need to know why you are at the Academy. *I* don't need to know. *You* do. Like it—or not—you will both be leaders."

As chairman of the Academy, Jad Entrovel taught leadership. He leaned forward with an intensity that intrigued them both. "True leadership is not bestowed or earned. It is *taken*. If you have confidence and purpose and you act, you will lead.

"I believe every person was created to lead. To seek how to lead is one's own responsibility. To lead others to lead—that is also his own responsibility.

"Having said that, the kind of leader you become will depend on many things.

"Your father, Velirith, cares about people, has good people skills, and good morals. It makes him a man both loved and respected by our people and those outside Velakun. If I may be frank, it is his vagueness of purpose that would be considered a weakness. Because he is such a good man, he suffers me to say this.

"In contrast, look at Feleanna. Her purpose and confidence and her willingness to act make her an outstanding leader. But the kind of leader she is leaves much to be desired. She bullies, threatens, manipulates and cares only about her own desires. She cares nothing for others except what they can do to forward her own ambitions. She is respected, feared, but not loved."

Velirith and Orlazrus stood across from Entrovel, arms folded but admittedly in complete agreement with his assessment. Velirith was unsure how this teaching applied to her, but the Ortessi heir had a question immediately after Entrovel stopped speaking.

"What are we to take from this, Cota Entrovel? What kind of leaders will we be, based on the principles you've described? Will our leadership be an extension of who we are?" he asked.

Entrovel's eyes gleamed in a smile. "Absolutely yes but no," he said cryptically. "Who you are depends on who you choose to be. Unless you know this concept, you will be a product of your circumstances. Let me be brash without intending to offend. Lady Velirith, you could be a spoiled, capricious, self-centered leader around whom people are unsure how to act. Verr Ortessi, although I know less about you, your boldness could, as a leader, be considered rash, unmindful of the responsibilities and consequences that are magnified by leadership."

Orlazrus cast a questioning look at Velirith, as if asking, *How are we supposed to take this?* But he turned back and asked Entrovel, "You have more advice on this subject, I assume?"

Still addressing them with an easy confidence, Entrovel elaborated. "Take who you are and look into the future and decide who you want to be. Then move every day toward becoming that person. And that will define the kind of leader you will be."

"But isn't that being someone you're not?" Velirith challenged. "It's like acting—you'd be a pretender, a poser."

EPISODE 3 – ATTRACTION AND REPULSION

"At first, perhaps, but the opposite is worse. To never fashion and make yourself, to never design your own destiny, is by default to be a product of outside influences. Your parents, your friends—who are probably people you just grew up around, not people you consciously chose—and your economic and social status sculpt you into someone that fits into that environment, like a living piece of a puzzle. You can rebel, of course, my dear, but that too is just a reaction to the pressures molding you."

That struck close to home. "So... what's the alternative?"

"Step back and determine what is truly valuable. Let that shape your purpose. Examine the principles by which you live your life. Are they true and sustainable? Are your principles based on what society and your friends accept, or are they based on a deeper philosophy or faith? Determine right principles and then, the hardest and most important step, live by those principles."

The two pupils looked at each other as if they were blank slates, written on for the first time. This would take some thought.

Velirith and Orlazrus walked out of Entrovel's classroom office in silence. They followed the staircase that led down the outside of the gently curving, three-sided building. When they reached the bottom, Velirith broke the silence, turning to the Ortessi, "Wise words, true?"

Orlazrus nodded, and Velirith saw a faint troubled look behind his mere thoughtfulness.

She went on, "It got to you, didn't it? Now, will it change the way you proceed?"

He gave her an annoyed look. "Will *you* change from poking me every time I do some introspection?"

Shrugging, she replied, "Not until you fess up."

CHAPTER FOUR

"You have bones, my lady," Kieler cooed. He ran his fingers down a duralium wing-spar. Halfway down the long spar a burr nicked his finger, immediately drawing a drop of blood. Kieler jerked his hand back and sucked at the finger. He examined it closely and smiled. "And teeth too, it seems."

He stepped back and admired his developing creation. The airship frame stood like a skeleton waiting for skin. Encircling the airship on the floor was a ring of scraps, fasteners, tools and spare duralium. He walked over to a leather tool bag in that circle and pulled out a metal file.

After the first few days of Orcad, Kieler had explored the underpinnings of the citadel. He had found this abandoned bay halfway between Arrival Point Station and the generator dome. It had the advantage of a large bay door and being close to—but not on—the podcar track.

There were lots of these empty bays, evidently awaiting a future expansion that had never come. Since discovering the place, he had locked the bay doors, re-keying the lock with a lockset from under the Plate. With pilfered tools and materials from Jarovel, he had set to work.

"Movus suggested you, my lady," he told her, "but he didn't suggest a name. I'm sure he intentionally left that to me."

He thought about what the ship meant to him, what the ship was. It was the rebuilding of his lost treasure. And it would be far better than his first ship. He knew so much more now.

The trip to Avertori right before the start of Orcad had been to meet with Arvel and file his official statement of intent to claim property unlawfully possessed by House Cortatti. That chore had been accomplished in one long, slow, uneventful day. They had been escorted everywhere under heavy Velaki guard.

But the night before his court appearances, he had slipped out of Vel Taradan in disguise. Nearly certain that the building had been watched, he was still greatly relieved at how easy it had been to sneak back below the Plate compared to how hard it had been in reverse on the night of the New Year's Gala.

Velator knew he needed to talk to contacts under the Plate, but it would be better if Feleanna didn't. Sneaking out without the guards' knowledge lessened his exposure.

It was also a relief to see Movus and discuss how working within House Vel affected their plans. Movus gave Kieler both perspective and direction.

In a way, Movus pointed out, Kieler was a prisoner of House Vel. No, he was not in chains, but neither was he free to come and go amongst his old contacts simply because of the immense distance. So Movus had suggested he build another airship. Something that could take him silently from Velakun to a nearby point down the powercoach line where they could stash a high-speed sled. Kieler could take night runs back to Avertori and the counsel of his mentor.

He had returned to Velakun hopeful and excited. This ship would give Kieler at least a modicum of liberty.

"*Liberty.*"

He liked the name. It sounded feminine, yet it was strong and independent.

"And it's who you are. You are flight among the clouds. Free from the bonds of earth. A dance on laughter-silvered wind."

He shook his head. Poetry was not him. Machines and plots and daring acts of righteousness. That was him.

But he was like his fledgling airship in some ways, he reflected. He was incomplete too, incapable of independent flight and built for a purpose not of his own choosing.

Still, ocean vessels had names. Why not ones that sailed the seas of air?

"*Liberty.*"

He filed down the burr and smoothed the edge. Anything that bit the skin of his finger would bite the skin that would hold *Liberty's* lifting gas as well.

He was pleased with his progress, though he knew he had a long way to go. It was three months into the year. Working with Jarovel, he had access to all the tools he needed. This first step, the duralium frame, had come mostly from the discarded lattice work of the viewing deck of the *Pride.* The pieces were phenomenally strong and could be shaped and arranged into almost any configuration. For his purposes, he had fashioned them into a three-chamber airfoil capable of holding enough hydrogen to support a two-person airship. *Two people or one person with cargo*, he corrected himself. *Just in case.*

"Velirith would love the freedom of flight," Kieler told his airship. "She's got an independent streak in her the length of your wingspan."

The cockpit, which would be a small affair under the much larger envelope, would only be one seat... the second person would have to lie in the long, slender, rectangular frame behind the seat that supported the undercarriage.

What am I saying?

Velirith is the enemy!

That had been another conversation with Movus; the seductive allure of the "nice" house, House Vel. Movus saw his adoption by Vel as a good thing to be approached with great caution. "They serve themselves. Their isolation says they don't need anyone else and is a subtle kind of arrogance. If the Omeron fell, they unconsciously feel they would still be fine in their mountain fortress."

Pointed out directly, Kieler could admit seeing that in their attitude.

EPISODE 3 – ATTRACTION AND REPULSION

"They show a face that is concerned for all Omeron, but at the first sign of resistance they go into hiding. Vel and Ortessi were friends, yet Velator never saw justice through to a righteous conclusion. I would deduce that both he and his lawyers see your case as hopeless, and he just sees you as a protective layer, a shield to take the battle damage that could be aimed at him.

"And their sanctimonious attitude, their respectful treatment of others... it is a clever, seductive means to their own enrichment and advancement. Seduction is the underlying word."

Not all of Movus' diatribe did Kieler accept, having lived with House Vel a couple weeks. He felt their magnanimity was genuine, but he agreed with Movus that Velator definitely saw "Orlazrus Ortessi" as a usable ally. Movus saw what Velator did not, that their generosity was a strategy. Kieler thought Velator probably didn't consciously view it as just another form of manipulation. Well, maybe he did, but it was a better form of manipulation than Telander's kidnapping of other men's wives.

Kieler filed and sanded through the night, smoothing the spars to perfection, doing what he could with what he had. In his deepening fatigue, his mind wandered to many subjects.

"You know, *Liberty*, I almost died defending House Vel, just down that service corridor outside your room, in the generator dome." *Liberty's* bay was domed as well, part of the structural underpinning of the towers far above. "It was..." He shivered, not able to complete the thought aloud. *The pain was terrifying. Knowing that I was disfigured and not knowing that I was going to heal.*

There had been no assurances. Dr. Yuric didn't know what was happening. Yuric couldn't convincingly tell Kieler, "You'll be fine, son. A few days in bed and you'll be good as new."

At the time, Kieler knew he was maimed for life. He *knew* it. At one point before the doctor and Velator had found him in the rubble, he swore he had stuck the remains of his tongue through the side of his cheek. The pain had been like a never-ending fire all over the left side of his head.

He found he had stopped filing. Skin-melting metal scared him. That he was alive today was a miracle that he just couldn't accept crediting to the indifferent Cota Chance. He ran his finger over the rough surface of the file and then over the too-smooth left side of his face. His beard had not started growing on that side yet.

Though his body had healed, he felt as if some non-physical part of himself was still scarred. And that same part of him felt hurt when Velirith scorned him. She tried to avoid him, and he her, yet they always seemed to end up together. He couldn't deny wanting to be closer to her. He had even caught himself flirting with her! *What am I thinking?*

He shook his head vigorously, focusing back on his airship. Rei would be coming up soon, and he needed to get back to Vel Estate to at least appear to have been there all night. But the image of molten copper kept flying at him. He was tired, but he had just the vertical section of the tail to smooth out. Wearily he forced his mind to think of something beautiful.

And there was Velirith. Fortunately, she wasn't here in *Liberty*'s bay. But when he thought of beauty, he thought of her. He realized he could have thought of Veshun Falls, the dam, the dragons, Symphony Garden—but he thought of her.

But why? She's such a brat! He still wondered if she had something to do with the fog prank at the New Dawn Ceremony. And any day now he expected something to fall on him. She just didn't seem done tormenting him. Aside from physical beauty, he had no reason to be so taken by her.

Well, he reconsidered, there was that passion-for-the-truth thing she had. He did admire that about her, even though it was a direct threat to him. She could be relentless about sticking to the truth when so much around her was false. Her poor father had to put up with her candid comments all her life.

EPISODE 3 – ATTRACTION AND REPULSION

And even her pranky, capricious nature was sometimes a refreshing break from the heaviness of his justice-driven purpose. Her attitude was a mental holiday where he didn't have to perform; he could simply watch and enjoy.

And she would grow into a leader eventually, like Cota Entrovel said. She'd be responsible, truth seeking, justice motivated with a streak of fun that would keep people guessing, and laughing.

Would she have grace and forgiveness? Hard to say. She could go down the cynical, hard road of judging everyone who didn't live up to her standard of truth. But no, he didn't think so. For whatever reason of her own, she had shown him grace, though she was convinced he was an imposter. Even when she had been angry with him, she had not pressed to expose him.

She was an enigma, and he liked breaking open puzzles, deconstructing machine works.

He laughed. "Sorry, *Liberty*. Thinking of Velirith as a machine. She'd make a terrible machine. Can you imagine the hodge-podge of controls? 'This is her Random Act Mechanism. And this component makes her nice on odd-numbered days when the Roivas Cross points eastward.'"

Machines were predictable, like *Liberty* would be. Velirith was not—and he found that extremely attractive.

And she had said as much to him. She "liked him." She said he had a "handsome face."

What if that changed? What if he did something to arouse her anger toward him? Would she then be bent on exposing him? It was eerie how she knew something or someone to be true or false.

He shook his head again. He had resolved not to think about her, and who had he thought of all night? Her.

He ran a finger over the now smooth tail spars. He was done. At least, he had finished the spars of the airfoil. He still had to build a cockpit, controls, electrolyze hydrogen out of water, and the skin to hold it, and of course a motor.

286

CHAPTER FOUR

He sighed, exhausted. He had few answers except that Velirith was a skynut he'd be foolish to try to crack.

Next trip to Avertori would be to figure out the motor. He would also follow up with Twink concerning the Velaki arms order.

For now, he packed up and locked up and headed back to Vel Estate.

He'd be tired for another day of Academy, but he was happy with his progress on the airship. Velirith would love riding in it.

He stopped.

There he was again. Thinking of her.

It had to stop.

CHAPTER FIVE

Kieler enjoyed both the lifestyle of a House Prime and the best education on Zotikas, not that he, as the school's new owner, could take credit for that reputation.

He was pushing himself hard now. The last seven days he had only slept a couple hours each night, going straight from the Academy to work for Jarovel, grabbing a bite to eat near Arrival Point Station, and after that descending to his secret workshop, constructing *Liberty* well into the night.

Today, despite how excited he usually was to learn engineering, Kieler struggled to stay awake for the highly structured, compact teaching of Cota Rejin.

Having spent much of his childhood watching his father design and build, and then figuring out how things worked on his own, he had a very hands-on understanding of mechanical things. But now, to be learning the mathematics that could be used to precisely define flow rates, gas expansion, load bearing, acceleration, elemental energy release rates—it was like coming out from under the Plate into the illuminating light of Rei.

Further, Velirith obviously hated the structure and rigidity of the subject. She also didn't care much for Cota Rejin's emotionless presentation style. It made it just that much more fun for him to ask that one last question at the end of their session that would cause them to stay an extra fifteen minutes.

But today... well, he was going to have to get some sleep soon.

Cota Rejin, the staid, stoic science expert "entertained" Velirith and Orlazrus with calculations and demonstrations of how the arches that support the powercoaches coming into Velakun were designed to withstand the high loads of the enormous trains. Kieler would have been fascinated if he weren't so fatigued.

Following some interactive theory work and a short break, Rejin returned from her office shaking her head, bemused.

"Everything all right, Cota Rejin?" Kieler asked.

She shrugged with an irritated smile. "I suppose." She looked at Velirith. "Your Aurelios was in my office. I always feel I have to check everything when he leaves. I don't know why he comes by. One time he managed to remove the graphite out of all my pencils. No idea how."

She guided them through designing, building and testing arches. It was rigorous, and to Velirith—grueling. Kieler watched her yawn more than he.

Under her breath she complained to him that working the math that described why a catenary arch worked was "like watching a haventhall grow." But he could tell she was even more annoyed watching him get excited over the same subject.

His first two attempts at building arches himself were not bad, but he was so tired he accidentally knocked them both over just as he was completing them. Velirith gave him a look wondering what was wrong with him. He wasn't usually that clumsy. He was trying to hide his exhaustion under his excitement.

His third arch stayed up without mortar and his classmate sighed out, "Finally!" She was ready to be done, probably wanting to get to the theater and her beloved Aurelios. But that was not their next stop. Entrovel wanted to see them again.

As they left Rejin's workshop, Velirith grumbled at him, "Did you knock those first two arches down on purpose just to annoy me? To make me suffer just a little longer?"

Kieler grinned, feeling the ache in his muscles. "No, just a serendipitous benefit."

She grunted. "Just wait for sparring in Triose's Arena tomorrow. You'll fall a lot harder than those arches."

EPISODE 3 – ATTRACTION AND REPULSION

"Mmm," Kieler replied, deliberately ignoring the barb. Triose's art was a lot like dancing... with a kick.

"So why do you like learning so much? You're like a child! Like you've never seen this stuff before." It was good to see her frustrated.

"I was raised in exile, remember?"

She gave him that silver stare again. "That seems to make sense, but... it just isn't the whole truth."

He shrugged, not thinking of a response.

"I am going to have to take you to the theater. I doubt you have any spiritual depth to you, but it will be good to find out. If you don't, then what excites me will bore you. Maybe it will cool your intolerable enthusiasm for everything."

He turned his head and looked at her. "You actually want me to be shallow?"

Velirith scrunched up her face. "You're a pain. Truth."

Sitting in Entrovel's office, a light spring breeze coming in through the high, arched window, he almost felt airborne.

"Verr Ortessi." No response. "Verr Ortessi!"

Is that me? Kieler broke through a cloud and woke with a start, his head jerking up to look in the face of Entrovel.

"You know, Verr Ortessi, school for you is voluntary. If you aren't getting anything out of our lessons, you can sleep more efficiently lying down in a bed. I'm sorry I don't have one in my office," Entrovel chided.

Still groggy, Kieler heard Velirith giggling off to the side. He avoided looking at her.

"My apologies, Cota Entrovel. I slept poorly last night."

Velirith muttered, "I doubt you slept at all."

He turned and shot a look at her. "How would you know?"

In response to his annoyance, she wiggled a smug shrug and kept laughing at him silently. *Let her have her weak revenge.*

Entrovel had mercy. "If you can stay awake, Verr Ortessi, I want you to read through the synopses of House Leaders in *Primus*

CHAPTER FIVE

Vel. You too, Lady Velirith. Yes, I know they're all Vel leaders and I'm biased, but we've had many great and some not so great leaders. Some mixed, like Velacon. Pick out five to ten leadership qualities that you want to incorporate yourselves. You can learn something from everyone. Now go get some sleep."

As the two students headed toward the stair, Velirith asked, "It's very nice out. Do you want to come up to the campus garden and sit for a few minutes?"

Sleepy but surprised that she delayed going to the theater, Kieler agreed. As he followed her up to the roof of the building, he wondered if she was spitefully trying to keep him from taking a nap. The top of Orcad, like many of the buildings, boasted a well-landscaped garden. It was open, with a number of benches and tables for student use. Lush grass covered much of the area and low shrubs sectored the garden for privacy. No haventhalls grew here as the only water was a small fountain near the stairs.

Velirith sat on one end of a bench and Kieler let down his guard a little, stretching out over the remainder of the bench with his feet on the ground. With his head next to her leg, his still short-cropped hair brushing her thigh, he closed his eyes.

"I can tell you're going to be good company," she muttered, leaning back and raising her face to the warm light of Rei.

"Mmm," he groaned, dozing. He could operate on little sleep, but he was at his limit.

Velirith spoke softly, reminiscing. "I love all the gardens in Velakun. My father and I used to spend a lot of time quietly sitting in the garden at the estate." She paused, "Especially right after my brother and mother died. We didn't have much to talk about."

Tired as he was, Kieler managed some interest. She rarely ever mentioned her brother or her mother. "How old were you when it happened?"

"Six. We would just sit and look out over the lake. Feel the breeze. Rei. Try not to think. Father was so sad."

EPISODE 3 – ATTRACTION AND REPULSION

Kieler remembered his own devastation at the loss of his parents and the one time when they had gone over to Govian to picnic in the coastal forest. "One of my best memories is from about that age. My parents sitting on a bench at a table, holding hands, and the breeze blowing through the trees above. Rei was shining through the branches…"His voice caught with emotion and he cleared his throat.

He continued dreamily. "They gave me a tartimelon and were laughing because the juice was running down my fingers and all over my arms. I tried to lick it off but that didn't work. So I picked up some seedballs to throw in the pond. And even though I was standing right on the shore, I kept missing because they kept sticking to my fingers." Kieler laughed.

"Sounds nice. Do you miss them?"

There was a slight edge in her voice.

"Of course," Kieler replied. "I especially miss my dad. He taught me so much. And the way that he died was so horrible—" he cut himself off and tensed. He looked up at Velirith, very awake, and very aware that he had been talking about *his* father, not Orlazrus'.

Velirith was looking down at him, her eyes like silver bullets, precise in their aim. But there was more in her gaze than accusation. She *knew.*

Kieler could not look away from those shining eyes. He could not speak any of the dozen lies his brain was creating to cover his slip in identity. He could only wait.

A cloud covered the face of Rei and finally she spoke. "I still have my father. You lost everyone you loved." And Kieler saw her eyes were shining not only from their natural reflectivity, but from a mistiness as well.

CHAPTER SIX

Symphony Gardens fell away beneath them and The Empyrean still towered above them. The podcar ascended. Unlike the interior track he and Velator had used on Kieler's first day, the rail that climbed the exterior of the tallest tower in Velakun had views that rivaled those from his airship—better, really, since he had never gotten to fly during the day. Velirith and An'essa sat opposite Kieler on the red leather bench of the clear-topped vehicle. Rei neared the western horizon.

Velirith sat half-turned toward the window exuding the airy confidence of having the upper hand. Kieler shifted uncomfortably, wary and wondering.

The hood of Velirith's deep-blue cloak was thrown back, and she rested her chin on the back of a silver-gloved hand, gazing toward the Northern Rim of the caldera. Under the cloak, Kieler noticed, she wore a dark blue leather suit, cinched tight with buckles. He had never seen her wear it before.

He glanced down at his own meticulous green and gold overcoat and, sitting in his lap, the matching burrit fur hat Velator had given him. Kieler deliberately wore a uniform every day to solidify in the minds of all that *he* was Ortessi.

But *she* knew.

It had been three days. And Kieler was still waiting to see how Velirith would use his accidental revelation of his true past against him.

An'essa, stoic, scanned for threats with practiced casualness. She sat erect in her seat, ready. *What could she do so high above ground?*

EPISODE 3 – ATTRACTION AND REPULSION

Velirith had invited him to see the lighting of the Starstone. Hezek had worked out the repairs of the magnetic confinement mechanism, and they were ready to light the massive chunk of luzhril. Kieler was admittedly excited to see this blend of natural grandeur and engineering employed.

Other than telling him that the Starstone was only lit on special occasions, she had intentionally withheld describing how the light worked. She liked her dramatic surprises. And, Kieler feared, she seemed to brim with them today. Oddly, and against reason, he was excited to see what she might have in mind.

For whatever reason, she'd been much nicer to him since his colossal foul-up on top of Orcad. He frowned, trying not to focus on the point where the smooth skin of her gracefully curved neck emerged from the silvery fur lining of her cloak.

As she continued to stare at the caldera Rim, Kieler noted an eager expression building on her face. *She has such a capacity to enjoy the now. But then, so would I if I'd grown up the way she did.*

No. That isn't necessarily true. Whatever her circumstances, Velirith is unique. I know a few highborns, and none are like her.

Kieler's train of thought was broken when Velirith exhaled the breath she had apparently been holding. They had cleared the confines of the top of the caldera and he could now scan range after range of snow-clad mountains and glaciers receding into the distance. The caldera below was the only oasis of color in an ocean of brilliant white.

Why is she showing me this? Why is she spending any *time with me?*

When he brought his attention back to Velirith, he saw her eyes sparkling at him—in amusement certainly, but there was more too.

"It's my way of showing you trust. Not complete, but trusting you with some of my private world is an attempt to get you to trust me."

CHAPTER SIX

Kieler kept silent. She was so naïve. He would love to trust her. He had considered trusting her. But that was not in the plan. And despite his identity slip, he needed to move his mission forward. He needed to be doing more, getting back to Avertori more. At least he had begun work on the airship.

An'essa watched them both. Though expressionless, he couldn't help feeling like she was judging. Judging them both.

As they approached the top, Kieler regarded the nearest stream of water as it flowed down the side of the monumental tower. The water emitted trails of mist that dispersed into the wind. The falling water didn't arch out into the air like many of the other tower-top cascades. Instead, it clung to the tower's side like the waterfalls of Symphony Gardens, whether by surface tension or some engineering trick of which he was unaware. Had it arched, he realized, it would disperse long before reaching the towers below. He wondered how they pumped it up this high.

As the podcar rose, the nearest stream down the side of the tower traced a path between large windows three or four stories below the summit. The water was smoothly diverted by gently arched lintels so that it didn't obstruct the view from inside the tower.

Sensing the direction of his gaze, Velirith commented, "Behind those windows is the Council Conference Room where you spent your first day here."

Kieler nodded, putting it together now. At the time, The Empyrean had been in the clouds.

Far below, the vertical stream fed Symphony Garden, no doubt contributing to its ethereal harmonies.

The pod crested the rim of the tower, smoothly docking at one of the three corners. As the podcar opened, Kieler caught his breath at the chilling bite of the thin air. He was suddenly glad he had heeded Velirith's suggestion to bring his heaviest coat and the burrit fur hat. He filled his lungs with the bracing air.

EPISODE 3 – ATTRACTION AND REPULSION

The plaza onto which they stepped bustled with people. Some in clumps, as if co-workers, some with steaming drinks in their hands, as if this were some sort of impromptu party. The groups migrated and flocked together, then broke off. It seemed that everyone knew someone else. Velakun was a small city, a much tighter community than Avertori.

The crisp air was full of excited talk and laughter. He saw a group of their classmates from Orcad talking and passing around some sort of small ball, hitting it with both their hands and feet.

Kieler didn't feel like blending in, and he was glad Velirith made no move toward that gathering. He wanted to look around, get a feel for this plaza in the sky.

Where Symphony Garden exuded peace, this monument, soaring high above the protection of the caldera, radiated grandeur. Dominating the center of the tower-top plaza stood a statue of a majestic, winged being several stories high. Polished white and surrounded by energetic fountains, the being seemed to be made of a ceramic-metallic composite similar to the tower itself. Its arms stretched upward in a gesture of supplication to a brilliant stone above.

The glassy stone was held in place above the statue by a triple arch rising from the corners of the plaza. Nearly as large as a podcar and surrounded by a ring of lenses, the stone dazzled in the light of the setting sun, perhaps concentrating the light of Rei. Beams from the huge crystal refracted and rainbowed down through the myriad water patterns created by the fountains below.

Feeling like an awe-struck child, Kieler looked up and around. He was aware of Velirith beaming like the stone.

"I love when you're awed," she said. "It renews my appreciation of the beauty of our city. After a while, everything loses its glory. It shouldn't."

Water pushed up around the base of the statue, as if the solid creature was emerging from the pool at its feet. Adding to the illusion of motion was the spray coming out of the statue itself in shimmering arrays. The creature's wings seemed to beat slowly, and Kieler realized the wings were not solid, but formed by thin sheets of water, spraying out in a feathered pattern from its back. The entire figure hovered in a cloud of mist that wafted back and forth in the light breeze, and the light from the stone cast constantly shifting bows of color around the heavenly being and down upon the stone paving where they stood.

The effect was one of rising. When Kieler looked at the feet, it seemed to be rising from the churning pool. When he looked at the body, the creature seemed to be lifting on shimmering wings. And when he looked at its outstretched arms, it appeared to be stretching upward toward the stone.

A barrage of tiny, frozen crystals struck his face and entered his slightly opened mouth, highlighting how frigid the air was up here. The water from the misty fountains was freezing in the breeze.

He closed his mouth and frowned. The art and function seemed impossible. Kieler's analytical mind couldn't grasp the nature of the well-cut stone at the apex of the arches. It wasn't just a huge hunk of luzhril, it was an enormous gemstone of the energy-dense, light-giving element.

How can this be? The magal needed to suppress that amount of energy would be enormous or need to be extremely refined. Probably both.

"That cannot be..."

"Be what?" Velirith asked, for once not anticipating the end of his sentence.

Kieler shifted, trying to focus on the edges of the stone. "Luzhril that big."

Velirith smiled, obviously missing the significance. "We told you we were lighting the Starstone. So why the awe and amazement?"

Under the Plate, chips of luzhril the size of a clipped fingernail were prized light sources, even fought over. Luzhril was much better than light lugs. The red luzhril orb that Movus possessed was enormous and completely unique. And even the fist-size globe used to illuminate the Cortatti library was there to impress visitors with its extreme value. But this hunk displayed at the top of the city—it was a sheer impossibility.

"The size of that thing. The purity," he whispered in awe. *The power!* he thought.

"Yes..." She still wasn't on the same wavelength. "Beautiful, true?"

Kieler unconsciously stepped backward. Could Velirith be unaware of the energy bottled up in this stone? If the power of this mass wasn't suppressed by a magnetic field just as powerful, it would incinerate the city. He wondered if a similar mass of luzhril, unconstrained, could have released enough of a blast to have created the entire caldera.

"I've never seen anything like it." Feeling a bit out of control himself, he deliberately spoke with pretentious casualness. "So where did you find it?"

Velirith cocked an eyebrow at him. "Oh, stuffed in the sofa cushions. You know, we highborns lose stuff like this all the time." She shrugged. "Or maybe it was found a couple thousand feet beneath Center Isle. I forget which."

Kieler didn't even respond. He was thinking that the uniqueness of the stone was reflected in the uniqueness of all Velakun—and its people. These people, isolated geographically and culturally for hundreds, perhaps thousands of years were different.

He saw it in their architecture and engineering, of course. Towers built of structural ceramic were found all over the world, and the best quality material came from here in Velakun. It was one of their original exports. But the strength and flexibility of these towers was greater than anywhere else, even Avertori.

Perhaps the export version was diluted. Towers as slender and as high as these in Velakun could not be built without that higher quality. They had kept the best for their own city. Something about the very ground under Velakun seemed to harbor greater strength than anywhere else on Zotikas.

Kieler followed the water as it flowed from the pool surrounding the statue and radiated outward in straight channels like wheel spokes to the edges of the tower. It then cascaded down the sides as he had seen on the ride up. He walked to the very edge and looked down to Symphony Garden. The vertical distance made it look small, and yet he knew it was much wider than Starstone Tri.

His knees weak, he traced the mazelike, three-dimensional path the water followed downward. Starting from the top of The Empyrean, it clung to the sides of the tower as it flowed down to Symphony Garden. There, it split through many channels into that terrace's pools and falls across the expansive garden. Flowing over the side of Symphony Garden in various places, it then ran down from one terrace to the next, feeding the lower terraces. It worked its way across raised aqueducts to the east end of the island, flowing around both sides of the theater, and finally ending its journey by cascading into the lake.

Bridges spanned the gaps between towers, seemingly at random, but with an uncrowded, pleasing aesthetic. Diagonal cross-structures also reached from one tower down to another, giving the city a lofty majesty.

I would rather have been a builder of this society than a destroyer. To build a city, a new world... He shook his head. *But my mission is to cut the rot out of this behemoth, regardless of how beautiful it may be.*

Velirith came to stand next to him. An'essa stood several paces away from the edge, appearing nonchalant. A narrow stone railing ran around the circumference of the plaza, and Kieler and Velirith leaned their forearms on it. Other than the railing, nothing stood between them and a several thousand foot drop. He felt her shoulder touch his.

Kieler thought Velirith was going to study him again, but instead she just joined him, looking out beyond the Rim into the jagged mountains that surrounded Velakun. The peaks and icefields extended as far as he could see. Velirith's cheeks were flushed, probably by the chill breeze.

They turned back toward the sculpture in the center of the plaza.

The piece was saying something that hit a chord deep within him, but he could not identify the longing. The meaning of this celestial creature was just not clear to him. It called to him so strongly that he had to ask. Before he could, Velirith anticipated his question.

"The sculpture is called 'The Light of Truth,'" Velirith told him.

He nodded thoughtfully. "So the creature is worshipping that stone?" Kieler asked, knowing he was intentionally goading his escort.

Velirith bristled. "Of course not, slink-brain! The stone represents Truth."

Kieler nodded, grinning, then found himself once again trying to figure out how this display worked—granted it was beautiful. Even more mystifying was how anyone was able to stand on this high plaza without being fried by the Starstone. *The top of the arches must contain extremely strong magal.* He nodded to himself.

Out of the corner of his eye, Kieler noticed two men in silver and blue stride up to An'essa. They were close enough to hear.

They both inclined their heads toward him and Velirith, and the taller one spoke to Velirith's bodyguard. "An'essa," he said with obvious respect, "we are ready to deploy the shield and light the stone. But with security required at both the generator dome and on the *Pride* now, we are stretched very thin at the control room. Can we trouble you to stand with us?"

Something niggled Kieler about the request. Velirith was watching too, and a small smile quirked the corners of her mouth. It reminded him of the smile she had given her father at the conclusion of the Family Harmony Dance. She was obviously unconcerned.

An'essa looked to her charge.

"Go, Ani," Velirith consented. "You'll be close if there is trouble, and we'll meet you after the lighting."

An'essa hesitated. Velirith raised her eyebrows and tilted her head as if to say, *What are you waiting for?*

Deliberately, An'essa scanned the plaza. Though the plaza clamored with people excited to view the lighting, none seemed threatening, even to Kieler's refined situational awareness.

Velirith's bodyguard was not bound to accompany her everywhere. An'essa looked intentionally at her charge and seemed to convey some sort of admonition of warning. Then she nodded slightly and told the men, "Of course." To Velirith she said, "Please summon me should you need me."

Velirith nodded.

Kieler was puzzled by the exchange. He felt that the right thing to say might have been, "I'll watch out for her." But he had missed his cue and An'essa was already walking away.

He looked questioningly at Velirith, but she just arched her eyebrows at him too. She was twirling something around her finger by its strap, too quickly for him to see it clearly.

She stuck the item in a cloak pocket and straightened from the railing. Following An'essa at some distance, she led Kieler across the plaza. As An'essa and the two security men headed down the stairs next to another podcar station, Velirith stopped Kieler.

"What?" he asked stupidly.

"You almost stepped into the water."

Looking down, he noticed his reflection staring back at him from one of the water channels. He had been so absorbed in Velirith's sly behavior that he had indeed almost stepped into one of the streams radiating from the plaza's center.

EPISODE 3 – ATTRACTION AND REPULSION

As he peered into it he saw that his reflection came from *below* the surface. Curious, he knelt and reached down through the clear water. When his outstretched fingers touched the reflection, it distorted and gave way. Apparently it was some sort of heavy, metallic fluid under the water.

Velirith broke into his thoughts "That's the material they use to shield the plaza from the Starstone when they turn it on."

"Turn it on? It's not an arc-light. That thing will fry the entire city." Was she being intentionally dense? He thought about how they could "turn it on." Perhaps by retracting the magal in the supporting arches, or rotating the magnetic field. But that was what this event was all about, "Lighting the Starstone." He had to admit the design was beyond him. He was nervous.

"That's why there's a shield," she replied with a bit of a smirk.

"But how can they use a fluid to shield anything?"

She shrugged. "Let's go, engineer. When they turn it on we really don't want to be by a metal stream."

Curious, he followed her to where one of the corner arches met the plaza. On the right side of the massive arch was a door labeled "Facilities," and next to that was the stairway down that An'essa had taken. To the left of the arch was a podcar dock and two rain-sheltered benches.

She sat down on a bench and patted the spot next to her. She smiled breezily at him. "You'll like this."

Kieler didn't doubt her, but there was just something about her attitude that made him wary. Still, he sat.

He looked at her askance, just letting her know that he was ready for one of her little surprises. She just smiled at him again, crossed her legs and began shaking one leg in an absentminded, fidgety way.

An air-horn sounded three blasts from a niche in the arch about halfway up. He looked around and saw the other tower-top observers hustle over to the benches or stand near the bases of the

302

arch. *They're just getting out of the way to watch the center of the plaza.*

Several seconds elapsed in anticipation, and then the air seemed to charge.

"Oh!" Velirith exclaimed, obviously remembering something. "Not wearing your beloved sigil, are you?"

He smiled slightly and shook his head. He had seen the "No magnetic materials" signs, but he didn't make it a habit of wearing the sigil around Velakun anyway.

So what is happening? He could hear something moving in the arch above them—feel a vibration in the air. The water in the nearest stream rippled, the quivering intensifying as the machinery above continued.

The cool liquid metal he had seen beneath the water was pulled into the center pool at the angel's feet, gathered, and rose closer to the surface. It happened quite quickly. Once the radial arms of water had been emptied of the flowing metal, another hum emanated from the angel itself, and the metal spiraled from the base, streaming up around the angel in gleaming streaks. Again it collected, this time in a large, undulating disc suspended above the creature, but below the Starstone. Finally, the disc stretched and flattened, spun by invisible magnetic hands until it spread into a hovering dome of metal that shielded them from the Starstone and blocked their view of it.

Totally unfamiliar with the properties of the magnetic liquid, Kieler was fascinated. It was a lot of metal! All held in suspension by magnetic fields perfectly projected from the arches.

Kieler could now see the entire worshipping statue in the center, but could not see the Starstone. Where they sat, at the tower's edge, the reflective metal sheet was just a few feet above their heads.

It was a mirror, a shield, yes, that would reflect the coming light of the stone. *Amazing.* He was excited and admittedly grateful that he still had so much to learn from House Vel's engineering expertise.

Once the hovering, shimmering dome stabilized above their heads, another air-horn sounded from the now-obscured arches. This tone was long and loud and echoed back to them from the Rim a few miles away.

Light flashed from above, flooding the valley below.

He looked out through the gap between the top of the tower and the bottom of the shield. A golden-red Rei faded in the west, and a new, small sun, tightly controlled, had bloomed above the suspended metal shield.

The caldera Rim shone in the silvery, ethereal light, reminding Kieler of Iliss' light when it was full and closest to Zotikas. But the Starstone was many times brighter. The buildings on the far slope seemed to glow as if their walls were infused with luzhril and then outlined in shadow.

The Artist's Towers, spaced regularly around the top of the Rim, glinted back the moon-like light. Kieler felt as if the world were suddenly unreal, a dreamland where flaws were erased and perfection floated in a twilit gloaming.

Captivated by the image, he saw the entire caldera illuminated by the transforming light—and then he caught a glimpse of the shield edge, limned in coruscating heat.

His eyes locked on the scintillating edge. The air around the hot light warped and distorted, causing the metal edge to look as if it was melting and reforming.

Perhaps it is. His thoughts were dim compared to the white-hot shield edge. *Containment couldn't be perfect. And if a bead of that superheated metal were to drip onto us—*

Kieler shivered, an image of the melting copper of the generators flashed through his mind. *These people have no idea the power they have unleashed.* Only a slim sheet of magnetic metal *floating* above their heads separated them from being incinerated by the ferocious heat of unfettered luzhril. One

304

CHAPTER SIX

tenuous magnetic field held the molten metal from pouring down on them.

Everyone applauded.

Kieler froze in the restrained heat.

Velirith looked at him and laughed. Then she *saw* him. She started, paling in the shadow of the silver dome. "What is it? What's wrong?!"

She put a hand to his face, trying to turn his head to meet her alarmed and desperate gaze. She flicked her eyes to where he was looking, to what was causing his paralyzing fear.

Her other hand on his arm was suddenly gentle. "Orlazrus," her voice soft, like a consoling mother, "We've been lighting the Starstone for hundreds of years. They meticulously maintain whatever magnetic marvel those arches hold. We have a *perfect* record. Not one accident. It's like riding a podcar!"

But Kieler didn't let go of his tension. It felt too familiar; the eerie, glowing metal above him; the increase in temperature from the heated air coming in under the shield. With a hot chill, he pictured molten copper flinging toward his face—the memory only a few weeks old. And an older memory crept in, of a vision he had only imagined—the fire in which his mother died.

Velirith was reading the fear in him, connecting her intuition with his anxiety.

"Oh Truth!" she exclaimed, reaching up to touch his face with both hands now. "I'm sorry! I thought you'd love all the clever engineering involved. I didn't think it would remind you—"

Kieler reached up slowly and took her hands. Her gaze flicked to the left side of his face, still pink and raw and a billboard of his nearly deadly encounter with hot, liquid metal.

But her touch was electric and cooling. He held the outside of her hands as he very slowly brought them down, looking into her oddly reflective, molten silver eyes.

She really doesn't think sometimes. Despite her superhuman intuition, sometimes she just doesn't think. She was, in a way, the most innocent person on Zotikas. He was annoyed with her, yes, but he was angry with himself too for losing control.

For several slow breaths, he calmed down, letting her reassurances about the incredible safety mechanisms of the Starstone go from his intellect to his emotions. They sat for a while under the peculiar penumbra umbrella. And it was okay. It was nice. Frightening, but nice.

He let her hands go automatically, then regretted doing so.

CHAPTER SEVEN

With the Starstone successfully lit, the crowd, talking excitedly, faded off in podcars or went down the stairs. Kieler soon found they were truly alone. He had most of his control back, and Velirith—*by Truth* if she didn't have a hint of her mischievous smile back already.

Rising from the bench, the couple walked slowly past the podcar dock. Kieler found this curious, but assumed they were going down the stairs to meet An'essa. He was still melancholy, a tension between the receding fear of the heat above and the cool touch of Velirith's hands on his face.

She too was quiet, but her quiet was of a different kind—a silence that restrained a different kind of danger. Two strands of black hair curled toward her chin, framing her slightly downturned, oval face. She flashed him a silvery glance and looked back at the ground. Kieler tried to read it, but aside from a vague air of mischief and a slightly stronger air of impossible affection, he gave up.

Their hands brushed each other, and Kieler felt—his own intuition in play—that had he grasped her hand, she would not have pulled away.

"I do thank you," she began softly, "for saving my life on the *Pride*, and at the generators. You are consistent in that. You act decisively and bravely."

Not knowing how to respond, he replied, "You are welcome." *And worth saving,* he almost added aloud. Instead, he shifted the awkward pride he felt to wry humor. "Does this mean you'll accept me as Orlazrus Ortessi?"

EPISODE 3 – ATTRACTION AND REPULSION

She snorted, very unladylike. "No. I won't play your game. "

His humor shifted to concern. Kieler knew she couldn't prove he wasn't the heir, but she probably could insist that her father reject him. All Kieler could do was get better at his role as Orlazrus Ortessi. He certainly couldn't let down his persona with Velirith just because he had fallen out of character once. Or twice.

"Stop worrying," she chided, not even looking at him. "I told you I wouldn't interrupt your little play. Besides, it's going to be fun to see how long you can pull it off before you slip out of character in front of someone who cares. I *do* want to see how it ends."

Kieler frowned at her. She was right, of course—slipping out of character was his fear as well.

"Maybe you should get acting lessons from Cota Aurelios." She smiled with an over-familiarity he found unnerving.

"As I see it, you're still thinking like whoever you really are. You have to convince yourself that you *are* the Ortessi Heir. Vulnerable, yes, I like those accidental touches, but you've got to be more slighted, like... like you've been cheated. Yes, that's it. Like you're *entitled* to lead a house that doesn't exist anymore." She laughed heartily, any trace of the nurture she had displayed minutes before had evaporated.

Kieler still didn't know how to react to this girl.

She continued, relentlessly, "I know you want to do something good, but you've got to be better at your own game!" Then, with sudden seriousness as if she realized something else, "And you better not mess up so bad that you hurt my father." It was a blunt warning.

As if thinking aloud, Velirith went on, tapping her chin. "So, we know you are not who you claim, but that brings up a much more interesting and pressing question. Who are you?"

"I—"

"—don't lie! Lies are revolting. To me, a lie looks like something disgusting just crawled out of your mouth. Took me years to figure out other people don't 'see' lies.

"And I don't mean, what role are you playing? Why-ever you're playing this role is probably because the role you were previously playing demands it. But it's just another role. Most people play roles. My father plays The Politician, but it doesn't make him one. At least he knows it and does it to protect our people.

"But who are you? What makes you act? What are you trying to *stand* for?"

Kieler closed his mouth. Velirith was not just the shallow fun-seeker he'd taken her for at the gala. Her questions really did make him think. *Am I just playing a role? Even in the Coin?* He supposed he was. But it was a true role, and it was his reaction to the world under the Plate and above it. *But what would I do, who would I be, if I chose my actions independently of my circumstances?*

"Who would you be if you chose your actions despite your past?" she asked.

Despite the eerie echo of his thoughts, he paused mentally and looked over and into her reflective eyes. *I'd chase you around the world, young lady.*

Velirith blushed and looked away immediately.

"I'd like to *hear* your answer," she muttered, recovering herself. "But give it some time and thought—not too much, mind you. You never know how much time you really have with me, considering my mercurial temperament."

What is she talking about?

Without his notice, Velirith had started him down the stairs next to the corner arch. Distraction. Being distracted is not a survival quality for a spy. They had gone down a couple floors before he voiced his curiosity. "Is An'essa down here? Where are we going?"

The stair followed the curve of The Empyrean, open to the air on one side. Velirith continued quickly down the stairs, obviously not feeling compelled to answer.

EPISODE 3 – ATTRACTION AND REPULSION

Eventually, as she opened a door into the interior of the tower, she answered his question with a question. "Have you ever noticed how some questions will be answered shortly after they are asked simply by waiting? Like, 'What's for dinner?' or, 'How long is this podcar ride?'"

Kieler clenched his teeth. It was as if Velirith had switched to her Annoying Girl character. Perhaps she just put on these different personae to practice her theater.

The corridor led straight toward the core of The Empyrean and stopped at a door marked, "Facilities." Kieler frowned at the door, which was heavy and sealed, almost like a hatch on the *Pride.* Velirith opened the door and entered. Kieler still followed, still puzzled.

The room was little more than a closet. Discarded telegraph cable and maintenance equipment used to clean the building had been 'stored' haphazardly in the room. Another, more substantial hatch at the far end of the room stood locked, barred and unlabeled. Velirith went straight for it and produced a key with which she unlocked and then unbarred the foreboding portal, but left it closed. She stowed the key in one of the pockets of her soft-leather jumpsuit and pulled two pairs of goggles from the pocket of her cloak.

She threw one pair to Kieler, who caught them absently. She put on the other pair, and threw her cloak back over her shoulder.

He realized that asking "What are these for?" would be ignored. Instead, he eyed the full-length, skintight jumpsuit, the leather outlining and caressing her curves exquisitely.

She looked intently focused for a few moments, then launched into a passionate monologue for which Kieler was totally unprepared.

"I *can't* trust you! You're the one I'm fooling for my own nefarious reasons. Noble but nefarious. That's me, a nefarious nobleman!" She had deepened her voice and puffed out her chest.

CHAPTER SEVEN

It was exaggerated melodrama. It was Velirith playing the part of a bad actor. Kieler realized she was parodying him.

Then she switched. She wasn't quite herself, but almost. She was like some melodramatic, ditzy version of herself. "Oh, you poor misguided hero!" Her voice was higher than normal now. "I will show you trust and nurture and you will open up to me and together we'll rule the Omeron with truth and justice."

Deep voice again. "No, no, no. You are just a spoiled daughter of the oppressing class. I must remove you and your fellow oppressors and replace you with my own oppressors. Pure and noble and truthful like me, the Deceiver."

"But can't I help you?" she batted her eyelashes and tilted her head. "Maybe I'm really smart. Maybe I'm a real person (unlike you) and have feelings and care about world peace and babies and endangered shungvaals."

"No," she replied to herself, deep voice again. "You are a shallow, selfish highborn unable to do anything but protect your own interests. You'd rather play pranks and scoff at the lesser houses and dance on the wind."

She paused, seemed to drop out of character for a moment to consider his/her own words.

Then she popped back into the ditsy role, hands on hips. "Show some respect. I'll have you sent to the Arena for that!"

Deep voice shouted back. "Typical Prime arrogance! Go jump off your ivory tower!"

She feigned being emotionally crushed with fake tears. "Oh my Stars! You reject me. You hate me. All I want is to be your friend." She threw the back of her hand across her forehead. "You'll regret losing me!"

Velirith, still exaggerating her gestures, turned as if leaving him, and flung open the door that had been behind her. A strong blast of wind rushed out and through the maintenance room, stirring up dust and scraps of paper and knocking over a broom.

EPISODE 3 – ATTRACTION AND REPULSION

"Farewell, Cruel Hero!" she said over her shoulder and stepped through the door. And fell.

After a startled pause, Kieler shot forward not knowing what happened to her. There was no question she really fell, but her actions just didn't seem real. He stuck his head through the door into a mass of rushing wind and looked down into a dimly lit shaft extending downward, seemingly infinite.

Fear for her rushed through him. Had she gotten so wrapped up in her silly drama that she forgot there was no floor beyond the door?

She was gone, lost in the dimness that undoubtedly dropped the whole height of The Empyrean.

She was gone.

Lost, Kieler stared into the vertical abyss, a shaft about twice as wide as he was tall. He couldn't even grasp how to think. This woman, who he was just beginning to care for as a woman and not, as she put it, "a spoiled daughter of the oppressing class," was no more.

And why? She had acted as if this were some fictional drama put on to make a point and make him realize that his mistrust of her was misplaced. But throwing herself into an airshaft was no fiction. She was gone.

"Velirith!" His desperate shout was lost in the rising wind, and only the wind answered.

He knitted his brows, trying to think through the emotional pain. He absolutely knew he didn't want her to get burned by the grand plan of revolution he was igniting. But—

Why did she jump into the shaft, and not off the tower? The tower was much more scenic...

What a ridiculous thought! he chastised himself. She was obviously unbalanced, insane in some highly functional way—well, highly functionally until moments ago.

"Velirith!"

CHAPTER SEVEN

Hardened as he was to losing men on a mission for the Coin, nothing prepared him for this senseless waste of vibrant, beautiful life.

...but why the goggles?

To protect his stinging eyes, he put on the goggles she had given him and peered down into the wind. They were actually more robust than the ones he had used during his flights in Avertori.

As he puzzled on the goggle mystery, tears, a fluid he hadn't know his body still generated, began to form. The goggles began to fog.

What will I tell Velator?

He stared down into the dim hole, the wind coming up. Some air pushed around the seal, drying his eyes at about the same rate they watered, preventing the tears from actually falling. Instinctively he tightened the strap.

It was in this frozen state, between grief and confusion, between confidence and a gut-twisting feeling that everything he was trying to do was wrong, that he saw something dark fluttering far below. It sent chills coursing through him.

He had never been a man to believe in spirits or shades, but the trembling shape rising toward him gave him the strongest feeling that it was Velirith! What else could it be but her spirit?

He straightened, never taking his eyes off the rising apparition, preparing himself to, to... to what?

To say goodbye to her departing spirit.

He would proclaim his admiration of her. He would declare his appreciation for her ability to perceive the truth. He would confess his—

The quavering shape was close now, and it looked far more physical—though not solid—than some ethereal spirit.

The last few moments before the form resolved filled him with brimming fright. The shape slowed, looking like it would stop very nearly level with him standing on the lip of the airshaft. There was no alternative but to wonder if he was in the presence of the supernatural. But then—were those ankles and feet sticking out one side?

He suddenly recognized the fluttering phantasm as a widely spread cloak.

As the dark blue cloak rose above his head, the specter rotated slowly toward him, and Velirith's face, goggled, turned to look him in the eye. Her grin was ghastly only in its triumph.

After a long appraisal of her victim, she threw her head back as she hovered before him and laughed a very earthly, very ignoble guffaw, unnaturally distorted in the rushing wind.

He felt the layers of emotion peeling off him in the constant, steady wind.

Joy. Velirith was alive! He almost jumped off the ledge to hug her to him.

Confusion. She's *not* dead?

Foolishness. She had played him like a triolica on festival day.

Fury. Velirith, Prime daughter of House Vel, had humiliated him.

Mouth set in anger, he lunged at her.

But she had been reading his emotional progression. She was holding her cloak by the edges, arms out at right angles. The other corners of her cloak were clipped to her ankles somehow. Just as he tried to grab her, she raised her far hand and tilted away from him.

Kieler tottered on the edge of nothing, windmilling his arms for balance. He felt, for a moment, that nothing could stop him from slipping over the edge. But with a lurch backwards of both shoulders, he stumbled back from the lip of the shaft.

Shaken, but still furious, he stepped back to the edge and raged impotently at her. "You child! You inconsiderate, immature little girl!" The intense emotions, until a moment ago bound in horrified grief, were now spewing forth unrestrained. "I thought you were dead! I almost jumped in after you—"

CHAPTER SEVEN

"LIE!" she shouted over the wind with a smile.

He spluttered. "I— Well— I wanted to! But I'm not an idiot like the one I'm looking at!" He regained his righteous ire.

She had drifted close to the open door again. Too close. Within two feet. Kieler snapped his hand out and grabbed her wrist.

He really didn't know what he was doing. Just that she was still not safe, hanging on nothing but air.

But *she* knew what she was doing. She let go of both corners of the cloak, and with the hand of the wrist Kieler had just triumphantly locked onto, she grabbed *his* wrist.

Then she twisted, balled up, and fell.

His first thought was that the woman who seemed merely arrogant and immature was really totally insane.

There was no way that Kieler could hold her plummeting weight with one straight arm. And there was no way he could disengage quickly enough, even mentally, from his goal to grab her, especially now that she had him. And so she effortlessly pulled him into the near bottomless airshaft.

Kieler was falling.

"You're insaaaaaaaaaaane!"

With that accurate insult, she let go and spread as wide as her lithe frame would go. The roaring wind snatched her back and up (though later Kieler realized she was still falling, just not like the rock he was). He was left alone, flailing his arms and legs for some purchase. Never had his body been totally out of contact with something solid. But the conniving scamp had somehow let him go in the exact middle of the shaft, unable to reach the side for anything like leverage.

The dim lights along the shaft flashed by like a speeding powercoach—at first. He tumbled. He kicked. He flailed his arms like a drowning man without the water.

He tried to think what his last thoughts should be. He did realize he had some time. How long would it take to fall these thousands of feet? He almost laughed that his mind defaulted to engineering calculations.

Had he lived a meaningful life? He had cared about doing right. He could honestly say that in facing the end of it.

But he hadn't ever loved anyone deeply, nor intimately. He had thought Velirith might be—

But Truth! She was the one who was ending it prematurely for him! Since he was tumbling uncontrollably, he tried to look back up the shaft to see what was happening to Velirith. She was still up there, actually getting closer to him. She'd die too, just a second later. But no, he considered, she hadn't died the first time she fell.

Then it struck him. This wasn't the "first time" she'd done this.

And something else struck him: the lights were slowing down. The rushing wind hadn't slowed as it roared past his ears. But the lights were coming to a halt. He could make out pipes running the interior wall of the shaft, and vents, and other access doors. Almost at walking speed.

Had he hit and died and the world gone slow motion?

No, he felt like the Cortatti cutter as it left the mag-lev track, battered as he flipped end over end.

Finally, the walls stopped moving except for his spastic bobbing motion. As he rolled in the vertical wind, he saw Velirith above him. She descended like a leather-clad goddess, commanding and standing on the wind. Her left foot was pointed down, her right leg cocked back along the left. Her arms were straight out and angled back like a raptor preparing to dive on its prey. Tied to her ankles, her blue cloak fluttered and flapped vertically behind her head.

She was obviously in delicate balance, her leg muscles sharply defined through the deep blue leather of the jumpsuit as she made fine adjustments. But she was in total control.

Kieler shouted but even he wasn't sure what he said, lost in the wind. For a brief moment, he stabilized, face up. As if waiting for her cue, Velirith curled up, then dove, hands out, head first, right at him. He cringed, and the motion set him to tumbling again. He crashed into her with a rolling smack that pushed her away.

She shouted at him. Something like, "Hold still!"?

He had smacked her good with a flailing arm, and was taking some satisfaction in that. She disengaged and pulled back to hover above him again.

But now that he realized he hadn't died, and unless he did something foolish he wasn't going to die, he did start thinking. He was like a leaf held up by the wind. He wasn't an airship, but he did have control surfaces: hands, arms, feet, legs, even his head and trunk were directing air to push him left and right, forward and back.

He forced his limbs into rigid stiffness and symmetry. Again he rolled onto his back, but the spinning stopped.

He was looking up at Velirith. They had eye contact. She didn't look crazy. But neither was she smiling or laughing at him— much. She was assessing his presence of mind. It was like she was deciding if a drowning man was going to drag her down with him.

This time she brought her arms and legs in slowly. She caught her streaming cloak and furled it, causing her to descend. Truth, she really knew what she was doing in this world of wind.

She passed slowly down beside him, keeping out of his reach. Kieler assumed she was going to come at him from below, but for what purpose, he didn't know.

He had been holding himself rigid, not moving even a finger. But now that she was below him, he couldn't see her. He turned his head to look for her, and that slight movement caused him to flip over, face down, right smack into her ascending form.

But this time she didn't pull away. She grabbed him around the chest. She had evidently meant to get on his back, but he had rolled, and they ended up face to face, nose to nose. She still had that mischief-eating grin at the corners of her mouth.

EPISODE 3 – ATTRACTION AND REPULSION

He grabbed her reflexively. She was the first solid something he had touched since he'd fallen. He hugged her so tightly her silver eyes pushed out in surprise.

"Loosen up!" she shouted. He heard her through his partly open mouth, it seemed, more than his ears. He tried to loosen his death grip, and though still stiff, managed to give her some room to breathe, literally.

Now she smiled wide, her face so close he could have reached out with his tongue and touched her lips. And the thought crossed his mind. But more immediately, he wanted to know how they were going to get out of this alive.

"Stay relaxed," she shouted. "I'll lead this dance."

As always, Kieler thought unwillingly.

To grab him, she had once again let go of the cloak attached to her ankles. Thus it was beating up above them, inverting them by her ankles, which, he now realized, were wrapped around his legs. He couldn't help feeling excited despite his desperation.

So, floating inverted somewhere in the middle of The Empyrean, where the velocity of the air below supported their weight, Velirith was in control. She laughed again.

She put her mouth next to his ear and shouted, but not quite as loud, "So, are you going to tell me who you really are? Or should I let you go?"

The scamp! Weren't House Primes supposed to have manners and decency and— But what was he saying, that had never been true except *maybe* for Velator, and this was Velirith. And he had no idea to what lengths she would go to... to... to what? Find out the truth?

But Kieler had his mind back now. Granted, he was still plummeting down an airshaft desperately clutching the shapely daughter of House Vel with no idea how she could fly and he couldn't. But *he* was holding her as well as *she* was holding him. He could use that.

CHAPTER SEVEN

He clutched her tighter to him, deliberately. Her eyes widened. She was surprised for the first time in her little adventure drama. He saw her realize that he controlled her as much as she did him. Kieler knew she could try to hurt him to make him let go of her, perhaps bring up a knee to a sensitive spot, but he thought that was too much, even for her. Maybe. He braced himself in case she tried it anyway.

He held her gaze, hard, as hard as he held her around her chest. She looked back at him just as stern, knowing now that her ultimatum wasn't going to work.

Finally, she heaved a sigh. Kieler felt her chest rise against his, rather than actually hearing her sigh. She scowled at him.

She put her mouth to his ear again. "Fine. Don't move. You could crash us into the wall. I'll fly *this* airship."

Kieler was okay with that. Just when reason seemed to be returning, he became aware of how hard their bodies were pressed against each other.

Then she bit his ear.

He jerked back, but neither he nor she let go. It was just a nip, but it hurt. The burned ear, too.

"That's for you being more stubborn than me!" she shouted into his ear, a hint of laughter in her voice. "Now be still!" she repeated.

He felt her move against him. She unlocked one foot from around him and hooked it around the cloak streaming from her ankle above them. He moved his eyes down her backside (looking up actually) to see what she was doing.

She wrapped the cloak around that same leg, keeping her foot hooked. Then she did it again. And again. When her cloak was about half reeled in, it escaped, and two loops uncoiled from around her leg. She had obviously never done a two-person maneuver before! Kieler was strangely thankful for that. But it also showed she wasn't perfect in this alien environment. They weren't actually safe yet.

EPISODE 3 – ATTRACTION AND REPULSION

She re-wrapped the cloak around her leg twice more, but as the coil got fatter around her leg, she couldn't keep it from unraveling. The warm air from below was feeling hot, and Kieler knew she'd be sweating if the wind wasn't evaporating the sweat before it formed.

Finally, Velirith got a couple more loops, just over half her cloak, and tried something different. She crooked her leg up.

"Hold me!" she shouted.

He did, willingly, and she let go, reaching down (up, really) with one arm to grab the cloak from her ankle. This she managed first try.

She hauled it in and their feet-up attitude began to settle to a horizontal one. Clutching her cloak tightly, Velirith looked around, up and down. Somehow, when she looked around, they remained stable. She was moving some other part of her body to keep them balanced.

She found what she was looking for, checked Kieler with a look (he felt like a child being checked for good behavior), and began unfurling her cloak from her hand, this time near their midriffs.

They rose. Their bodies horizontal, she let out more of her cloak. Catching the rising air, it pulled them upward a couple more floors. She shot him another stern look that said, *You better not move!* Knowing the precariousness of their situation, he didn't even consider it. She got them sliding across the wind toward the wall.

Now Kieler saw her objective: another service door. Kieler stayed still, holding her, as she used her hands to grab a lever that obviously opened the door from inside the shaft. The partially unfurled cloak kept her atop him.

With one arm holding her cloak, the other on the lever, she slowly moved her leg to brace against the lip of the door for leverage. She simultaneously moved her other leg to counterbalance. Kieler didn't move. He was the only one holding them together.

The bar moved up and the door swung inward. She pulled her legs together and the upward rushing air pushed them through the door. Their momentum flipped their legs over their bodies, and with the supporting column of air gone, they fell to the floor of another service room. Kieler landed on top of her, pinning her down, his face an inch from hers, his lips less than an inch from her lips.

His brain wasn't working again. He should have felt relief, or anger, but his eyes were lost in the silver pools of hers. They seemed to be stirring like hot, liquid metal. The corners crinkled in the slightest smile: mischief. And... joy?

He could see his eyes reflected in hers. They looked very intent.

She looked back, unflinching.

CHAPTER EIGHT

Velirith looked up into Orlazrus' intense brown eyes. He was breathing hard, his chest rising and falling rapidly against hers. And hers, she realized, was rising and falling just as rapidly, mostly, but not entirely, from the exertion of getting them safely out of the airshaft.

She hadn't expected to end the flight in this position, but it wasn't all bad.

He was very close. Hard to focus on.

Will he do it? Will he actually kiss me?

It would be a true emotion for him; that she knew and savored.

It was a long time. And if ever there was going to be a time, this was it.

Something snapped, and his eyes went hard.

I'm the enemy again, she read, sighing, probably before he even realized it himself. She felt her own heat cool suddenly.

He couldn't kiss her.

"Fun's over," she told him without emotion.

Wordlessly, he rolled off her and then helped her up.

She let him.

It was so odd. She knew he should be blazing with anger at her—or he should be cursing his missed chance. Or crying in relief that he was alive. But all his emotions seemed to cancel out. He wasn't controlling his emotions. He was simply composed.

As he pulled her to her feet, he kept her hand. He looked at her and smiled, pleasantly, she thought.

CHAPTER EIGHT

Would he, someday, come clean and include her in what he was really doing? She studied him, still excited, but he gave her no hints to his inner thoughts now. He had buried them again.

So, the second objective of her scheme hadn't worked, but the first had. "Well, that was fun."

Velirith led, and the Ortessi followed.

Despite the ending of her prank, neither of them seemed to be in a hurry. Their breathing slowed, and yet Velirith still felt the hard press of his body against hers. For now, that feeling dominated her concern over his true identity.

She had another activity planned for Verr Ortessi, something she felt she wanted to do but had hesitated to let the fraud in on. It would reveal much about what was important to her, and she wanted him to treat it with respect.

So after plunging him into the airshaft, now may not be the perfect time, but she knew she was going to jump in anyway. The Ortessi had revealed something of his past, albeit inadvertently. Three days ago he had opened the door a crack. She felt she was responding generously, opening her door quite a bit more.

This airshaft service room opened into an interior corridor of The Empyrean, which led straight out to a garden balcony.

They were much lower now, under Symphony Garden. The crescent-shaped, small garden was fed by a cascading waterfall from another balcony above. A single haventhall grew out of the main pool. From that pool, in turn, ran a small channel that flowed to the edge of the balcony, generating another waterfall down to the next terrace.

When Velirith paused to look over the side, Orlazrus examined the tree, counting.

"...six, seven, eight, nine. Amazing."

Evidently, he had never looked at an individual haventhall up close. Though she was used to them, she had to admit it was a fascinating tree. Nine thick stems twisted together, usually with a beautiful perfection, to form a trunk that stretched upward into the sky. At the top, the nine cords of the trunk separated, spiraling out to support the leafy canopy far overhead.

She observed him fondly, noting both his childlike wonder and his manly face, like chiseled stone in the grey, metallic light of the reflected Starstone. She also noted how quickly he had recovered from falling about half the height of The Empyrean. Still, she had surprised him. The scene had played well. But he was obviously practiced at keeping cool and regaining composure after experiencing danger. Which brought up the questions once again; who was he and where did he come from?

It struck her, something that should have been obvious, that he wasn't from a rival house. No one at the New Year's Gala had recognized him. Not even the Merckles and Mizgots, who vouched for him, really had any idea who he was or why he was there. And that was the bigger question; what was he trying to accomplish? How could he *not* belong to one of the other houses?

Maybe Aurelios might have some insight into that question.

"Come on, Wonderboy," she chided, calling his attention from the top of the tree. "We're going to meet the second most influential man in my life, after my father." It was odd she felt compelled to clarify that statement.

She ducked through the tiny door.

This small door opened into a passage where neither of them could stand erect. The short passage led to an equally tight staircase descending around a podcar tube.

"This is a podcar service access," she explained as they began down. "There are back passages like this all over. You can get from one end of the city to the other without ever using a main corridor."

She glanced back at him. The Ortessi was trying to appear blasé, even bored, but she could see these passages and service doors were exactly the kind of environment he thrived in.

After following the stair down several levels, they crawled through a complex series of connecting cross-shafts. This in-and-out of service tunnels should have confused most everyone. But her tail took it in stride. *Maybe he really was raised under the Plate.*

As she led him past a switching mechanism for the podcars, then a reinforced pipeline that channeled water to the top of the tower, and through yet another 'shortcut' under one of the pipes, she noticed that he was, almost absently, analyzing the devices that made Velakun work.

In a flash of intuition, Velirith asked, "Did you build that airship?"

He jumped, completely unprepared for her sniping. His face went guarded, and he answered, "Yes," and that was all.

Well, Velirith decided, *he's learning to tell the truth around me. But there's much more he was thinking about behind that answer.*

She couldn't think of a follow-up question, but the fact that he had actually built something that flew, however briefly and dangerously, was quite impressive. Then she asked, without the shock value, "Did you design it too?"

Again she looked back at the end of her question, and his new-skin, baby-face reddened, self-conscious. "Yes," he said again.

She threw him some ego-fodder, "I'm impressed. Flying free through the open air, not just in an airshaft... that would be a wonderful experience." He was blushing again, both in pride and... something else. Then she couldn't help casually adding the barb, "If it didn't crash and blow up every time."

She felt the sting on her rump and realized she shouldn't have turned away from him. "You didn't—!"

"—smack the spoiled royal cheek? Of course not."

And she didn't need her royal gift of lie-detection to recognize his bald-faced lie.

So he can be pushed only so far. She could respect that. "That better not leave a mark."

The mumbled reply sounded like, "Hope it does."

EPISODE 3 – ATTRACTION AND REPULSION

She smiled. They had come to another hatched door. This door scared her a bit.

"Do you mind?" she asked with false impatience, indicating the hatch. "This one is a bit heavy. Show off those dumb muscles."

She doubted he could resist a chance to demonstrate strength. And she was right.

The hatch lever dutifully resisted his weight and the increasing pressure of his muscles. As she plunged her own weight against the door, she commanded, "Push on it!"

He did. It opened. And the moment it did, she grabbed his waist and added to his shove. They fell through the open door, and for the second time today, they were free-falling.

"You—!"

Whatever adjective he was about to modify her with was cut short by plunging into a fast-moving aqueduct.

They surfaced. Him shouting. Velirith sputtering from trying to laugh underwater.

"What are you thinking?! Why do you do these stupid pranks? Have you no sense of—sense of—" he fumbled in the water for the word.

"Shame?" she finished for him.

"Propriety!"

She gulped more water then spat it out with the word. "Propriety! This from a man posing as a House Prime?"

Should she warn him? He was sputtering now. They were being carried by the gentle stream through another balcony garden. In frustration, Orlazrus cupped his hands and shot a blast of water into her face.

Nope. No warning, she thought.

She dove under, knowing this would keep his attention on where she would come up. But instead, she swam the few feet toward him and grabbed his waist again. She tried to pull him under, just to amplify the effect, but he pushed her head down to keep her under instead.

CHAPTER EIGHT

No matter.

Indeed, two seconds later they plummeted over another waterfall. She let go of his body and pushed away. This one was a good, long one. She curled and, just for style, did a double summersault before hitting the next pool.

Truth! she swore inside her head. She had landed, in the process of straightening out, on her stomach. The water knocked the wind out of her and she gulped for air, getting only a lung-full of water.

She finally came up, gagging and flailing. On the verge of passing out, she caught a glimpse of the Ortessi. That one glimpse registered his fury, his concern, and his wariness that her drowning was but a final act, a last curtain call scripted to further humiliate him.

Unfortunately, it could well have been her final act. She couldn't get air, even when she struggled weakly to the surface.

He didn't let her flounder long. She felt his arms around her midriff, and then felt herself riding with her head out of the water as he back-paddled toward the side of the pool.

Gagging and spitting up water, she felt embarrassed. But as soon as she was pushed safely up onto the lip of the pool, and her spasmed diaphragm started working, and she had spit out enough water, she began laughing again. She couldn't help it. This man was going to save her even if she killed him.

The Ortessi just looked at her with a silly grin and shook his head.

She did thank him. Within five minutes she had retrieved the clothes she had stashed in this garden, both for her and for him. Hers was a normal set of blue and silvers. But his, and at this point she hoped he didn't know, was a pale blue theater robe. Pale blue was the color for absolute novices.

He was shockingly quiet.

He didn't seem mad anymore. He was past that.

EPISODE 3 – ATTRACTION AND REPULSION

She eyed him, assessing. He looked back coldly. He reminded her of her father when they both knew she had gone too far. He really looked a lot older despite half his face being so baby-smooth.

She bit her lip. She was going to tell him that this garden was level with a causeway that led straight across to Theater Tri. They had arrived! And by the shortest cut possible.

But she was afraid. Afraid that if she broke the brittle silence it might shatter, and she would be showered with shards of his disapproval.

So she just led him between two towering tri-cornered edifices and toward the causeway. She looked up at the dizzying heights. She tested the silence's strength. "I like how small the buildings make you feel. There's something humbling and true about it."

He gave her a "you're crazy" look.

"Because *we* are small. Nothing we do affects much beyond our lifetime. In this world, nothing lasts. In the physical."

He cracked, not shattering. "How can you say that? Standing here in the shadow of Velik? Your house shaped the face of the last thousand years. *One man!*"

"That has some significance, I suppose. But not much compared to time stretching out infinitely in both directions. How can our mortal blink impact the purpose of the universe?" She knew she was being dramatic. Probably her theatrical bent.

"'*Purpose of the universe?*' How about just staying alive? How about just being fair and compassionate to another human being?" The Ortessi was getting fired up, thankfully, not just glowering at her. "Just be practical. What if we could just make today better?"

Smiling, she realized she had accidentally pressed the right buttons. She murmured, "So, there's some kind of idealist under that conniving façade. Hmm."

He snorted in exasperation.

CHAPTER EIGHT

She sighed in relief. She had brought him back from "too far."

"Anyway," she continued, "you'll like the backstage of the theater. Gadgets, trapdoors, illusion makers—it's your style."

Velirith wanted the faux-Ortessi to know the man who had inspired her to her passion: *Theater!*

It's illogical. But then, logic limits the creative mind.

As the Ortessi walked her from the causeway to the theater, he glanced at her quizzically. She voiced the question she knew he wanted to ask, "Why am I trusting you with the secrets of my private life when you know I know you're someone else?"

She imagined Orlazrus gave her an imperceptible nod.

Velirith looked up to the sky, clouds gathering, and sighed. Rain was coming. She passed fingers over her eyes, across her brow, and pulled her wet hair back. "I don't know. You don't trust *us* with your real identity, which I suspect is probably better than your fake one. I suppose I'm trying to draw you out by showing you trust."

Knitting his brow, he finally spoke, "There's some logic in that..."

Velirith laughed. "It's not logic."

Kieler locked his resolve with his steps as they crossed the open plaza that hosted the six-sided theater. He would not let this girl get to him. *I have control of one thing in her home arena: my attitude. Just let her childish pranks pass.*

The expansive triangular plaza of the theater openly sprawled in contrast to the vertical development of the rest of the city. The center of Theater Tri was dominated by the massive dome of the theater.

Why the Velaki had dedicated so much of the island's precious real estate to such an impractical pastime, Kieler could not guess. The plaza around the theater was artistically landscaped with fountains, pools, greenery, and statuary, including one of Velik himself holding a scroll. Clubs and groups of friends gathered regularly in these plazas. In fact, he had rarely seen Theater Tri vacant as he had passed over it going to and from Vel Estate by podcar.

Theater-goers could enter the building on five of the six sides through towering, arched doors. The sixth side housed a minimal backstage area. Velirith and Kieler entered opposite the backstage through one of the tiled arches.

They passed under the arch, through an elegant ante-theater, and emerged at the top of the lower seating area. The seating sections encircled the large center stage except for where a catwalk cut through the seats from the center to the rear stage with a curtained backdrop.

Velirith led him down an aisle to the front row. She jumped up to the slightly raised middle stage and indicated for him to follow. The stage thumped hollow beneath him as he leapt up.

Once in the exact center of the arena-like theater, Velirith spread her arms and broke into a soliloquy, evidently unable to control herself. She projected her voice to reach even the farthest row high in the empty theater.

"We enter these haunted domains to fight chaos itself! What it keeps divided, we will unite. Where it seeks disorder, we will order, by design, row and pattern. It is a groveling, selfish force of hate and destruction. *We* are intelligence infused with love. We will conquer," she paused to look intently into the faces of the imaginary troops around her, "and we will *build!* A city of light and beauty! By orderly array of form and function, we will overwhelm the ranks of chaos. Our enemy will not be overcome by mere violence, but by the persistent pursuit of grace and artistry. It will flee our presence! For out of its ruins we will forge symmetry and system, a new dawn of people united in law and mutual respect!"

The great hall echoed with her enthusiastic rendering.

CHAPTER EIGHT

"Velik himself never spoke it so boldly," Kieler forced the praise out of him. He knew it was Velik's famous address to the troops upon entering the collapsed city of what was now Avertori. Her performance was worthy of praise. He just didn't want to encourage her.

Velirith beamed at the compliment as if it were totally sincere. "He probably didn't," she admitted with a broad smile. "That speech is more fiction than action, true? But I love to belt it out. It was the first thing I memorized when I was just five."

She bowed thrice to the applause of her imagined audience, then spun and strode proudly down the catwalk to the narrower stage at the far end of the theater. Kieler followed, and he couldn't help grinning at her drama. She was fun.

Irresponsible, but fun.

Hopefully, the pranks were over. She was getting predictable.

Two strides before the backdrop, Velirith stopped suddenly with a conspicuous scuff of her foot and whirled on him, more mischief in her eyes. Kieler drew up short, cautious and ready, but she had stopped so quickly that he was too close to her.

Her next move surprised him anyway. She slipped her arm around his waist, drew herself to him and looked up into his eyes as if to—

"Nope!" she declared. With a disappointed sigh she pulled away and said, "I've actually overdone it. Truth."

Suspended between her confession and her next prank, Kieler waited expectantly.

Velirith, with what appeared to be humility, asked him, "Do you want to see how the trapdoors work?"

Kieler looked down at the stage floor. Her foot hovered over a raised button that her initial scuff had evidently activated. He looked down at her and gave her a wry, resigned smile. "Mischief must build up in you like lightning in a storm. Go ahead. Get it all out."

EPISODE 3 – ATTRACTION AND REPULSION

"Oooh, I like that," she responded with a tilt of her head. "Lightning in a storm." She stomped her foot. But not on the button.

Braced, Kieler wondered why he wasn't falling again.

"Stand back two feet," Velirith instructed.

He did. She too scooted back, then balanced on one foot and reached out with the other to press the button on the floor. True to a trapdoor, it swung downward and into blackness beneath.

Still wary, Kieler looked down into a very dim under-stage. A cage full of fluffy cushioning lay beneath the gaping hole. "No," Kieler remarked. "I didn't need that."

"That's for hauling me out of the pool back there."

He mocked an enlightened expression. "So *that's* the secret. Every time I save your life you spare me a prank! Well that's fair. Perhaps I'll save your life every day, yes? That will allow me to keep my dignity. Except give me one day a month off."

He watched Velirith consider the consequences of *not* saving her life on his day off. He felt good about his jibe, but he did suspect it wasn't really saving her life that had spared him. Pranking him had simply lost its "dramatic effect" by this time. Bad theater.

"Is this your favorite playground, Velirith?"

She rolled to her feet. "Absolutely. This has been my main playground since I was little. Come this way. You know I believe in experiential education."

"I'm not sure I'm ready to learn anything else. Ever."

"Baby."

It was amazing how her pranks and spontaneity kept him on the thin border between totally annoyed and having the time of his life. She had planned this day well, he determined. But it was her witty personality, her quirkiness, and her *flirtiness* that kept him from going over the edge to rage. He hoped the trapdoor was the last of this series.

CHAPTER EIGHT

She led him downstairs to the very back of the dim maze of special effects. They were behind and under the far backdrop, he was sure. Along the back wall were rows of levers and gears and pulleys with cables extending up to the stage above.

"Pull that one," she demanded, indicating a massive wooden lever.

He hesitated.

"Oh fine. I'll do it." She pulled fast and with all her weight, and from the dark side of the under-stage came a whooshing sound. In an instant they were both blasted with chill air. Straining against the rush of air, vainly trying to keep his silly robe down, Kieler again heard her laughing against the wind. She struggled to throw the lever closed. He put his hands on hers and lifted, shutting off the air.

Her hair was plastered all over her flushed face and her chest was still heaving as her laughter died off. She looked up at him through wild wisps of dark hair, her silver eyes flashing. "Guess what we use that for?" Pause. "Making wind! It comes straight from those airshafts we played in. And guess what's next?"

Kieler shrugged but played along. "Another water trap? Being shot out of a maggun?"

"Nope. We meet Cota Aurelios."

"Your theater master? That doesn't sound dangerous."

"It's not," she replied, "usually. As long as you're not uncomfortable in the presence of peaceful souls." She regarded him for a moment and then strode off again. "I guess it *could* be a problem for you." She found a flight of stairs and bounded down several levels. Kieler followed, acquiescent.

This is my punishment for slipping out of character.

Stars, she boils my blood. Spoiled, but bold. Smart, but pretty. And totally irresponsible. She wants nothing to do with changing the Omeron, even though she's in a uniquely powerful position to do so. I can't let her get too close.

EPISODE 3 – ATTRACTION AND REPULSION

Another part of his mind responded, *She's already too close.*

He tried not to think about it.

"Does Aurelios live in the basement?"

"Yes," she answered. She waved a hand as they passed several levels. "Props, costumes, make-up and changing levels are just below the under-stage. This is a storage level... and this down here is the Theater Guild quarters. Cota Aurelios lives here."

Immediately the hall opened into a wide, spacious living area furnished with elegant couches, chairs and inlaid tables. Hung around the outside walls, illuminated by lens-softened luzhril fixtures, were wall after wall of exquisite art, both paintings and sculpture. This common living room was surrounded by many doors that must house the members of the Theater Guild. Several members of the guild clustered around a table, evidently working on some script. They paused and waved across the room at Velirith.

Velirith led Kieler along the side of this living room past several doors to one which bore the name *Aurelios*. She knocked gently. Kieler noted that every hint of impish demeanor was gone; she stood demurely, almost like a normal person, as if waiting to meet the Executive Chair.

Presently the door was opened by the elderly man Kieler had seen at Orcad's opening ceremony. Aurelios' posture was straight but relaxed. His eyes were a soft grey, as was his short, wavy hair. He smiled.

"Velirith!" He gave her a hearty hug, and Kieler's immediate impression was of a man with a lot more life left in him than his years proclaimed. Aurelios was joyful to see Velirith, yet at the same time, he radiated an extreme calmness that set Kieler on edge.

The man looked at Kieler with a half-smile, leaning back to assess him. "So this is the confounding gentleman by the name of Orlazrus Ortessi you've so often mentioned."

CHAPTER EIGHT

Velirith colored slightly and Kieler bowed a little, trying to remain as relaxed and casual as he could muster.

The man nodded as if he had just confirmed something, then turned to Velirith. "You look wet and windblown! Living at full tilt?"

She laughed. "Absolutely. I've been sharing gems of my life with this nefarious nobleman here." She waved a hand at Kieler, who scowled wryly at the reference to her earlier performance.

"He looks like he could handle your exploits."

She couched her reply, "Most. He's somewhat deeper than he plays. Which is why we are here."

Aurelios smiled and shook his head. "Are you manipulating again, my young apprentice?"

She gave the slightest hint that she might shake her head in denial, but then simply said, "Yes."

Aurelios gave her a knowing look, his eyes twinkling. He turned to Kieler. "What are you finding most interesting in Velakun, young man?"

The man seemed to intentionally not use "Verr Ortessi." Kieler let it go as he considered the question. "The beauty. Engineering rounds. And history."

The older man nodded, and Kieler decided that he only accepted Kieler's response as a partial truth. "Engineering, eh? Do you find Cota Rejin's teaching style engaging?"

Velirith responded to this banal comment with a studying tilt of her head.

Kieler replied, "I do. I'm very impressed at her depth of knowledge and commitment to her field."

"Well said. She *is* very passionate."

Something about Velirith's high level of interest caught Kieler's attention. He knew she certainly wasn't interested in the subject of engineering. She said to Aurelios, "My companion here tells me you stink-bombed her lab." She seemed to be probing.

EPISODE 3 – ATTRACTION AND REPULSION

Aurelios didn't miss it. "You know I have a bit of a mischievous streak too."

Her eyes narrowed. "That answer is just a tiny bit evasive."

Biting his lip, he deliberately said no more. His eyes twinkled even more, and Kieler wondered what he was missing.

Velirith's eyes grew very wide. "You? And Rejin?"

Aurelios looked very serious. "No," and after a long and perfectly theatrical pause, he added, "Just me."

Velirith's jaw opened and she blurted out, "You have a crush on her!"

Both the accusation and her barefaced bluntness surprised Kieler as much as anything she had done today. But the color that tinged Aurelios' pale face surprised him as well. She was right.

"How could I have *not* seen this before?" Velirith seemed astonished at herself too.

"Maybe because he's at least twice her age?" Kieler said offhandedly.

Aurelios scowled fiercely at Kieler. "A man's appreciation of a fine woman, passionate and devoted, does not fade with years! Nor should it." He sounded defensive.

But it was Velirith who apologized. "I'm sorry, Cota Aurelios. I'm just surprised."

Aurelios looked down with a small smile, and the peace he wore like a favorite cloak seemed to return. "I guess I didn't realize you would be able to perceive my affection for her. A misjudgment on my part."

"Does *she* know?" Velirith asked.

Aurelios shrugged. "I don't know. I would think a woman of her intelligence would figure out why I put so much effort into annoying her." He looked up at Velirith with a shy smile. "It's an odd attraction, I admit."

She looked back at her mentor with a thoughtful, loving smile. Her respect and admiration for the man stung Kieler with a pang of jealousy.

CHAPTER EIGHT

They still stood in the doorway to Aurelios' apartments, the conversation having progressed more quickly than decorum. The Theater Cota paused, tilting his head as if listening. Despite the embarrassing revelation, Kieler once again felt tranquility radiate from him.

Aurelios' eyes focused on Kieler, suspicious and concerned. "I've just been told I should show you the theater's library. Not something I would have even considered otherwise."

Kieler looked around. "Told by whom?" He felt he was missing something.

But Aurelios closed the door to his chambers behind him and moved with purpose across the parlor. Kieler and Velirith followed.

"Our theater holds the key to our wellbeing. I think you would benefit greatly by studying the plays."

Is he saying I need an education in the arts or intimating that I need acting lessons?

Aurelios led them at a brisk walk through the residences to an inner circular stairwell leading deeper. The stone steps bore the wear of ages, and Kieler was intrigued by the feel of the place— ancient... hallowed?

Almost grumbling, Aurelios told him, "Be very careful around the scrolls. We don't even let most of our guild members come down here."

Kieler, trailing the old man down the stairs, responded automatically, "Then why are you showing me?"

"Because the Truth is *always* right. I've learned not to question it."

Well, that was cryptic. Kieler cast a glance back at Velirith. He was beginning to question the man's mental competency. She deliberately avoided eye contact.

The Cota said, "You don't know the Truth. You don't know that much about Velirith. And by the elements, you don't even know your own heart! You don't doubt your Orcad mentors, do you? Would you question instruction when you don't even know what you don't know?"

This guy was more random than Velirith. But unlike the repartee Kieler enjoyed with Velirith, this man was annoying him. Aurelios knew *nothing* about his background; how he grew up; how he lost his parents. "I don't think you know anything about me either."

"You're right. At least *I* admit it. *You* don't. I'm told you're playing a game and don't even know the rules or who's side you're on."

This is too much. "Told by *who,* Aurelios?"

Kieler thought he heard the man growl. "You wouldn't know him."

Him? Not Velirith? Kieler was about to pin the man down to a straight answer when he ran into the back of him. "Sorry," he mumbled testily. They had come to a stone door to which Aurelios was applying the key. Engraved into the door were the words "Know the Truth, and the Truth will set you free."

Kieler scowled as if the phrase was the coded conclusion to their ethereal conversation, a riddle answer to a riddle question he couldn't even phrase. He glanced back at Velirith, who seemed upset. He didn't care.

As the stone door groaned inward, Aurelios visibly regained his peaceful composure. In fact, he moved in the slow awe and wonder of someone seeing something for the first time. Kieler pushed into the chamber to see what caused the change.

He found himself on a narrow walkway around a circular room overlooking a three-story drop. The curved walls were riddled with evenly spaced alcoves, niches in which Kieler could see rolls of paper scrolls. The circular chamber was tiered, three tiers below them and three more above, capped by a painted dome. Every wall of every tier was riddled with cubbyholes. A thin, sturdy handrail kept them from falling to the tier below.

CHAPTER EIGHT

Velirith took hold of a rolling, vertical ladder that extended up to the next tier. She mounted it, shoved with her foot against the floor, and sailed around the perimeter.

"What are in all these niches?" Kieler asked as she slid away. He looked up to the domed ceiling far above. It was painted with a fresco of a theater-in-the-round, seats surrounding a stage with actors in the middle of a performance. It was detailed and finely done.

Aurelios stood in mute reverence looking up at the cubbies as if he were in the presence of the divine. The ladder slowed to a stop, and Velirith climbed a couple rungs then reached into one of the small, door-less recesses. Compared to her reckless, headlong actions of earlier today, she seemed to slow to a crawl.

Gingerly, she extracted a sheaf of scrolls. Kieler squeezed past Aurelios on the catwalk to a point near where she stood on the ladder.

"This collection of scripts pre-dates Velik," she said, her voice hushed. "How far back, I don't even know. Maybe Cota Aurelios does. This sheaf contains all the parts for *Arrival*, the play we will perform at the Festival of Aerial Lights in a few weeks."

"These are all plays? But there are thousands of them! Who wrote them all?"

She shrugged. "The Guild, mostly. Theater Velaki is a deep part of our tradition, far older than that of Theater Ortessi. All of the plays from the house you are pretending to be from were written after Velik's reclaiming of Avertori to preserve the history of the cleansing and rebuilding. The plays in *this* library chamber are of events and wisdom so old they are, frankly, difficult to believe. Even the perspective is different."

Velirith leaned over to Kieler, and he gingerly took one of the ancient sheets of the upcoming play. It was old, but still whole, as if preserved by a method now forgotten. Two questions suddenly struck him. "Why is the play called *Arrival*? Are you in it?"

EPISODE 3 – ATTRACTION AND REPULSION

"I have a part, yes. And you'll see. It's a moving, very visual play. I'm not going to spoil your first impression. The Festival is one of the highlights of the year here in Velakun." She gently took back the scrolls and replaced them in their nook.

Aurelios walked across the catwalk, slowly looking left and right, up and down the vast vault of the library. He stopped halfway around, looked up and smiled. "The teaching of wisdom doesn't have to be dull and serious."

He looked at the two young students, Velirith on the rolling ladder, Kieler in front of her. The Cota of the Theater continued, "I have found my life's joy in these plays. And I have also found joy in passing that joy to you, Velirith. Drama, joy and wisdom: who can ask for a better combination?"

Kieler thought he was being a bit *over* dramatic.

Aurelios leaned over the rail and put a hand across the space below. He stretched toward the niches on the opposite side of the circular space. "It seems no one is reaching for the Truth today. And it's right there!" He wiggled his fingers on the end of his outstretched arms.

Then he turned and touched a scroll in an alcove next to him. He continued softly, "It's right here, in these sacred plays."

He turned and addressed Kieler, as if responding to him. "Do you think that by removing the Omeron, you remove the problems of Zotikas?"

Kieler felt his eyes widen at how closely Aurelios' sudden words described their plan. Aurelios waited a moment for Kieler to respond, then went on. "Do you think it's the Omeron's fault? The Omeron is just people. Do you know any people who are pursuing the Truth?"

Unsure of the point, Kieler shrugged.

"A few seek the Truth. But if you eliminate the current government people, who will replace them?"

Kieler thought but didn't reply out loud. *Our people, from below the Plate.*

Aurelios responded, "They're still people! More people who aren't seeking the Truth! Nothing changes for the better if people pursue wrong principles."

Aurelios couldn't know that Kieler was here to take out the corrupt heads of state. Yet he was suggesting his mission would accomplish nothing!

Ridiculous. He felt his jaw clench.

"Do you want to make the government better?"

Yes, thought Kieler.

"I believe you do. But does replacing one lie with another make it true? Does replacing one selfish, ignorant leader with another selfish, ignorant person suddenly make the world good?"

The issue had crossed Kieler's mind. *Who did Movus have in mind to run the government?* Kieler assumed it would be Movus, with Kieler in some role, backed by the Coin. But Movus hadn't really detailed the full plan after the fall of the Omeron.

"Seek Truth and pursue it. So where do you find Truth? There used to be a book…" Aurelios mused. "But it's not in circulation now."

Kieler looked up into the pigeonholed plays. He still wondered whether Aurelios was mad or if the man had somehow guessed Kieler's true intentions. Either way, it was unnerving.

Aurelios followed Kieler's puzzled gaze.

"Knowledge of the Truth. Hidden in a play," Aurelios finished.

Kieler, grasping for something to say, couldn't help but retort, "Truth? How can you get truth out of fiction?"

Facing Aurelios, Velirith leaned out from the ladder and slapped Kieler across the back of the head.

Aurelios responded simultaneously. "You're a fiction yourself! Use the logic of your heart and you may actually be able to perceive Truth!"

He strode up to Kieler's face and for a moment Kieler thought the old man would strike him. Instead, he whispered intensely, "You follow a path of willful ignorance that leads to devastation. You are bolting down a cliff like a blind kovar."

The words stung Kieler like firethorn. He could not bring Aurelios' words together into coherent thought, but he felt their underlying truth. How did Aurelios know so much? Had someone come to him with information? Kieler's confusion boiled into heated frustration.

Aurelios drove the thorn deeper under Kieler's skin. "Foolish man, you bring destruction to House Vel." The words reverberated off the chamber walls. Kieler felt flustered and trapped.

He could not give voice to the fear rising in him. Somehow Aurelios was making him feel as if he were doing wrong, but Kieler knew his motives were right, and their plan as good as they could make it. The theater man's words were like a spell—or a spell breaker.

Confused, Kieler took a stumbling step forward on the narrow walkway. He felt like a fool stomping on brittle ice beside an abyss. He had to get out of this chamber.

"You charlatan! You listen to voices that aren't there and then you spit accusations and insults when you know nothing about me!" But Kieler was reeling with how close Aurelios had come to the truth. He grabbed the rail for support.

Despite Aurelios' dire prediction, the man stood relaxed and calm, as if watching Rei setting over the Rim.

But Kieler felt as if he had been struck, tottering inside. To cover his unbalanced state of mind, he pressed forward as if in anger. Pushing past Aurelios, Kieler lurched for the ancient door and fled the library.

CHAPTER NINE

Four days later Kieler was under the Plate and happy to be there. Velirith and her people were driving his thoughts in ragged circles. He never imagined the twisting, decaying passages of the under-city would bring him solace.

But after conferring with Movus, Kieler had managed to arrange to get together with Bags, his closest friend besides his mentor. And just to top off his sense of returning home, they were to meet at The Stale Ale, an old favorite.

Kieler made his way from Movus' apartment through the rubbly tunnels of the underworld to the pub. The best news he got from his boss was that a motor was being built for Kieler's nascent airship. It would be a few months before delivery, and Kieler knew that if he could have been on that team, building it would go faster. But he wasn't. He was playing his role in the greater plan, even if Velirith thought he was playing that role poorly.

Agh! Why do I care what that spoiled girl thinks?

He arrived before Bags and ordered up the unusually dry brew for which the pub was famous. As the mugs arrived, so did Bags.

"Bags!" Kieler rose, grasped forearms with the big man and pulled him into a hug. Bags had a grim, crooked grin on his face as they broke apart. "Arriving with the ale! I think leading Slink Squad has improved your timing."

Bags swallowed and nodded. As they sat, Kieler noted the haggard look of his friend, but held off asking.

"It's so good to see you! I never thought I'd be glad to be back in this pit we were always so eager to get out of," Kieler told

EPISODE 3 – ATTRACTION AND REPULSION

him, "but a break from the crazed, twisted ways the up-worlders think and act is like a breath of stale, familiar air. Do you know I spent nine hours today waiting with a stuffy Vel lawyer for a two-minute appointment to stamp an eighty-page warrant? I'm surprised the weight of the paperwork up there doesn't collapse the Plate on our heads."

Kieler studied Bags' reaction—barely a rise in blood pressure. Something was wrong.

They pulled at their mugs, Bags with a slow lackluster that further solidified Kieler's assessment. As he set down his vessel, Kieler toned down his mood and studied Bags.

Bags noticed the change and managed a weak grin. He grunted and his voice came out hoarse, "Good to see you too, Sparks."

"What's the bad news? Eznea?" Kieler prodded.

Bags looked down into the ale. "No—well, in a way." He lifted the mug but seemed not to have the will to raise it to his lips. He looked up at Kieler. "Telander killed a couple of newlyweds last night."

Kieler cocked his head and scowled. "Someone you know?"

Bags shook his head. "Not personally. But she was an attractive young lady. They got married a few days ago. Telander heard about it and checked her out. Decided he wanted her for his 'collection'. Last night he sent his monster squad to get her. The husband defended his new wife with his life. And the young lady defended her man. She got clipped in the crossfire. She might have lived, but she would be useless to their boss, so they finished her off."

Horrified, Kieler's instinct was to ask how Bags found out about it, but that wasn't the point. Kieler knew Bags had a couple guys watching Telander's people and following them when they moved.

"So the real bad news is that we're not making any news." Bags looked up with intense, tear-filled eyes. "We're not doing anything!" and he slammed the ale mug to the table, sloshing out a large portion.

Stone still, Kieler listened. "You're the high-profile spy, Sparks. We're the Dead Ones, rotting in our hole in the ground!"

He'd never seen such despair from his friend. Bags had always been confident and determined to get Eznea back from Telander. But Kieler could understand how waiting and doing nothing while his wife was a prisoner of a creature like Borgus Telander was tearing him apart.

After a long silence, Kieler tried to encourage him. In a low, intense voice he said, "Bags, we're making progress. I'm accepted as a Prime in Velakun. Sure we'd be doing more if I had ended up in Avertori, but I'd probably be dead by now. Feleanna wouldn't put up with me strutting around Avertori under her nose."

But that comment just seemed to emphasize how little Bags was doing. "You don't know how hard it is not to storm his complex and take down as many of his people as I can before they take me down." Bags was holding back rage.

Kieler stared at his friend. "But you know that wouldn't fix anything."

Sighing and deflating, Bags knew. With a long silence, Bags idly traced circles in the ale he had spilled. He whispered, "At least I would be doing *something*. Better than hiding in this hole we call home." Bags had said that more than once.

His friend was a man of action, like Kieler. *Not* doing anything was killing him. And at this point in Movus' plan, the Coin needed to lay low while Kieler built up a power base up top.

"Look, Bags, can't you help Twink procure weapons for the Velaki order?"

He nodded sullenly. "I suppose. But Twink is just hitting all the outposts for weapons. The Cortattis own all the big caches, and they've really tightened security since someone broke into their house a few months back." Surprisingly, that comment broke Bags' mood and he looked up to smirk across the table at Kieler.

EPISODE 3 – ATTRACTION AND REPULSION

"Yeah, shame about that," Kieler replied in kind. "You'd think with all those guns they'd be more careful."

"Maybe we could offer them protection," Bags snorted and Kieler laughed. They shared a look of triumph, and Bags perked up a little. "Yeah, that was a good mission. But it was the last good assignment I had."

Frowning, Kieler looked intently at his successor. "Bags, think about this! You are the leader now. You need to pull your smarter guys together and figure out what else you could be doing. Don't sit around moping. Find something to do, clear it with Movus, and do it!"

Bags set his big jaw and nodded. He was not happy, but that familiar glint of determination shone in his eye.

They drank their brews, and it was Bags who changed the subject and moved on.

"So how *is* your mission going? You're still alive. That itself is an unlikely but good start."

Kieler nodded. He had beat the odds so far. "It is touch and go sometimes. Velator readily accepted me as the Prime of House Ortessi, but I suspect he has his own political reasons. I'm not sure he really believes it.

"And his daughter is another story," Kieler finished.

"Velupterith?" Bags said casually.

Kieler nearly sprayed his beer. With a laugh in his eyes and a control he didn't know he had, he swallowed and corrected, "Velirith."

Bags nodded and smiled slyly. "Right. That's just what the guys in Slink Squad are calling her."

Shaking his head, Kieler went on, almost whining. "Somehow she knows I'm a fraud, Bags. From the beginning, from the very first night of the New Year's Gala, she knew!"

"Did you screw up that night? Fall out of character?"

Shaking his head, Kieler answered, "No, not that night."

CHAPTER NINE

Somehow Bags didn't follow up and ask him the obvious question. Instead he asked something just as piercing. "So why doesn't she turn you in? Why doesn't she expose you?"

Kieler wanted to reply that she didn't have hard evidence, but the real reason popped out unexpectedly. "I think she likes me."

A real laugh burst out of Bags. "You're kidding!"

Taken aback, Kieler defended himself. "Why is that so hard to believe?"

Bags had brightened considerably and was shepherding the spilled ale into a pool on the table with the side of his hand. Kieler wondered if he was going to slurp it up. "Well," Bags began, a bit more slyly reserved, "you've never even had a girlfriend down here, so far as I know." He was avoiding Kieler's gaze. He was trying not to offend him! "And, well, your first night above the Plate you crash the biggest party on the planet and think the most eligible bachelorette in the Omeron is hot on you." He shrugged and looked up. "Just sounds a little unlikely."

Kieler felt hot. Yes, he was a little offended. And yes, it did sound more than a little unlikely. He had no response.

Bags was looking at him now. Studying him now. Those dark blue marbles of his drilling into Kieler. "And do you like her?"

The directness of the question, the implications after Bags had just reminded Kieler of Telander's heinous habits, sent a cold chill over him and gnawed a hole into the pit of his stomach. The truth was... the truth was he did.

"NO!" He denied it so loudly he knew that it sounded like a lie.

Bags drew back, eyes slightly widening. He couldn't have believed him. *So why did I just lie to my best friend?*

Because if Kieler admitted in any way that he had feelings for this Omeron scion, this pampered, selfish, irresponsible brat, he was endangering the bigger mission. He would basically be telling

Bags that chasing this blue-leathered babe was more important than cracking the Omeron or getting Eznea back.

His own selfish emotions could destroy everything they had worked for. And Bags would know this. If not immediately, he'd figure it out quickly enough.

Now Bags completely changed the subject. Kieler was relieved, but noted that the leader of Slink Squad should have pursued this flaw to its bitter conclusion. Perhaps making the point was enough. Perhaps Bags was more subtle than Kieler gave him credit.

"How's your shoulder?"

Kieler animatedly rotated the injured shoulder in its socket. He forced confidence into his voice. "Funny thing, Bags. After the raid on the Cortatti compound, it hurt like it was never going to heal. But after my run-in with the molten copper coils from the melting generator, it seems to be good as new."

"Hmph. I never saw you with your face burnt off. Maybe your miraculous recovery was more thorough than you thought. Sounds like you got a dose of that bio-element stuff Movus has been experimenting with."

Kieler shook his head and shrugged. "I have no idea what I was given, but *somebody* was down there in the generator dome with me. Somebody gave me something to help me heal. And the crazy thing is I think it was one of Feleanna's agents, but it makes no sense.

"Maybe you could do some checking on my mystery angel, Bags. I suspect a man named Cota Chance, and I don't think his motives were completely kindhearted. I'd appreciate it greatly, and it would give you something to do."

Bags sat up straighter at the suggestion and listened while Kieler gave him details.

CHAPTER TEN

He'd been back from Avertori for a week. Back to the Academy. Back to Velirith. Back to working on the *Pride,* and afterward his airship, *Liberty.*

After Orcad, it was Kieler's habit to head down to the *Pride's* bay and work with Jarovel. He had little overlap with the other workers, and often started by cleaning up their messes and tools. But lately their messes had been very light. Evidently, Jarovel made them clean up their own messes now, wanting Kieler to work more on the plating in the aft section, or the duralium lattice in the fore.

Today Kieler was up about eight feet high in the lattice, fitting glass panels into the growing duralium framework. The drive wheel spun smoothly behind him, still pumping power into the city above. It struck Kieler as amazing that the powercoach was now a main source of power. But the house responsible for building replacement generators seemed unconcerned, ignoring any urgency House Vel might feel. It did not surprise Kieler that the uncooperative house was House Telander.

As the *Pride* came back together, Kieler felt that Jarovel appreciated his efficient, meticulous work, though the Chief Mechanic was always spare with his compliments.

In turn, Kieler appreciated Jarovel's ignorance in the "loaning" of tools and parts Kieler needed for *Liberty.* He would have loved to have this quality and variety of tools available when working on his first airship.

About a month into cleaning and stripping the *Pride of Velik*, Kieler had suggested an impossible task for himself that no

349

one wanted. It was such a massive and obvious job that the rest of Jarovel's team and Jarovel himself couldn't even see it. While Jarovel was meticulous about keeping the *Pride* in perfect repair, his workshop was a train wreck.

In addition to housing the *Pride* itself, the dim, deep bay held rows of shelves of support materiel for the powercoach. To walk down an entire row of shelving took Kieler about a minute, and there were a dozen rows.

One afternoon when the maintenance crew had finished for the day, Kieler volunteered to spend time "organizing."

Organizing *centuries* of clutter.

His motives were purely ulterior. He wanted parts for *Liberty*.

When Kieler brought up the idea of cleaning the shop, Jarovel had laughed at him for a full ten minutes. "There's junk to fix, junk we don't even have any more! It would take a hundred years. Most stuff is useless anyway. And if you clean it, I'll never find anything. I know exactly where everything is."

But Kieler prevailed. "I'll not touch any of your tools. And if there's something with just a little dust on it, as if you used it only a decade ago, I'll ask you about it. With the *Pride* in the shape it's in, I'm certain I'll find pieces we can use to make her better faster."

It was that comment that did it. Jarovel was still heart-sick that his life's work was a broken skeleton.

So every night after his regular shift, Kieler spent an hour or two shuffling or labeling tools, fasteners, parts and pieces. He threw nothing away. But what wouldn't be missed, often disappeared.

And every evening, Jarovel eventually retired to his bunk at the back of the workshop or to his home—Kieler was surprised he had one—on the *north* side of the Rim, the prestigious side. But most nights, Jarovel stayed on Center Isle with his beloved *Pride*.

The work on the *Pride of Velik* was progressing even though they had to work around the spinning drive wheel still being used to help power Velakun. So after spending some time organizing, Kieler would slip out with needed parts or tools and take them down into the underpinnings of the citadel where he harbored his airship.

He found it exceptionally easy to pilfer goods. Nothing was guarded! Even though security in Velakun had increased with guards around the *Pride*, crime was in a deplorably primitive state inside Velakun. Avertori could pride itself on being much more advanced in that sector of the economy.

So night after night, he added to his collection, and finally *his* shop was producing something substantial.

He couldn't wait to try flying her. Unfortunately, he would have to. It would take months for Movus to get him an engine, and he still needed special fabric for the envelope and tanks for the hydrogen.

Getting Jarovel to order that fabric was Kieler's goal for tonight. As he worked on the scaffold at the very front of the powercoach, he thought about how he would sell the idea to Jarovel.

But his thoughts didn't stay on that course. Kieler realized he was working on the section of the lattice in which Velirith had perched on his first ride out of Avertori. He could picture her, looking down, judging him, already so sure that he was an imposter.

He also realized that this section of the fore-ship had been totally destroyed, ripped clean off the ship by magbolts. If she hadn't leapt at the first volley, he would have lost her.

What would this mission be like without her?

"Simpler," he said to the *Pride,* aloud. He had caught Jarovel talking to the *Pride* too, so he didn't feel self-conscious about it. But Kieler needed to be careful; he couldn't let someone overhear what he said in confidence to the enemy's ship.

When he finished the assigned section, he found Jarovel gently bending a metal bar into exactly the right curve to replace one of the damaged arms on the great "V" of the prow. He was an artist in his own way.

After a greeting of exchanged grunts, Kieler went into the shelves of parts and pieces and resumed moving stuff around. After a time, Jarovel finished his work and came to watch Kieler. In minutes, the older man began to yawn.

"Tedious," he grumbled, and shuffled back to his cot. But he certainly didn't stop Kieler from working. To Kieler, it wasn't work; it was treasure hunting. He found disused, high-quality magnets; special, smooth headed bolts; a pump for gasses that was over two hundred years old and *never used!* Valves, tanks, cables, bolts, cutters, files, presses, pliers, precision measuring equipment—it was all in there waiting to be found! He figured with a little time every week, consistently, eventually they would see major progress. He reminded himself that he was not here to make the shop work more efficiently but at the same time took pride that he was making a difference.

A few days ago he had found a ledger, a maintenance log, from shortly after the *Pride of Velik* had been inaugurated around five-hundred years ago. He shared this with Jarovel and they poured over the misadventures the early engineers had designing and operating a high-performance, mobile generator.

Tonight, under an old cowling, he found three brass knobs, classy and small enough to fit in his pockets. Admittedly, these knobs and the plush seat he had picked up a couple nights ago were luxuries—luxuries he felt were justifiable for such a sophisticated airship.

Having done as much sorting as he was willing to do tonight, and wanting to get a few hours work in on *Liberty,* he headed to the back of the *Pride's* bay to suggest they order tough-rip fabric.

He found Jarovel at his workbench, once again with his feet on the desk, engrossed in the maintenance log Kieler had found.

CHAPTER TEN

"Orlazrus, look at this!" he took his feet down and shared his rare excitement with Kieler. The log showed a roughly sketched diagram of a drive wheel breaking loose of its housing and rolling over the front of an older version of the *Pride of Velik*. It was fascinating and horrific at the same time.

Together, he and Jarovel read how, once again, the monster of consistency control in concentrating magal had raised its dangerous head. On its third voyage, the crew was testing the *Pride* for speed (Kieler could just imagine the eager engineers revving their new toy). On a stretch of the Ardan plain, the drive wheel entered a state of magnetic runaway, something that occasionally still happened in generators, as Kieler and Velirith had experienced. One quick-thinking engineer managed to get everyone onto the trailing support coach and cut loose. Slamming on the breaks, they barely managed to stay behind the flying wreckage as the powercoach was torn apart by the drive wheel.

"Could you imagine? A wheel breakin' loose..." Jarovel muttered in awe.

With a sideways nod of his head, Kieler admitted, "I could."

Jarovel kept the newly found old log on his workbench desk, on top of all the other stuff, and since this find, he had been much less antagonistic toward Kieler's clean-up project.

Now was the time to bring up Kieler's proposal. "Jarovel, can I suggest an improvement to the *Pride*?"

"No." The big man thumped the book closed and closed his eyes. "The *Pride of Velik* was built when people did things right. They cared. Exact. Beautiful. Now—all is junk."

Kieler went on anyway. "But we care too. You and me. And there are no safety devices. When those maggun bolts ripped through the prow—I saw the only daughter of Vel almost shredded by flying glass."

Jarovel shifted his bulky frame. "What do you want? Cover all the windows with steel or duralium? Nobody could see out. Lovely beast. A warship."

EPISODE 3 – ATTRACTION AND REPULSION

"I was thinking of creating a gas-filled bag of ripstop woven with haventhall fibers."

Jarovel looked stunned, trying to figure out what Kieler was suggesting. Then he guffawed. "Put the *Pride* in a bubble?"

"No, put a bubble in the *Pride*. Upholster the main structural beams of the viewing deck with an envelope of ripstop. Then if the *Pride* hits something or gets shot, gas would blast into the bags to form a huge bubble inside that would protect the passengers."

Jarovel thought Kieler was out of his mind, but he didn't laugh. By now he knew that Kieler was skilled in building and fixing and creating. Kieler had already proven himself fast and precise by completing the tasks Jarovel had given him repairing the *Pride*. Now, though, Jarovel just blinked at him with his puffy eyelids.

Kieler stood there, waiting, expecting him to say yes.

"The *Pride* is perfection. Improving perfection makes imperfection. If it looks ugly, we won't do it."

Kieler replied, "So we make more perfection. Look, with all the materials I found already by sorting out the junk in this bay, especially that pallet of plating you didn't know was under those rags, we'll come in way under your estimated repair cost. Order me a bunch of this stuff. Let me test it. If you like it, Velator will like it. The *Pride* will protect its riders better, and if we do it, well, *perfect*, it will look like part of the upholstery. With Feleanna on the rampage, this could make you the savior of House Vel."

Jarovel scowled, but relented. "I don't want to be a savior. I want the best *Pride*. Try it." Then he leaned forward, "But you do it like they did it five-hundred years ago: with class, with *pride*!" He pulled a materiel order form from under a stack of tiles and shoved it across the desk to Kieler. "You do the paperwork."

Kieler buried the thrill of victory behind a casual shrug, "Ok."

CHAPTER TEN

After quickly filling out the order, before Jarovel could change his mind, Kieler headed out of the powercoach bay and through the underpinnings toward his own airship's bay.

The vaulted underpinnings of the citadel soared into dark, unseen heights of massive ceramic arches that bore the weight of the sky-reaching towers above. They spanned the vertical distance between the level at which the powercoaches docked deep in Center Isle and the highly populated, well-developed commercial and government sectors on the surface. Immediately he passed several arched bays dedicated to the storage and repair of the podcar system.

After those bays, however, was a lonely stretch of a path on which Kieler had rarely seen another individual. It eventually led to the generator dome, but there were faster ways of getting there than walking, namely the podcars, but they didn't follow this path.

Feeling completely at home in the dark underground, Kieler sparingly used one of the luzhril lights from his residence to make the journey. It would have reminded him more of the under-Plate, but it was just too clean. There was no rubble, the way was relatively straight, and the columns were arrayed in an austere but pleasing pattern. Few of the areas were enclosed like the bay he was using.

He unlocked the wide door to his airship bay and unsheathed the array of lights he had taken, mostly from his own ambassadorial residence, but also some that happened to be unattended elsewhere in the underpinnings.

Kieler started by tightening a bolt attaching the skeletal cockpit to the skeleton airfoil.

Stepping away from her, he assessed his progress and enjoyed a moment of contentment.

"Looking good, *Liberty*." He ran a critical eye over the seven, super-light, super strong duralium wing spars that defined the shape of what would be the inflated wing. They were large— had to be to define a gas envelope large enough to lift a man or two—and rested on stands just shorter than Kieler was tall. The upper structure was almost filamental, and Kieler had to be thankful there was no air movement down here in the massive cathedral-like domes that made up the foundations of the city above. A breeze would have knocked it over.

"You know where I got the idea for your light spars? From a dead bird. One of those trenneks that gets trapped under the Plate sometimes. This one was just a skeleton, like you so far. I found it amazing that such a thin, light wing-bone could lift the whole bird. So, I can't give you wings that flap, *Liberty*, but I can give you wings that lift."

Like his first ship, the shape of the wing contributed to its lifting ability. This second idea he got from his childhood underground. After his father had died, Kieler had ventured far in the underground looking for sellable scrap. One time he had found an engraving on a metal plate set into a massive, fallen tower-top of the Dead Ones. It showed a cross-section of a flying machine. He thought it such a unique shape that he copied it, sketching it with a pencil onto a broken board. He instinctively knew that it had something to do with how the Dead Ones could create ships that flew.

Despite his constant hunger, constant boredom had competed for his attention. Over a week's time, the young Kieler had carved and smoothed a wing and a short body out of his late father's modeling wood. When he threw it, it went up, instead of falling straight down, like a rock. He never forgot that peculiar behavior.

Now, beneath the wing of his full-size airship, he was building an open-air cockpit. Three long, thin rods of duralium curved from horizontal skids to vertical supports that framed the pilot's seat and control pedestal.

So far, Kieler had allowed for one weighty indulgence, a plush captain's chair. He was about to add a second luxury—the three small brass knobs he had found tonight in the *Pride's* bay.

CHAPTER TEN

Extravagances to be sure. But everything for the *Pride of Velik*, even the spare parts, were of such quality that incorporating these luxuries into the airship made Kieler feel like a Prime in truth.

He worked at attaching the brass knobs to the linkages controlling pitch, motor speed and the yawing motor swivel that gave directional control.

At every stage of construction, Kieler took into account that he would be collapsing the structure for transport to a launch spot. One of the oblong utility podcars could carry some larger items, but not the fully assembled airship.

Behind the cockpit was a light rectangular truss that extended to the rear of the aircraft. This not only gave structural support to the wing above, it also provided the motor mount at the very rear, balancing the weight of the pilot near the front. If Kieler's calculations were correct, this bigger airship could also carry a fair bit of cargo in this lateral truss—or carry a certain young lady.

If this airship was all he had to be concerned about, he would have been a happy man.

In truth, Kieler was feeling a lot like Bags: He felt he needed to be doing more. Out here, isolated in the mountains of Ardan, he couldn't make the alliances with other houses that would be necessary to start pitting them against each other, cracking the supports of the already decaying Omeron.

And even though plots and schemes should have been his main train of thought, he kept thinking about two women: Eznea and Velirith.

His best friend's wife was a prisoner of a very twisted man, an untouchable man simply because of the family he was born into.

And the woman with whom he had become illogically close to here in Velakun would have been just as untouchable if Kieler's true identity were known.

Images of the day of the lighting of the Starstone kept popping into his thoughts. And images of Velirith, the things she did and said, played over and over in Kieler's head. *She pulled me into an airshaft thousands of feet deep!*

Terrified at the time, now, looking back, he knew it would be one of the highlights of his life. And there was that inviting moment on the floor after their jump, her eyes shining, their breathing hard…

He caught himself staring at the wrench in his hand, doing nothing.

He tried to stop thinking about her: their conversations, the shenanigans, her mentor Aurelios' odd character and his habit of listening to voices that weren't there. Everything reinforced itself in Kieler's mind, making him feel as if the whole episode had some deep significance emphasized by extremely ridiculous action.

But he could make no sense of it.

What if I share our plan with Velirith? She's just as unhappy with the government as we are.

"*Liberty*!" he addressed his airship again. "Help me stop thinking of her! Let's talk about getting you dressed. You need skin. Do you know I ordered you skin tonight?"

It was an interesting exercise deliberately shifting his thoughts from Velirith. But his airship could not respond. He needed to focus on his mission and the reasons for it. And that brought him back to Bags' wife.

Eznea. They had very little intel on where Telander kept his women. Somewhere in his palatial complex on the Island of Threes, no doubt. Kieler wondered why the Coin hadn't attempted a rescue mission, but then he coldly realized that to raid the Telander Estate would stir up a swarm of retaliation for no strategic gain.

Still, if Telander's goons had killed a potential addition to his harem simply because she wouldn't be "useful," then Eznea's life depended on her remaining valuable to Telander as well. Sick thought, that.

Worst of all, no matter how many rumors flew about Borgus Telander's indecencies, there was no investigation, and even should incontrovertible evidence be brought to light, the courts would not act against such a foundational Prime.

Corrupt courts would act in Kieler's favor in claiming Ortessi properties and legitimizing his status. His case was a "Prime vs. Prime." But the people hurt by Telander were from sub-houses or lower without the clout or money to fight a Prime.

The court system was not originally designed to run this way. The courts were to be completely independent, with members of the court appointed by the Omeron and guided by an ancient code of principles espoused by Velik himself. Those principles had eroded like the ruins of the nethercity.

He wondered if Velirith would turn her back on those principles when she came into her own. Would she give up jumping off waterfalls? He hoped not. No one else thought like he and Velirith did.

He laughed out loud and said to his airship, "That girl loves flying in airshafts as much as I love flying in airships."

"*Liberty*, what do you think? Maybe Velirith and I could take a trip to Avertori between rounds."

He caught himself again. *No, I need to avoid Velirith, not gallivant with her.* When the Omeron came down, he would try to spare her, but it really wouldn't be up to him at that point. Movus' plan would have the Prime Houses ripping each other apart. He couldn't, and shouldn't protect her.

How can I say that?

I will always protect her.

But her family supported the Omeron. Truth, her family *created* the Omeron! They could never oppose it.

He tried to be objective about his internal conflict. Yes, Velik, of House Vel (then Clan Vel), had created the Omeron. But it had worked well for hundreds of years. Something had changed. It was as if the foundation had washed out and been forgotten.

EPISODE 3 – ATTRACTION AND REPULSION

When Jad Entrovel spoke Velik's words, they didn't match what the Omeron did now. Yet for the most part, Velator seemed to try to serve the greater good.

But Velirith was young and had been over-protected by her worried father. Perhaps, now that he was encouraging her to take a more active part, she would realize her responsibility and start to serve. Kieler knew it was more than his feelings for her; she would mature into a strong leader. She had it in her.

So what if we could get the Coin to change the plan? What if we backed House Vel in a massive reform?

No, neither Velator nor Velirith could muster the violence to cut the corruption out of the other houses. They didn't have the power base to do it anyway. And Movus had a particularly intense aversion to House Vel and what he called their "noble-seeming manipulation." Movus considered the whole act a self-righteous deception of others.

In the end, Movus' way—that they bring down the whole system and start over—seemed the only possible solution. It was the only way to bring people like Feleanna Cortatti, Borgus Telander and especially Ek Threzhel to justice.

Which meant he could not protect Velirith, despite his feelings. To do so would be to sanction the actions of those using the system to protect themselves from answering for their crimes.

And Velirith wasn't that different. She was a Prime, raised in privilege. She was spoiled and selfish. She wouldn't be targeted specifically by the Coin, but when the other houses started grabbing for larger portions of a shrinking pie, she could be hurt in the scuffle.

But the bottom line was Eznea. Kieler was doing this for her, and the many others abused by the system without recourse. He was doing this for Bags.

If he let his own selfish feelings care for Velirith, he wouldn't get the job done. He decided: It was time to shut her out of his life.

CHAPTER TEN

He had to shut her out.
He had to.
He would do it.

CHAPTER ELEVEN

"I love being young," Velirith told Moshalli. "I've realized I'm old enough to understand adults, but my father and others still look at me like I'm a child."

"I hate it," Moshalli moped. "My mother doesn't think me old enough to have a suitor. She just doesn't trust me around boys."

Silently, Velirith agreed with Moshalli's mother.

Moshalli went on. "That's one of the reasons she agreed to allow me to holiday alone to Velakun. *I* wanted to visit you for the Festival of Aerial Lights in a few days—and to talk. *She* just wanted me away from Rammy. She thinks we're too 'hot and heavy', whatever that means. She thought we needed some time apart."

Moshalli had taken Velirith to the top of The Empyrean. Sitting in Starstone Tri, eating a picnic lunch, all Moshalli had talked about was 'Rammy', short for Ramico. As Velirith again agreed with Fechua's wisdom, she looked out over the edge of Velakun's highest plaza and around the Rim. It was calm, as it often was in the bowl of Velakun in springtime. At first, Velirith had thought it strange for Moshalli to pick this high, stark terrace, rather than the more serene but lower Symphony Gardens. And then she thought of the Ortessi; Moshalli probably shared his need to feel above the world, to feel in control.

Ooh, that Ortessi. She still stung from how rude he was to Aurelios. Granted, it seemed Aurelios had intentionally provoked him. But for reasons she couldn't quite define, she had desperately wanted her mentor to like Orlazrus.

CHAPTER ELEVEN

The Ortessi had such a long way to go. Bold, good-hearted, hardworking, and competent in many areas, but—in her opinion—an incompetent actor. And his whole reason for being here was some deceptive act. She sighed.

"Are you listening to me?" Moshalli interrupted her thoughts.

Replaying in her mind some of the ramble about Rammy, she replied, "Some. Sorry. I was distracted."

In a leap of intuition Velirith thought her incapable of, Moshalli asked, "Thinking about a boy, perhaps? That mysterious Ortessi, maybe?"

Feeling her eyes go wide and a flush in her cheek, she admitted, "Yes. But not romantically." But the denial voiced the truth. Nevertheless, she knew, as much as she loved Moshalli, the girl couldn't keep a secret. To her there was no such thing. Just gossip to be passed from one listener to another.

"Mm-hmm," Moshalli nodded smugly.

"Truly, I still don't trust him, though I know he's good-looking and good-hearted."

"Not to mention a good dancer and a good fighter... at the same time! Oh—" Moshalli sat up straight. "That's another thing I've wanted to tell you ever since that monstrous Family Harmony Dance. I had this premonition when I saw Orlazrus and Feleanna dance-fighting that night."

Velirith leaned forward in sincere interest.

"I felt like that scene was just a... a preview. That those two would someday be in a fight to the death for real. There was even an audience. It was scary!"

"That's fascinating, Mo'. Somehow, I feel you're right."

Moshalli nodded, then shrugged and giggled. "But who knows, maybe we're just a couple of 'young' girls fantasizing. Anyway, Feleanna hates your Orly—"

"Orly?"

"Just a pet name. What do you call him?"

EPISODE 3 – ATTRACTION AND REPULSION

"I try not to." Truth. She knew it wasn't his real name. "And he certainly hasn't been calling on me much lately."

"Anyway. Feleanna is fighting him already—and your family too since you're 'harboring' him—anyway she can."

"What! How?"

"Well, I served lunch to Ek Threzhel and Ber Casem. That guy has such weird fingers; they like curve backward somehow..." She looked at her own fingers and tried to arch them the wrong way. "Anyway, Ber was complaining that Feleanna was on him to impose a fifty percent tariff on the duralium your father ordered for the *Pride*. She was insisting to him that such a large order had to be used for weapons, so her family industry should get a royalty off the sale."

"Weapons! Is she insane? Moshalli, it's being used to fix the powercoach *she* destroyed! You know we hardly buy enough weapons for our own security forces. I think it's one of the reasons our economy is still decent. We don't waste money on Feleanna's killing machines."

Moshalli looked levelly at her friend. "Well, you might consider 'wasting' a bit now. Feleanna is acting like she's at war, with you and with the House-of-One who's living with you."

Velirith actually felt a pang of worry. Moshalli went on, rather mercilessly.

"Well, at least it's a good time to be a lawyer. My friend, Kazzi—you know her, the one with the long, frizzy hair? Her dad and all his buddies have been hired to block Orlazrus' claim on the properties the Cortattis stole twenty years ago. Oh! Did I say stole?

"And I swear Feleanna is paying people to bug Ek to raise taxes again. And between you and me, I think it's one of the few things Ek Threzhel agrees with her on. But people are always getting into the palace on one excuse or another. I swear I ran into one in the *kitchen* of all places, and he said he was an inspector until he caught Threzhel coming out of the bathroom and started on about 'mutual interest' and 'critical fiscal shortages'... I had to *accidentally* spill gravy on the blood-sucker to get him off my Prime's neck!

"You should have seen the look of gratitude Threzhel gave me, Velirith!"

As Moshalli paused ever-so-momentarily to gasp in a breath, Velirith's mind raced. What she was saying, despite her gossipy perspective, was that Feleanna wasn't sitting idle. She was using every means available to push her agenda. At least it was non-violent—so far—but her father needed to know all these things, even the rumors, right away.

"And the *worst* thing Feleanna is doing is..." Moshalli paused to lick some red sauce off her sandwich that was dripping down her fingers. Velirith, admittedly in suspense, didn't really want to hear the *worst* thing, but now couldn't wait to know.

"The *worst* thing," Moshalli repeated, "is the constant, shameless promotion of her Arena games. She must be forcing every shopkeep in Avertori to wallpaper their storefronts with pamphlets, banners, and pictures of some bloody fight. Now you know I like to watch a good competition as much as anyone, but it's so tacky! I swear there's not a patch of wall without some poster of *hers* on it."

Velirith bristled. "I hate her arena. Those aren't games. Those are people's lives—ending."

Moshalli paused, sort of, and looked to be thinking. "But every one of those people that fight are criminals. They've done something horrible or they wouldn't be there."

Studying her friend, Velirith realized that Moshalli wouldn't accept Velirith's perspective on bloodsport. She was either naïve or didn't want to know. "Mo', do you know that telling me about Ek Threzhel's personal conversations could be interpreted as spying?"

Her friend cocked her head. She didn't know what Velirith was getting at. "It's just interesting news. You won't tell anyone. You never do."

"You're right. I won't. But under the law, it is spying."

EPISODE 3 – ATTRACTION AND REPULSION

Moshalli didn't look particularly uncomfortable. She was missing it. "So?"

Velirith leaned forward with her own sandwich. "Where do they put spies when the catch them, Mo'?"

Her eyes widened. "In the Arena."

"And what happens there?"

"They die."

Velirith appreciated that candid answer. They didn't always die right away. Sometimes they won many fights. But eventually they died.

"Moshalli, if someone wanted to make us die, they could accuse us—you and me—of anything. If we didn't have someone else, like Ek Threzhel or my father, who wanted us alive, we would be sent to the arena."

Moshalli, predictably, sighed relief. "So we're safe. Ek Threzhel will protect me and your father will protect you."

"But who will protect those who have no protector? What about someone who steals to feed their family, or someone who just thinks they are passing on a bit of friendly gossip? What happens to them, someone like us but who has no protector?"

"The Arena."

Velirith nodded. And she could tell Moshalli got it.

Moshalli actually took it a step further. "Then we have a bad system."

When Velirith didn't say anything, she went on, "You should change it! You're a Prime. I'll help you."

Oh. *Didn't see* that *coming.*

A lump seemed to have instantly formed in Velirith's throat. She didn't *want* to do anything. But her friend, a young woman of far lesser means, did. Moshalli had more courage than she did. Orlazrus had more courage than she. *That is an ugly thought.*

"Velirith," Moshalli continued her tactless barrage, "you might as well do something. Feleanna is attacking you anyway. It can't get much worse."

CHAPTER ELEVEN

Velirith sat bolt upright. "What do you mean?"

"She's telling everyone that you attacked her peaceful delivery coach and she's even parading the pieces of her destroyed freighter as 'evidence!'"

It felt like a deep pit had opened in Velirith's stomach. As much as she had intentionally kept out of the political arena, her outrage at Feleanna's lies made her want to jump on the next powercoach to Avertori and confront this awful woman. "Peaceful? We attacked her?? Moshalli, I was there. I have the scars to prove it!" she raged, turning out her inner arm toward Moshalli. "Do you know what happened?"

She shrugged. "I heard a powercoach pulled up armed like a bandit and tried to blow the *Pride of Velik* off the track. But that's your story. Hers is different."

"And what do you believe?"

"You, of course. But no one else was there. And Rammy says no one really knows for sure. And Feleanna has a bigger mouth. She's been blabbing her story non-stop everywhere. Since no one is saying different, some people believe her."

The realities of worldly ways were making Velirith sick. She looked up at the mighty angelic creature above them, the protector of Vel, then let her gaze drift down onto the surrounding lake, to the tall, graceful, white-trunked haventhall groves in the lake edges. It was peaceful in Velakun. A peace she had come to take for granted, even resenting the boringness of it sometimes.

A faint breeze drifted from the still frigid north mountains. It seemed to bring a scent of bitterness, of invading cold into their oasis of paradise.

She looked back to Moshalli, who munched on a haventhall nut. Before she finished chewing, she seemed to remember something. "Oh—this is just a rumor, from the housekeeping staff, and what do they know, but that attack cutter, like the one she sent after you? I hear Feleanna's making new ones, several, so she can steal all sorts of stuff and add to her war chest—"

EPISODE 3 – ATTRACTION AND REPULSION

"Moshalli, how do you hear this stuff?"

For a moment she looked smug, like she was privileged. But then her expression turned meek. "Well, honestly, since I'm just a servant of House Ek, people talk as if I'm not there."

Velirith suddenly saw the side of Moshalli that felt trapped in a subservient house. The Omeron really could be oppressive. Then she realized something else. "Mo'," she said softly, "this boy Ramico, I know he's from an 'important' house, but be careful. Go slow. We've always been great friends, true? As a friend, my intuition isn't comfortable with what you tell me of this guy. You deserve the best, Mo'. Go slowly."

CHAPTER TWELVE

Festival-goers gathered in the warm spring evening around Theater Tri. Most were outside enjoying the last rays of sunshine as Rei slid behind the Southwest Rim on the last of this gentle spring day. Tonight, they would not be using the Starstone for supplemental light. Tonight, Kieler was told, it was important for the bowl of Velakun to be dark.

Moshalli and Kieler pressed through the throng to the theater. Nothing was reserved for this very public production. Fortunately, Anessa was allowed in early to secure seating in the first row. She had to be close to the stage in case anything happened to Velirith while she was on stage.

The ante-theater's arched walls were tiled in artful mosaics that depicted different dramatic scenes that Kieler could only assume were from famous plays. But the artwork was cracked and some of the tiles missing, making it difficult to appreciate.

"I'll bet Velirith would know what these mosaics represent," Kieler commented absently.

Moshalli, who had hardly stopped talking even to let Kieler answer her constant questions, replied, "Oh, I'm sure she would. She knows everything about theater. She studies directly under Cota Aurelios. He's ancient and the keeper of the art here in Velakun."

"I met him." He added, intentionally impassive, "He doesn't seem to be keeping up this art very well. This part of the theater is in sad shape."

Moshalli shrugged, "Back in Avertori, the arts don't get much money anymore. Everyone goes to the Cortattis' Arena. I

369

suppose they have the same lack of money here. You do realize theater in Velakun is *older* than ours in Avertori? Not the building, but the art. Our theater began with your ancestor, Oonyez, I think, to record the taking of the Isle of Threes. But Theater Velaki is a much older *tradition*.

"Velirith told me," Kieler managed to slip in.

"Still, this place is hundreds of years old," Moshalli went on. "No wonder it's run down. At least they do regular plays here. There's been very little produced in Avertori since—" she faltered, "—since the Ortessis stopped putting on plays about twenty years ago…" She looked over at Kieler, embarrassed at bringing up his horrible past.

Kieler picked up on her faux pas and dismissed it. "I remember so little of the time before the Cortattis slaughtered my family. The images are so vague that I don't even know if they're real memories or dreams."

He looked into the distance as he pretended to recall. "I kind of remember the fire at the estate. People running. Nasty smelling smoke. It's funny how you remember smells from childhood. But I seemed to be far away. Then someone grabbed me and swept me away…"

Kieler shrugged. "Anyway, it's good they didn't burn the museums or the Academy. But unfortunately Orticot, the puppet Cortatti, didn't have the same passion for history that my true family did. I guess they stopped performing in the Oraflora."

"No," Moshalli winced. "They didn't stop; they just got so bad that no one goes. That theater troupe is more like a gang of thugs."

Kieler raised an eyebrow at this information. He didn't know that. But he should have.

The mosaics separated the entrance arches, meticulously carved of haventhall wood with the trim layered for depth. They passed through the old, open arches and started down an aisle toward the front.

CHAPTER TWELVE

Immediately a strong hand clapped Kieler on his shoulder.

"Verr Ortessi," Jad Entrovel greeted him in a friendly way, "I'm so glad you're out for this festival. It's good to have fun."

"Cota Entrovel," Kieler replied.

Looking at Moshalli, Entrovel said, "Are you the young MgFellis... Moshalli, I believe?"

"I am."

"My, you have become quite the attractive young lady!" Entrovel complimented her sincerely.

Moshalli blushed and was blessedly quiet—not that the spell would last.

Pleasantries were exchanged and with eager excitement they parted as they headed to their desired seats. Within moments Kieler spotted Jarovel as well. The big man was sitting near the back of the giant theater, content not to vie for a better seat.

Kieler grunted and Jarovel returned his version of a smile—sort of a twitching nod with the corners of his mouth pulled back.

"Good to see you out of your cave," Kieler said.

Now Jarovel grunted and replied, "And you out here doing your Prime thing, being important. Hope you are better at that than you are at fixing."

After Moshalli and Kieler passed by him, Moshalli whispered, "Why do you let him talk to you that way?"

Kieler ignored her question. He really liked Jarovel. Kieler realized how happy he felt. He realized that seeing people he recognized, normal people, felt good. He wished he could call this place home. He'd only been here six months—yet he was recognized, even accepted to a degree. If things were different, these people could be his friends.

They found seats in the front row and sat down to wait. Never having seen a play, Kieler felt the thrill of anticipation perhaps more keenly than most. At one end of the huge hexagonal theater was the small stage with a backdrop that reached from the stage floor to the high dark dome overhead. From that stage the catwalk extended out through the crowd to a center stage covered with sharp, icy peaks as high as a man. Kieler was fascinated with the effect. He wondered how and why they had decorated the center stage in such a way.

As more residents of Velakun filed in, Moshalli pointed back up at the ceiling. "I love that effect; it just gives me the shivers."

Kieler hadn't noticed before, but the underside of the dome was *moving*, like dark clouds blowing in a threatening breeze. The lighting, too, was dimming and he felt an icy draft waft over him like the leading edge of a storm. He knew, firsthand, how that effect was produced. He smirked recalling the mischievous Velirith.

Though Kieler wanted to remain in the deepening spell being cast by wind, ice, clouds and light, Moshalli kept talking. "When the performance is over, we can go right out those doors back into Theater Tri. We're supposed to meet V by the statue of Velik. Pays to be early, doesn't it? Have you seen the Festival of Aerial Lights before? Oh, no, of course not, silly me. You didn't even *exist* before the New Year's Gala and this is your first time to Velakun."

And so the one-sided conversation went on. Kieler forced himself to pay attention and was glad he did. At one point Moshalli chattered about the significance of the festival and the play and the Aerial Lights. "It's a silly legend, really, but the story goes that the ancestors of House Vel came from the sky, stranded by their skyship—something like that. And they were sad about it and so they celebrate this festival every year to remember and hope that they'll go back up in the sky again, though I don't see what would be so great about that since it's always so nice here in the bowl and the air outside the bowl is just freezing! I think they ought to stay here. But that's not how the story goes. Am I talking too much?"

A non-vocal reply worked well, Kieler giving her a look that could only be interpreted as, "I don't want to hurt your feelings, but yes you are."

CHAPTER TWELVE

"Of course I am. I'm sorry. I'll shush. But this is exciting for me too. I've only seen this twice before, and I was really little and I came out with Velirith and—oh! I'll be quiet."

Oddly, Kieler suspected Moshalli was nervous, and more precisely, she was nervous about being with him. "It's okay, Moshalli, but it seems like they've put in a lot of effort to create a certain atmosphere. I think silence would enhance the performance and help us get in the mood." Kieler surprised himself with how polite that sounded.

Moshalli put two fingers to her lips and looked around nervously.

She was mercifully quiet until it began, though Kieler could tell it was taking all the restraint she could muster. Within the theater, the wind increased, bitingly cold. Kieler saw couples drawing close (as good of an excuse as any), and Moshalli glanced at him and then turned away with an embarrassed smile.

Overhead, whatever they were waving to make the tumultuous clouds, cloth perhaps, was whipping like a fierce storm. A great bassando rumble of thunder rattled their seats and crescendoed into a roar. Then, suddenly, the roar silenced and a bright light cut across the theater into the clouds above. It illuminated a sky-ship, shaped like an ocean vessel, high overhead near the backdrop, descending as if out of the clouds. One woman stood on the high platform dressed in a full-length indigo gown that, despite its deep color, glowed luminously in the spotlight. Around her head was a delicate circlet of silver that reflected light like compass points around her black hair—no, Kieler realized, the circlet must have slender luzhril fragments embedded at the cardinal points, making her face radiate and her eyes shine silver— Kieler caught his breath.

It was Velirith!

He had no idea she played such a major part. Costumed as a celestial creature of light, she was stunningly beautiful. She stood tall and brave, looking calm, confident and wise—hardly the selfish pest he knew she could be.

Around her on the ship knelt a blue-robed crew, looking intently ahead, piloting the ship through the roiling storm. They leaned into the wind, concentrating fiercely. On the sides of the ship glowed multicolored lights highlighting its slow descent toward the ice below.

The nose of the craft tilted downward, angling toward the center of the theater where the glinting peaks threatened. The dome was still darkly alive and writhing, seeming to drive them down. But now the theater itself was echoingly quiet.

As the craft continued its slow descent, Velirith's character began to sing a slow, melancholy song:

> *Our house is in the heavens,*
> *Our place is with our God.*
> *We've turned our face and left Him.*
> *Upon the ground we'll trod.*

> *We travel now in sorrow,*
> *Descending under Rei*
> *A fading light, tomorrow,*
> *For we have lost our way.*

Those around her on the ship joined in chorus:

> *Falling, falling*
> *Through the darkening skies*
> *Calling, calling*
> *And now our body dies.*

Velirith:

> *A rugged land we fall to,*

CHAPTER TWELVE

Cold as our hearts it feels.
By pounding out a haven,
Love shelters we who reel.

We live in but a shadow,
Our joy, reflected light.
We'll live amongst our brothers,
Descendants of our flight.

Falling, falling
Through the darkening skies.
Calling, calling
And now our body dies.

We are falling, falling,
Losing all we love.
We are calling, calling
To our home far above.

Our hope is in the heavens,
Our place is with our God
We're humble and returning,
Our place is with our God.

Velirith sang the last verse again and the chorus was sung over it in harmony. As their voices faded, they were just inches above the peaks of ice. Thunder rumbled and the ship hit the peaks. Instantly the ice shattered across the stage and Kieler jumped in his seat. The high tinkling of breaking ice contrasted with the rumbling crash of the thunder peal.

The spotlight went out as Velirith fell to the deck of the ship.

EPISODE 3 – ATTRACTION AND REPULSION

From beneath center stage, a pale blue light came up slowly through a misty fog, and a wisp of song floated through the mist like an echo. Velirith rose slowly, as did her coterie.

But as they did, two factions formed. One led by She-Who-Waits, the other by a tall, thin man spitting bitter accusations at She-Who-Waits. She bore the accusations as she bore the bitter wind that continued to blow across her grieved, lovely face.

In turn she pleaded with the one she called Dybek for patience and unity, but the man wanted nothing to do with her leadership. He wanted to conquer the unexplored world, to make the best for himself and his contingency out of their disaster, which he blamed on her.

Her pleading, her apologies, her acceptance of responsibility did nothing to assuage his desire to leave.

He turned to go and she commanded, "Wait!"

Violently, he swiveled and pushed her away, casting her to the floor. It was a convincing shove, and Kieler felt himself jerk forward in his seat, catching himself in an instinctive reaction to protect Velirith once again. He didn't know whether to laugh or chastise himself for his reflexive defensiveness.

He saw Moshalli notice his movement, giving him a quick, thoughtful look.

But the play moved on. Dybek and his followers danced wildly up the aisles, frightening the audience with their anger and intensity.

Velirith's character rose again, conveying a melancholic determination. She danced from one to another of those who remained, who in turn danced around the circumference of the stage raising small, three-cornered towers around the rim of caldera that had formed around their crash. Haventhalls rose too, guided by the ministrations of those who remained.

The serene blue light from below had entirely replaced the fallen skyship, which appeared to have sunk into the stage.

CHAPTER TWELVE

One dancer, a young man, stopped at the stage edge and spoke. "Ever she did wait, patient and sad. The sons of the stars reached out to the world beyond the mountains—building, seeking.

"So much was lost, so much retained. And so much yet to be regained."

She-Who-Waits picked up the refrain from center stage.

> *Therein lies our shining hope.*
> *Our yearning for our stars, our heavens.*
> *Our burning spirit longs to rise*
> *And fill complete with love's pure heat.*
> *A love that waits—as I have waited—*
> *That we should turn,*
> *And be saved.*
>
> *Ever in belief*
> *That we are not abandoned.*
> *Ever in love*
> *That we strive for compassion.*
> *Ever I will hope*
> *That those departed may return,*
> *Rising again to the stars.*

Many of the dancers that had gone out from Velakun reappeared, joyfully and in greater numbers, as if they had multiplied and brought with them other seekers. They came from all directions, but Kieler didn't see the one named Dybek among them.

Velirith's character lifted up a three-sided paper lantern beneath which a delicate basket held a pitch-soaked fleece. She pirouetted, stretching her arms up to the top of a luzhril-lit tower model. As she touched the basket of the lantern to the bright stone, the fleece burst into flame and the star went out. By what device, Kieler couldn't tell, but it thrilled him to see.

Velirith opened her hands as the warming air from the burning fleece filled the paper lantern. The light hung suspended just above her head, just above the Starstone. It seemed so tenuous, as if the lone lantern might slip to the ground and burn. But then, slowly, the heated air lifted the lantern higher into the air.

The audience oohed. Kieler felt his own hope rising, his skin prickling. He pictured himself as one of those who gathered from the six corners of the world to come to Velakun. He felt the community, the spirit of unity that the audience had with those on stage, the welcoming, even of outsiders, to their heritage and hope.

The only lights in the theater were the hovering Aerial Lantern and the soft blue illuminating the representation of the basin of Velakun. As the lantern rose by increments, subtle currents wafted the aerial lantern toward the audience and then gently circled it around the theater. It circled several times before it neared the dome of the ceiling. As their eyes followed it ever higher, Kieler realized that the dark clouds were gone. Instead, thousands of starry pinpoints dotted the ceiling. He saw the Roivas Cross, the prominent constellation of the Northern Hemisphere, represented in luzhril stars. The dome's center was a darker spot with dim stars that took him a moment to comprehend. It was an opening out into the actual night sky above the theater.

The lantern circled and was drawn by the currents inexorably toward the opening. The lights around the theater brightened just enough to see by, and the attendees were slowly making their way out the doors. Moshalli took him by the arm and drew him toward the door. Kieler looked back to see the Aerial Lantern escaping into the sky.

Out in the plaza of Theater Tri, people were kneeling and lighting their own lanterns. With the Starstone extinguished, the

CHAPTER TWELVE

bowl of Velakun was dark except for a few lanterns already beginning to glow.

"The lantern coming out of the top of the theater is the signal for the audience to light theirs," Moshalli explained quietly in the hushed awe of the spectacle.

Many children were lighting lanterns, while others danced or chased each other. One young boy couldn't seem to sit still long enough to get his flint spark to ignite the fleece. Parents laughed. People chatted, looking around at the growing flotilla of lights. Friends drew together.

He wanted to belong. He wanted to be a part of this.

He tensed. It was all so seductive. But these people ignored the cancer growing in Avertori and, Kieler suspected, in the outlands as well. *I am here to cure this body. I am the medicine. And though I may look pleasant enough, I am a violent and foul-tasting remedy.*

I don't belong. I have a mission to complete. And until MY people are free, I must remain the subversive.

The warmth of the night turned chill to him and he withdrew his arm from Moshalli.

"What's wrong?"

He ignored her. *Women.* And one woman in particular. *Velirith.* His increasing closeness to her threatened to undermine his resolve to do whatever it took to bring down this pretty façade. He liked her; he almost trusted her, and that was a big problem.

Just as he was consciously hardening his resolve not to be seduced by this hope-filled ceremony, they were hailed by someone in a knot of people.

"Orlazrus! Moshalli!"

Kieler looked ahead, surprised to see Ek Connigar calling them. The young man had a genuine smile on his face and had been talking to several other students from Orcad. They had a couple of lanterns between them and were working to ignite the pitch.

EPISODE 3 – ATTRACTION AND REPULSION

Before they got too close, Moshalli hissed sideways to Kieler, "Connigar! He was always the grouch of House Ek."

Kieler remembered him from the first day at Orcad. Sullen and withdrawn, unhappy to be in Velakun, the Connigar they approached didn't look like the same person.

"Hi Moshalli! Good to see a familiar face out here in the wilds!" He touched her arm familiarly. Moshalli, her expression shock and bewilderment, mumbled something back about being nice to see him too.

Kieler grasped his arm, and Connigar spoke again. "Nice night, yeah? It's going to be gorgeous when all these lanterns are launched."

Agreeing mutely, Kieler looked at the youngest Ek curiously.

"Awesome play too," Connigar went on. "I just finished a history round, so I was really looking forward to seeing a real Theater Velaki production."

Unable to contain his confusion, Kieler spoke bluntly. "Connigar, I thought you hated being sent here. Are you being serious?"

The young man laughed. "Yep! But that's just it. I was too serious. I thought Father Threzhel just sent me here to get out of the way. But I found out that being out of the way is pretty nice. Weather is good. Nasty politics are far away. It's a beautiful place..." He paused and nodded to where Tarawy Firstholm was cupping her hands to shelter a budding flame under their lantern. "And I've made some good friends. I dumped the Glums and decided to enjoy myself."

The smile on Kieler's own face reflected Connigar's own, but still held a touch of unbelief. A pang of jealousy twisted in his stomach too. *Why can't I just enjoy this?* "I'm really glad for you." And he was, but it was an extremely mixed emotion as Kieler remembered that this man's father was responsible for his real mother's death.

CHAPTER TWELVE

The somberness must have shown through in Kieler's expression for Connigar leaned in conspiratorially. "Hey, I know you're smart. You had to figure my father sent me here partially to keep an eye on you. But honestly, what's to know? You're going through rounds with the rest of us. It's a good school. And you'll get to run it when you know the ins and outs. Relax and enjoy it. Things will turn out right. I'm even thinking of staying in Velakun if I can figure out how to convince my father."

Kieler couldn't shake his amazement, but a part of him responded intelligently. "Maybe you could take the ambassadorial assignment once you're through with Orcad."

Connigar brightened even more. "That's brilliant! I may be too young, but nobody else wants to stay out here because it's so far from home. The current ambassador is an old fogey who wants to go back to Avertori anyway."

They shook arms again and parted, Kieler and Moshalli moving back into the happy press of people.

"I don't believe that's the same guy!" Moshalli said aghast.

Nodding, Kieler agreed. *Could I make that kind of shift?*

Movus had scoffed at the Velaki, pointing out that they felt they would be just fine without the Omeron. The funny thing was, *he was exactly right!*

They didn't need the Omeron. The Omeron needed them. They would be just fine in their self-sufficient mountain citadel, but instead it was Velik who reached out to unify the old clans and try to create something better.

If the rest of the Omeron no longer wanted to play nice, maybe it would be better if Velakun just retreated into isolation again. Let the selfish Houses of Avertori destroy themselves.

That might be a better plan than Movus'. *I could like it here. Velirith and I could—*

He let out a long breath as he wavered. Why *couldn't* he just enjoy *this* night? The real Ortessi would. His emotions felt as windblown as the ragged skies of the theater had been.

381

EPISODE 3 – ATTRACTION AND REPULSION

They moved between clusters of people to the statue of Velik that Velirith had suggested. At its base, Kieler opened up the satchel he had been carrying and unfolded lanterns for the three of them. They waited for Velirith before they lit them. In moments they saw her winding her way through the gathered groups, food vendors, and the quickly multiplying aerial luminaries. The excitement was more audible, a growing fervor of community.

Kieler watched her come with an intense mixture of joy and dread.

CHAPTER THIRTEEN

Kieler sparked the pitch into flame and the three lanterns slowly lifted into the night sky. He had the briefest flash—that they were here, three friends, excited to be together sharing a warm moment. He squelched it, but it returned.

All around them the graceful lights floated like tiny airships. Although there was no discernible breeze, the aerial lanterns lifted and slowly moved counter-clockwise around the bowl of Velakun. The normal lights of Velakun had been doused, including the Starstone, of course, and as Kieler looked outward toward the Rim, he noticed that people on the far shore were lighting and launching lanterns as well. The combined effect was that of tens of thousands of drifting stars, swirling slowly skyward. The entire basin of Velakun was lit by the combined contribution of every citizen.

"Magnificent!" Kieler whispered, unable to contain his words. He heard Velirith and Moshalli sigh deeply as they all watched the circling lights. The words of Entrovel came back to him, "Determine what is truly valuable, find right principles, and live by them." While sky lanterns were not the most important thing in the world, the community here was strong, homey. *Am I living by right principles?*

"I wish Rammy was here with me to see this."

Kieler and Velirith choked back a chuckle and glanced at each other sidelong. But what had been meant as a knowing look about Moshalli became something more as Kieler saw the thousands of golden points of light glittering in Velirith's silvery eyes. He tore his eyes away from hers.

EPISODE 3 – ATTRACTION AND REPULSION

As the festival drew on, vendors sold food and drink. Looking up, the three leaned against the pedestal of Velik's statue. Unconsciously they had drawn closer together. Though excitement charged the air, the buzz of conversation remained hushed.

"You sang beautifully, Velirith," Moshalli said heartfully. "Who would have imagined when we sat in there as children that one day *you* would be singing ever?"

Kieler noted the odd phrasing but was more moved by the two girls remembering shared memories of childhood. He had no friends like that. He could mainly remember sneaking and scrounging for food through the jumbled passages under Avertori. He had some memories of his father, good memories of working endlessly on his father's devices. But friends in the nethercity were few. To have grown up among the privileged, or even among an average family—he would never know.

"That was moving, Velirith," Kieler agreed quietly. He felt the warmth of her shoulder against his.

"Thanks."

"Oh! Now watch!" Moshalli bubbled. "As the lanterns reach—"

"Shh, Mo!" Velirith interrupted. "He'll see. Let him be surprised. It's good for him."

Moshalli bit her lip to keep from talking. Kieler, now very curious, looked at the two girls with their wide, I've-got-a-secret eyes, but neither would now say a word. He repeated in his mind what Moshalli had started to say, "*As the lanterns reach...*"

He forced himself to watch the lanterns, rising to heaven. Some would wink out, having expended all their fuel. But some kept rising, and as they did, they swirled around The Empyrean. They were like tiny sparks of hope, rising toward an unseen goal.

As the tower was surrounded, Kieler thought he saw the shield unfold. As the lanterns rose higher, it became clear that the top of the tower now resembled a huge silver bowl.

CHAPTER THIRTEEN

A breath later the night sky was rent by an explosion of light.

Blinking to recover his sight, Kieler forced himself to look back up. The top of the tower was now a sharp silhouette in contrast to the beam of light that shot heavenward from it. As he watched, the shield flattened and the light of the Starstone shone through the surrounding ring of lenses.

Numerous smaller beams separated and angled away from the center. They fanned apart, expanding into the night. His eyes followed one of the beams out toward the Rim. It continued to descend until it was about to intersect the top of the caldera rim. It was then that he noticed one of the Artist's Towers in its path. *Ah, the lenses focus the light on the Artist's Towers!* As soon as the beam struck the tower's apex, it reflected upward, shining back to the heavens. Kieler knew Hezek had restored power to the towers just in time for the festival. The other beams found their own towers around the entire caldera, and Kieler found himself staring up an infinitely long tunnel of light.

He felt drawn, as though he should immediately start making his way through that tunnel, following the hope to a place of light. But his feet stayed stuck to the ground, just as he was stuck. He couldn't play Ortessi forever, and he couldn't go back to be an exile under the Plate. The spell of hope was broken by the paradox of his emotions.

The beams dispersed and widened, now unfocused. Each of the Artist's Towers glowed as the light washed down into the caldera. The light continued to diffuse until the entire city returned to the bright moonlight they used to illuminate the evening city.

The Velaki slowly eased out of their reverie and began to talk again in soft tones. But Velirith hung on to the last.

Kieler felt torn and suddenly empty, an angry violence ripping at the pit of his stomach. Why had all *these* people grown up in security, with enough to eat, and with loved family around them, while *he* had nothing but darkness and fear and hunger? And

385

now he had feelings toward Velirith that could not help him, that she could never feel for him, knowing that he was a fraud. *How did she know?*

The fire of anger burned darker inside. Around him, on the warm spring night, was a city filled with silvery light, hope and the voices of those sharing the sight with those they loved. He gritted his teeth. They were *still* loved. And he still was not. The only reason he had been invited here was because they thought he was someone important, no less than a House Prime himself.

The words of Movus haunted him, *"These families are directly responsible for the deaths of your parents. Remember that when your resolve falters."* It was quite clear his resolve had faltered.

And then a clarity settled upon him, cold and sad. That which had eroded the foundation of his resolve, what had made him question whether it was worth it to bring down the great houses, was this young woman right here. Velirith.

She was still looking up, smiling slightly. Beautiful, yes. But she was the quintessential representation of the system that had killed his parents and made his childhood a lonely struggle from one scarce meal to the next. Even her selfish practical jokes showed her disdain toward those considered of lower station.

And he had feelings for her?

He must kill these distracting feelings, feelings that could only lead to the failure of his mission. This shouldn't be hard. He had no realistic hope for their relationship getting beyond the standards of society. She the heir to a Prime house. He a no-family, no-property underworldling. And she *knew*.

What if her father knew what he really was? He would surely find out eventually. Certainly once he knew Kieler was an underworld agent and not a member of an Omeron house, he would not let Velirith associate with him. *What am I saying? My deception is an Arena offense!*

CHAPTER THIRTEEN

Kieler had to finish his mission before that happened. He had to gain power in this society and squeeze the Omeron from both sides, using the covert might of the Coin and the power of a legitimate, influential position. He knew what he had to do.

Velirith's smile melted into concern even while she continued to look up. Kieler felt an icy envelope encircling him despite the warm night air. Velirith turned her head slowly and looked at him.

He spoke. "How did you get the part of 'She-Who-Waits'? How did *you* get the lead in the festival play?" It could have been an innocent question.

"What do you mean?" she replied.

Moshalli looked between them, confused at the sudden chill.

"Well, you're so young. Seems like there would be many women more qualified for the part." Kieler's implications were cold and blunt.

But Velirith didn't completely bite. She went around his frontal attack and flanked toward the core. "What are you doing? Why are you suddenly so cold?"

Moshalli helped him. "Are you implying she got the part because of her *family*?"

Kieler shrugged. "One leading role, one daughter."

Velirith held silent, obviously trying to figure out what caused this change of weather. But Moshalli fanned the cold flame.

"You just said her acting was '*moving*'! That's why she got the part, you oaf!" Kieler did like Moshalli for her directness.

"The *play* was moving." He knew Velirith took great pride in her theater. "But—" he shrugged again.

"You liar!" Velirith hissed with such vehemence that Moshalli literally jumped backwards. "You don't even believe what you're trying to say!"

EPISODE 3 – ATTRACTION AND REPULSION

Kieler was not as good an actor as she. He knew his face registered a moment of guilt in the ferocity of her counterattack. He hid his lapse by raising a blank wall, cold and hard.

"But why?" Velirith probed him with her eyes, stepping right up to his face. "Why are you deliberately—"

Kieler had to take the offensive or lose. He cut her off. "Get out of my face. Your version of the truth is distorted by your naiveté, sheltered by Rim-walls, *true*?" he mocked. "You deny your position but wear your rank like a costume on the stage. You're proud that you are 'above' politics, just a spoiled princess. Take the perks, forget the responsibility." He had stoked his anger and picked the sharpest truths to pierce her weakest armor. "If you do *anything* significant with your life, it will be a total accident."

Moshalli, mouth open, burst into tears, shaking her head.

But Velirith abandoned her role of probing inquisitor and flew at him, violently pounding on his chest with her fists. She may know he was not being emotionally honest, but his words were unforgivable nonetheless. "Your thoughts—your feelings... are all twisted! The truth is in there—somewhere—" She clawed at his chest now, fingernails scraping down the green cloth, as if trying to rip off the armor around his heart, "and you are denying it." Her voice cracked.

Kieler couldn't escape without a moment's self-doubt. *What* am *I doing?* He wanted to be close to her. Even her anger against his chest felt good. But he also *knew:* If he were to stop Ek Threzhel from murdering people like his parents, if he were to free Eznea, if he were to remain loyal to Bags and Movus and his squad, and, in truth, if he as the point man of this revolution were to change things for every soul exiled to live in the darkness below the Plate—*she* could not be close to him.

"You should see the real world someday, Velirith. Start with a tour under the Plate. Not everyone lives in a palace, *princess*." Ripping his gaze from her tearing eyes, he turned away and stalked toward the shadows of the towering city.

388

EPISODE 4:
A LIGHT IN THE DEEP

CHAPTER ONE

The dark, fake clouds above reminded her of the fake Ortessi. Not real, but still depressing.

Velirith and Aurelios sat on the edge of the stage, their feet dangling over the side. Around them the skyship from the play.

Aurelios seemed younger for sitting that way, but she felt older, heavy with emotion.

The theater was empty, the doors all around were open as usual and a cool morning breeze blew through carrying the tangy scent of haventhalls. *An empty theater is itself depressing.*

Aurelios waited for her to collect her thoughts and express them as words. Her mentor could read her well. She had spent nearly as much time with him growing up as she had with her father.

She wondered what he was like when he was young. Probably quiet, thoughtful... sensitive. *Unlike that deceiver—the reason I am here.*

"He's so messed up!" she began, her voice cracking though barely above a whisper. Aurelios smiled. He reached over and rubbed her back gently, like the reassurance of her father. But she hadn't gone to her father with this. She didn't want Velator to know how much the Ortessi's cruel words had hurt her—how much she cared when she knew the man was living in a house of lies constructed of mere slivers of truth. Somehow, he was trying to protect himself, but—*This cannot end well.*

"He knows I don't believe him. He doesn't even believe himself. And I know he doesn't really want to say those awful things. But he says them anyway!" She bent over her knees and sobbed.

Aurelios replied softly, "We don't know his motivation. He's hiding a wicked purpose."

"But there's so much good in him!" Velirith surprised herself with the vehemence of her defense.

Again, he waited before responding. "Perhaps. Perhaps you see more than I do. But something, someone has twisted that good into lies."

Velirith wondered. Maybe, yes. "Or maybe he feels he must lie to accomplish something good. Like my father, playing those ridiculous political games thinking he can accomplish real good." She thought about a life so entangled that good and evil were intertwined.

"So how do we untangle such a beautiful mess?" She tried a weak smile.

"Forgiveness. Reconciliation," Aurelios said simply.

She shook her head, not disagreeing, just— "It's so hard." She paused, then added, "Harder for him."

After a while her sobbing abated. She sat up. "Well, he's got his shield of emotional space again." She wiped her eyes. "The jerk."

Aurelios laughed. She smiled, knowing that naming the problem bluntly had separated it from her own regret.

It was time to move on. Aurelios would know that too.

Her cota tilted his head, his dark gray eyes seemed to pierce Velirith's reflective silver ones. "You've acted in many plays, Velirith. You do realize they are more than just stories?"

She paused, noticing she felt better. Aurelios had known just when to change the subject. *More than just stories?* Velirith always made a conscious effort not to be flippant with her theater master. He was the deepest soul she knew. "I've felt it more than thought it," she admitted slowly.

Nodding, Aurelios' eyes twinkled. He had been kind to her, patient, and pleased that the daughter of Velator was genuinely interested in the Theater Velaki. "It has been so long since I was young; I sometimes forget that stories told to children are often taken for granted as fables. You've always grasped the tone of our plays, but you need to know their true meanings.

"You are intelligent. And you are concerned about what is true. You know the seed of Truth automatically, don't you?"

"Yes." She nodded sincerely. "Truth feels right, like a puzzle piece that fits perfectly. A lie—it's like spoiled meat that turns my stomach."

"Outside Velakun, theater is *mainly* for entertainment. Some of those plays have an intellectual point. And Theatre Ortessi has a historical basis, though that has been corrupted, especially since the Ortessi Theater lost its leadership twenty years ago. Their art is vapid. Empty."

She knew what he was saying was highly derogatory to outside theater, but he said it completely without judgment. It was fact.

"Do you want to know how to best interpret our plays?" Once again, his eyes sparkled as if the stage were covered with mist and he was about to pull the truth out of the fog. But she knew he was serious.

"Yes." She prepared herself for a tricky explanation.

"Take them literally."

That surprised her. What was being revealed was not for the skeptic. She thought about the recent performance of the Festival of Aerial Lights.

"Are you saying that our 'ancestors' really came out of the heavens?" she asked.

With only the slightest smile, he simply nodded.

"I thought it was a literary figure symbolizing that when we turn away from the truth, we are essentially fallen, less of what humans were intended to be. That life doesn't go as well as it could and that we long to rise again," Velirith said.

"That's true also," Aurelios agreed. "And far deeper than I

would expect from someone your age. But you need to take the action as truth too."

Velirith looked to the domed ceiling, still decorated with dark clouds. She suddenly felt as if the clouds were storms coming her way. To think of the play literally was bizarre. A ship coming down out of the clouds? The only flying ship she'd ever seen was the Ortessi's, and that one hadn't flown well or long.

Knowing this truth about the plays of Theatre Velaki made her realize something else. "My play, the one I've been trying to write forever, it can never measure up, can it? That's why I'm still stuck. It's a fiction. It doesn't have the literal truth behind it."

Her cota studied her. "You're so young, Velirith. Why would you think that, in your life, you wouldn't have some Truth-revealing experience worthy of a play? Just pay attention. Your play will happen."

Wow, her own life immortalized in a play? It was grand thinking even for her.

She suddenly remembered another play that was very abstract and fantastic. "Cota Aurelios, what about *Night and Day*? On the surface, it is the story of Velik searching under the Plate for Boreas immediately after he disappeared. That play depicts creatures of light and creatures of shadow engaged in battle. The creatures are a mix of machines and animals and spiritual beings and monsters. Those creatures don't exist. I even think people live under the Plate now, and they couldn't co-exist with abominations like that. So how could that play be anything but an allegorical fantasy?"

"How indeed," he mused. He frowned and took a deep breath. "How could that be literal?"

That's what I'm asking.

But she got no answer.

CHAPTER TWO

It was a month after the Festival and an hour after midnight, and Kieler wanted to ask Velirith a question. Given that he was intentionally keeping a distance between them, calling on her might give the wrong impression, which actually would be the right impression. They were two pieces of magal with opposite charges; he had to fight not to be pulled to her.

But in his little play, calling on the attractive young daughter of the house ruler, even for an innocuous reason, could only be misinterpreted.

Restless, he left his quarters to wander in the general direction of her tower suite at the center of the estate. He strolled slowly through the dark vegetation, thinking.

Only seven months ago, Kieler had come here a total stranger. Now he was trusted—except by Velirith—and he was proceeding with his plan to infiltrate society, elevate his position, and eliminate the corrupted Omeron.

Yet he could feel the pull this place was having on him. Velakun was somehow less touched by the greed that was corroding the rest of Zotikas. Velakun seemed to have greater momentum, a spirit carried forward from the time of Velik and even farther into the unknown past.

And that's what he wanted to ask Velirith about. This whole city felt older, and he wondered if she, in her mischievous wanderings, had found anything related to that mysterious time. Velator could tell him the history, but his daughter might be able to verify it with her experience. Despite Kieler's strong curiosity, he had intentionally severed any meaningful communication with Velirith. He had to maintain that resolution.

He sighed. The truth was he didn't just want to talk to Velirith, he wanted to see her, to be with her. Maybe he could use a relationship with her as leverage in toppling the Omeron.

No. I couldn't. Movus might approve of such a tactic, but Kieler realized that he had found a limit within himself. Using Velirith in such a way was past that limit.

He stopped walking and looked up. Above him the constellation Roivas shone down through the clear sky. The perpetually warm air within the rim barely stirred through the wispy greenery. Outside the rim, despite the long hours of daylight, it was cold at night in the deep north of Velakun.

He was standing still, looking up, when he noticed a shadow move off to his right. Moving nothing but his eyes, he watched as the shadow followed a narrow path between the arched wall that surrounded the garden and the shrubbery. Once, between clumps of growth, he caught a glimpse of a cloaked form, silent and purposeful.

His underground instincts kicked in. When the person moved around a corner, he slid into the shadows behind, trailing silently. He had been on the main path; he now followed in the narrow, natural path between the wall and the greenery.

He didn't have to follow far before his quarry stopped at one of the stone sheds used to house gardening equipment. The figure stooped, moved a flat rock and reached down into the space beneath. Expecting a hidden weapon to be revealed, Kieler faded back. But instead he heard a scraping sound as a portion of the back of the shed slid sideways creating a shadow-filled niche.

Who is this person? Is he dangerous? Should I call out? Or go for help?

Before he could decide, the figure descended into the shadowy niche and disappeared. No time for help. Time for "Orlazrus" to be a hero again and find out what was going on. He was approaching the secret enclosure when the door began to slide back, scraping like the lid of a stone coffin. He acted, slipping through before it shut.

Immediately he stumbled, but the noise as he regained his feet was more than covered by the false wall of the gardener's shed grinding into place. The figure ahead had produced a light, and Kieler could just make out that he was on a sharply descending, narrow stair. Then the light moved away and Kieler slowly felt his way down.

Fifteen steps below, the stair ended and he could see the silhouette of the prowler far ahead. The person was slightly shorter, but the cloak hid all other distinguishing features. Lithely and silently, the figure moved quickly around a turn in the tunnel. Now Kieler was committed. If the person turned around to come back through the narrow tunnel, there would be a scuffle. Kieler would not let this intruder get away. Bags had warned Kieler about an operative in Velakun, perhaps this was he. It was dangerous, not knowing who or why he was there, but it would look good to Velator to catch this prowler.

Kieler's training in the underworld of Avertori, both for his own survival and in the Coin, paid off. This was his environment. He stayed far enough behind that his light footfalls could not be heard, but he could still track the prowler.

Kieler controlled his breathing and with every step concentrated on bringing his foot down with complete silence. In ten minutes he was sweating, even in the cool of the tunnel. The twists followed a fissure in the rock and helped keep him out of sight. His sense of direction served him well, honed from years surviving the three-dimensional labyrinth of his home.

Keeping the intruder's light just around the corner in front of him made it hard to see his footing. He was following a path though, sure enough; sometimes cut out of the steep wall on his right, sometimes built out in stone and masonry over the natural fissure to his left. The tunnel was ancient and in rough repair.

CHAPTER TWO

Quite suddenly, the path crossed *over* the fissure. The stone arch looked as old as some of the structures under the Plate and was frighteningly narrow. With no light of his own, his footing over the tiny bridge looked precarious.

But there was nowhere else to go. The path did not continue on this side, and the only light was getting farther away by the second.

Tottering, Kieler crossed the bridge.

Despite the dark, Kieler could feel the drop beside him like a yawning maw. Far below, or perhaps above, he could hear the constant *plink, plock* of water dripping. No sooner had he crossed the fissure when forty feet later it doubled back and he had to cross over it again on another thin bridge.

Though anything but straight, the switchbacks and turns of the fissure generally seemed to be heading outward, through the caldera wall. That meant they were heading for the outside of the rim. *What could this trespasser be doing out there? Perhaps he has a camp out there and comes through this tunnel to spy on House Vel.*

After some time, intent as he was on his own movements, he missed that the prowler had stopped. Kieler had accidentally closed the gap more than he would have chosen. He flattened himself against the rock wall.

The intruder had reached the end of the tunnel, an apparent dead end. Being close, Kieler saw the shadow turn and grab something off the side wall, inserting it into an opening in the rock face—a key, probably. This seemed confirmed as the end wall swung out quietly and the form passed through, leaving the door open. That meant he would be coming back, no doubt.

Kieler waited until the light had faded, then pressed forward and through the door. It was cold outside, despite being early summer. But it was not the cold that concerned him. It was brighter out here under the stars. Iliss was mostly full, but small and far away. Either the intruder had doused his light, or had gone

397

on out of sight. Kieler hesitated, not knowing whether to stay near the door or go looking. He decided he at least needed to hide somewhere outside the door, in case the man returned quickly. Silently, Kieler sidled into a grove of squatty trees near the exit.

Once there, he surveyed the scrubby growth typical of the vegetation just outside the caldera. He perceived a narrow game trail and chose to follow it, surmising this was the most likely path taken by the interloper. It went perhaps three hundred steps before the path fanned out into an open meadow. He slowed and paused, still in the stunted trees. It was not a meadow exactly, but a clearing, odd shaped with rocks arranged like seats around a center dais. Nothing moved, but one shape before the dais seemed out of place.

The place felt ancient and a tingle seemed to envelop his entire body. *What is this place? Where did the intruder go?*

His instincts warned him to stay hidden and he slid off the path into a space between the dense trees and a boulder that still afforded him a good place to study the clearing. As he did, he scraped his uniform jacket on a branch. The shape in front of the dais moved! It turned, and in an instant Kieler realized it was his quarry, sitting huddled upon one of the rocks in front of the dais! Kieler suddenly did not like where he was, sandwiched between the rocks and the trees. It was poorly defensible and hard to get out of quickly.

But the figure must have been spooked as well, for it uncovered the luzhril lantern it had been using earlier to look back toward Kieler. The light illuminated its face and Kieler stifled a gasp.

Velirith!

Her silvery eyes peered back in his direction, but with the light near her and he in the shadows, she could not see him. He closed his eyes to mere slits so they would not reflect her lamp. After a minute, she covered her light and turned back to the center. She arched her neck, looking into the sky.

What is Velirith doing creeping around outside the safety

CHAPTER TWO

and shelter of Velakun? It's freezing out here! Then he realized. He hadn't recognized her shape because she was wearing that thick cloak. She had come prepared. But prepared for what? She was just sitting there, looking up, doing nothing...

But between whips of wind, Kieler realized she *was* doing something. She was humming, no—*singing,* softly. At first, it was so soft it sounded like the breathy wind, playing in the hollows of the trees. But as she gained confidence in her solitude, her voice rose. She sung sweetly, not with her projecting theater voice, but with a natural letting go, seeming to make up words and melody as it came, serenading the stars.

Kieler was amused and confused. This was not her normal mischief. What would she do if she found out she was not alone? Kieler knew he would be embarrassed, and for a moment thought she would be too. But then, this was Velirith. If she felt like singing at dinner she would do so without self-consciousness.

And what should he do? Jump out and shout "Boo"? That would serve the sneaky girl right.

But what could he do?

He could only...

Listen. Her song was beautiful. Heartfelt. Sung with abandon. His body tingled in reaction. He could really do nothing to interrupt this strange woman's midnight aria. He could only shiver and wait. But despite its beauty, the song that seemed to fill her heart, left his own feeling empty.

He was close enough to hear the words, but seemed unable to make out their meaning. Did she know another language? Everyone in the Omeron spoke the same language though some places had such thick accents they were hard to understand. It wasn't even the language of the dead ones. Her words simply sounded like nonsense, made up.

At one point, she swung her arms out wide and back and raised her voice to a pure-pitched cry. Her head atilt, the note strong and joyous with a touch of sorrow, or loneliness... it almost didn't seem of this world.

Her song rose and fell to a music only she seemed to be hearing, then slowly faded.

She seemed to be sobbing. Gently.

Kieler wanted to take her and comfort her. Just hold her. He thought about stepping out and boldly taking her in his arms.

But the song was not for him. And she seemed to have all the comfort she wanted and needed. He let himself just watch and not judge. There would be plenty of time to speculate. It was outlandish behavior for a Daughter-Prime.

Maybe.

Her singing lasted perhaps half an hour. Then she got up and walked slowly back, humming, toward the path. Kieler held his breath and froze. But he was far enough off the path and Velirith was looking down, content and oblivious. She had obviously forgotten the noise she'd heard earlier.

When she was out of earshot, Kieler stiffly slithered out of his hiding spot and followed her up the starlit path. Before he was completely out of the trees, he saw that the stony door was shut. Concern shivered through him and he scrambled up to the secret entrance. After much searching, he found an unobtrusive rock that tilted away revealing a key-like hole. He grabbed a stick and pried it around, trying to release what must be a catch, or a lever. But the lock was trickier than that. After much wasted time, he was forced to give up.

He looked up the cliff face. It wasn't sheer. It was climbable, just barely. He was cold already and it was dark. But the starlight was clear enough. He'd have to do it the hard way. He had probably two hours left before the early dawn.

Before starting the climb, he jogged back down the path to the clearing to examine it more closely on his own. The arranged rocks were definitely seats, worn enough to have seen much use long ago. And the dais? An altar perhaps. It was clean white stone about two feet high. Smooth, with no scratches or stains.

CHAPTER TWO

Kieler stood on it and found it easy to imagine speaking before a surrounding audience. But why? "The Theater Beyond the Rim"? Singing solos would be appropriate after what he had witnessed tonight. But this place was disused for ages.

He shook his head and sat in the seat in which Velirith had sat. He felt the same tingle through his body as when she had sung, faint, but present. This was a mystery.

He got up, and just before leaving noticed two paths leading farther down the side of the mountain through the taller trees. He would have to investigate these later. Getting back before light was going to be close if even possible.

Returning to the door in the rim wall, Kieler took a deep breath and climbed. There was no path through the rocks and several times he got himself in trouble and had to backtrack to find a less dangerous route. He was alternately sweating and freezing, but he reached the summit with a pink glow illuminating the sea of mountain peaks behind him.

An Artist's Tower was nearby along the rim path, and rather than head immediately down to Vel estate below, Kieler stumbled into the tower to shelter from the wind and watch the rise of Rei.

He climbed the three stories up to the observation level of the Artist's Tower. Looking through a lattice that was both decorative and structural, Kieler rested and surveyed a mist-shrouded Velakun bathed in pre-dawn light. Only the highest towers of the citadel were visible, appearing to defy gravity as they floated on the clouds. The Starstone still glowed softly from the previous night's use and the Empyrean appeared to bob gently when the clouds below stirred with the breeze.

The Starstone wouldn't be used much longer now that the generator was repaired and being tested. He would miss the artificial moonlight.

Remembering with a hot shiver the night when the blazing stone was first lit, he wondered why so many resources were committed to a belief—a superstition really—that the Velaki came

401

from the stars and would someday return. In conjunction with the Starstone, the Artist's Towers produced a powerful beacon pointed at the heavens. Strange.

He looked around. A tight spiral staircase led from the observation deck up to the top floor where the reflector mechanism must be housed. As the sky brightened in anticipation of Rei's rising, he climbed the stair.

After a brief delay to deal with the lock, he opened the hatch. A shining sphere of reflective liquid hovered in middle of the room; the same substance used to shield The Empyrean when the Starstone was lit. Peering up at it, he saw his distorted reflection in the liquid metal. He poked at his oversized nose. The fluid rebounded more forcefully than he expected, a few rings rippled across its surface and settled quickly.

Above the mercurial ball, a three-sided cupola topped the tower. The shroud could open like the shell of a haventhall nut. Somehow, the magal in the cowl suspended and shaped the reflective fluid.

For the last several months, Hezek had his engineers had molded that fluid into a convex mirror to diffuse the light of the Starstone over the entire bowl of Velakun. But during the Festival of Aerial Lights, the reflectors must have been concave and angled, beaming the light into the heavens.

Kieler massaged his eyes. He admitted his exhaustion. Further study of these magnetic marvels would have to wait.

Returning to the observation level, he saw Rei crest the never-ending peaks of the horizon in a glorious display of peace and immensity. As far as he could see in all directions—mountains. Jagged, cold, inhospitable.

Ice fields, snow, and frozen rock--that the House of Vel had found this one oasis and settled and developed it in the middle of nowhere was a miracle. There was nothing else. The outer slopes of the rim supported short trees and undergrowth, spillover from the geothermal heat inside the bowl. But beyond that sparse growth—desolation. And why this one bowl had heat coming up from the ground below, making it verdant and inviting, who knew?

Kieler turned and looked back over Vel Estate and across the lake of clouds to Center Isle. As Rei tilted higher, light struck the tip of the Empyrean and refracted. Pinkish beams coruscated onto the sides of the rim, and the inhabitants of this isolated masterpiece began to wake.

CHAPTER THREE

Airships were the substance of dreams, Kieler decided. He ran his hand over the feminine arch that would shape and support the gas-filled envelope. He had just finished working the light, durable metal into the swooping form of the first strut. Now he had to wait to make the others until he could skim more duralium from Jarovel's supply. Even though it was far from complete, Kieler could see the rest of the ship in his mind's eye.

He wouldn't complete it here in his workshop, but he could envision it. It would be bigger than his first ship; its lines smoother. It would also carry more; this craft should be able to carry not only his body weight but additional cargo.

He stroked the strut he had just finished, feeling for unsanded burrs that might rip the fabric of the envelope. Tough-rip was strong and light, but not bullet proof. To prevent one magbolt from completely deflating his airship—like last time—this inflated wing would have seven separate chambers of hydrogen.

Kieler examined the motor—a motor he had dreamed of for eight years. The last one he'd taken two years to build, but this one he completed in only six months. With a finger, he spun the hand-crafted prop easily. This one was better. The tools he had borrowed from Jarovel's shop and the ideas gleaned from Cota Rejin's engineering classes allowed him to fashion a more precise magnetic impeller. These improvements reduced friction and nearly eliminated the overheating challenge.

He moved forward to eye the relatively delicate, open-air cockpit which would hang below the inflated wing. Behind the cockpit, a narrow truss ran out to the tail where the engine was mounted. Conveniently, this allowed cargo to be stowed inside the truss.

Because he was now pilfering parts from a house that prided itself on quality, his work had some nice touches of class. For instance, the valve knobs above his head that controlled hydrogen flow were now solid, polished brass. Not that these fancy accouterments made filling and venting any easier. But they sure looked nice.

The burgundy velour covering the pilot's seat and armrests likewise conveyed that dint of elegance. Out of those armrests rose three levers (brass knobbed as well) connected to the linkages that controlled pitch, yaw and motor speed.

But he was eager for that duralium. Once finished with those struts, he could attach the envelope. To fly the ship, he would need to disassemble it in sections, carry the smaller pieces from his workshop under the citadel to a launch area, and reassemble it.

He was eager to be airborne again. His first training flights with his original airship had been pure magic. The freedom he felt aloft! And Velirith, she would love flying! She'd appreciate both the beauty and the thrill—

Kieler halted his thoughts.

Velirith would never even see this airship.

She was not part of the plan.

She was a nothing but a hindrance.

Fortunately, following that hinderance outside the rim two months ago had proven very worthwhile. One of the faint paths from that strange outdoor auditorium led to another clearing. It was farther up the valley between the rim slope and the Abiding Mountains beyond. The side of the clearing nearest the rim had such high rocks that it shielded it from view from someone atop the rim. It would make an excellent mooring for his completed airship. And because the path seemed to dead-end before reaching his hidden spot, Kieler felt confident even Velirith would never go there.

He sank slowly into the lightly padded seat. He sighed. Which was better? Having her reluctant goodwill or having her resentful silence? She could have made his life very hard if she pressed the issue of Kieler's identity with her father. But instead, even since the Festival, she had chosen to keep his secret. Nevertheless, she found other ways to make his life difficult.

Her habit of watching him when they were together was disturbing: She was either watching him intently or ignoring him completely. Was she plotting? Or just scornful?

He smiled wryly, looking up at the high ceiling of the windowless chamber deep in the heart of the Velakun citadel. Velirith had already loosed one of her mischievous schemes on him. Two days ago, his favorite green and gold coat, emblem of House Ortessi, had mysteriously gone missing from his own closet. He had looked everywhere, even checked the closet for some secret door, and found nothing. But not to worry, it turned up later that day—at the top of the Orcad flagpole in place of the Ortessian flag.

How? He didn't know.

Who? Who else.

He could only imagine what else she was cooking up.

No, Velirith would never get a ride in his beautiful airship. She was a stumbling block. A gorgeous, delightful, exciting, pain in the ballast.

CHAPTER FOUR

Back in the Great Hall of House Ek in his green and gold best, Kieler felt almost a nobleman himself. Velator stood next to him in his blue and silver, An'essa at his side. A troupe of acrobats performed flips and catches and pyramids with supernatural coordination on the honeycomb-tiled dance floor. And House Vel had front row seats. Only Velirith was sitting down, moping, really.

Arriving four days before his *second* New Year's Gala, Kieler had made time to visit Movus in his library below the Plate. To prepare for the gala, he needed to know more about Ek Threzhel.

"What does the Executive Chair want?" Kieler had asked his mentor.

Movus had been pleased with the question, explaining that finding a person's deepest desire was *the* way to gain power over them.

"Control."

Yes, he has reached the pinnacle and wants to stay there. A lesson in the pitfalls of trying to maintain a position rather than striving for a new one followed. Now, as Kieler stood at Velator's side, surveying the array of partygoers, Kieler realized he had done pretty well in the year since his introduction to Omeron society.

Sailing into Avertori on the glistening *Pride of Velik*; striding into the Executive Chair's gala with the Prime of the most famous house in the Omeron; and knowing that many of the Houses here were already accepting that he was indeed the true Orlazrus Ortessi.

As he had walked through the crowd earlier, several young women intercepted him, ambushed him really. Two had cut him off from Velirith and her father, and two more had stepped in front of him, forcing him to stop. He had cast a glance at Velirith when it happened, perhaps even hoping for help, but she had flicked a disgusted glance at the ceiling and led her father to their reserved place.

That further amused Kieler. But though the words the women spoke put them in support of his position, he recognized the political and petty manipulations they employed.

"Verr Ortessi!" It was Callia Telander, obviously the leader of the assault. The layers of cloth on her exotic dress reminded Kieler of a cake with too much icing. And yet, when she moved, the layers parted to reveal skin beneath, designed to make a man want more. Kieler recognized its flamboyance as one of the latest Parchiki designs. She plied, "How did you manage to speak with almost no one else last year and then be the talk of the gala this year?"

He deigned to grace them with a coy smile. Immediately he had a thought that had never crossed his mind in a year with Velirith. *I could fake a relationship with one of these social insiders and use it to further my climb up the Omeron ladder.*

"If I remember," Kieler replied smoothly, "I arrived late last gala, and no one wanted to stick around and socialize afterward. Otherwise, I'm certain *we* would have spoken."

His subtle flirt elicited a slight flush from Callia, but she had approached with purpose and was not to be distracted. "And then we hear about you singlehandedly destroying The Red 'F's new toy. Very impressive."

The Red "F"? Kieler froze his expression, mind racing, until he figured out she meant Feleanna. *Brash! No love for the Cortattis in this pack.*

"Now Lhea Callia," he responded with a modesty intended to be seen through, "You have your story wrong there. The crew of the *Pride of Velik* deserves credit as well."

"Where do you think I got my information?" she volleyed.

408

CHAPTER FOUR

Another young lady in the group was obviously feeling left out. "I'm Sonyal. I have to tell you I had the strangest dream after last year's Gala. I dreamt the complete opposite of what really happened; that the ball went off without a problem, and that I was dancing with someone in green and gold who could dance better than anyone here. Any idea who that could be?"

Kieler feigned not knowing the answer, but her approach made him very uncomfortable. He wasn't sure who she belonged to (parents, that is), and she had to be one of the youngest girls at this party.

"Oh, there's the fire maiden now," said the third young woman, inclining her head to a point across the room. "Escorted by her man-friends that look like they keep sticking their faces in front of powercoaches."

Kieler looked over as the girls tittered at the insult. Feleanna and her bodyguards would have fit better in the arena than this fancy gala. But Kieler once again squirmed internally at the bold and unwise remarks of these debutantes. If Feleanna had heard them, she might not care, but she'd probably kill them nonetheless.

Callia whispered, "Can you say 'gaudy'! Try harder, Feleanna. You're not a Prime no matter how red your dress gets." The jibe was typical of a general prejudice amongst the other houses against the Cortattis. During the confusion when House Ek had gained the Executive Chairmanship, House Cortatti overthrew the Prime House under which they had formerly served. It was accepted by Ek, but few others.

Finding himself at a loss for which way to steer the conversation, Kieler discovered he didn't have to. Feleanna was the fodder these sea-dragons were looking for.

"Is that supposed to look hot?"

"She couldn't look sweet on the dessert table."

"Can you imagine her ever getting *married*? Poor man would have to be a Martial Cota to get inside *her* guard!"

EPISODE 4 – A LIGHT IN THE DEEP

Not sure if this display of "affection" was to curry his favor or if they had forgotten he was there, Kieler got away from the vitriolic vixens as fast as he could. It was almost as if he were running a gauntlet of a different kind this year. Granted, he hadn't been shot at, and he hadn't experienced any rapid rising or stomach-dropping falling-of-out-of-control maneuvers. And he hadn't been chased by the undesirables of the Glums. Nor had he been nearly roasted by fireworks.

No, this year, he had ridden calmly and fashionably on the FamTram from the top of Vel Taradan to the opulent and ostentatious entrance gallery and air gardens of the Executive Chair's palace. Kieler had come a long way toward infiltrating the corrupt society he planned to destroy from the inside-out. And with the help of the Coin, from the outside-in as well. He would squeeze the Omeron until the houses squirted out and fell like the juice of a yellowberry fruit. There would be retribution for the murder of his parents.

To think those girls would someday be running this world if he didn't shut things down. He couldn't suppress a shiver.

Kieler glanced over at Velirith. She was definitely moping... he hoped—not plotting. She was, of course, glaring at him. Behind her subdued exterior her eyes sparked with barely contained lightning.

He looked away. She was the trump card; and he didn't hold it. He had counseled with Movus about her, about her unshakeable conviction that he was a fraud. Kieler hadn't mentioned his secret attraction to his enemy. Movus had simply said to avoid her. She could not and would not be able to prove anything and she currently held no power. Movus had hinted that within the year the path would be open for Kieler to return to Avertori in an elevated position and avoiding her would be much easier.

So things were going well. And for some strange reason, the Family Harmony Dance had been postponed till next year, replaced with entertainment from this marvelous troupe of robed, traveling acrobats from the outlands. He wouldn't even have to worry about stepping on anyone's toes at this party, at least, not physically.

And that reminded him once again of Feleanna. Kieler's eyes rested on the woman who had made surviving the trip to the palace so difficult last year. She had not tried another direct assault on him since the attack on the *Pride*, but he knew she was not idly biding time. She was just being smarter about her attack. Flanking. Probing. Exploring weak points and exploiting her political influences. She wasn't done with him.

Across the grand ballroom, her flunkies stood around her, arrogantly bantering. But she herself stood, in a flaming red dress, tight and controlled. Silent and surveying.

He looked away before her gaze came to rest on him. No use provoking the beast.

Velirith could almost feel the Ortessi's heart race as Ek Threzhel, Executive Chair of the Omeron, rose to his feet in his booth. The Ortessi fraud was hoping for recognition, and indeed, it was the talk of this whole boring party.

The acrobats tumbled fluidly into a circle of seated forms at the feet of Ek Threzhel, in deference to the host's upcoming announcement. *And really...* Velirith mused, *they tumbled out of the spotlight a little* too *quickly.* Almost as if they anticipated the Executive Chair's rising. She mulled on the odd feeling.

The room quieted and Ek Threzhel spoke in a moderately loud voice. He could have been louder, but didn't seem to care if those in back could hear or not. "Families of the Omeron! I have gifts tonight in keeping with tradition and the promoting of family harmony."

Velirith snorted at the obvious irony, considering it was the first year in history that the Family Harmony Dance was not being performed.

He went on. "The first gift is for a young man who is proving to uphold the reputation of House Ortessi, aiding Velator in various

411

projects, and excelling at the lessons of history available at the Ortessi Academy of Leadership in Velakun. My gift is to encourage his continued pursuit of the preservation of the history of our esteemed society." He paused and surveyed the waiting crowd. Threzhel may not be enamored with life anymore, Velirith observed, but he still enjoyed playing with the power he had obtained.

"My gift to Orlazrus Ortessi is the original grounds of the Ortessi Academy here in Avertori!"

Applause, some enthusiastic and some simply mandatory manners, rippled through the crowd. Feleanna shot magbolts from her eyes at the recipient of what she undoubtedly considered *her* property. Of course, it wasn't. Her puppet Orticot had sold it to Ek Threzhel for a measly personal gain, not seeing the political value. That slink would be lucky to keep all of his body parts. Feleanna was furious.

Kieler bowed deeply before the Executive Chair. Though Velirith herself was ambivalent about the gift to the fake Ortessi, she was surprised at the mix of emotions she picked up from him: Pride, certainly. An ugly, self-satisfied sense of his own accomplishments. But she also picked up a distinct scent of loathing from the Ortessi... *for Ek Threzhel!* For the *grantor* of this boon. How odd that she would pick up *true* hate for someone who was obviously supporting the Ortessi's claim.

"My second gift is for Corthuane, the Cortatti Prime. As his health is poor, I ask his daughter to accept the keys to a finely apportioned apartment in this very palace. Corthuane has been a dear friend and ally for many years and has always been fond of the expansive view from the North Pinnacle. It is my hope that his twilight years will be made as comfortable as possible.

Again applause, all of it merely polite except from the Cortatti contingent. Feleanna registered the slightest surprise. Velirith could see she didn't see this coming but knew the danger behind such a bequest. Velirith too, could read the knife-twisting Ek

412

Threzhel intended with his every word. Perhaps he intended to hold Corthuane hostage, insurance against further Cortatti aggression.

Someone standing behind Velirith muttered, "As it should be. Cortattis will always be proximal in *my* book."

Feleanna accepted the "gift", of course. Even her rudeness was curtailed by the social and political pressure of the moment. She kept her poise in front of Ek Threzhel but was fuming on the way back to her table. *Poor woman. Everybody makes her angry.*

Threzhel handed out gifts to other favored houses, though none of them created the stir of the first two. When it was done he raised his cup, "Enjoy the entertainment, here's to a prosperous New Year."

Threzhel is just plain ugly, inside and out. Velirith mused on how some people were taken in by pretty packaging—though that did not apply to Threzhel. But Moshalli could be fooled, for example.

Rammy—*Ramico*—was as handsome as they came. Strong, chiseled. But Velirith knew from the snide sneer of his words that he was rotten within. Having finally met him, her heart broke for her lifelong friend. Moshalli so wanted love and status that she overlooked his black and petty soul.

The manipulative gift giving and the aura of loathing between the prime players left her feeling even more regretful that she was part of it, or even that she had come at all. She slouched in her chair and caught Lhea Firstholm's eye. Instantly the fine matron's words came back to her, "What are *you* going to do to make things better?"

Nothing, Velirith thought, looking away. Then recanted. *No, I'm going to confront that Ortessi fraud—someday. Not that it will make any difference.*

During her introspection, she hadn't noticed the drink arrive on the table next to her. She picked up the crystal glass and sniffed the contents. It seemed to be only some cool, sweet juice.

413

Evidently Fechua knew her preference. She sipped casually while turning her attention back to the acrobats.

The performers had changed into body-concealing white robes with scarlet hoods and masks, completely concealing any individuality. The fifty or so players ran a weaving pattern on the floor, a three-leafed procession. Their intentions were mischievous, and Velirith, despite her foul mood, was intrigued.

One leaf peeled off single-file and approached Ek Threzhel seated in his booth. Those sixteen or so players bowed in perfect unison, then beckoned him to come and join them. He gave them no quarter. His soft face remained rock hard and he simply shook his head. The mute acrobats in their red masks, drooped their heads in mock disappointment and began to file away. One player, however, shielded from the view of Threzhel by the others, pointed at the Executive Chair and slither-scampered across the floor in a perfect imitation of the motion of a slink, in full view of the audience! The implication was that Ek Threzhel was too scared to participate!

The audience could not withhold their shocked laughter at the audacity of the acrobat. The single procession continued around the dance floor in the direction of the Cortatti contingent while the other two leaves of acrobats wound round and round in a figure eight.

They're going to pick Feleanna. Velirith realized suddenly. *And they're going to pick me!* She couldn't identify the subtle clues that led her to that conclusion, but she knew she was right. *They never intended for Threzhel to play; they just wanted to imply he wouldn't because he was afraid. Or maybe they invited him for a different reason. The Ortessi?*

Sure enough. When they beckoned Feleanna to come and play, her hesitation was overcome by her pride, that she wasn't afraid of taking a risk that the current Executive Chair would not take. She strode out from the sidelines and into the middle with a casual confidence. She was presented with a white robe and red mask, identical to the others, and the players easily slipped the costume over her head. They put her in the middle of the procession, and though she looked like them now, she was out of stride and out of the rhythm which the practiced troupe so naturally assumed.

But that standing out didn't last. Instead of Feleanna matching their pattern, the players altered *theirs* to assume the long-strided, purposeful gait, the slight sway of her shoulders, even the intensity of her person. By the time her file had re-entered the weaving pattern of the others in the troupe and reestablished the third leaf, the players that had picked up Feleanna had mixed her into their ranks like a shell game. It was masterful theater, and Velirith was instantly out of her personal Glums.

When the second leaf broke off, they came toward her... but chose the Ortessi. *That is outright dangerous!* Velirith had no idea what game was afoot, but to mix such elements as these two, could only have explosive results. Out of the corner of her eye, Velirith saw Fechua MgFellis' hands rise to her horrified face. She was seeing a vision of the Family Harmony Disaster repeated.

But Velirith didn't think that would happen. The Ortessi accepted, of course, with a look of surprise and consternation that was only slightly over-acted. He finished his drink and handed it to An'essa and accepted their invitation. But he had accepted for different reasons than Feleanna. Yes, he didn't want to look weaker than Cortatti, but also; he was the man-of-the-day. He was expected to play nice and participate even if it was potentially embarrassing.

One of the players weaving the pattern in the middle stumbled ever so slightly as she turned her head to see the troupe choose the Ortessi. That must have been Feleanna. Other players imitated the variation, but Velirith was sure that Feleanna had highlighted herself momentarily. Then the real Feleanna was swept back into the pattern and disappeared once more.

Orlazrus was adorned with robe and mask and his file

marched off toward the center. His group walked more stiffly, confident but calculating, all of them looking around more, gathering information on which to base their decisions. It was so him. It was uncanny.

She knew instantly that keeping track of Feleanna and Orlazrus would be important. That noting subtleties would allow her to pick them out no matter how good their group of players managed to imitate them. Her intuition allowed her to cheat.

The audience was spellbound, trying to anticipate what kind of game this could be and reveling in the visual display of white and red.

Shortly after Orlazrus' group reformed the three-leaf weave, the final leaf, split off and, sure enough, came for her.

Velirith jumped to her feet and bowed deeply and melodramatically to the players, who, it turned out, anticipated her gesture and bowed either simultaneously or *before* she did. These actors were well-studied indeed. Or… Velirith realized, they were more than well-studied. They somehow had an edge, but she was so far from sussing out what it was that she didn't try. She just determined to enjoy the game.

And a game it was. After dressing and prancing into the center weave in Velirith's own particular… idiom, her group of sixteen or so effectively made her disappear as well. It was a thrilling but weird experience to be copied so precisely, even when she intentionally did odd skips or twirls. Before she even began to move, the players threw in characteristically Velirith randomness, drawing attention away from the real and to the copies.

Suddenly, shockingly, Velirith found herself in the middle of the floor with two other robed figures, stopped, and with everyone around her stopped. She felt a flash of fear and knew that the other two in the center, Feleanna and Orlazrus, felt it too. They stood facing each other, adversaries in real life, contestants in this mad game.

Again, Velirith seethed with excitement.

CHAPTER FOUR

Three of the acrobats came out and stood, one before each of them. Their hands were entirely concealed in their robes and simultaneously, without signal, each of the three quickly withdrew their hands, drawing and flourishing short, blood-colored knives, one in each hand. Velirith was the only one who didn't jump.

Feleanna actually kicked at the person in front of her, thinking she was being attacked, but she was anticipated and avoided. Orlazrus leapt back and assumed a foot-forward stance they had learned in Cota Triose's class. Good for him. It came naturally in a real situation just as they practiced during sparring.

But this was not a real situation. And the acrobats were not threatening them, Velirith knew. They bowed carefully before their contestants and presented two knives to each contestant, handles first, into the hands of the players. Velirith took the two props with some fear, but once in her grasp saw that the bright red blades were just stiff sponges infused with blood-colored paint. These were not deadly.

The three acrobats, having given each of the players two knives, turned to the center and faced each other. Somehow, they each had a blood-bladed knife in each hand again. The three circled warily, like hunters face to face with a grevon. They were demonstrating. One feinted and dodged back. The third stepped in and slashed the first down and across the chest leaving a long, wide red streak. Blood, at least, *theater blood*.

The victim looked down at the streak and fell, dying dramatically, admitting defeat. The other two now faced each other. But the victor of the first engagement had only one dagger left. The blood marker had broken off with a single use. Velirith could only guess the same would happen to them. They had only two shots.

Within seconds, the players resolved their anonymous conflict and a second "body" lay on the floor with a red slash mark while the victor leapt silently into the air, celebrating his win.

So this is to be our game. Our fate. To battle until but one

417

remains. Velirith was no longer sure she would enjoy playing.

Feleanna leapt across the center space and took a preemptory swipe at Orlazrus. But he was ready and dodged easily. This seemed to surprise the acrobats, perhaps for the first time, but only for a moment. Instantly the others around them swept in and swept each of the players into their midst. They were now three groups: The Feleannas, The Orlazruses and the Veliriths. Each about sixteen strong. All identical.

That's better! Velirith decided. *We aren't just arena fighting, we have to pick the real adversary out of the crowd!*

She wasn't even in the middle of her group. She was actually quite close to the point as she saw to her dread that her group, like a flock of birds, had whirled and was heading straight into Feleanna's group. She felt so exposed!

But she wasn't. As the two pods of actors merged, Velirith instantly picked out the real Feleanna. She was out of reach as the groups passed through each other and was anxiously searching the masked faces for the real Velirith. She didn't find her. *Interesting.*

The Feleanna and Ortessi groups flowed through each other next and from across the dance floor Velirith watched Feleanna intensely seeking Orlazrus. Orlazrus, near the back of his group, stood out to Velirith by some subtle posture of evaluating. *Amazing how good I am at this. I can even tell that they didn't see each other.*

The trick was to fit into your group and yet position yourself to draw and slash as you passed by one of your identified opponents. Velirith felt she would have no trouble winning as it was easy for her to pick out the real Feleanna and Orlazrus. But evidently, her group of Veliriths felt the same thing. She suddenly realized they were not imitating her very well, she was being highlighted by her own troupe!

Why? This is intentional!

But the answer hit her. Because this was for the entertainment of the audience. If she won too easily, it would be over too soon, without the drama of a good play. *Ohhh! Well, don't worry, I'll draw it out!*

Oddly enough, with that thought, her troupe reformed and she reblended. *How do they know? How did they know to pick us three, perhaps the most conflicted of the people attending?*

She shivered with the realization that these acrobats were more than mere gymnasts.

Then she realized something even more alarming: she could not distinguish between individual actors, even in her troupe, even right next to her! They blended into each other even better than they blended in with her.

Time to think about these oddities was short. Her troupe now angled toward Orlazrus' entourage. As the two flocks passed through each other, she subtly shifted to pass face to face with the Ortessi. And it struck her what she would do.

One of the things that gave both Orlazrus and Feleanna away was the great tension that surrounded them, a tension the other players could only approximate. They wanted to win. Well, for Velirith, she just wanted to play.

Her front rank merged into the Ortessi front rank and they rapidly passed one another. No one reacted abruptly until she, one step before passing by the real Orlazrus, leaned her head in front of his, focused, and winked her silver eye at him simultaneously sticking her tongue through the mask.

Orlazrus jerked back, pulled out his knife and slashed. But she knew that his reaction would be quick and she tumbled away, as did the rest of her troupe. Rolling on the ground, popping up and crossing over each other in a tangle of paths that prevented Orlazrus from tracking the hodge-podge of Veliriths.

The audience roared like an arena crowd. But her mischief caused two other actions that Velirith hadn't anticipated. First, her troupe, *individually*, broke out laughing uncontrollably and showed they definitely were not *her*. But the confusion of motion was still sufficient to hide her. Second, as the Ortessi band whirled to give feeble chase to the phantom Velirith, Feleanna's gang ran forward to engage. She had seen the interplay and marked them both. Evidently, she lost Velirith first and was going for Orlazrus.

As the Veliriths rolled and cavorted (and laughed), the Orlazruses pursued for a few brief moments, then saw Feleanna coming, ran together in a big mash-up, spun, and whirled back out thoroughly shuffled. Feleanna was foiled and her rage—her most endearing and enduring quality—identified her before her own troupe shuffled her back into the pack with intense fist shaking and storming about.

It would have been quite humorous… had it not been so real. Those two really wanted to kill each other. Velirith noticed, sadly, how much the crowd loved it.

Kieler found Velirith's antics childish and frustrating. This game, played right, could cause doubt in Feleanna's cold heart about her ability to defeat him in real life. It could give him an edge in a critical moment. But he had to admit, the Vel girl had him pegged.

He saw that the mash-up had hidden him from the enraged Feleanna. Her troupe tried to hide her but he followed the real anger she exuded. He guided his group toward hers, locked on the form he was tracking. To look away even for an instant would mean losing her. *Ingenious game!* he thought. *If only it weren't so realistic.* But he saw the advantage to be gained politically by defeating Feleanna, even in a game.

Velirith? He'd get her too, just to teach her a lesson—*after* he got Feleanna.

His group was camouflaging him expertly. Evidently they had played this game many times before. His strategy was to blend in until the last possible moment when there could be no counter-strike. He was still certain he had the right Feleanna, though they all seemed intensely mad now.

The groups filed through each other. His Feleanna was second from the rear on the right. But before he passed her, a

CHAPTER FOUR

Feleanna on his left feinted an attack on one of his own decoys. He whirled his head to make sure he wasn't targeted and realized a split second later that he had just given himself away. His group anticipated his next move and they all crisscrossed, shuffling him but foiling his attack run.

He flared with frustration, but still, his first priority had to be to keep himself alive. Dead, he would not have his chance.

The feint by the decoy Feleanna also made him doubt whether he had tracked the real Feleanna. Strategy! He needed a good strategy. Though more dangerous, he needed a way to cause her to reveal herself at the last moment so he didn't waste an attack.

The Feleannas were pursuing. As one, Kieler's crew whirled back to the fray. Velirith's troupe, prancing around like the children they were, ran through just as the Feleannas and Orlazruses clashed.

And clash they did. Kieler couldn't believe it! A Feleanna kicked one of his Orlazruses and the rest copied her. A genuine brawl broke out immediately and in earnest. Kieler parried a kick, then tripped another Feleanna who kicked at him.

Above the din of the all-out brawl he heard a shriek. Fechua? He didn't have time to check.

The audience roared with appreciation. *So much for a dignified party.* He doubted Fechua, or Ek Threzhel for that matter, could have planned *this!*

The ludicrous thing about the fight was that he and the real Velirith and the real Feleanna could not remove their hands from their robes lest they reveal their knives. So they and all their copies leapt around like armless fools kicking at each other.

Kieler was almost to the Feleanna who instigated the altercation when the Veliriths bowled through. Rolling (shoulder first), leaping, cart-wheeling (no handed!) and generally hopping around like lunatics, the Veliriths just weren't taking this fight seriously!

421

EPISODE 4 – A LIGHT IN THE DEEP

One Velirith managed to leap onto the shoulders of a Feleanna between him and his target. Kieler's foot swept the bottom one and they both tumbled down. He leapt over the two of them toward the Feleanna who started the fight just as she planted a hard side kick into the mask of the opponent she battled.

That confirmed her. He whipped out a knife and slashed across her front as she went backward from her kick. The knife blade disintegrated as he struck leaving a long streak of red and then a huge blotch of fake blood. *Gottcha!*

Feleanna collapsed and played dead and immediately his heart fell into his stomach.

Loser or not, Feleanna would not play dead. The real Feleanna would have been spitting her own blood in his face. Kieler ripped off her mask and found an arrogant acrobat grinning wildly back at him. He'd get kudos for fooling him no doubt.

A motion in front of Kieler caused him to look up into a plunging leap from the *real* Feleanna. Knife descending, fury in her eyes, he was done.

Suddenly, in that time-protracted descent, a Velirith flew through the air from his right—she had to be thrown by one of the other acrobats—and knocked Feleanna out of the air and into a rolling heap.

Kieler wanted to move but was still standing in shock over his "innocent" victim. When the Velirith and Feleanna stopped rolling, Feleanna rose in a fury!

She was marked! Dead! Dripping with the fake blood from Velirith's knife. It had been the real Velirith!

Three other Veliriths simultaneously rolled in next to the real one, trying to cover her. How they did that, anticipating every move and rolling in to try and decoy, was unsettling. But Feleanna was up, dead or not, and chasing the middle Velirith with both knives out, one red-bladed and one silver. Two of the Veliriths split off and circled back toward him to distract her.

Silver?

CHAPTER FOUR

Kieler sprung to his feet to save his savior. He had bolted three steps after them when he was tripped by a white-robed acrobat. He tumbled over her.

"You fool!" he shouted. "Feleanna has a *real* knife! She's going to kill Velirith! I have to save her!" he struggled to get up. As he did, the person who had tripped him pulled her mask up and off and there revealed the white-toothed, beautiful, oval face of the Velirith.

His breath caught and for a moment he couldn't fathom how she could be running from Feleanna and standing in front of him at the same time. Something dripped off a fold in his robe and onto his hand. He looked dumbly down at the drop of red blood.

Am I hurt?

Realization struck harder than the knife he hadn't felt.

Velirith turned and bowed deeply to the wild applause of the audience as Kieler looked down at the blob of blood-paint splattered on the front of his robe. He felt like an idiot.

But that meant Feleanna was chasing an acrobat. The actor wouldn't stand a chance against her fighting skills! But as he looked over, there was a group of acrobats carrying the unmasked Feleanna back to the center on their collective shoulders to the appreciative cheers of the crowd.

Had she a real blade or not?

It was frighteningly unnerving to think he thought he knew what was going on, and have it turn out completely different. He squelched his fear, his disorientation, his lack of control.

He unmasked and followed Velirith's lead: He bowed deeply and smiled broadly.

And he had no idea how all this just happened.

Feleanna had no choice but to do likewise as she was set down before the roaring approbation. But she bore no smile; just that cold glower that meant only one thing: This had only been a game of show. The real game wasn't over.

CHAPTER FIVE

Spring was coming. Velirith could feel the growing energy of it in her blood.

Even though ice still gripped the mountains outside of Velakun, today, Rei was alight and pleasant, and a whisper of a warm breeze meandered up from the lake and through the Artist's Tower in which she reclined. Spring touched her. New life.

Sitting in the heavy lattice that supported the tower top, she soaked in the balmy rays of the sun.

It was a day off. So she wasn't even deliberately evading the academy. She looked down into Vel Estate and out across the lake to sparkling Center Isle. Outside the rim she beheld the limitless peaks of the Abiding Mountains.

Closing her eyes, she hummed a tune from the upcoming festival play. The Festival of Aerial Lights would mark the one-year anniversary of the still mysterious "Ortessi" successfully pushing her away. She hadn't thought he could have maintained it. His motivation and will power were strong.

She thought. And inevitably her thoughts led back to how angry she was with him. The measure of satisfaction gained by beating him at the New Year's game had faded months ago. The sting of him pushing her away had grown back like a weed in springtime.

She had consciously let it go a hundred times. *I forgive him. I forgive him. I forgive him.*

He hadn't asked for forgiveness, but a certain voice within her patiently explained that unforgiveness was a poison that affected only her. He could go blissfully on in total ignorance.

I forgive him.

There, that feels better. He doesn't control me. I control me.

He will suffer the consequences of his deceitful acts. And he has certainly been a smug jerk since getting the old Orcad property in Avertori. Strutting around as if he—

She captured her thoughts. There they went, right back to thinking negatively about him. *I forgive him.*

My mantra, she smiled. *But I still care about him. And am attracted to him. And—*

"Agh!" she cried in frustration.

A quiet crunching and an awareness of an approaching presence caused her to open her eyes. She looked back down the path to the estate. *Of all the people to see up here...*

It was him. The faux Ortessi. He entered the base of the tower and climbed the stairs to the observation level. If she could only get him to admit, even to her, *especially to her,* that he was lying—it would make tolerating him... *tolerable!*

I forgive him.

But I don't have to talk to him...

"Hello, Your Unapproachableness," he opened innocently.

"Mm-hmm." She closed her eyes again.

"Didn't know you were here, but the fortunate meeting allows me to tell you some news."

She sighed and opened one eye.

"Now that I'm a landholder, again, I'm going to move back to Avertori. Probably after this term. In the summer."

She found herself sitting up straight. She didn't want *that.* Amazing. *Here I am stewing about having to put up with him and now he tells me he's leaving and I'm upset? I'm such a woman!*

She wanted to say, "Fine, go!" but she didn't mean it and it wouldn't be true. She wanted her words to say what she meant.

"You insensitive *abbig!*" she spat instead, unable to control her words.

Kieler's eyebrows shot up nearly to his hairline. "What?"

She said nothing.

"I'm sorry, but I don't have the slightest idea if you've insulted me well. What's an abbig?"

She cocked her head at him. He really didn't know. Every child with a picture book knew what an abbig was. Whatever burrow he crawled out of, he wasn't raised normally. Furrowing her brows, annoyed, she replied, "You know, furry, brown, arms as long as their legs. Live in trees in forests. Abbigs."

Kieler shrugged.

How could this deceiver be so lovably naïve?

He went on. "I figured you'd be happy to see me go."

No, I won't. But I can't tell you that, you arrogant impersonator.

"And I am sorry we… couldn't get along better. I'm very grateful that you showed me the ropes around here. I enjoyed that time."

He is grateful, even if he's been a jerk for an entire year! He's probably just trying to make sure I don't press the issue of his false identity with my father.

"Now that I'm almost done with the construction—I mean *done* with the construction on the *Pride…*"

Hmm, he was going to say something else—

"I feel most of my obligations are finished. And I don't want to bother your father with my upkeep anymore."

He's nervous, prattling on. Perhaps he'll slip up again.

"He's been exceedingly generous, giving me the income from the Velakun Orcad to fund the legal battle for my house. Now that I've been granted some of my property back, I want to see if I can generate my own cash flow.

"So I'm thinking of leasing out some structures of the old Orcad back in Avertori. I visited the campus New Year's Day, just after the gala. It's nice, all with second-level Rei exposure. It's run down, completely emptied—by your father to supply the current Orcad, I assume—but it will be nice when fixed up.

"At first, I was thinking conventionally; to rent to one of the houses in Avertori. Bintle perhaps. But then an unusual idea hit me. A rogue idea. What if I didn't rent to a prime house? What if I rent to those who cannot rent, those of minor houses who are dependent on the 'good' will of their superior houses?"

Is he testing me? Goading me?

"I couldn't get much on an individual basis, but I've got a fair chunk of real estate and collectively— "

"It's a good idea. Rent to them." Velirith couldn't stop the words because she believed them. She still didn't want him to go. But his idea seemed right.

The Ortessi, for his part, pulled back as if she'd slapped him. His face told her that he in no way expected a daughter of the Omeron to support such a rebellious idea.

"Are you agreeing so that I'll be attacked? The other prime houses will hate this idea."

"No, it really is a good idea. Figure it out." Velirith considered why she thought it was a good idea. Velakun was completely different than Avertori. Prime houses in Avertori were supposed to supply their proximal houses with the basics: a place to live, food and a stipend for other necessities, or "luxuries" as the stingier house primes called them. Depending on the house, oftentimes the accommodations were substandard.

What the Ortessi was suggesting was that the proximals could get better housing with their stipend and any black-market monies they may scrounge up.

Since Orlazrus was still staring at her, puzzled, she continued, "Your tenants would be endangering themselves, you know."

He nodded, now concerned. "If their Primes found out they weren't living in provided housing, the Primes would wonder where they got the money."

EPISODE 4 – A LIGHT IN THE DEEP

Velirith nodded slightly, still very annoyed with him.

"I—" his eyes showed sincere consideration going on in his mind. Something about her that he had misjudged. "I didn't expect you to be supportive..."

Forget his entrepreneurial scheme. He's leaving! All my efforts to get him to open up, all my displays of trust, bringing him into my private world—futile. He is just going to leave and be the same fake—even with me—that he has always been. And I still don't know who he is!

A rage built up like a boiler of hot steam within her. She had to move. She couldn't stand him looking at her, with that denied affection, knowing he would not break down and be honest with her.

She jumped up and stood before him.

"Who are you?"

She never thought of herself as violent, but she certainly wasn't passive. She shoved him back two steps, then bolted past him down the stairs.

He might never *tell* her who he was, but she was determined to find out.

CHAPTER SIX

A pre-dawn breeze blew across Kieler's face as he stood near the edge of Orcad's Martial Terrace. He looked across the lake at the Velakun caldera silhouetted against the brightening spring sky. Yesterday, he had told Velirith he was leaving, and today he was telling himself he was doing the right thing. Velirith, for her part, had been emotionally erratic lately—well, *more* erratic. *Shouldn't she be glad the fraud is leaving?*

Though he couldn't see Rei yet, its light struck the top of the Empyrean above and refracted through the Starstone. Light crawled down the tower, and the lower spires glowed with new warmth. Kieler enjoyed the slow, peaceful dawn, reflecting.

Most of his time in Velakun was spent "becoming the wise and just leader of house Ortessi," as Velator had put it. Kieler felt good when he said that. He could almost believe it. He could almost believe his father would have said it.

His father. His father had tried to change the Omeron with his revolutionary compact generator. For this "rebellion", he was killed. The cota here at Orcad knew of the injustices of the Omeron but had no plan, no will to change things. Movus, on the other hand, had a plan, the will, and the cunning to make things happen.

Still, apart from their "somebody-else's-problem" attitude, Kieler realized the cota had a lot to offer. Politics, economics, war and engineering; he was learning to play the game as they played it—trained by his enemy in the very skills needed to defeat them.

The price of that training was time. Seventeen months had passed in Velakun and he bristled at how little progress he'd made.

EPISODE 4 – A LIGHT IN THE DEEP

His contact with the Coin was limited to infrequent trips to Avertori and a few coded telegraphs. His airship was still not complete, though close. Worst of all was how little control of House Ortessi he had managed to grasp.

All of the Ortessian proximal houses still followed Orticot, Feleanna's puppet. Kieler's plan to open Old Orcad in Avertori might woo some of them to his authority, but the proximals weren't stupid. They knew Feleanna would extract retribution for defecting from her.

Kieler ground his teeth and looked around the terrace where students trained to fight. Divided by pillared colonnades, the terrace was a collection of open arenas. The colonnades also supported the aqueducts, fed from higher towers and cascading to the lower ones. Here on the Martial Terrace, they also fed the pools that defined the arena boundaries, an ever-present motivation. No one wanted to "take a bath" by getting thrown out of bounds into the pool.

A channel also ran around the entire edge of the terrace where Kieler now stood—a final safety net for over-zealous sparring bouts.

With his eyes closed and face up to the approaching sun, he drew a deep breath and thought about his options. *What if I just stayed Orlazrus? I could just live and learn and enjoy life here in Velakun.* With the acquiring of the original Orcad, he could become the legitimate leader of House Ortessi. No more of this sneaking around and constant plotting. Financial prosperity would come. He could even allow people to get close…

Kieler caught himself. *This is what happens to the highborns. They have so much given to them that they forget about the suffering endured by others that makes their lives possible.* He could not let playing a Prime make him into one. It was the greatest danger he faced. Except, perhaps, for Velirith.

"So, what brings the Ortessi out here so early?"

He didn't startle out of his reverie at the sound of Velirith's

CHAPTER SIX

voice. *If I could just be Orlazrus...*

Kieler turned from the terrace edge and faced Velirith, just coming around one of the colonnades. He was surprised to see her dressed in full practice armor and a conniving look she wasn't attempting to hide.

"I woke early, so I came to watch the sunrise," Kieler answered guardedly, gesturing to the vista before them.

"It is glorious, true?" She gave a quick twirl to the practice staff she carried. Made by lashing together several of the springy upper boughs of the haventhall, the resultant weapon was a staff with more give, and students with less injuries. But it hurt like a whip when it connected.

She walked up to the edge of the pool and stood next to him. "How was your ride over from the estate this morning?"

His intuition raised a tiny warning flag. But irritated by her intrusion, he answered curtly, "Fine."

She flashed him a dangerous look. "What time did you leave?"

He shrugged coldly. "Early."

"No, you didn't," Velirith replied flatly.

Kieler gave her a small shake of his head. "Whatever you want to believe, Velirith. How would you know anyway?"

"No!" she nearly screamed, "No, you didn't leave early. No, you did not *leave*. And no, it's not 'whatever I want to believe'. I believe the Truth.

"*You* never even came back to the estate last night. You're lying. Again. There's been no truth in you from the minute we met. You have continually lied to my house! You lied to my father! And you keep lying to *me!*"

Now he was alarmed. She had been acting calm, but she was hot. By the vehemence in her voice, Kieler finally realized *truth* was not just important to Velirith; it was non-negotiable. And her uncanny knack of sorting truth from falsehoods made her *feel* lies like slaps to burn-raw nerves. Lying was revolting to her. Painfully

431

repulsive.

Still, he could not trust her with the truth, not that much. "I— "

"Stop!" She cut him off instantly. "I sat in the Vel Estate station since sunset last night. Not one podcar arrived or departed without me checking it. This is your last chance. You either tell me the truth now, or I will not rest until I have exposed you!"

The finality of her declaration stopped him. If she persisted with fraud accusations, it was hard to tell how much damage she could cause. He had to calm her without telling her who he was. He tried, "Why is this so important to you?"

She just glared at him with bewildered fury, her head shaking with it. Then, with shocking speed, she whipped her staff up in an uppercut to his chin. Instinctively he turned his head and the staff tip glanced off the side of his face.

"Velirith!" Kieler cried angrily, reeling back. Before he could collect himself, she continued the momentum of the first strike, spinning around to thrust the other end of her staff into his stomach.

He doubled from the blow but did manage to hang on to the end of her staff. "Velirith, stop it!" he grunted as his temper flared. "I don't want to hurt you."

"Oh really?" she exclaimed as she tried repeatedly to wrench the staff back. "Because that is exactly what you've done with every lie you've ever spoken to me."

With that verbal blow, Kieler lost his grip on the staff. He ducked to avoid another swipe as Velirith whirled, trying to catch him as he regained his balance. Her missed strike gave Kieler the split second he needed to lunge forward and catch her knees in a diving tackle.

They both went down hard, and the staff skittered away across the sand. It came to rest near one of the colonnades. Thanks to her practice armor, Velirith recovered quickly. She brought her knee across Kieler's face before scrambling away after the staff.

CHAPTER SIX

Kieler was up an instant later, moving to catch her as she slowed to pick up the staff. It was time to put an end to this. But it didn't work as he had planned. Just as he reached for her, Velirith suddenly leapt into a handspring, grabbed the staff, and continued into an uppercut.

Kieler dodged to the side, narrowly avoiding the blow and stepping in behind her. This time, when she spun around to attack, he was ready. Once again, he caught the staff and used her momentum to swing her around, pinning her to one of the columns. Her own yanking on the staff pulled him in close.

His face was just inches from hers.

"Enough!" Kieler growled, looking into a face that was now the picture of startled innocence. "You dare to accuse me. You, who constantly sneaks around pursuing your own conniving pleasure. Do not lecture me. At least my *rebellion* has a purpose."

Rebellion! Velirith thrilled. It was the real him. *Finally!*

She blinked in surprise, recognizing multiple truths. Lhea Firstholm had pointed out Velirith's lack of meaningful purpose. The Ortessi had a point. If she were completely honest, she was living a double life too, just to a lesser degree. But this confrontation was not about her. This man lived in her house, and she still didn't know who he was. That was going to end.

Pinned to the column by his sheer strength, she opened her mind to her fighting options and chose the most effective and most desired—she kissed him.

She held the kiss longer than she planned; her brain turned off and her body turned on. His warm lips against hers seemed like a kind of truth in itself. But she finally remembered that she was going to win this fight one way or another. She ended the kiss by blowing a sharp puff of air into his mouth. His surprised coughing gave her just enough space to snap her head down onto his nose.

Reeling from the emotional and physical blows, the Ortessi staggered back. Velirith pressed her advantage with a kick to the stomach and then tried to jerk the staff away from him.

433

EPISODE 4 – A LIGHT IN THE DEEP

Unfortunately, she underestimated his strength, now rage-fueled.

The Ortessi yanked her toward him, catching her throat in his hand. He then stepped behind her and threw her onto her back, pinning her to the sand.

With his hand on her throat, she couldn't recover her breath. It was the first time she had been truly afraid of him. "Stop...hurts," she finally managed to whimper.

"Hurts? Really?" the Ortessi asked with a cruel laugh. "You highborns haven't the slightest idea what true *pain* is. You sit here in your palaces with no thought to the suffering that built them. You're right. I'm not the highborn slink Ortessi. You want to know who I am? I'm Justice!

"Do you accept *that* name as Truth? What does your precious intuition tell you now? Am I lying?"

He was bleeding... but he wasn't lying.

"I am the only Justice in the whole rotting Omeron. *Truth*?"

She couldn't talk, her vision graying at the edges. But his blazing brown eyes were huge before her. He believed every word he was saying.

"It's the only truth you need know."

With that, he released her, and stormed off to the men's bath.

She remained lying in the sand, eyes closed, gasping and thinking about what the Ortessi had just said. She frowned. No, she really couldn't even call him that now.

He had just admitted that he was not Ortessi. That was important, but she had already known. What really concerned her was that she had kissed him and there was as much truth in the kiss as in the confession. That brief moment, when neither had pulled away, was truth too.

And he only told me who he isn't. He didn't tell me who he is!

When she opened her eyes again, she saw An'essa and Cota Triose staring down at her, very concerned. She simply smiled and looked up at them, waiting for them to break the awkward silence.

"Are you alright m'lady?" asked An'essa tensely as she knelt beside Velirith.

"I'm fine. Just taking a break after some early practice," replied Velirith, fairly sure she didn't have any major injuries.

"Extra practice is good," An'essa said. "Though I'm curious how you managed to hit yourself in the head."

Velirith sat up, blinking in the sunlight that had just crested the rim.

"Is Orlazrus here yet?" asked An'essa. "I didn't see him leave the estate this morning."

"Oh, he's here. Over in the bath. Had some mishap. Might be a bit late."

Eventually, when "Justice" came out of the bath, his only obvious injury was a swelling nose. All other hurts were hidden beneath his armor.

CHAPTER SEVEN

No point worrying about Velirith, Kieler told himself.

A full month had passed since he had consciously, purposely told her he was not Ortessi... and she had been much more pleasant toward him since. Strange woman.

Even stranger was how violently their relationship surged and ebbed as they navigated the jagged rocks of circumstance between them. Despite Movus' advice to avoid her, she had suggested they visit the Avertori Orcad campus again, together, and he had assented. An'essa would go too. In recent days, Velirith seemed to be including her bodyguard and friend—and chaperone—much more. He hadn't forgotten their kiss, manipulative as it was. He suspected there was more to it.

Before they had left Velakun for Avertori, Velirith told him, "I have a feeling... that there's more to that old academy than you think."

"It's an empty shell. Dilapidated. I went through every building in the days after the new year." But Kieler wasn't fool enough to discount her intuition. It was, after all, that intuition that had pegged him a fraud from the minute they met. Besides, to follow up on his idea to lease out the buildings, he needed to sketch out their floor plans and list requirements to make the ancient structures serviceable.

They arrived at Zotika Central, spent the night in Vel-Taradan, and headed out by tram to the old Orcad quite early on a clear, late-spring day. It was warm, and for Avertori, fairly fresh. The air was always clean in Velakun, but here the freshness of spring contrasted with the hint of stench coming up from the lower realms of Avertori, a reminder of the dank, almost-sewer in which he had lived most of his life.

But An'essa and Velirith were quite chipper, excited to be out exploring on a Velator-sanctioned trip. They avoided using the *Pride of Velik*, and instead came in on a regular train very incognito. If their enemies didn't know they were in Avertori they couldn't plot their demise. They even wore disguises. Velirith had suggested white robes and red masks, but Kieler declined. At least *she* thought it was funny. And grudgingly, *to himself*, he admitted it was.

The tram delivered them to a little-used station near the old Orcad administration building. At one time, not much longer ago than Velirith had been alive, this place had been teeming with academia. Even until it closed, it had never lost its reputation as a repository for knowledge and wisdom, despite the lackluster management of House Ortessi in its last years. Students had come and gone from this tram station to their school much like they did now in Velakun.

Rei warmed the steps of the tiered architecture, the theme of three-layered arches repeated in the façade around the doors and stone trim. The campus comprised the upper levels of several spires, all joined together by an elevated plaza. It was situated in one of the oldest and most historic areas of the city. Though it used to be prestigious, weeds now claimed every spot where dirt had accumulated in the cracks of the venerable structures.

He stood there, hands on hips, surveying the place from the front terrace.

"You want to make something great out of it, don't you?" Velirith asked.

By Truth, I do! He nodded in agreement with his perceptive companion. "But for now, I just want to make some money with it. I really don't like being beholden to your father, good as he's been to me."

EPISODE 4 – A LIGHT IN THE DEEP

She nodded back, and Kieler wondered what it would be like to never *have* to make money, as her situation provided. Granted, at some point, as sole heir, she may have to run her house industries, but she'd never have to build them. The powercoach tracks that spanned the continents were built by visionaries in Vel's past.

By Truth I'd love to build something world-changing like that...

He broke his reverie and walked up to unlock the front doors. An'essa, doing her job, entered first to clear the way. The main entry hall was dominated by a large bronze of Velik and Oonyez Ortessi grasping forearms and holding a large sheaf of paper between them, visible to all who entered. The statue was covered with trennek droppings, the ubiquitous birds having penetrated the building through the many broken windows. One perched atop Oonyez' form now, cocking its head and regarding the strangers in its presence. An odd flash of memory flickered through Kieler's head, recalling the bird he'd released as he left the undercity so many months ago.

"Do you remember me?" he said aloud to the bird.

The creature continued its almost studious regard of them.

"Someone you recognize?" Velirith asked, with obvious double meaning referring to the statue as well.

Kieler turned and grinned at her. "Do you not see the family resemblance?"

"With the bird? I don't see you as flighty, but I can picture you flying about and perching in high places."

An'essa looked at them quizzically and Kieler guessed that Velirith had not told her of his "not-Ortessi" admission.

They wandered the dusty, debris-strewn lobby and wings of offices. Things weren't bad, structurally. These buildings were built to last. But the surfaces needed to be redone, everything needed cleaning, and the windows would need replacing. Plumbing was probably shot. It would take a lot of physical labor and Kieler had the sudden urge to just dig in and get to it. He realized that this building itself would take him months to renovate for acceptable rental. He would need laborers. Maybe he could sneak some of his Coin buddies up here and pay them with what he had until the rents came in. Of course, Coin laborers wouldn't take the worthless dras he would collect in rent.

He sketched the floor plan and made lists of materials needed.

"Let's try the other buildings." He led them through dorms, classrooms, lecture halls, gyms and labs. All empty but for birds and rubbish.

Kieler wasn't disappointed. He had known what they would find. "I want to lease the dorms as individual apartments. The offices will be for small businesses if we can get away with it. The labs," he shrugged, "maybe some kind of industrial use. Maybe I'll build something myself."

Velirith glanced at him, her silver eyes expressionless. "Let's go back to where we saw your relative."

"Oonyez."

"The bird," she replied casually.

They walked back to the lobby across what had been a grassy courtyard, now weeds. Velik and Oonyez stood motionless on the low platform.

Velirith considered it for several moments then, in characteristically unconventional Velirith style, she leapt up to stand next to Velik on the pedestal. Kieler noted she didn't seem put-off by the bird detritus that covered much of the statue. An'essa did not admonish her either. So Velirith stood on the bronze feet of the founding fathers, using their solid arms for hand holds and looked from the face of one to the other.

"Are they whispering anything to you?" Kieler asked. "You know you're probably the first one to climb on them. I'm sure this was a stuffy, academic display on which no one ever laid a foot."

"Mmm," she murmured, still looking repeatedly from one

face to the other. Kieler furrowed his brow. She seemed like she thought she was on to something. She said, "You know, they're not looking at each other."

"So where are they looking?"

She followed their gazes with hers and concluded, "At the document."

Suddenly curious, Kieler asked, "What is it, by the way?"

She turned her head sideways and studied it. "A map, I think."

"How can you tell with all those bird droppings on it?"

"Just a hunch." She used the sleeve of her jacket and wiped at the bronze document between the figures. As the offal fell away, it did indeed appear to be a map—no, less a map and more a blueprint of the academy.

He leapt up and stood opposite her on the other side of the pedestal. He took a quick glance around. It was an odd perspective, standing on a pedestal in an empty building with his "supposed" ancestor; Velirith with her true ancestor.

He slipped out his knife and gently scraped the droppings from the surface. "You should carry one of these," he muttered.

An'essa called up. "I've tried to convince her of that myself, Verr Ortessi."

"As long as you could refrain from carving me up," he added so only she could hear.

Inlaid gold lines scribed the outlines of the buildings. Onyx stones marked the statues. Amber ones the stairwells. Green denoted the elevators. It was a work of art itself.

"But it's wrong," Velirith told him.

Kieler looked up sharply at her. "What do you mean it's wrong?"

Velirith pointed. "Look at the dorms. It only shows two wings, not the four we just walked through."

Kieler looked closer at the faded, smeared diagram. "Maybe they didn't keep it updated. We're here, at this onyx stone, and these onyx stones represent the statues in the center park."

"And the amber stones..."

"...are not quite right either, are they?" Kieler noted.

"These stairs are in the right places. But the directory shows at least five, maybe six stairwells that we didn't see."

"One on each side of the campus. There used to be one down that hall by the Headmaster's office." He jumped off the statue and ran over to where the stairwell was indicated.

"It looks like it has been redone into an office. The construction is slightly different," he noted.

"A stair remodeled into an office? Where did it go?"

"There's nothing above that section. It didn't go up."

Velirith jumped to a conclusion. "Then it went down."

Considering this a valid possibility, Kieler said, "then the other stairs probably went down too. I wonder why they sealed them off?"

"Wasn't the *original* original Orcad below on the first level of Avertori? On the Plate itself?"

"Yes," Kieler nodded. "They must have sealed it off to stop people from coming up— "

But Velirith didn't agree at all. "No, I think they wanted to keep students from going down, creating mischief."

"You would know."

"Yes, but why *all* the stairwells? They would leave a way." She mused, staring at the bronze placard. "And, by the way, the true Ortessi heir would own that lower section as well."

She was goading him but she was correct. *How would they get to the old section?* "The elevators," he said with sudden insight.

"Yes!" she knew he was right. "And they could control access that way."

Kieler grinned excitedly as they headed toward the elevator. But An'essa threw water on the fire of their enthusiasm. "The elevators won't work after all this time."

EPISODE 4 – A LIGHT IN THE DEEP

Slowing, Kieler had to concede that was probably true. "Maybe we can get them working."

"Maybe we won't have to," Velirith added slyly.

Kieler wondered at that, but waited to see how things might work out.

They found the elevator door and had to pry it open to get in. The car was waiting, silent and still, lifeless.

"An'essa was right," he said.

"And so was I. Look up," Velirith commanded.

A small hatch was outlined in the ceiling, an escape hatch.

"Boost." Velirith demanded. Kieler complied and hoisted her up to the ceiling of the car. She pushed hard and the hatch popped up. A shower of dust rained down on him. Velirith was conveniently sheltered by the hatch.

"Oh, so sorry," she said and wasn't.

"Just when I thought you were growing up," Kieler muttered, spitting out dust.

"Perhaps you'll correct your thinking. Up, please."

He shoved her, indelicately, up into the dark shaft above. Her bracelet was set with a luzhril stone and she slid the magal cover back to light her way. Kieler hefted An'essa up after and she reached down to help him jump up to the lip and pull himself through.

"Great, Velirith," he complained, "Remember we wanted to go down?"

"Oh, stop. You are cleverer about getting around than you're letting on. Look at the gap around the sides of the lift."

Indeed, the cables that held the elevator's counterweight ran between the car and the walls of the shaft. There was ample clearance for the explorers to descend. The cables also gave them a ready rope. Without waiting for permission, consensus or complaint, Velirith led the way down. They shimmied one after another down the cable.

It was dark. And though Kieler too had brought a light, once

442

they cleared the bottom of the elevator car it didn't seem to penetrate the depths of the shaft very far. "We were right. This shaft goes down to the old section." His pulse raced, wondering what they might find.

Velirith didn't go far, just to the first level under the upper academy. She set her feet on the lip of the doors one floor below, then hooked a bar with one arm. As Kieler and An'essa slowly shifted from the cable to the narrow ledge, he could feel the abyss behind him.

"What say we work together on this, V?" Kieler realized he had just used a pet name. He glanced over to see her raise an eyebrow, but she did not look displeased. "I pull the door with one hand and you do the same. That way we can each hold on with the other."

"Sounds good."

But as soon as they started pulling, Velirith's hand slipped and the sudden shift of weight sent her over the edge. She swung out, her other hand firmly on the handhold, and then she swung back in. Her body slammed into the metal door with a thudding clang. Kieler caught her free hand and she was able to get her feet back on the lip. She did not cry out.

He studied her in the light of her bracelet. Her silver eyes reflected a bit more light, wide as they were, but she seemed relatively unshaken. *What a partner in crime she would make.* He also, said nothing. *All in a day's work.*

But An'essa, reserved as she usually was, couldn't play coy. "Fools! You both represent the end of your respective lines and you're treating your lives like old toys! What are we doing here?"

Kieler glanced at Velirith, and despite An'essa's wise words, there was a flash of understanding between them. *This is awesome!*

Velirith gave her bodyguard some consolation. "I'll be more careful, Ani. Perhaps we can find a latch that holds the doors together."

EPISODE 4 – A LIGHT IN THE DEEP

"Perhaps we could go home," An'essa murmured.

But Velirith's suggestion was an excellent one and Kieler immediately felt near the top of the door and found a release. Even then, moving the old door wasn't easy. Any lubricant was long gone and he realized that although the upper level had only been abandoned for twenty years, the lower could have been sealed for much longer. Who knew how long it had been since anyone came down here?

Pulling on both sides, they gradually opened the door a crack. Once they could get fingers and a toe in, they worked the old metal doors back until they could squeeze through.

"Any thought to how difficult it's going to be to shimmy back *up* those cables?" An'essa was no fear-monger. She was just voicing the common sense that neither Kieler nor Velirith wanted to listen to. They wanted to know what was down here.

Kieler expected to emerge from the shaft into a hallway or room, but it wasn't either. The space into which they stepped was very low with a sloped, curving roof. It was cramped and irregular shaped.

"What is this?" Velirith asked.

Kieler applied his extensive knowledge of Avertori, both above and below, to the odd, dark-metal beam that cut through the tiny space. He squatted down, looking under and past the beam. He saw stacked papers in a cramped space that shortly dead-ended.

Using his light, he looked at the stack of paper folders. "Student records." Frowning, he ventured a guess. "They used this space to store old records... but what is this space? It looks like the space between the upper and lower Plate, but it must be one of the columns that support the higher levels of the city. The newer part of the Academy must be built on the tops of them."

Velirith looked at him and nodded agreement. "But is there no stairwell? How do we get to the next level down?"

"Same way we got to this one I'm afraid," he replied.

CHAPTER SEVEN

An'essa groaned.

Nevertheless, they repeated the procedure and swung down to the next level. For this they were rewarded with a slightly larger chamber between the enormous, sweeping beams that were built by the Dead Ones. *Amazing engineering. The Avertori built by the Omeron is falling apart even with people living in it. These columns stay solid and their builders have been dead for thousands of years.*

This space too was used for storage, but whatever was being stored was in a half dozen wooden crates. With his knife, Kieler pried one open. Inside, packed in soft material, was a statue of a man-like creature. It was cast in a metal Kieler could not immediately identify, perhaps nickel, and was the size of a child's toy. Its head was full of eyes and teeth, its arms ended in mechanical claws and it had a third leg. It was posed as if fighting.

"Art?"

Velirith shrugged. "Not very pleasing to look at."

"Toy?"

She shrugged again.

"Maybe it's a paperweight." An'essa piped up, still irritated that her concerns were ignored.

Kieler put it back. It might be valuable, but it was heavy and wouldn't be easy to carry up with them. Besides, it had remained there for twenty years, it would be there when he came back for it. Maybe there really was something valuable down here. The other crates in this chamber contained similar figures, different accessories. One, again three-legged, was a thick-muscled, heavily-plated creature with just a tiny head and multiple eyes in the cracks of its armor.

"This seems to be some of the pieces House Ortessi would display in its museums," Velirith suggested.

That made sense. "Let's go down one more level then head back up. We can come better prepared with ropes and pulleys next time."

EPISODE 4 – A LIGHT IN THE DEEP

Kieler noted that An'essa scowled but didn't complain. They were all fit; they should be able to shimmy up three stories if they rested on the ledges. He realized that An'essa was commissioned to guard a person who put herself in more danger than any outside threat. Her job was nearly impossible. At least it wasn't boring.

The next room down was again slightly bigger as the tower widened toward its base. That base, Kieler knew, was not *on* the Plate, but far below it. The island-spanning Plate and these columns, all made up a semi-rigid grid that even with his mechanical knowledge he couldn't understand. He now suspected it was far more than just something to cover up their old garbage.

This room had more crates labeled: ANCIENT WEAPONS. *Now this is more like it!*

The first crate contained a metal contraption that seemed to strap on to one's arms. Two blades, still sharp, one for each arm. Gingerly picking one up, he found it lighter than it looked. As he figured it out, he muttered, "Your arm goes in like this... and the blades run across the rails... they must extend. Not sure how you activate them."

An'essa, resigned to the fact that neither of the heirs could be discouraged from their adventure, took a professional interest in the device. "Long. Extends your reach. The metal rails also act as shields to deflect attacks."

"I'll come back for these." The technology of the Dead Ones never stopped fascinating Kieler. He had lived in the refuse of it for most of his life, but Karst had been picked-over for hundreds of years. Rarely had he found much of value.

Velirith discovered a small case in another crate. She opened it, slipping out a dagger with a slim hilt and even thinner blade. As she turned it, the blade seemed to disappear when viewed on edge, like a sheet of paper.

"Looks like that would shatter the first time it was used," Kieler commented.

To prove or disprove his conjecture, the impulsive woman

slammed the flat of the blade against the edge of a beam. It flexed a bit, but did not break.

"Guess not,"

"Tough stuff," Velirith smiled. "Has a good feel to it even though it's so thin. And look, it's got writing on it."

Kieler noted the markings were similar to the writing of the Dead Ones, but he couldn't decipher the symbols easily.

"You should keep it," An'essa said, looking at Kieler for permission. "You need one."

"Sounds like a good idea to me. It's the first time I'll have been able to give you something. Just don't use it against me." He was joking—he hoped.

"All right."

Kieler peered down the yawning shaft, wondering what the rest of the rooms, ever larger, might hold. But with a shrug and a sigh, he conceded, it was time to go back up.

CHAPTER EIGHT

Kieler's trip to old Orcad with Velirith and An'essa had made him realize how long it would take to make the place habitable. For one thing, since he had no proximal houses subject to his authority yet, he had no security. Kieler couldn't even camp out at his new property without the very likely probability of getting taken out by Cortatti.

It looked like Verr Ortessi would need to rely on Vel hospitality for a bit longer. So in the weeks after returning to Velakun, he pushed hard and finished his airship. But Liberty couldn't fly underground. He needed to bring her up from the workshop in the underpinnings to a hidden mooring site outside the rim where he could use it to secretly fly away from Velakun.

Of course, it all had to be done at night, in one night, and that night was tonight. Since he could not carry the larger pieces outside the rim, he had decided to transport the pieces to a launch site within the rim, then fly to his hidden shelter.

That launch site was the top of Symphony Gardens, where Kieler stood by a rock formation taking inventory. He had hidden extra fasteners, cable, tools—anything he might need. *I've launched from a tower in Avertori, why not launch from a tower here?* And here he had one enormous advantage: no one was trying to kill him.

To move larger cargo around Velakun, special podcars were used from the powertrain docks. Jarovel used these cars to get materials to *The Pride of Velik's* maintenance bay. Now, Kieler had used them to get the sections of his airship up to Symphony

CHAPTER EIGHT

Gardens. It took Kieler several trips to lift everything to the top of the tower. He wore a dark coat with the hood up and his Coin mask to ensure anonymity. This would also deter the cold he knew he would encounter outside the bowl. Not the time for his trademark green-and-golds.

Fortunately, he saw no one on any of the trips. He hadn't expected to see anyone down by his workshop; that area was abandoned and always deserted. But he had thought that loners or lovers might occasionally make use of one of the highest public spots in town.

He glanced out to the rim above Vel Estate. Just to the northeast was a spot amongst the rocks where he would tether and hide his ship. The breeze was light and shouldn't be a factor.

He had chosen to take off from a wide space between a rocky rise and the edge of the tower where he knew the watchman rarely patrolled. Kieler arranged all the sections of his ship for quick assembly, then started putting pieces together. She took shape rapidly. He had practiced this at least a dozen times down in his workshop. Although he worked with speed and great focus, he still had enough presence of mind to notice the garden's water music calming his anxieties. The artistry and care in putting together the orchestra of the garden was impossible not to admire.

As soon as her structure was complete, Kieler pulled the envelope around the frame and tethered her with a single, sturdy cord. Only an hour after he had begun, he was at the point of filling the seven envelope bladders with hydrogen from a tank. It was the fastest he had ever assembled his invention.

He breathed a deep, excited breath. In fifteen minutes, he would be flying again. While the balloon part of the ship filled, he took a moment to look it over and enjoy the tinkling music around him. Though the air was cool, he was warm from exertion inside his hood and mask.

As he listened, a beat struck out of time with the water rhythms around him. It was a small thing, a falling stone striking a rock below, but odd to hear in the lulling perfection. He looked around to see if he could spot the cause but saw nothing.

When the envelope had inflated enough to be out of the way of the three-bladed propeller, Kieler reached into the cockpit, pulled on a bronze control knob, and started his motor. It spun up with a quiet whirr and pulled the tether taut. He glanced down the rail around Symphony Garden, checking to ensure all was clear. He felt good. His ship was performing nicely. The only thing he could legitimately fret about was in-flight maneuverability, which he was unable to flight test in the underpinnings. Still, he was confident his controls would work.

The midnight-black envelope was tightening up with no kinks or tears. The basket lightened and a breath of wind caused his airship to strain against her tether. The hydrogen tank was more than half empty and the envelope was full. His ship hovered before him, trim and beautiful, as if a section of the space between the stars had been carved out and made to float at his command.

Kieler disconnected the tank and stowed it and the other tools in the frame behind the cockpit. As he returned to check his hiding place for any last items, he heard a small trickle of rocks overhead.

He looked up just as a large man leapt down on him, knocking him sideways. Kieler saw the glint of a knife. He rolled, gaining his feet. Simultaneously, Kieler pulled his own knife from its calf sheath.

"Who are you? What is that thing?" It was Commander Scoravik, Velator's Chief of Operations.

Kieler did not respond, except to feint with the knife and move right to get between Scoravik and his airship. He had to protect it.

Scoravik dodged back but was no stranger to a knife fight. He slashed and back-slashed, driving Kieler stumbling backward into his own aircraft. She pivoted on her tether. The whirling prop rotated toward him.

CHAPTER EIGHT

Kieler was almost backed up against the rail. He wished for something to throw. Scoravik had the advantage. But what Kieler hoped was that his enemy might not be able to see or recognize the spinning propeller in the dim light.

Kieler shoved Liberty's nose farther around, driving her prop toward Scoravik. He didn't want to kill the man, but this was the end of the mission if Scoravik managed to recognize him. Kieler was suddenly thankful he hadn't taken off his mask.

The airship began to pivot, but Kieler had forgotten about the tether! In a fraction of a second the prop snapped the taut tether and the line immediately wrapped around the shaft. The blades whined to a halt with a wisp of burning cord.

Scoravik startled, seeing the blades for the first time only a foot from his face. But there was no time. Kieler's ship was rising. Having been released from its tie-down, it was floating up and over the edge. In the second of his opponent's shock, Kieler planted his foot into Scoravik's chest, driving him back and Kieler toward the rail. Unthinking, he jumped onto the rail and dove for the fleeing Liberty. It was a long leap over a yawning abyss.

The idiocy of his jump hit him in mid-flight. He shot his right arm forward and hooked his wrist on the bottom skid. Immediately, he slipped back and his hand grabbed the skid with desperate strength. The airship's ascent slowed under his weight, but that wasn't what mattered: he was dangling thousands of feet above Velakun!

A knife clanged off the metal landing skid an inch from his clasping fingers. A glance back to the tower showed Scoravik staring in disbelief, but not so stunned as to give up. A moment later and he was looking for something else to throw.

Kieler heaved and kipped. He only had one shot at this. He looped his other arm through the metal runner, hooking his elbow. It was a more secure grip on the drifting ship. A small rock bounced off his coat back, doing little damage. The momentum of his flying body had spun the craft and he found himself facing back toward the rail as Scoravik ran up to it. When the commander comprehended what he was seeing, the man broke into a scornful laugh.

"Looks like you're in for a rough ride!" he called. "How about a last confession? What are you here for, slink?"

Kieler didn't bite on the bait, only watched as his ship spun him slowly away, continuing its lazy, drifting rotation and ascent into the night.

The frame was not made to be entered from below. Still, after several attempts, Kieler managed to swing a leg up and into the pilot's seat. But even then, his foot caught one of the bronze knobs, kicking the control that pivoted the motor. The motor swung rapidly to one side, and with his bodyweight throwing off the balance of the ship, *Liberty* tilted wildly and his leg fell back from the cage.

A shout erupted from the man at the edge of the terrace. "Who are you!"

But even the sound of his voice receded as the ship floated away.

After another, more controlled attempt, Kieler got his foot up again and, contorting his body in ways only thousands of feet of empty air could motivate him to accomplish, managed to pull himself into the seat within the cage of the cockpit. The restraining belt had never felt so comforting as he strapped in. He glanced back at Symphony Garden, but could only vaguely see the cause of his near-death experience.

Kieler craned his neck around to look at the prop. It was hopelessly twisted, tightened by the magnetic torque. It looked undamaged, but there was no way he would be able to free it in flight. He considered it for several seconds, deciding that the truss he had designed for the behind-the-seat cargo would support his weight. But even if he could crawl back to the prop, he wouldn't be able to reach the prop shaft from that position.

He cut power. It was the best he could do. He was adrift.

CHAPTER EIGHT

Taking a deep breath, he looked down. The swirling breezes of Velakun were pulling him around the perimeter of Center Isle.

He was an unlit Festival Lantern now, a gift back to the starry heavens, drifting round and round the bowl of Velakun. It took about ten minutes to circle Center Island and come back to near where he had started. Thankfully, he didn't come close to Symphony Gardens again. The fabric of the airship's envelope was dark and unreflective, and he hoped that neither Scoravik nor any sleepless stargazers could see him from below.

The only control he had was his hydrogen volume. The flight tank could be toggled to fill the envelope even more and cause him to rise faster. Or, he could vent the lifting gas and descend. Without an engine and forward airspeed, his control surfaces were useless. At least he had mostly stopped spinning.

He thought hard about venting and dropping down, hopefully landing in Lake Skyfall. But then what? His ship would be lost, and worse, would be an interesting topic of conversation at Velator's breakfast table tomorrow morning.

"Did you see the balloon ship floating in the lake this morning, Velirith?" Velator would say over a hot cup of tea.

"Yes, father. I heard it was made entirely from parts intended for the *Pride of Velik*. I wonder how they got in the lake. Hmm. Who had access to those...?"

He couldn't deal with that. Kieler let Liberty rise high above the swirling currents of the bowl. As she did, and she began her fourth lap around Center Isle, Kieler noticed he wasn't circling the center anymore, but the northeast shore where the skybridge to Vel Estate was. Then he remembered the aerial lanterns of the festival. The thousands of floating lights would drift round the bowl, but a few that had enough fuel to reach the higher altitudes had lifted and drifted to the northeast. The prevailing wind outside the bowl was in that direction!

He remembered it too from his excursions outside the rim. With luck, he would be blown somewhere near the rock theater and his hidden mooring spot. The only disadvantage was he would blow right over Vel Estate. Maybe Velirith would wave to him. She would probably recognize the craft.

But no, he was too high. In the dark, it would be nearly impossible to be seen from the ground. He was so far above the rim, it would be difficult to drop down fast enough once free of the swirling effect to even make landfall in the first basin beyond the rim. He hoped he didn't end up four mountains away.

Until he reached the rim, however, there was nothing to be done. He looked down over the sparsely lit city of towers, at the glinting lake and at the surrounding houses of the rim. Small, luzhril lights dotted the peaceful, sleeping city, but for the most part, it was the stars that lit it. It was absolutely gorgeous. He wished Velirith could share this sensation of flight with him. She would love both the thrill and the peacefulness of it.

What am I saying? Velirith would only see this as evidence of conspiracy against House Vel. Why did I admit I'm not the real Ortessi?

He sighed and looked around one more time as the rim began to pass below him.

Now that the wind had definite direction, his speed increased. To drop into the valley far below, he pulled all the vents with one hand. At first, he only stopped climbing. Then as the envelope deflated and became slack, he felt the drop more distinctly. He had enough hydrogen left in the tank to refill half the bladders. He hated to waste the hydrogen, but he hated to die too. Every resource he had—which weren't many—would be used to save himself and hopefully his airship.

With only half-filled bladders, the ship dropped quickly and the wind seemed to have less effect. And now, with forward airspeed created by his descent, he could steer. He made toward his target, slowly refilling the envelope to abate his descent.

Rocks began to loom up below and in front of him. He pulled the fill valves harder. Ground rush filled his vision and still his main altitude control was filling and venting. The rapid fill took effect gradually and his descent stopped. Unfortunately, he began to bob back into the sky. He didn't have enough hydrogen to fill again, but he had to release now to continue his landing.

He pulled the release valves, pulsing them to come down gently. Towering rock fingers reached up for him. The bottom of the frame scraped over the top of one jagged formation, and he fell slowly to a relatively clear space below.

Before the ship hit, Kieler jumped out to catch it, hanging onto two mooring lines he had ready. The ship, relieved of his weight, popped up again. Kieler acted quickly, anchoring it by wrapping one line around a boulder and hanging onto the second himself. The ship bobbed above him and settled, pulling lightly against the wind. He was safe, and his ship was undamaged.

Several hours of night remained. He took stock of his position and where he needed to go. Maneuvering the floating airship like a kite on a string, he should be able to walk it down the rest of the mountain and back to his out-of-sight mooring. But did he have time?

He was dressed well against the cold of night, which was tolerable during the summer months. He decided to move the ship as far as he could tonight. If he didn't make it all the way, he would secure it and run back through Velirith's tunnel.

Moving expediently but without the rush of a time crunch, he carefully guided the airship around high rocks and clutching tree limbs. It went faster than he expected. There were times when having a line floating above him allowed him to swing up onto rocks he would otherwise have to climb. He kept sharp, but actually enjoyed the light-footed hike back.

An hour before dawn, he reached the clearing protected on the rim side by a steep cliff. He had more tie-downs prepositioned there. With the craft secured by no less than eight lines, Kieler pushed himself to jog back up the path, through the outdoor theater and back to the hidden rock entrance.

EPISODE 4 – A LIGHT IN THE DEEP

He no longer relied on the special key within the tunnel. He had learned from that first night outside the bowl and made a copy.

Pulling the long-shafted key from inside his coat, he inserted the coded end into the hole. With a twist and a click, the latch released and the door swung free. He took a last look over the valley, deceptively calm, and made his way back to his quarters.

CHAPTER NINE

Sneaking around had become a habit.

Whether sneaking outside the rim to enjoy some solitude, or short-cutting through the airshafts, or even just walking quietly through one of the terraced gardens, Velirith realized she was habitually moving with stealth. Thinking about her dubious new skill, she found herself outside the door to her father's study, listening to the voices within.

"It was twenty freight cars pulled by a single engine." said a rough voice she didn't recognize. "The Parchikis fibrum shipments come from the interior of Govian and are powercoached down the eastern coast to Avertori to be made into clothing."

She heard her father sigh, then ask, "So did they steal the cargo?"

"Three cars full."

After a pause, Velator asked, "Why only three?"

"Whatever they used to blow up the engine scattered seventeen of the freight cars along the coastline. Clearly a precision operation."

Velirith caught the sarcasm.

Velator gave a low whistle, obviously amazed at the destruction.

"The emergency coupling disengaged the surviving freight cars as the train disintegrated. Then the attackers pulled up behind, hooked to the remaining cars, and pulled them north back to an uninhabited part of the coast. From there they must have loaded the fibrum onto a ship."

"And the crew of the power engine? Anyone tending the cargo? What became of them?" Her father's voice was anxious.

A second voice, smoother but still unrecognized, replied, "The engine crew was all killed when the engine was destroyed. When the last freighters glided to a stop, the pirates boarded and totally ignored the one man tending the freight. The survivor has no idea why they didn't kill him too." Still hidden outside the room, Velirith felt a pang of sorrow for the lost lives.

"Hmm," mused Velator. "As thorough as they were, it seems they would not have missed that detail intentionally. But I'm glad for that man and his family."

"I talked to him. He was thankful but still a puddle of nerves."

Velirith could hear Velator pacing slowly across the tiled floor. He spoke again, "Feleanna attacked us by rail over a year ago, I assume that she is the prime suspect?"

The smooth-voiced man answered. "Not really. We think it was done by rail to throw suspicion on the Cortattis, but there are strong clues that point us elsewhere. First, one of my sources says the engine wasn't shot by magguns."

"What then?" asked Velator.

"We don't know," continued Smooth-Voice. "It was almost as if it were rammed. Second, the man who survived mentioned two things that lead us away from Cortatti involvement. He heard the word 'Coin' as if in reference to an organization, and all the boarders wore masks."

"The Coin? Wouldn't you know if your organization perpetrated this attack?" asked Velator.

Rough-voiced man replied curtly. "Anyone can wear a mask. And although 'organization' is a high-compliment for our loosely connected groups below the Plate, I happen to be well-informed of the goings-on down there. Any raids by my dark-dwelling friends would not have been conducted so sloppily or blatantly as to attract such attention from the major houses. It would be sheer stupidity."

There was a tense silence as the smoother voice had obviously, in light of his intelligence, accused the other's friends of murder and piracy. But the smooth voice eventually spoke again, intentionally softer but intense. "It barely needs pointing out that if your group was guilty your allegiance would require you to protect them!"

Velirith tensed. There was obvious mistrust between the two informants.

Velator let the tension go on longer than Velirith felt comfortable. Then he asked, "The Coin keeps a low profile, yes?"

"Yes." The response was barely distinguishable from a growl. "Their attacks wouldn't be so obvious or messy. Most victim houses try to keep it quiet to avoid looking weak."

"Who would benefit by setting up the Coin to take the fall?" Velator pressed.

Rough-voice: "I answer with another question: Who makes money regardless of who's fighting who?"

Smooth-voice responded, "It's not Cortatti 'style' either."

Another sigh from Velator, then, "On another topic, my Ops Officer encountered a flying craft here in Velakun, black, but like a balloon. Could this craft be related to the Parchiki attack?"

The voices didn't respond, but Velirith did, jerking erect outside the door. *Flying machine? In Velakun? Where did the Ortessi get another one of those? The slink. Well, wouldn't he be surprised if it were to go missing?*

"Well, it may be how Cortatti has been getting spies in and out of our city," Velator continued. "What is House Ek's response to the attack? This seems like the most destructive one yet. Is Threzhel doing anything?"

Rough again: "Yes, he's called for a conference of house primes. You'll probably get word tonight or tomorrow. Consensus is that he'll try to organize a defense coalition."

EPISODE 4 – A LIGHT IN THE DEEP

"'Defense coalition,'" Velator grunted sarcastically. "Sounds like Threzhel wants us to fund his private army. It's no stretch to imagine he was behind the attack himself for that exact purpose."

The smooth-voiced messenger spoke again, "There is violence out there, Velator. It has grown ever since House Ek wrested the Executive Chairmanship from your grandfather."

"Thanks for pointing that out," Velator grumbled. "Back then, House Vel was so committed to peace we didn't fight to hold that leadership. Veldicar, my grandfather, was not a very strong leader—though who am I to judge?"

There was a shuffling of movement that Velirith guessed was the preparation of the guests to leave. She slipped away from the door and back down the hall a distance while the men said their goodbyes. Then she turned again and walked calmly and purposefully back toward her father's study. She timed it well to get a good look at the men as they left Velator's office.

"Hello," she greeted.

One man nodded to her and said hello—roughly. He didn't try to avoid her, and Velirith decided he was probably a great spy. Average looking, unassuming. The other nodded but said nothing. He had the grey eyes typical of those born in Velakun. *Not quite so easily overlooked.*

She entered the study to find Velator looking out the windows across Lake Skyfall, deep in sad thought. Velirith spoke as if with no regard for his pensive state, "Father, I'd like to visit Moshalli. Last we spoke, she'd been upset with a boy she liked. Go figure. Do you think I might be able to visit for a day or two?"

Velator turned, his thoughts still on other subjects (Velirith knew what). Shifting his attention to what she had said, he replied, "Yes, that's very likely. I think Orlazrus and I will be going into Avertori soon for an Omeron council. You can come with us then."

Of course, there's no way I'm getting dragged to that Omeron meeting.

CHAPTER NINE

She had to act. The next day at breakfast found her mulling on the information she had gleaned outside her father's study and what to do with it.

At breakfast, Velator confirmed they were going to Avertori in two days. Better yet, the Ortessi bluntly mentioned to Velator that he was going to disappear for a while and contact the Coin. This in itself was not unusual. He had visited "his people" before to set up the spy arrangement and try to get black market weapons. But mentioning it front of Velirith at this time was like wearing a sign on his back that said, "Follow me!"

The exciting thing for Velirith was that she detected no lie in his declaration. These were the people she wanted to meet.

After breakfast, Velirith and An'essa took a podcar over to Center Isle. Velirith wasn't looking forward to talking to her bodyguard friend. "When we get to Avertori," Velirith began carefully, "I need to run an errand."

An'essa tilted her head and looked at her quizzically.

"And I need to do it without you," Velirith concluded.

An'essa's quizzical look turned very dark. But she waited.

Velirith would rather An'essa asked questions so Velirith could steer the conversation in a way to make An'essa understand. But An'essa kept silent. Velirith slapped her hands on her knees and blew out a sigh. "Look, we've talked about this before. I'm telling you so you won't worry. Isn't it better than me sneaking out, and you finding out later that I'm gone? Then you have to explain to father how I slipped past you."

An'essa glowered.

Velirith knew why. "I know." She looked down at the podcar's control pedestal. "I'm manipulating. I don't like doing it. But I'm old enough to know when I need to do something on my own. And this is one of those times."

A long silence, and finally An'essa replied, her voice tight, evidently controlling her anger. "How am I to guard the body I'm supposed to be bodyguard for when I'm not near that infuriating

461

body? If I follow you, you find a way to lose me. If I tell your father, he will either assign other bodyguards--who you will fool easily--or he'll lock you up, which wouldn't last long either. You seem determined to put yourself in danger, put me in an impossible position, and put an end to your family line!"

Velirith nodded, still not meeting An'essa's eyes. "This is the hardest thing to do, An'essa. I love you, but I hurt you. You want to protect me, but some things I just have to do on my own. I have to."

Velirith turned her gaze to look out the window as they approached the theater on Center Isle. The tension did not break, even as the car slid to a stop and popped the glass hatch. Velirith stepped out. An'essa was headed to Orcad to practice her already excellent fighting skills. Skills, ironically, she could not employ when Velirith made sure she was not around her.

"You've got to stop sneaking off," An'essa stated flatly.

Velirith just stood next to the podcar as the hatch reclosed. *I also have to find out who this Ortessi really is.*

How to follow someone who is always looking for a tail? It's a tough problem.

Velirith entered the theater and walked slowly down the aisle. She climbed onto the stage and headed back toward the curtain.

Once backstage she noticed the floor. It was painted with a myriad of lines; some indicating trapdoors, others showing safe paths for the actors to follow. She knew that the stage in front of the curtain was just as busy, but those lines were painted with an invisible paint only seen when actors wore a special lens. *I wonder if Eos could do something with that?*

She went down the stairs to the Prop Department workshop, the realm of Propmaster Eos Goran. Eos was a shriveled man who always *looked* serious, but he had that same mischievous gleam in his eye that Velirith was so proud of in her own.

"Verr Goran, could you help me with a problem?"

Eos looked her up and down as if evaluating what her problem might be. "Lhea Velirith, I will do all I can to further your exploits."

Frowning in thought, she continued. "It's a serious challenge, one that requires confidentiality. I have a strong feeling you can solve it. Can you help me?"

"I will endeavor to."

Workbenches and tools encircled the perimeter of the open workshop. Velirith had been here before, most recently to fit the safety harness she had used in the Fall Festival. The Ortessi would love this place, given his affinity for gadgetry. She growled silently. *Oh that he would trust me with whatever he's up to. I would probably like the real him.*

As it was, she was still bent on tormenting him in little ways and finding out who he really was. If Eos could come up with a solution, she stood to find out a lot in the next few days.

"If you had to secretly follow someone who was very wary of being followed, how would you do it?"

He mused, his eyes glinting with a childlike glee. "The best way to follow a fella is by making him unknowingly leave his own trail... A prodigious challenge. I like your thinking."

Velirith smiled and thought about his answer. "Make him leave his own trail without knowing it." That, she admitted, was fairly pure mischief. Just her thing.

Eos paced the aisle between workbenches, thinking. On the benches, Velirith noted tubes of chemicals and cans of paint littering the countertops.

"And I suppose you don't want other people seeing his trail either, right?"

"That would be ideal, I thought we could somehow use the invisible stage paint."

"Do you know how that stuff works? It's actually a tincture of luzhril that emits light just outside our visible range. That tiny monocle we wear shifts the light to be visible. My predecessor in the prop department came up with that ingenious device."

Velirith didn't really care how it worked, but she could tell that by talking, Eos was thinking it through out loud. She let him continue.

"The luzhril can then be applied to a surface invisibly. If we could have him deposit just a little at a time, it could lay down a line indicating where he went. Yes, but how...?" He continued pacing through his huge workshop, ignoring the odd, half-finished contraptions on the workbenches. "You know, we don't actually have to lay a continual line, do we? If we just dripped drops of the stuff..." He whirled back to face her, an idea clearly lit his face. "Can you get his shoes?"

Raising her eyebrows in surprise, Velirith nodded, curious.

"I suppose we'd have to do this late at night—when he's not wearing them," he continued.

Velirith nodded again, letting him roll with his idea.

"Good, because I work best late at night. When does this have to be done?"

"Tonight or tomorrow night."

"Tonight then," he affirmed. "No use waiting until the last minute."

"May I ask what you're going to do with his shoes? They're boots really."

"Even better. And certainly you may ask since you're going to need to know in order to pull off your little espionage. I'm going to insert a bag of the UV paint into the heel of his boot and have a valve dispense a single, tiny drop every time he steps. It should leave a nice dotted line to your quarry. You will have to wear a monocle to see the trail."

She could picture the device and execution in her mind. It fit. It was an elegant solution. "Perfect." She gave the old Propmaster an excited hug, and he rubbed his hands together rapidly in conspiratorial glee.

Getting the Ortessi's boots was no more of a problem than

464

getting his coat. He hadn't figured out how she'd done that either. She even had a plan to keep him from sneaking out tonight.

Later that day, she cornered the Ortessi and picked a fight. She simply ended it by saying, "I know you're up to something around here. Tonight, I'm going to camp outside your door and go with you!"

She delivered the boots to Eos around midnight. He was ready with the tools of his trade, but she fell asleep watching him as the night wore on. He woke her an hour before dawn to demonstrate.

Clomping around the workshop with one foot booted and the other bare, he looked ridiculous and happy. He told her that the paint had a limited range, so she would have to find a way to remove the plug from the paint dispenser and start the flow just before the intended pursuit.

"Sorry I can't be more precise. Not enough time to analyze body weight, volume dispensed and such."

"This is excellent work, Eos. I'll find a way to remove the plug." Velirith examined the modified boot and found the unnoticeable opening on the front of the heel facing the instep. It was a great prop. "I've got to get this back to him. Thank you so much!" She kissed his cheek as he grinned with pride.

"Let me know how it works—in general terms, of course. A co-conspirator always wants to hear the outcome of the deed."

She promised and dashed off to get the boot back to the foot. As far as Velirith knew, she was the only one in Velakun who ever used the Vel Estate tunnels. Quite convenient for her.

I like it underground, she thought. *It's quiet* and *sneaky.*

These particular tunnels had been built centuries ago, probably in times when tension between the houses was high--like now--and spying on the ambassadorial suites was deemed necessary. She took the tunnel from the main estate to the Ortessian ambassadorial villa and a one-way mirror that looked into his suite. Silently releasing a latch, she slid the mirror aside, slipped in and set the boot back under the bed where she had found it.

Light was seeping through the windows, and the Ortessi stirred, nearing wakefulness. She spared a tense glance at him as she slunk back to the mirror and was surprised at the pulse of attraction she felt for him. He looked so innocent, so vulnerable, lying there asleep on his bed. So...kissable. She noticed she had stopped walking.

She shook the thought out of her head and moved quickly to the mirror. He was dangerous--but he was bold and brave. And they should be on the same team.

Someday, they would trust each other.

CHAPTER TEN

She could have brooded. But Velirith was too excited to brood. Instead, she just pretended to brood.

She sat behind Velator and the Ortessi on the passenger train to Avertori. She got the impression that the Ortessi would be heading out to meet his accomplices (friends) shortly after their arrival. If she didn't activate the boot now, she might not have another chance. Besides, just pulling the plug didn't use paint. He had to step on it.

While her father and he talked, she pretended to drop a pencil and reached lithely under the Ortessi's seat; he had his feet back under it anyway. It was a delicate but not difficult matter to pop the plug out of the heel. He didn't notice.

An'essa did, but said nothing. A slight roll of her eyes expressed her opinion of Velirith's antics.

They arrived in Avertori late afternoon and Velirith realized a flaw in her plan. In the dimmed theater or at night, the luminescent paint showed up plainly. But in daylight, when she surreptitiously slipped on the monocle, the paint was nearly invisible.

It was stifling hot in Avertori. *This is why I don't come here much in the summer,* she reminded herself. The heat brought in the moist air of the surrounding oceans making it as stuffy as a shoe closet; the tall buildings and overhead plazas held it all in.

Everyone in their party took the private tram from Central Station to Vel-Taradan. Velirith found herself counting steps. Every step shortened the distance she could follow him. Velirith dressed in a dark brown shirt, slacks and a light cloak, her lock pick set in one of its pockets. She waited in the common area, sweating casually, pretending to read a book. At dusk, the Ortessi came out and passed her on the way to the elevator.

She looked up, feigning boredom. "Where ya goin'?" she asked him. Dressed in loose-fitting, drab clothes, unshaven, he looked a bit ragged.

The Ortessi glanced at her as if she were years younger and therefore a child (she was *not*). He evidently couldn't think of wisecrack answer so instead he just greeted her coolly and pressed on. As soon as he was on the elevator and ascending, she slipped the monocle on and checked his footprints. In the light of the room, she could dimly but easily see the tiny scuffed drops glowing a dull purple.

Ten minutes later, she pulled on a cap, rose and went after him.

Her father couldn't know she'd left. She would follow the Ortessi and return when he did, which had to be before the morning conference. Perfect. She would not be missed. But if she got on the tram in the usual way, the guard would report it to her father. So she would get on in an *unusual* way.

Velirith left the elevator on the floor where the FamTram came through the building. She walked past the guard and slipped the oval monocle in front of her eye. Sure enough, despite the well-lit little station, she could see the pale violet dots leading to the boarding platform. She suppressed a frown as she saw a tiny pool of the glowing liquid where he had evidently waited for the tram. She thought about him standing there, and remembered that he had the restless habit of rocking slightly as he stood. Now that rocking was inconveniently pumping paint out of his heel.

She returned to the elevator, smiled at the guard, and waited until the doors closed. As soon as they did, she quietly jumped onto the handrail and pushed open the emergency escape hatch in the roof. Again maintaining stealth, she pulled herself through the opening, stood on the roof of the elevator, and replaced the hatch. She climbed up the short distance to the next floor and released the door catch. These elevator doors pulled open easily from inside and she crawled up to the highest floor of Vel-Taradan. The only thing above this was the ornamental spire.

She had been up here many times, often bored during the unavoidable trips to Avertori. This floor housed machinery for the tram station. The tram cars were suspended from the tracks by large struts that hung through an open channel in the floor to the loading area one level beneath her.

She had thought about this stunt many times, but it was frightening, even for her. The attempt needed a reason more than just another lark. Now she had one.

Standing next to one of the channels, she saw a car coming down the Grand Stair. If the car stopped at the station below, it would be easy to climb aboard the hanging struts.

No luck. As the car came into the station at speed, she jumped for its support strut and grabbed it with one hand. The momentum of the car below jerked her forward and flung her spinning over the open channel. She hit the far side rolling, stopping face down just before falling through the opposite channel. She saw the guard below, thankfully oblivious to her accidental acrobatics.

Groaning and dragging herself up, she belatedly remembered one of Cota Rejin's lessons. Something about relative motion and inertia. Forgetting the lesson almost killed her! She wondered how Cota Rejin had made it sound so boring. If this had been the example, Velirith was sure she would have paid more attention.

Thinking it through this time, she walked all the way down to the other end of the channel where the next tram car and its struts would enter. Once she saw the car coming she started running. As the car overtook her at a more leisurely pace she was able grab the strut and swing aboard.

469

EPISODE 4 – A LIGHT IN THE DEEP

Then she was out of Vel-Taradan and into the open sky, hanging on for dear life against the sudden rush of wind. She peeked down at the plaza below. It was a very long way down.

She eased her way down the strut and collapsed flat onto the roof of the car. *Weird how knees go weak and wobbly just when you need them the most.*

Lying flat on her stomach, she faced forward and found herself hugging the slightly rounded roof. She was sure she had thumped the metal loud enough to be heard by the occupants below her, but there were no windows in the top, so what could they see? Funny, the reason this private tram was suspended was to maximize the view; there were even windows under a grate on the floor. But there were none on top. Guess they didn't plan for their daughters to be jumping onto the roof.

Below her passed the Grand Stair and the classically designed, most beautiful architecture in Zotikas, Plaza Floraneva. Of course, for most of the ride, all she saw was the metal supporting strut four inches in front of her face. Eventually, she craned her neck around to see the tram approaching a gentle curve and the entry into the Arena Station.

Arena Station was not on the top floor. She could not jump onto the station roof. She stayed flat and rode the gondola to a stop in the busy depot. Peering over the side of the tram, she confirmed the trail of paint continued here. No one was waiting to get on the private tram, so she waited until the Merckles (of all people) waddled off. No one looked at the top of the car (who would?), so she sidled down as far she could and dropped and rolled. An old man jumped back as she fell right in front of him.

"Sorry!" she jumped up. "The stairs from the second floor were broken." The man looked up, baffled, and she dashed off.

I should have waited until it started to pull out, she scolded herself. But at least she didn't land *on* him.

The private station had two exits; one to the arena, the other to the public trams connecting all over Avertori. She guessed correctly that the Ortessi would avoid the arena. They might put him in it. She repositioned the oval monocle in front of her eye and picked up the badly scuffed trail leading to the transfer station.

Then she looked up and gasped. *Thousands* of people were heading home. Hers could be a short trip. She was probably fifteen minutes behind him, but already the trail of breadcrumbs had been eaten up by bright light and shuffling feet.

A sign displaying timetables and track numbers caught her eye. Avertori was divided by plazas and sectors. Two trams were heading to the lowest sectors within ten minutes of now. Another three had already departed. She strode quickly to check out the two platforms that were soon to depart. The first was nearly empty, a tram recently departed. With her monocle, she inspected the loading platform and found not a trace of the luminescent paint.

She doubled back and went to the other platform. This tram was just pulling out. She kept behind a column until it was out of sight just in case the Ortessi was on it. He would certainly be looking for a tail, especially since she had threatened to follow him just two nights before.

Keeping an eye out for him, she scanned the floor of the platform. A couple of the arc lamps were going bad, causing the light to flicker. Where the last car had loaded, she was just able to make out a large splash of scattered, glowing paint. He had waited here! She sighed relief. A sign indicated another tram for the same destinations would be by in just twelve minutes. She pocketed her oval monocle and paced, alert and thinking.

Why am I doing this? I just risked my life to follow this fraud without any specific *reason. And I'll probably be risking it again before the night's through.* But she had to know where he went and who he talked to. She had to know the truth about who he was.

Her long, slender legs covered much of the platform as she paced. People were gathering for the next train and looking at her.

EPISODE 4 – A LIGHT IN THE DEEP

None of them had her energy. She stopped and pretended to fit in. When the tram came she boarded where the paint indicated and watched carefully as they slowly descended through the lower boroughs toward the Glums.

She had never been to the Glums. They were considered dangerous. She noted that the lower they got, the people remaining on the tram were dressed more shabbily. Even her dark, plain clothes stood out because of their quality. But nobody remaining on the tram paid any attention. They were tired and lethargic, probably having worked all day at an assigned job for a meager subsistence. *Why would anyone put up with living like that?*

But in Avertori, people didn't have much choice. Family status governed their opportunity. *What if a person could choose any occupation they wanted? Would they?* Velirith's intuition told her that most of these people would remain oppressed by their own programming. This was who they thought they were. Perhaps the next generation could break free.

At every stop, she worried she would miss seeing the paint on the ground where the Ortessi had gotten off. But three stops before the end of the line, peering through the glass in the tram doors, she saw it. She saw it even as the tram approached its stop, such was the gloom that inhabited these lower reaches. She scrambled off but there was little need for haste. The few people in this sector ambled with the hopelessness of the walking dead. And despite the dearth of Rei-shine, it was stiflingly hot.

The gloom, the muggy heat, the grime, and especially the lack of hope pressed in on Velirith like a tangible weight. *How can anyone live here?* She focused, not only on the drops of paint— which shone brightly in the dimness, but on an intangible aspect of the heaviness of this lower region. Something brooding seemed to hover around her. Something old and intelligent and intentional. Velirith was far too conscious of her intuitive ability to dismiss the feeling, yet she had no framework from which to identify the

CHAPTER TEN

cognizant foreboding.

She had to choose to forget it and concentrate on her quarry.

The droplets of light led her to a seedy pub. She was surprised. And suddenly alarmed. Only one set of drops led in, which meant the Ortessi was still in here and that he could come out any time, running right into her. She ducked into a dark niche, of which there was no lack.

But this was why she was following; to find out who he met with. Perhaps she should enter and blend in—mingle and see what he was about. But before she could act, her decision was made for her; the Ortessi strode out, keenly sweeping the area with his eyes, looking for trouble. She slid completely out of sight before his gaze got to her hiding place.

He seemed different. He seemed... to fit. *This is his home!* she realized. He *did* have a home, and this was it. And she hated it. How had he survived? And how had he emerged with any sense of decency whatsoever? He could actually be quite gentlemanly. She felt a wave of compassion that accompanied her realization. Where she had grown up, protected and loved and surrounded by beauty, he had not. She had judged him for not trusting her and yet, had she grown up here—she almost cried right there in the shadowed alcove.

She pulled herself together and considered what to do next. She needed far more distance between her and him. She was right about him looking for a tail. He was out of sight now, but what to do while he increased his lead?

She looked at the bar: *The Bottom of the Barrel*. It had elegance smudged all over it. *Oh, there I go judging again.* She pulled up her collar and pulled down the cheek shields of her cap. It made no sense to be wearing so much, but it hid most of her features. She walked into the bar. It stank of sweat and spilled beer. She almost gagged.

Blending in... was not going to happen. She walked too

473

confidently, she was fit—both mind and body—and she was clean. All eyes from all corners of the dim joint turned to check her out. She was so suddenly self-conscious that she almost missed seeing the elevator car smashed into the middle of the establishment. *What bizarre décor! If I live, I need to write a play using this setting.*

Adapting at last, her theater training kicked in and she slouched and slumped, surreptitiously sliding the monocle up to her eye for a quick peek at where the Ortessi had gone. The trail led to a small splotch at the far end of the bar. Knowing her presence was already conspicuous, she went to where he had stood and looked across the bar. Immediately the barkeep sauntered over to her.

"Been here all your life, have ya?" He grinned, a surprisingly nice smile for the grungy surroundings.

Though naïve, she was fast thinking. "Yeah, if I was born yesterday."

The barman chuckled. "Name's Ogard, miss. Though I won't be asking yours."

She nodded, "Appreciated. I can't stay long—" she hesitated, but her intuition told her this man was decent though extremely cunning. "I need to ask you about the man who just left. And I need you to never tell him I was here." Another flash of intuition made her pull a few thousand dras from her pocket. "Will this amount ensure that confidentiality?"

His suppressed laugh told her it was off the mark. "Young miss, perchance you *were* born yesterday. But yes, in the parlance of secrecy, you've spoken loud and clear. Be that as it may, there's propriety to observe." Ogard pulled out a few copper coins and one silver one, pushed them across the counter, then collected the dras. "If you're going to use a bribe, do so in proper fashion. Paper flies in the wind, the metal of ril holds fast. Use those."

Velirith tried to recover what little dignity she could. "If you keep my confidence, I'll match that sum if I return. But if I *ever* find out you've given me away, you'll never see another…"

CHAPTER TEN

"...ril?" Ogard suggested.

"Right, ril."

"An 'if' I'd recommend against, miss, as a protective father would recommend."

His candor was alarming, but again appreciated. He read her well.

He continued. "That chap is a regular that I'll not betray to a high-born familial like yourself. I'll keep your visit a secret, but I'll also be keeping his secrets a secret. And I mean no offense.

"I will tell you one thing we talked about because I think you'll learn something from the conversation itself, though not about him. We talked about a friend of ours, a dear friend, who ran a bar not far from here. He wasn't wise. Bold and courageous, but not wise. I told your man about this mutual friend because our friend disappeared last week. Why, you ask? Because Ashperis, the house who owns the liquor business had a gripe with our friend. They had squeezed him so hard that he wasn't makin' enough to feed his family. So he decided to get his booze from another source, a dark-market source, you might say.

"The Ashperis thugs figured this out—a drop in product orders—and 'negotiated' his return as a customer. He didn't negotiate in good faith. Now he's gone. The system stinks like my bar."

Tense, Velirith considered the value of what he *had* and *had not* said. So the Ortessi was known here. And Ogard had figured out her 'status' despite her weak attempt to blend in. If she ever did do this again, she would first visit the costume department in Theatre Velaki. And she knew he was telling the truth about not exposing her visit. As for the story about their friend, well, perhaps she did need that education.

Nevertheless, she pressed her questioning. "Is that all I get? I'm sure someone else could tell me more."

Ogard pulled a bottle from beneath the bar with a casualness that seemed magic. "No, you get a drink too. Though I suspect it may be your first real one. And yes, you could get more from someone else. But I warn you it would be *much* more than you bargained for. I'd stick to talking to me since I really am a father."

Velirith gulped, knowing he was right. She eyed the eyes staring at her across the room. This wasn't the cafe in Orcad. Several tables of rough men were already guffawing at her, probably challenging their drinking mates to approach her for one thing or another. She'd have to be sharp not to be followed out of here.

"Thanks, Ogard," she turned to go, but even though she was shaking, turned back with a curious thought. "And though you've warned me, I suspect you will see me again."

He shrugged noncommittally, and she knew he'd watch her back on the way out.

In the gloom of the Glums, she wore the monocle all the time. She was not followed out of the bar. The Ortessi's trail was now as easy to follow in the deep shadows of full night as a Powercoach track. She was now slouching and shuffling to match the general lethargy of the Glums and go on less noticed.

His path led her several blocks into the crowded alleys between the crowded buildings—apartment tenements mostly, but dwellings and businesses were squeezed in side by side and seemed to grow off the large ancient towers like fungi. It was as if for the last thousand years these things had been decaying rather than growing. The dots of light led to a massive building identified by its smell: garbage. Several open chutes allowed residents of the neighborhood to dispose of refuse. The lighted path led to a door next to the chutes. She reached to open it and found it... locked!

Another flaw in her breadcrumb plan. She examined the lock in the dim light. Velirith had become extremely adept at locks by practicing on every one that affronted her freedom to explore Velakun. She had at least thought to bring her basic tools. Pulling her lock pick set from her cloak, she had the simple device open in less than a minute. No one was about. Whether someone was within, she didn't know.

The office inside was blessedly empty. A messy desk indicated the place was operational, probably during business hours. Ortessi's footsteps went back behind the chutes, through a smelly work area, to another set of tubes. These had no apparent openings, yet the light drops ended at the tube on the far right. A secret door, no doubt. Without the light trail, she would never have figured out where her quarry had gone. *Thank you, Eos.* But how was this door activated?

Three levers were affixed to the wall next to the tube. This seemed too obvious to Velirith, a diversion. She pushed and lifted to no avail. She ran her hand along where the tube entered the wall and found a tiny gap that looked like nothing more than a crack. She retrieved her lock pick set again and pushed a thin metal pick into the hole. She expected another lock to pick, but mere pressure against a hidden latch released it with a *click*. She pulled on the tube and a large section swung outward revealing the top rung of a ladder inside.

Cool, dank air blew out of the now open tube. While it smelled not so foul as the refuse center, it still smelled of decay; ancient decay and the strange foreign scents of the deepest depths.

If it was dim in the work area, the disused garbage chute was pitch black. She took a deep breath of pungent air and climbed into the tube. And if there was a way to light the chute, she couldn't find it. She uncovered the luzhril in her bracelet and started down slowly. The hatch above her closed with an echoing clang. She paused a moment to find the release on the inside so she could get out in a hurry if necessary.

Down she went. After twenty rungs, she covered her light to check if there were any other lights below. There were not. As she went down another fifty rungs the air continued to cool and her drying sweat made her shiver. She realized she was now well below ground level, below the Plate.

The Plate! She had never even seen it before today. Now she was below it. She shivered again despite herself.

The ladder emerged from the tube into open air and ended a few feet lower on hard-packed ground. A little-used trail led down the side of what seemed to be an underground mountain. The stench was still horrible. She held up the stone of her bracelet to light only the path ahead, but sensed vast space around her. Again, she covered the light to see if she could see others.

Velirith still saw no one. But she did see light—no, *lights.* Faint and moving, a myriad of unidentifiable lights flickered in and out of existence on the ground around her, like stars on a windy, cloud-scudded night. She couldn't see what was creating them.

She opened her light to full brightness and looked at the rough mountain. But it was not rough because of stones. She saw the ends of other tubes some distance away, the tubes pointing at other small, dark mountains. The garbage chutes.

But that meant... she looked closely at the surface of the mountain. Bits of glass, paper, decayed, unidentifiable matter—she stood on a mountain of garbage! Only the mountain on which she stood was older than where the garbage tubes currently emptied. This one was packed down by time and its own weight. But the irony could not be avoided: part of the foundation of their great society was merely refuse.

Though the variegated surface partly hid the luminescence of Ortessi's trail, she could still make it out as it followed the only path along and down the ridgeline of the garbage mountain. She moved carefully and quickly down the path.

Her light, as good as it was, dimmed into the immensity of space in which these garbage mountains had formed. She wished she could determine how big they really were. She felt disoriented and more than a little scared. After hiking for nearly ten minutes, always downward, the path leveled out. Now it wound slowly through the valleys between these mountains. She heard the

CHAPTER TEN

skittering of small animals, or perhaps settling debris, all around her. Then she heard a more consistent sound, a crunching of footfalls, and she doused her light, standing still. The footfalls through the garbage stopped near the base of the mountain, near where the active trash chute emptied.

Frozen in the darkness, she wanted desperately to uncover her light. But to do so against an unknown threat would only highlight her position. Imaginations of strange creatures in this strange place assaulted her mind. To calm herself she imagined herself in Symphony Gardens back home, listening to the water orchestra in the warm light of Rei. It worked until she heard the crunching much nearer in the pitch black. She would have to turn on her light.

Just before she did, she saw, from where had been nothing but darkness, a tiny speck of light. It bobbed and dropped but she was unable to determine its distance and size because it was so small. Then suddenly, the light lifted, and she saw in its glow the face of a small boy, perhaps six years old. She was totally unprepared for the sight. He stood perhaps twenty feet away and in his palm, he held a tiny jar. In the jar was a bug that gave off the faint light. With it he was examining something he had picked up.

Velirith shifted her weight and he heard it, looking up in her direction as he closed his hand around his light. Despite how close he was, she barely heard him moving away in the total blackness. He was obviously practiced in navigating the trash field.

Standing there, straining to hear the child, Velirith didn't know what to think. How could a child live down here, in this eternal night? How could the world above, *her* world, be so blind to the existence of this nether-region?

She shone her light in the direction of the departing child. All she saw was the path through the valleys of detritus. She scanned her surroundings.

Nothing.

She had to move on. Out of both curiosity and fear of being

479

seen, she tried moving forward with no light. Within ten steps she stumbled, falling to the path and ripping a hole in her dark pants. She turned on the light to examine the damage and what she had tripped over. A stone, and the damage was nothing, perhaps a bruise. But it gave her an appreciation for how that child could move through this place in pitch dark. She continued on.

The garbage mountains tapered off abruptly and she crossed a refuse-littered plain. At the end of the plain she came finally to a tunnel. The path was harder packed here and the Ortessi's trail more distinct. The tunnel roof overhead was a shallow arch of cracked stone, a fallen tower perhaps? Velirith thrilled that what she was seeing was certainly pre-Avertoric ruins, but she still shook with fear that this—the world beneath the Plate—was inhabited by known criminals and outcasts from the world above. It was a lawless world, and she was a young naïve girl completely ignorant of what was down here, human or otherwise. Hadn't Aurelios told her that the strange creatures of Theatre Velaki were literal creatures below the Plate?

The tunnel/tower was cracked somewhere near the middle and through the gap, a path veered off into ragged, wild darkness. What lay that way, she couldn't guess. Fortunately, the Ortessi's trail pressed forward. She realized after some minutes that if this was a fallen tower, it was far longer than the current towers of Avertori and Velakun were tall. More than a mile of walking led her to the other end. The exit was mostly clogged by fallen masonry, but a narrow, cleared path took her out. The way continued as a low-ceilinged, narrow stair that wound through the debris both side to side and vertically up and down in small hills. Evidently, the builders of this passage had found it difficult to excavate a straight way. The stairs were hacked out of the debris, crudely laid through broken masonry and twisted metal for another quarter mile. The ceiling was low and jagged. Velirith came to realize that the Ortessi's trail of light droplets was still extremely regular. He was moving with confidence where she was picking her way through.

CHAPTER TEN

He was at home here too. She suddenly felt very sheltered and small. That he acted as well as he did in the world above was to his credit. No wonder he didn't know what an abbig was.

She rounded a huge straight block and saw a lit open area ahead. She extinguished her light quickly, and emerged from the irregular alley into what could only be a form of town square, but such a town as she had never seen or imagined. The open area in the middle was merely a cleared common area smaller than most of the terraces of Vel estate. Three rough luzhril chunks, small but steady, hung suspended by dark cables from a ceiling somewhere in the gloom above. Considering the penury she'd seen thus far, the relatively expensive lights were unexpected. The small chunks dimly illuminated storefronts that were not much more than cleared spaces between large crushed buildings. The irregular shape of the ruins made it hard to distinguish rubble from operating businesses and habitable dwellings.

A half dozen people moved between the structures, such as they were. One man was pulling a cart full of jars that suddenly flared with yellowish light when the wheel bumped over a large pothole in the rough paving stones. Velirith pulled back into the tunnel from which she had emerged and drew the wings of her cap farther around her face.

This was a community. They knew each other well and she would be marked as a stranger immediately. She checked the trail of the Ortessi and found it leading right toward the underground town square. But where had he gone?

She had just determined to keep her head down and hurry through the town on his trail, when Orlazrus appeared out of a shadowed alcove, a shop perhaps, and crossed the town hollow to the right.

He greeted a man, obviously a friend despite a concealing mask. She strained to catch their words but she was too far away. They chatted briefly then the other man pointed to a small place along the right side of the commons. Walking over to the only

EPISODE 4 – A LIGHT IN THE DEEP

table, currently occupied, some words were exchanged and the patrons got up hastily to make way for Orlazrus and his friend. Evidently they were feared, or respected—or both. Velirith had never seen him interact in this way, like he was pulling rank.

They sat, and immediately an older man came out of the slanted opening in the rubble and took their order—so it was a cafe of some sort, or a pub. Then she noticed a sign above the door, barely readable in the dim light: *The Stale Ale*. The waiter/owner went back in to fill their request and the two began talking in earnest. Velirith *had* to know what they were saying. This is why she came.

She considered options. Her disguise? Inadequate to have her simply stroll by and listen in. Besides, there was only one table in the common area. And she doubted she'd get anything from the owner when they left. He seemed intimidated by them.

If she had been in Velakun or Avertori with all their towers and terraces, she might be able to get above the two at the table. She looked up. The higher reaches of the town commons were not a smooth dome by any means. From what she could make out, the hollow seemed to be formed by two or three building remnants leaning against each other and the rest was filled in with large pieces of broken walls. This left gaps and ledges at odd angles. One of these ledges started near ground level not far from her at the beginning of the alley in which she was hiding. It angled up the side wall to a spot over the lintel of the pub. She would be able to hear from there—if she could get there without being heard or seen herself. But if she was seen, she would be trapped, in a narrow gap between the ledge and the rubble above it.

Velirith almost laughed out loud at herself. *Not* take the chance? It was like *not* breathing. Of course she would. She waited a few moments until the foot traffic was either busy or looking away, then moved smoothly across the alley to the beginning of the gap. She squeezed in, leaving her cloak jammed in a dark crevice. Lying on her belly, she inched forward and upward. The beginning was the narrowest, forcing her face into the dust and debris that littered the ledge. Despite her racing heart, she forced herself to breathe shallowly and not sneeze the powdery dirt. An unseen protrusion from above gouged her back and she stifled a cry. She pressed on despite feeling a small trickle of blood down her back.

With her forearms in front of her she was able to brush fragments of accrual deeper into the crack. Still, it was a nasty, dirty niche. She was glad she wasn't wearing fine clothes. Even the clothes she had on weren't tough enough to avoid rips and scrapes on her arms.

The first twenty feet was near eye level. No one was near, but had they glanced over at that end of the square, she would have been looking right back at them.

Moving slowly and smoothly she inched up the ledge. The slab above eased its pressure on her back, giving her more space. She moved more quickly, not wanting to miss any more of the men's conversation.

Throughout the whole crawl up the shadowed crack, she had a clear view across the square. She saw a sign above one alcove, "Clothes". Another, "Grain". Another, "Tools and Supplies". All basic goods and services. This was not a place of luxuries. She pressed forward, grim, remembering the little boy in the garbage fields. She didn't know what could be done to help, but she felt something stir deep within her as she pressed on.

She began to hear the tones of their conversation, and shortly after, the actual words. She slowed to make sure she didn't knock sand into their drinks from above. She was perhaps fifteen feet above the ground in the niche directly above their heads.

"...Juf fixed my mask. It's worth the trek to have him do it. Last time, I tried to do it myself—" the man laughed, "—and that's why I had to have him repair my work."

"You're a great spy, Bags, but a lousy costume designer," Orlazrus laughed. "The mundane challenges of such an elite occupation. I was surprised to run into you this far from your place. I'm going to see Movus, of course. This business with the raid on the fibrum shipment. Doesn't sound like a Coin op."

"Nope. You've been out of the loop. Nomen alerted Sengus that the freighter captains might be sympathetic to dealing with us. They were afraid of us, but hated the Primes of their houses too. So for their 'protection', Sengus set up some very nice arrangements with the freighter captains *and* the suppliers to overload shipments.

"We don't even raid the Parchiki route anymore. We just meet them with sleds to offload our cut. Safer for everybody. The house primes don't even know we're eating away at their storehouses. So, no, we wouldn't raid that cloth shipment. It would just draw negative attention to us."

"That makes more sense," agreed the Ortessi. "But it raises the question of who did it?"

"We don't know for sure... yet."

There was a silence and then the clank of bottles settling back on the table.

"Interesting how that deal with the freighter drivers came together," Bags mused. "No one has ever seen Nomen, but evidently he talks to Sengus and sometimes Movus."

The Ortessi replied. "Movus told me Nomen has an above-the-Plate identity and doesn't want anyone to see him. He knows it would eventually leak. So Nomen knows how the money flows upstairs. He finds weak spots and points them out to Movus or Sengus so we can exploit them. Very nice to have a spy so closely placed to the Omeron."

The one called Bags snorted a laugh. "I heard a joke I didn't get. Movus told it."

"Movus?" the Ortessi responded, disbelief in his voice. "He never really laughs."

"I know, and it's weird when he does. Twink told Movus that he, Sengus, and Nomen were like the triumvirate of the Coin. I had to ask somebody what that meant, but anyway, Movus came back at him with, 'We're not the triumvirate, we're the trinity,' and he laughed and laughed at his own joke, his voice going up and down like a crazy song."

The Ortessi grunted at this, but must have found it more thought provoking than funny.

Bags went on, "Hey, back to the subject of sleds: you're getting one! Your mission must be high priority. Nobody gets a sled for their personal use. And guess who's delivering it?" A pause. "That's right, me! We're to meet at Vwislin, that spur just outside Velakun."

"Stars, Bags!" the Ortessi hissed. "Keep it down. Slinks have ears, you know."

"Sorry," the one called Bags mumbled. "Just excited to see you again, Cap'n."

"And I'm not Captain anymore. You are." Orlazrus changed the subject, his tone low and serious. "Any word on your wife, Bags?"

There was a long pause and when he spoke, Bags' voice cracked. "No. That prog Borgus is said to have a whole harem of stolen women. And he's married himself! It's *sick!* And it makes me sick to think what he might make those ladies do. And my Eznea among them, a—a—prisoner—" he seemed about to say something else, but couldn't bring himself to it. "Borgus has plenty of reasons to be paranoid. Of all the highborns, he keeps the tightest locks and the most guards."

"We will change things, Bags, I promise you. Fight the good fight down here," Orlazrus' voice was thick with intensity and compassion for his friend. "I have to see that bastage Telander tomorrow. I'll try not to hit him."

"Don't hold back on my account," Bags grumbled. "Sometimes I feel like Eznea would be better off dead. But I can't help being glad they didn't kill her when they took her. She's the best thing I've got in my life."

EPISODE 4 – A LIGHT IN THE DEEP

Orlazrus responded, "Her pain reminds us how great our purpose really is."

"How much can you say about what you're up to?"

Velirith held her breath in anticipation.

There was silence. "I probably said too much already." The drinks clanked on the table again. "But Bags, as much as we grew up hating everybody above the Plate, it's a big world. There's good and bad, just like down here. There's a lot of fat progs at the top that don't care..." Orlazrus trailed off.

"...which we will fix," Bags finished.

Velirith listened carefully. Bags' conclusion was not where the Ortessi was going with that line of thought.

"Bags," Orlazrus said slowly, carefully. "I have no compassion for Telander and those like him, the abusers of power. But I'm beginning to realize that we cannot just gather the lot of them into a ball and toss them into a hole like they've done to us."

His friend didn't answer, and Velirith listened as intently as she imagined Bags was listening.

Orlazrus went on. "I've seen their spite, their greed, their power lust and their simple guilty ignorance. Growing up in the privilege of a prime house, it never crosses their mind that everyone else is being crushed. Certain individuals could be... allies."

There was a long pause. Velirith had never heard him be so careful with his words and still be transparent. He had to be talking about her father. And her. It made her think about the way she treated him. And this trip so far had already revealed her "guilty ignorance".

Bags answered in kind, carefully. "I don't think you'll find any allies of your opinion down here. We need the Omeron gone and to start over."

She didn't hear the Ortessi sigh, but she imagined he would have.

But it was Bags who asked, "But do we even have a

CHAPTER TEN

chance?"

The long silence that followed revealed their unspoken despair.

Orlazrus finally spoke, quietly. "I saw Bokey in the garbage fields."

Bags replied, "Yeah, he's pretty much on his own since his Dad got killed."

"I gave him a few ril before he ran off," the Ortessi told him. "He can live for a month on those if nobody steals them from him."

"Yeah, but he needs more than money. He needs to see the light of Rei."

Velirith imagined Bags looking into his friend's brown eyes. She too wanted to look into his eyes, to read the truth she heard in his voice. To see the compassion he had for his people. The desperate passion.

The voice that spoke next was so low and hoarse with emotion she wasn't sure who spoke. "While we live. Let us *live*."

Someone cleared their throat. Chairs scraped below her. The men were getting up.

"I gotta go," the Ortessi declared.

"Great to see you, Kieler," Bags said with deep sincerity.

Velirith involuntarily jerked her head into the slab above. She winced in pain but wanted to cry out in joy.

"Bags!" the man scolded in a harsh whisper. "We don't use..."

"I'm sorry! Sparks. I mean Sparks. I just never see you--"

"It's okay. Nobody's around. But really, Bags. You're the most emotional lumbering hulk of a squad leader I've ever trained. You look like you're made of stone but I swear it's just putty!"

"Yeah, well, whatever. Sorry for caring."

Kieler laughed, and Velirith heard back-slapping as they wandered away from the pub.

Kieler! His real name!
Kieler!

CHAPTER ELEVEN

One thing was clear from the men's talk: Kieler was a subversive.

Now what did she do?

The men came into view as they walked away from the wall. Velirith marveled and thanked the Truth that people seldom looked up. Suddenly fifteen feet of altitude felt like eye level.

The two friends clasped forearms affectionately and parted ways. *Kieler* headed to an alleyway opposite the one by which she had arrived. Velirith scooted backward down the ledge. Though gravity helped her descend, she couldn't see her feet. She dislodged a crumbling edge of stone and sent it into the plaza below. She froze, but no one noticed. When she got about halfway back, she checked carefully below and rolled out, dropping to the ground. She didn't want to repeat the incident of dropping off the gondola into a group of people.

After retrieving and donning her cloak, Velirith walked purposefully across the plaza to the alley, her head down, hood up. With her torn and soiled clothing, she was now sufficiently bedraggled that she fit in. She was perhaps five minutes behind Kieler. Eyes followed her, but not people.

Her monocle revealed a path through something like a long hallway. Intersections and turns peeled off, but his trail seemed to be pursuing a more or less direct course. That Kieler hadn't been greeted by everyone in the plaza gave her some sense that not everyone down here knew everyone else. *How many people live down here?* She felt ignorant of the world—this world in particular—and anonymous, but kept her head down nonetheless.

What she had overheard kept trying to distract her from the focus-demanding task of following the faint footsteps. The Ortessi really was trying to change the world! But obviously outside legal channels. But they hadn't attacked that fibrum shipment, just as the Coin spy had told her father.

And Borgus Telander was doing horrible things! She had never felt comfortable around him, but what they accused him of— her intuition had never suspected, but it corroborated the accusations as truth. She felt a pit in her inner being. The world was uglier than she imagined, even among the Primes. Perhaps, *especially* among the Primes.

The hall-like artery emptied into a much larger open area with a town before her. She was once again amazed at the diversity of living space. It seemed that whatever was available, the denizens of this underground colony made use of it. Humans were resourceful.

The houses—no, *hovels*—of this town were made of stacked rubble. Many had roofs, but other than for privacy, they were unneeded. Very dim light glowed in most of the dwellings. Somewhere far above, the Plate loomed.

Some of the structures had names. "Dubak's Pub", "Tools", etc. Most were just houses. There was no organization. The terrain here rose and Velirith wondered if she might be walking on the ground below Avertori and not just fallen rubble. A stream flowing through a valley of debris added to that feeling.

Climbing a small hill, Velirith followed Kieler's path to where the rubble piles resumed. A large arch marked a thoroughfare through the next mountain of fallen structures. The easy road wandered gently with dozens of smaller tunnels branching off at intervals and several odd-shaped major intersections. If the paint didn't lead her, she would have been lost. *And until today I thought only a few murderous rebels lived under the Plate. Now I'm wondering if more people live here than in Velakun!*

Traffic on the road moved steadily, but no one paid her more attention than a curious glance.

Wondering why, she looked down at herself. Her clothes were covered in dust with numerous small tears. She actually looked worse than most of those she met. And for now, she was quite thankful about that. It was also cool down here. At least they didn't have to suffer the heat of Avertori above.

Most residents were dressed in shabby but clean clothes. They carried on much like those in the city above. All were pale, of course. Once, she encountered two men coming from the other way dressed in dark clothes and decorated masks. The masks themselves were fascinating. She only glanced at them and looked away, but she etched the picture in her mind.

The first was hideous, a face plate covered with ugly warts and protuberances that curved around his head. A clear spot above the left eye depicted a triangle and Velirith remembered that Kieler's friend Bags wore something similar.

The second mask was painted a smooth, flat black with two bright yellow streaks across the left cheek. She had no idea if the decoration represented anything, but the words of the spy in Velator's library came back to her: *Those of the Coin wear masks.*

Kieler is of the Coin. What does his mask look like?

This was obviously a main thoroughfare. It was the only one so far that was lit and Velirith could not at first understand how. She slid the magal over her own light and tried to determine the illumination's source. The walls glowed a faint green.

When the passage was mostly empty, she ran her nails along the wall. It was rough, and glowing flecks of it chipped off onto her fingertips. Paint? No, *lichen!* It looked much like the lichen that grew on the mountain rocks outside the rim of Velakun, but this breed phosphoresced. This society had somehow deliberately cultivated it on this main road.

It took her a while to realize something else too; above, in

EPISODE 4 – A LIGHT IN THE DEEP

Avertori, it was now night. Here, in this nethercity, these people carried on as if it were business hours. They didn't follow the conventions above. Here, it was always night.

She wondered what they did for work; how it was assigned. Then she thought, *if I were to watch those wandering around Avertori I could easily wonder the same thing.*

Eventually, Kieler's trail led to a small, solid side-tunnel. She hesitated, listening. Nothing.

She started down the smaller corridor. The paint drops seemed to be fading and finally ended at a door in a solid wall in the side of the corridor. This wall was part of a real structure, not just arranged rubble. The door, equally solid, was locked. A keyhole beckoned her to pick the lock. She hesitated. If Kieler was on the other side in a room, she would be found out. But if his path continued beyond the door, she would be left behind. She waited a few minutes, pacing slowly up and down the long corridor. No one else came down this way, which she found strange in itself.

After many minutes and no activity, she stopped by the door, lock pick ready. She had a moment's hesitation, a moment's thought, *Why must I pursue knowing the truth of this man any further?* It was a doubt she didn't listen to. Inserting a tool, she immediately knew the lock was not the same as the ones she was so familiar with in Velakun. It felt magnetic, like the tunnel door to outside the rim, but more... threatening. She kept at it, sensing the interior mechanism.

Snap!

Her tool broke off with such a sudden sharp report that it could easily have been heard inside. She tried once to get the broken piece out of the lock, fumbling nervously. She heard movement on the other side of the door, a chair scrape, *footsteps.*

Decision. Back the way she'd come and risk being seen and recognized. Or—

Down. She bolted down the corridor opposite the way she had come, into unknown territory. She ran full sprint down the empty, sloping passage. She heard the door open behind her after only a dozen steps just as she turned a corner out of sight. Slowing so as not to be heard, she pressed on, the corridor still descending.

"That way!" she heard shouted, and she realized it was Orlazrus; Kieler. Now, she wished desperately he wasn't such a man of action.

Multiple footfalls, running.

She ran.

She began regretting her choice of direction. As she ran deeper, the floor, walls and ceiling of the corridor were in progressively worse condition. She had to watch her footing, jumping cracks and dodging pieces of the wall or ceiling that had fallen in her path.

Suddenly, there was no corridor at all, just a narrow path and an uneven, underground plain before her.

She kept running. But the light faded fast. With the walls gone, the lichen had gone too. She had no choice but to uncover the luzhril stone on her wrist to keep her from falling on the increasingly uneven path.

Before her rose a jumbled wall of rubble; to the right it was taller than she, to the left it was a bit shorter and the path continued in a vague way. She could feel vast space above her. *How big is this place?*

She slowed, glanced back, still heard footfalls and saw light approaching as it reflected off the walls.

Decision. Climb up the wall and work through the rubble? Or—

She bolted left down the path. After an initial curve, the rubble lowered on both sides of her and the path straightened. That wasn't good. She didn't want them to see her and she held the only light down here.

Worse, the path was now almost indistinguishable amongst the jumble of debris. *Why would a path not lead anywhere?*

She had to slow or risk tripping over protrusions on the

rough semi-path. She was less than a hundred yards down the trail when lights began reflecting off the rubble behind her. Just before they came into view, she covered her luzhril and crouched behind a large broken block on the side of the path.

Catching her breath, she peeked around the block and tried to listen. It was easy to hear; sound carried far in the tomb-like silence.

Her pursuers paused and held up lights, faint chips of luzhril that didn't penetrate far into the gloom of the wreckage all around her. One of them was her Orlazrus, no, *Kieler*, she reminded herself. That it was he, she had no doubt.

His voice was clear over the moderate distance. "Caprice, go left. Block off the tunnel that circles back to the borough. Spit, wait here so our prowler can't double back. Grev and I will press forward."

"You sure that's smart, Sparks?" the one called Spit asked. "What if he's armed?"

"Of course he's armed. But I don't hear a maggun and we've got knives too. Someone bold enough to snoop on Movus' residence, we need to grab."

Velirith was frozen behind her shield of fallen stone. What could she do? To move would give her away. But if they came her way, she was sure to be found.

Kieler-Sparks and Grev started forward down the path at a cautious pace. Kieler was heading straight for her.

What will he do? If it were just him, I know he wouldn't kill me. But he's got his men with him. She shook her head. *His men. He's responsible to them, and I will* not *be allowed to leave. He may have to kill me or risk exposing his whole revolution. I've put him in a terrible spot and he doesn't even know it yet.*

She almost laughed. *Him? I'm the one who will end up killed.*

Kieler and Grev slowly approached her hiding place. She wasn't panicked, but she was close. She felt like a slink, and a grevon had her scent.

Decision again. Try to stay on the fading path, or—

Intellectually, she had no way to tell which way to go.

She closed her eyes. She calmed herself and listened to that voice of intuition that often told her the truth when she had no facts to rely on.

Go deeper. Go down.

She opened her eyes and peered around. She couldn't see much. The dying trail had leveled off, but to one side the ground descended sharply. She sighed.

She had no better ideas. She may as well trust that Voice.

Acting while she still had a few yards separation from her pursuers, she uncovered her wrist-light and leapt off the path into the tangle of rubble.

"There!" Kieler shouted. And she heard them break into a run.

Her way was steep. They could now see her light, but it would be hard to follow her. They might throw stones from above, but would have to slow or stop to do it.

Scrambling with all the reckless speed she had, she slipped and jumped down the jagged slope. Often falling, often catching herself before drops higher than she could survive, she veered left and right to find ways around the more treacherous falls, keeping blocks of rubble between her and them.

A rock whizzed by her ear. *That didn't take long.*

Do you know who you're throwing stones at, Kieler, my friend?

She found a vertical wall and sidled sideways along it for thirty feet. The sheer wall blocked her from their view and prevented them from getting a good angle for their throws.

Suddenly there was an increasing sound like thunder above her. *Truth? They've started a landslide?*

Smaller rocks and dust bounded over her head. No doubt the bigger ones were coming. She kept moving laterally, hoping to dodge the main fall of heavy rock.

Boulders of broken material crashed behind her. A roundish, jagged chunk of material bounced off the top of the broken wall above her and bounded over her head. Fragments from the impact sprayed the side of her face, but when the main chunk crashed into the ledge beneath her, it shifted, knocking her from her feet. Falling heavily on her thigh, she narrowly missed a jagged piece of wall bristling with twisted metal.

But that was the worst of their ad lib landslide. The main thrust of it was dying out. The slope wasn't steep enough to maintain the momentum of a full out landslide.

Velirith turned downward again, following the direction of the Voice and sheltering when she could. She had to keep her light on and that meant highlighting her, making her the only target in this eternal dark dungeon. Keeping her hood up blocked part of her peripheral vision, but it kept her anonymous.

She missed a footing and slid down a fifteen-foot scree slide. She scrambled in the sliding rock, managing only to scrape her hands without slowing her descent before sprawling hard on a ledge. A second later a chunk of rock the size of her head bounced a foot from her face and then bounced over the ledge. *Compliments of the man in green and gold.*

She followed the rock over the ledge, sliding again. Her leg dragged and the scree ripped another great gash in her pants, taking skin with it. She winced and almost laughed at the same time. *I'm a prime-apparent! And I'm getting rocks thrown at me!*

But she had put a great deal of vertical distance between her and the two men above. Once more she covered her light, shifted farther laterally from the men, hid under another shelf of rubble and looked up.

Now their lights highlighted them. They continued to hurl rocks, but they hurled blindly and off the mark. And for now, she had good shelter. In fact, a monolithic shelf hung out over a descent she could manage. Under the cover of the shelf, she picked her way down even farther, barely letting light leak out of her bracelet. Eventually, they could see her again, but she was almost out of throwing range.

Even now, with Kieler throwing stones at her, she realized she'd rather be running to him than from him. She knew his *name* now! For so long she had wanted to know who he was. Now she knew, and despite the desperateness of her situation, that knowledge heartened her. But what she really wanted was to use that information. What good did it do her if she died down here in this tomb?

She paused, panting. Her scraped legs, hands, and face all stung as if she had had dipped them in acid. And the two men just stood near the top, peering down. Their throwing stopped for now. *Why weren't they following?*

Kieler called down. "Hey Slink! You might want to rethink your escape. You'd have better odds up here with us than where you're heading!"

Velirith, light fully covered for the moment, leaned against the rubble and tried to catch her breath. *What did that mean?*

"We'll wait for you..." Kieler's voice taunted. Then the two men above sheathed their own lights.

Dim as it had been, at least their lights had been a reference. For a long few minutes, Velirith just listened. It wasn't entirely silent down here. She heard intermittent scurrying. She heard debris settling from the landslide. Her own breathing was still loud and heavy. And, in the far-distance ahead, she heard something very heavy moving about—not animal-like, more like the rumble of machinery, like the underworkings of the pod-car system, but not quite so... civilized.

Kieler could wait forever. She would not be returning that way.

Velirith had been leaning against a rock in the dark. As she looked forward the way she had been herded, all that faced her was deep, abiding darkness. But she didn't really have a decision to make. Going back put her in rock throwing range. Going up led right into Kieler's arms.

Shelter was easy to come by. Velirith put a monstrous block between her and the men above. She uncovered her light and tried to get a feel for the lay of the land rather than just flee headlong. Her light was good, illuminating the section of the hillside she had just scrambled down. It was more a ridge of heavy rubble, not just a hill. *I'm lucky to be alive.* It looked steeper looking back, and any one of a hundred drops could have broken her legs or worse.

She tried to look ahead. The ridge seemed to fade into an uneven plain of inexhaustible rubble. It just went on and on— daunting—beyond the range of her light.

She picked her way down, using her light sparingly. Though the men hurled rocks at her occasionally, they weren't murderous about it. More like kids trying to hit a stick floating down a creek. They laughed, chiding each other though she couldn't hear the words any more. In a way, their cavalier attitude toward possibly killing another human bothered her more than if they were intent upon her death for their security.

She moved on.

Fright. And not the stage kind. This kind made her wonder if her skin was still attached or beginning to crawl around her body to find someplace safe. So much unknown. That the men above, familiar with the under-Plate, had chosen *not* to pursue her— they must know something she didn't. Something very frightening.

Their voices soon faded entirely, the men now far behind her.

Moving carefully now that she was out of danger from being stoned, it took a long time to crawl over the pathless expanse. She held up her light. Her heart sunk and panic rose. Around her were small piles of rubble, on top of larger piles of rubble, on top of random hills of rubble. With no weather and no rivers and no wind there were no patterns in the miles of wreckage. The debris field extended beyond what she could see.

CHAPTER ELEVEN

Above her stretched a dark void with no apparent end.

She pressed on. The landscape had no distinguishing features. She came across some unique bits of junk--a metal cabinet with no handles, an intricately carved doorpost broken in several places, a circular window frame with bits of dusty glass still in it--but these curiosities faded into the gloom within a few yards.

I probably should try to go back. I have no food. No direction. No idea what is out here that even my brave Kieler wouldn't face.

But no, she had to go on. She strongly doubted she could even retrace her steps if she changed her mind and went back to beg Kieler for mercy.

Fear pierced her with every slip, every shift in the rubble around her, even the dousing silence. And every few minutes, some enormous something rumbled ahead of her, then stopped. Since the sound was the only source of direction, Velirith decided to approach it obliquely, angling off to the right with the hope of seeing the creator of the sound before it saw her.

She rested at intervals, but a soft scurrying or a sudden noise in the infinite well of silence would make her jump. So she moved on despite not knowing where she was going, despite not having any plan, and despite her waning hope. She wanted to scream, but held on to enough self-control to know that any sound might attract the very threat she was trying to avoid.

For hours she crawled over the indistinguishable rubble. Everything just smelled old and dusty, like the ruins they were. She had no concept of distance, and little concept of time other than the growing hunger in her stomach.

Velirith still had no idea what threat was out here. And not knowing was worse than facing it. She heard something sliding behind her and spun around. Nothing. Her backward glance caused her to stumble and fall. Her cheek smacked down next to a dark opening. A glowing insect startled, inches from her face. It flared to light with a buzzing hiss.

EPISODE 4 – A LIGHT IN THE DEEP

With her hair splayed over her face, Velirith snatched a chunk of debris and scrabbled back. "Get away!" She flung the rock at the thing, tried to get up, slipped again, and landed hard on her side. "Aaagh!" Frantic, she grabbed bits and pieces of the rubble around her and flung them wildly at the scared bug that finally skittered into the hole. "What am I doing down here!"

Like a frustrated child sitting in a sandbox, she kicked her feet in frustration and fear. Then she rolled onto a flat slab and cried, tears falling onto dusty chunks of the dead city.

For ten minutes she sobbed, losing her mind to her despair. Her emotions exhausted, she sat up wearily, hair plastered to her wet face.

Can I go back? she wondered.

No.

Will Kieler have a guard, knowing that I must go back that way?

Yes.

Will I be all right? Will I ever get out of here?

Yes, but not without trial.

She accepted this with a sigh, and moved on.

Occasionally she doused her luzhril, looking for other lights in the expanse. Sometimes she imagined a dim glow ahead, but in the utter blackness, she wasn't sure if her eyes were creating illusions.

After one of these dark tests, she held her light high and looked ahead. Some distance before her the darkness deepened, smooth and wide. She moved toward it. *An underground lake?* This she feared too, wondering what might live in a lake that hadn't seen Rei in millennia. But at least it was something *different*, and she was drawn to it.

Until it was one step in front of her, she still believed it to be water. But it did not reflect her light like water, nor did it smell like water. It seemed to be patterned, like the paving stones of an immense plaza. Not believing such a plaza could exist down here, she crept on hands and knees to the very edge—a place defined by the sharp cessation of rubble and the beginning of this new feature. She squatted before it. It was like the shoreline of Lake Skyfall. But as she cautiously reached down, her hand touched stone. Tile. It was smooth, black tile. Dustless.

What is this doing here? How can it be clean? How can it even be flat? Why isn't it broken like the rest of this world?

She stood and hovered her foot over it. As she would test ice, she lowered her foot and shifted some weight to it. It held. In fact, she felt quite ridiculous, for the tile was as solid as any plaza above in Avertori. At the thought of the city, she shuddered. The entire towering mass of Avertori was indeed above her. How far? Uncertain. How to get back there. She didn't know. It might as well have been on the other side of Rei.

She walked a few steps along the edge of the plaza, keeping close to the rubble. She didn't trust the endless expanse of flatness before her, like a sea that held secret dangers in its depths. But also, she reasoned, the edge of the tiled plain where it met the rubble gave her some orientation. Left or right with respect to the direction she had come. The rumbling had come from somewhere to the left; and she would rather face that unknown than blindly fear it.

She chose left. It gave her the tiniest feeling of security that she had a direction to go.

After walking several hundred feet, she realized that the edge was unerringly straight, not at all like an ocean shore. It was as though the builders had cut their tiles to precisely fit against an imaginary wall.

Although bothered by the mystery, Velirith was grateful for the smooth terrain. Her traveling was now easy, like walking down the hall in Vel-Taradan.

She noticed something else; each hexagonal tile, as wide as she was tall, was uniquely engraved. They alternated between tiles with writing and tiles with pictures. Velirith thought the script too difficult to read because of the elegant flourishes, but leaning low with her light, she realized the characters of these calligraphic masterpieces were in a language she had never seen.

The pictures amazed her in their diversity. Strange landscapes, cityscapes beyond anything in the Omeron, and gardens ornate beyond what she believed possible. And the resolution of the engravings was incredible. In one scene, a young lady held a flat tablet with writing upon it. As Velirith put her light down to the tile, not only could she see the young lady's delicate nose, she could see the lines in her irises, the title on the page and, with better eyesight, she probably could have made out the individual characters of the text!

Engraving this precise would have taken the artisan a lifetime, and it was inconceivable that time would not have erased such detail. Velirith's only conclusion was that this was very recent work by thousands of artists.

But why down here? The artists have a severely limited audience. Velirith smiled to herself. But it was a disturbed smile. She peered across the sea of tiles fading into an endless distance. This made no sense. No one lived here. She doubted that all the inhabitants above and below the Plate could have completed these tiles in their combined lifetimes.

So who built this place? And who maintained it?

With nothing to do but walk, she covered a great distance. For how long was hard to tell. In the absence of other scenery, she couldn't help looking at the pictures. Some described maps of unknown cities with the same intricate detail. She found only one picture she recognized. It was a continental map with the Isle of Threes at the center of the three converging continents: Govian, Coprackus, and her own Ardan to the northeast. That one recognizable depiction took the complete alien-ness away, but it chilled her to think that this 'society' existed right in the middle of her world without her knowledge.

Not all the pictures were perfect. Not that they were

marred, they were just wrong. People—distorted or missing half their bodies. Tiles with script trailing off into engraved, wandering scribbles, or the bottom half of a line of letters cleanly cut off. That it seemed intentional bothered her more than had it been defaced.

As she walked on, she began to feel, rather than see, a looming presence before her. Again she thought she saw lights— tiny, blue pinpoints—high up and moving. They could have been blue light lugs, but they were too high and moved too fast.

She couldn't tell how far away the lights were. Then they disappeared entirely.

After another five minutes of walking, it dawned on her what she was looking at: a monstrous, towering wall!

Her light did not illuminate the top. She stood at a corner of the structure, one wall continued the line that edged the tile plain, and the other wall struck out across it. That corner gave her a certain sense of grounding; there were defined borders to the place. Where the plain met the rubble, the wall shot straight up. Windows and doors dotted the wall high up and tilted at odd angles with no regard for function or symmetry.

The ground rumbled again, and Velirith realized the source of that great noise was on the other side of this wall, closer than it had been.

No point in crawling back into the rubble. I'd rather have answers.

She began the long walk along the base of the wall. A buzzing ahead made her look up. High above, three creatures flew toward her. Blue lights flashed on their underside. Standing perfectly still, Velirith watched the flying things bank steeply and enter the building through an opening high above. They appeared not to notice her.

Velirith remained standing for a long minute. *Where am I? How can all this exist? Am I still on Zotikas?*

Unsettled, she began walking again. She came to a doorway at roughly ground level. Only the top couple feet were accessible.

EPISODE 4 – A LIGHT IN THE DEEP

Strangely, the rest of the opening was built below ground level. Stooping down and peering in, her light illuminated a floor four feet below. Numerous doors and windows led out of this room with the promise of things opening up beyond.

She looked back onto the dark plain behind her, considering. *Can I go back?* What if she could talk to Kieler alone? Maybe she could convince him to—to—to what? Trust her? After she just followed him into rebel headquarters? When for two years he had been pushing her away to keep this very secret?

No. She would keep trusting the Voice, despite her growing fear.

She lay on the tile, put her legs through the partial door, and let herself down to the floor below.

After being on the wide-open, endless plain, the room felt confining. But it wasn't small. She walked over the sloping floor to a square door. Its frame was carved out of the same stone-like material as the building and depicted a climbing vine, again in detailed relief. Even the veins of the leaf were carved with an eye for realism.

She shook her head. She felt as if she explored the castle of a madman—fanatical for perfection, but irrational in his purpose.

Velirith moved carefully into the next room, which was a box barely large enough for her to stand. She climbed out of it through a window into an enormous chamber. The floor was tilted steeply, making it hard to stand, and three intertwining circular staircases angled upward from the floor to the top of the room. A row of sloping statues lined one wall—the first "furnishings" she had seen. Each statue was of the same bald man, bare to the waist with literally sculpted muscles and an expression of determination that seemed far overdone.

Velirith climbed the leaning, intertwined stairs on the outside of the staircase, crossing over from one stairway to the next when the slope threatened to dump her off. Reaching the top, she found a gap between the top of the staircases and the landing leading out. The gap was only three feet, but she realized that should she slip, should she fall and injure herself in any way, there was no help. She could make no mistakes.

She calmed herself and made the leap easily.

Passing through an opening, she found herself so close to the ceiling she had to crawl into the next room—a room that appeared to have no floor! A narrow shelf led around the edge. Though she couldn't see the bottom of the room, she could see a round window on the opposite wall. The ledge would bring her to it, but the window was far and the ledge narrow.

She began the long, slow crawl toward the window. The unknown height was getting to her. Her arms quivered beneath her, and sweat dripped from her face onto the smooth surface of the ledge, making it slick under her hands and knees.

Halfway to the window, she cocked her head, hearing a shrill buzz growing louder. She saw a flash of blue. Holding perfectly still, except for the trembling of her body, she rolled her eyes toward it. One of the blue-lit creatures hovered a mere yard away, appearing to examine her. It had a cylindrical body about six inches long, wiry legs and a long proboscis like a stinger. Multiple wings buzzed so fast she could not count them.

It darted toward her. Velirith slapped at it, nearly losing her balance, nearly losing her life.

"Shoo! Go away!" She didn't know what she'd do if it smacked into her—or stung her!

It dodged her clumsy slap and landed on her thigh, its body vertical. Its spidery legs wrapped around her leg and the buzzing quieted, as if she were a peaceful place to nap.

Velirith was frozen. She didn't want to enrage it, but she didn't want it on her body. Two of the creature's legs embraced her thigh sheath, so she couldn't get to her knife.

"Hey!" She wiggled her leg. The motion didn't dislodge the bird-bug but nearly dislodged her. "You! Bluedart thing. Off!" She clutched the ledge, eyes squeezed shut, mentally cursing Kieler for driving her into this labyrinth, mentally cursing her own foolish stubbornness. She had to get out of here. She had to return to the light of Rei so she could use the knowledge she had gained about Kieler. Knowing he was a rebel, and him *not* knowing she knew, oh, that would be a sweet advantage.

She opened her eyes, focused on the ledge, and continued moving toward the window. The mechanical bluedart rode along, attached to her thigh, perfectly content. She tried to pretend she was crawling around the outside edge of her bedroom tower at Vel Estate. Except no one would come to her aid. At night. With a little monster clinging to her leg.

As she crawled, she realized she inherently trusted the strength of these structures. They were not crumbling or dilapidated by time. Another mystery.

And she was going on faith that this was not a dead end. Turning around on this narrow ledge would be tricky.

She reached the window and immediately noticed a faint, acrid smell wafting through it, like the smell of the generator complex when it was sparking and melting down.

Glancing back, she checked her unwanted passenger. It seemed asleep, or sedated, the blue light on its belly pulsing softly. Velirith considered grabbing it and pulling it off her, but it wasn't threatening her now. It had curled its long, metal stinger into a harmless coil.

She poked her light through the portal and looked around. She saw a landing larger than the ledge and crawled thankfully onto it. But beyond the landing, a gap of thirty feet separated her from the next section of floor ahead. The gap did not look intentional (as if anything here did), and looking left and right, she saw a hole drilled straight through several rooms as far as her light penetrated.

What could have bored this horizontal hole?

Her thought was interrupted by a soft click above and to her right. Looking up, Velirith saw four creatures walking *down* the wall she had just passed through!

They looked like abbigs, but instead of fur, a satiny metal covered their bodies. They also had smaller heads than abbigs, heads dominated by large eyes encircled by rings of light that cycled rapidly from red to blue and back through the colors of the rainbow. Their four legs each ended in broad discs instead of hands.

In unison, all four creatures turned their heads to her. Her heart clenched in her chest as two of them started toward her. Clinging to the wall, they moved with an arm-over-arm motion that reminded her even more of abbigs swinging through a bizarre jungle.

Velirith watched, stunned, knowing her only escape route was backward. She moved her foot back, and it immediately slipped off the ledge behind her into empty space. She froze.

One abbig-like creature halted above the window, but the other, the colors around its eyes swirling wildly, shot forward, swinging down and shooting a haze of material at her legs.

Velirith twisted but it was too late. The material wrapped around— around the bluedart! The attacking creature's disc-hand glowed brightly and the haze congealed into stone around the weakly struggling flying creature. Encased in stone, the bird-bug fell with a clunk to the landing.

With the bluedart off her leg, Velirith snatched her knife from its thigh sheath. She brandished it at the attacking creature, expecting another blast of stony haze from its raised disc-hand. Instead, light swirled on the face of the disc, coalescing into a group of symbols. The creature held its disc out to her. She had no idea of their meaning, but the symbols looked like the characters on the tiles out on the plain.

Both creatures studied the blade, seeming to evaluate the threat she posed. In perfect unison, they twisted around and swung leisurely back along the wall.

When they reached their companions, all four turned to a

section of wall that had been cut away. Their discs glowed, again emitting a haze of material. As they passed their strange paws over the missing section of wall, the wall *grew back*, as cleanly as if it were never broken! It wouldn't be long before they closed the gap.

They're building, repairing! Kieler would love this, the subversive jerk, she thought. *A technological marvel. But are these what he warned me about?*

Velirith didn't wait to see the work completed. She sheathed her knife, and cautiously but expeditiously, turned on the landing and crawled back through the window the way she had come. Still sweating, but eager to put distance between her and the creatures, she retraced her path to the previous opening across from the intertwining stairs.

Jumping *onto* the stairs wasn't as easy as jumping off, and her landing slammed her shin into one of the risers, and she slid sideways toward the edge. Grabbing for the risers, she pulled herself to the crest of the winding stairs. Wincing with every step, she climbed down to the floor below. She didn't remember more than one doorway, but there were three.

Relieved to be on relatively solid ground, she massaged her head, an ache of hunger and thirst reaching her brain as well as her stomach and competing with the aches spreading through the rest of her body. *How am I going to get out of here?*

Almost like an answer, she heard the rumbling again. Instinct told her that the source of the rumble would be the source of the threat. She ran *toward* it, needing to know. She chose doors and openings that seemed to be in the direction of the noise, not knowing or caring where she was heading. Her going seemed faster and easier as the floors and doors were not as off-kilter as before.

The rumble stopped. She slowed to a walk down a narrow hall. Ahead, her light showed several darkened doorways. Something felt wrong. Something felt *near*. A long moment of silence crawled by as she crept forward to look into one of the shadowed doorways.

CHAPTER ELEVEN

The ceiling exploded in front of her with an earsplitting, grinding crash. She flattened herself against the wall as debris rained down, peppering her face. The air felt charged before her. Huge chunks of the building dissolved as they were sucked into the gaping maw of a massive creature driving down from the ceiling and through the floor. It demolished everything in its path. She had the impression of a determined malevolence as red lights barreled past just inches from her body leaving a vertical shaft in its wake.

Sheer fright propelled her back down the hall. She darted into the first doorway, knowing it didn't matter which way she went. She was hopelessly turned around. Now she knew what created the random shafts! The sound of its destructive progress ceased far below her as she continued to run and dodge through openings. She bolted for a doorway but drew up short as she realized there was no floor beyond it!

Disoriented and tottering on the threshold, she took in an immense plaza before her. She had to be five stories above it!

The hexagonal plaza below was larger even than Plaza Floraneva. But on all sides, it was closed off by vertical walls. The five walls facing her were mirror copies of the horizontal plaza below, giving the place an unhinged, kaleidoscopic effect.

An army of abbig-like creatures occupied the plaza, their disc-paws glowing in readiness. Most looked to be the same kind she had just encountered, but one abbig-shaped creature towered above the rest, and above her another five stories. To her horror, it turned its head and looked straight at her.

With its legs planted on the plaza far below, it turned, swinging a gargantuan arm toward her lofty perch. Velirith saw that the arm terminated in a flat plate like its little brothers below, but this creature's disc-hand had a diameter three times her height!

Velirith struggled for balance and tried to pull back, grasping at the smooth edge of the doorway. The building on which she stood shook violently. Tearing her eyes away from the being before her, she glanced down. Vibrations told her that something

EPISODE 4 – A LIGHT IN THE DEEP

was coming up from below.

A grinding thunder peaked as debris exploded out onto the plaza! A huge, slug-like creature—it had to be the one that had nearly eaten her moments ago—drove out from the building below and careened onto the plaza. It moved far too fast for its bulk, rolling forward to stop fifty yards before the towering leviathan.

The high-reaching creature turned from her to the threat at its feet.

An angry drone assaulted her ears, and from high up a swarm of thousands of bluedarts descended into the air above the plaza. They took position and hovered in squadrons above the massive slug, the nearest squadron only a couple dozen feet from her but blessedly focused on the abbig-like army.

Velirith tried to take in the standoff arrayed before her: The towering creature allied with scores of the small, abbig-like minions at its feet, occupied over half the plaza. This assembly stood in opposition to the single, immense, metal slug that seemed ready to devour the lot of them, and its swarm of air support.

At an unheard signal, three of the smaller abbig-creatures surged forward from the main force toward the squat, destructive beast. It was as if these creatures were being sacrificed to test their opponent. Two went at it from its left, the other from the right.

Velirith watched the unfolding battle in stunned disbelief. The scene was so foreign to her. These creatures that acted like both animals and machines displayed more agility and intelligence than either. But what were they?

The slug-creature turned its huge bulk toward the two smaller attackers. As they passed the threshold of its gaping maw, red lightning flashed across the opening, and the metal abbigs were disintegrated into a cloud of particles. With a rushing roar, the particles were sucked into the slug's gullet—gone.

The third one leapt onto the monster and spewed a yellow fog onto its right side. The slug's metal skin sizzled and boiled, but the behemoth simply rolled, shaking the world and crushing the metallic abbig like a bug.

Velirith had a moment to wonder at the power and strangeness of the tableau before her. She felt very small in a world that, in one night, had become so much bigger than she had known.

With that thought, the drone of the flying creatures increased, seeming to come from all directions. The building shook again, and just as she turned her head to look back, she was hit from behind by a score of the blue-lit bird-machines. They had come from the interior of the maze.

She released her grip on the door frame and swatted madly at the bluedarts. Her reaction was the wrong one, and she knew it within a second. The bluedarts were not large, but getting hit by so many at one time unbalanced her and she tumbled through the doorway.

With a short scream, she plummeted backward over the edge. The bluedarts poured out the opening above her, diving at her, grasping, clawing. Three or four clasped each arm; countless others dug wiry claws into the clothes on her body, scratching her skin beneath; they wrapped her legs in their wire-like appendages; they entangled themselves in her hair, yanking. Despite them clutching her arms, she could still swing against their pull. And she did—instinctively finding their wings the most delicate and vulnerable. Screaming like a woman berserk, she swung and grabbed and bit and thrashed. A burning pain seared the base of her skull, and it felt like one of them was drilling into the back of her neck.

She had crushed a half dozen or so of their wing assemblies when she realized something important: She hadn't smashed onto the plaza.

She looked over to see the opening from which she'd fallen... *below her!* She couldn't stop her hand in time to keep from smashing one more set of buzzing wings.

These things aren't pushing me to the ground, but carrying me off!

Velirith didn't know whether to be relieved or further terrified. Were they carrying her to a nest to be devoured?

But it didn't matter. She had damaged too many of them. The winged machines struggled to keep her aloft. The clumsy airlift was losing altitude. Velirith was going down.

Uneven lift caused them to spin as they fluttered madly above the plaza battlefield. The light from the myriad creatures allowed her to see the six walls of the plaza spinning around her, to see the towering abbig-creature reaching for her, to see the slug-thing turn its unwanted attention toward her—the screaming, flailing prey.

They hit the ground hard. Velirith's body smashed several of the bluedarts, and the air was forced from her lungs. She rolled, gasping as she gained her feet and flung the clinging creatures from her arms, tearing them from her legs.

She stopped. Swarms of the flyers hovered in a cloud around her, buzzing mad that she had smashed their cohorts. The hordes of small, metal abbigs focused their color-changing eyes on her. The giant abbig stared down at Velirith's tattered mayhem in the center of the plaza.

It was an awkward moment.

She almost laughed.

In unison, all eyes shifted to something behind her. She spun and saw the thirty-foot maw of the monstrous slug looming before her.

She screamed.

The slug charged.